EARTHQUAKE

Warren Thompson

Author's Note

Earthquake is based on the well-accepted fact among seismologists that there is the probability of a major earthquake during the next 600 to 1000 years along the west coast of the North American Continent.

Earthquake, strictly a work of fiction, is set in a well-known locality on Vancouver Island, which is situated in British Columbia, off the West Coast of Canada. While the names of streets, roads and towns are, for the most part, based on real ones, the author makes no claim of accuracy as to location. In this novel, Campbell River is a real town; the Comox Valley is a well-known farming and vacation area. The Rotary Club of Campbell River meets every Wednesday at noon for lunch in a downtown hotel. That is the full extent of genuine accuracy in this novel. All characters come from the mind of the author, and any resemblance to real people is purely coincidental. The Little River Valley in Alberta is an imaginary location.

Chapter 1

"Ladies and gentlemen! We've heard for years about the possibility, even probability that the 'big one,' the big earthquake, is going to happen along the West Coast of North America. Well, it is no longer a probability; it's an absolute certainty. And we are not talking about 300 years, 200 years, or even 100 years. We are talking about weeks, perhaps days. The big one is coming, and if you are still on this island when it hits, you had better be ready to meet your maker, because most of you are almost certainly going to die."

Rotary Club President Roger Burkham had introduced Dr. Paul Wolfgang. The meeting room at the Seaview Inn in downtown Campbell River was packed to capacity with the members of the town's two Rotary Clubs, their spouses and guests. Extra microphones had been set up in front of the lectern. Aligned along the walls were TV cameras from local channel 10 and CH TV from Victoria. Burkham had used glowing terms in his introduction. He praised Dr. Wolfgang as one of the outstanding seismologists in the modern world. After earning a bachelor's degree from Shawnee College in Oklahoma, where he majored in fine arts but became fascinated by geology and seismology, he went on to get his master's in geology at Bartlesville, Oklahoma, and moved to New Mexico for his doctorate at Desert University with special studies on earthquakes and their causes. Wolfgang had been speaking up and down the West Coast on radio and television shows and pulling in large audiences in appearances at service clubs and community centers.

Dr. Wolfgang had the undivided attention of his audience.

"I have been specializing in the study of earthquakes that will ravage this region when the tensions build high enough along the converging fronts that define the borders of the Pacific and the Continental plates. These two plates come together along the Pacific Coast from Alaska to South America. The greatest tensions are building in the area between the Queen Charlotte Islands and the Columbia River, with the greatest danger along the West Coast of Vancouver Island and the Olympic Peninsula.

"The world's earthquakes and volcanoes are not scattered at random over the Earth's crust. The majority of them are

1

concentrated along the edges of the continents—for example—the western edge of the Americas and along the island chains of the Aleutians and Japan. We've all known about this for years. But only recently have scientists been able to link these observations to the huge floating plates deep below the surface of the earth. Thus, the science of plate tectonics has evolved. That has been the focus of my studies for several years.

"The great Pacific Plate has been pushing eastward for centuries, forcing itself downward and under the Continental Plate, causing the Continental Plate to rise." He continued. *"When pressures become great enough, the Pacific Plate will surge forward and the results will be catastrophic.*

"Imagine these two great plates, thousands of miles in diameter, floating on a sea of molten rock, the edges being forced upward or downward. Something has to give."

Club bulletin editor Percy Hayes slipped forward with his digital camera to get pictures, and Wolfgang stepped back from the microphone, turning his head to provide the best view of his rugged profile.

Pompous ass, thought Jamie Morgan from his seat at the back, sounds like one of those Evangelical or political speakers that think so much of themselves. Most thought they were some special gift to the world and were somehow able to totally captivate their audiences. If he shouted 'halleluiah,' he'd have people on their feet shouting it back at him, Jamie thought. What's he want to do? Was it power or the wish to dominate, destroy or scare people to death? Or just look good?

"Imagine, if you will," Wolfgang went on, *"these two great geological plates, as two plates of glass, the Pacific Plate nudging under the Continental Plate. On the western edge of the Continental Plate are the mountains of Vancouver Island and the Olympic Peninsula. Just east of these is a long, deep valley, containing the Straits of Georgia and Puget Sound. Under this valley, the earth's crust is fractured with many faults, most running northwest to southeast, along the length of the valley. These faults are the result of previous earthquakes, many of them happening in the past several years.*

"Now, if you lift up hard enough on the outer edge of this sheet of slate, what is going to happen? It's going to break. The break will come along the deep valley that is already weakened. What happens then? The predictions are that the Pacific coast of

Vancouver Island and the Olympic Peninsula to the south will be pushed upward as the East Coast of the island plunges downward.

"What are the results? The West Coast of the island, and the Olympic peninsula, raised as much as 10, 20, 30 feet or possibly even considerable more. The East Side submerged an equal amount. It's hard to imagine the effects of such an event. Campbell River, demolished from the force of the quake, is submerged under the ocean. After the quake, a tidal wave, a tsunami, could well raise the ocean 30 to 50 feet and surge inland over all low-lying areas to complete the devastation of the quake.

"When you look at the possibilities here..."

Wolfgang threw his hands in the air and staggered sideways as the room swayed noticeably. Another earthquake was shaking the building. Wolfgang spread his arms wide, palms up, as the shaking subsided.

"This shake we just had is one of the many warnings. In recent days, a series of minor quakes have been occurring in the vicinity of Mount Hood and Mount Rainier. Mount Adams and Mount St. Helens have been showing activity. It is not clear if these volcanic mountains are connected to the plate activity. I can't believe it is a coincidence that this volcanic activity is threatening at the same time that numerous small earthquakes are warnings of impending disaster along the coast.

"What can we expect? Massive destruction along the coast! Besides enormous damage from the quakes, the erupting volcanoes may well add to the disaster. No one will be able to live here for generations to come.

"What do I advise? Get the hell off this island and into Alberta and west of the Rockies as far as possible.

"Will you have any definite warning when the big one is coming? The preliminary warnings are happening about every day, like the minor quake we just had. So be prepared. The final warning will be a series of three rather strong quakes, 4.5 or better, happening within an hour. Remember, three in 60 minutes. If you haven't gotten off this island before that final warning, you had better skedaddle fast, for you may have as little as 24 hours to get away."

The room was dead quiet as Dr. Wolfgang moved to his seat at the head table. Then everyone was attempting to be heard at once, getting louder and louder trying to gain attention.

Burkham held his arms high for attention. No one paid any attention until he picked up the gavel and struck a resounding blow to the big bell that sat by the lectern.

"Dr. Wolfgang is eager to be on his way," Burkham said, "but I'm sure he will take a few minutes to answer some of your questions. Stand and raise your hand and I will recognize you one at a time."

Jamie Morgan was out of his chair as if propelled by a spring, with his hand high in the air.

"Jamie," Burkham said, "you have the first question."

"Dr. Wolfgang," Jamie spoke into the portable microphone someone handed him. "How long did you attend Shawnee College?"

"That degree," replied Wolfgang, "was for the equivalent of four years of college work."

"Did you attend Shawnee for four years?"

"No. Shawnee has a system so if you demonstrate you have the knowledge, you get your degree in less than the ordinary four years required by most students."

"How long did you attend Bartlesville?

President Burkham interrupted from the podium. "Jamie, I think you're being a bit discourteous. Let's stick to questions about earthquakes. Who's next?"

Dr. Wolfgang stood. "Sir, I really don't have time for more questions. Will you excuse me, please?" He didn't wait for an answer and moved quickly out the side door to the hall.

Shouts and comments erupted once more, and President Burkham made no effort to control it. The meeting rapidly broke up as people made their way from the room, talking excitedly as they left.

Jamie sat unmoving in his chair, staring at the tabletop, deep in thought. He was aroused from his reveries by the approach of the club president.

"Jamie, do you think your remarks to the speaker were appropriate?" Burkham asked.

"I'm sorry Roger, but I think that guy is a total fraud."

"Be that as it may, but I was surprised at your actions, especially from a past president. On what grounds do you base your suspicions?"

"Gut feelings. The guy was too much like a wild-eyed preacher. But he sure was able to get people's attention. I don't

4

think you have a program lined up for next week, do you? How about I do some research and present the program? It's been some time since I've spoken to the club."

"I guess that would be OK," Burkham replied reluctantly. "But I don't think you should be too hard on the guy. Some people seem to think he knows what he's talking about. They could be right. You might not be very popular if you try to nail him too hard. I'll call the program chairman and set it up if he hasn't made other arrangements. I'll let you know."

Chapter 2

Jamie Morgan was the last to leave when he wandered out into the hallway. A group was gathered in the hotel lobby, and Jamie recognized the distinctive voice of RCMP Constable Pat Draper.

"I think Jamie has a level head on him," Jamie heard him say. "Maybe he knew something that the rest of us missed."

Jamie paused on the perimeter of the group.

Mary Andrews, with her back to Jamie and unaware of his presence, spoke up. "I think Roger landed on Jamie too quick. I'd have liked to have heard what else he had to say."

"Same here," chimed in Rosie Coleman. "That guy didn't want to answer any more questions about his background."

"Hi, Jamie," Constable Draper held out his hand for a firm shake. "Do you know something about this Wolfgang's background? You seemed rather uncertain about him."

"No," Jamie replied, "I never heard of him until he started showing up on radio and TV recently. I heard a man speak one time that sounded like him. Wolfgang sounds like a preacher and the fellow I heard was a preacher called Jim Jones who had formed his own religious cult in the states. He got so much control over his congregation that they gave him all of their worldly possessions and followed him to Guyana in South America. When the FBI started closing in on him, he convinced them all to take poison. More than a hundred people, men, women and children died. I just don't trust the guy. I think he's a fraud. I intend to do some investigating to see what I can find out. In the meantime, don't go rushing off the island just because he says you should."

"I agree with you completely," replied Draper.

Several other people, who had been listening in on the exchange, made no comment and quietly moved away.

I guess I didn't make much impression on them, Jamie thought.

Outside, drizzle was falling from a low overcast. Several groups of people were gathered under the awnings of the adjoining plaza. Passing one group, Jamie overheard the statement of one man. "I'm not going to wait around," he proclaimed in a loud voice. "I'm going to gather up my family and get the hell out of here, take them back to Ontario where we don't have to worry about falling in the ocean."

"I hope the panic isn't beginning," Jamie said to himself. "If there is a God, he had better start lending a hand soon, or there is going to be a disaster more dangerous than any earthquake."

* * *

Reaching home, Jamie sat gazing out across the deck to the hazy view of the ocean. The Cape Mudge Lighthouse was barely visible. For a while, he did not move. It was hard to get motivated in this empty house, so large and lonely since his wife Julie died the previous year. Would he ever get over missing the vibrant woman who had played so dominant a part in his life for so many years?

Jarring himself loose from his gloom, Jamie went to the den to turn on his computer. He started a search for the educational institutions where Dr. Wolfgang claimed he had received his various scientific degrees. Shawnee was a small town near Oklahoma City. He found a high school there, but no reference to college. In fact, there seemed to be little information to be found about the community. A click on the hotel link showed no hotels in Shawnee. Trying the long distance operator at the phone company, he was advised there was no listing for a Shawnee College. So much for Wolfgang's bachelor's degree.

Bartlesville, Oklahoma, provided about the same results. Jamie did find a few statistics. The city had a population of 36,150. The hotel link featured the Frank Lloyd Wright Place Tower, the only skyscraper built by the famous architect, 21 stories tall and with 19 guest rooms. It must be one skinny tower, thought Jamie. The education link showed no college or university. Nor was there any listing for Desert University in any of the southwest states, where one would think a desert university to be located.

Clicking off Internet Explorer, he brought up his e-mail. A large accumulation of spam showed on the screen, and he started systematically deleting the unwanted ads. The last item caught his attention an instant before he hit the delete button.

"Get a Bachelor's Degree, Master's or PhD—No Classes Necessary"

Academic Qualifications available from prestigious non-accredited universities. Do you have the knowledge and the experience but lack the qualifications? Get the prestige that you deserve today! Bachelor's, Master's and PhD are available in your field! No examinations! No courses! No textbooks.

Call this phone number to register and receive your educational credentials within a day. 24 hours a day, seven days a week! Confidentiality assured!

Jamie declined to try the phone number. The last thing he wanted was some high-powered scam artist calling on the phone. He felt that he now had enough evidence to present to the club to convince them that Dr. Wolfgang was a fraud, and he hoped he would be able to dispel some of the panic that Wolfgang had started.

Glancing at the clock, Jamie found it hard to believe that the afternoon was gone. It was five o'clock and time for the news.

Moving to his easy chair in the living room, he clicked on a news channel from Victoria. The news anchor was already on, talking about Wolfgang's appearance in Campbell River. The announcer switched to the reporter that had attended the Rotary luncheon who described Wolfgang as an "eminent scientist who had made extensive studies of plate tectonics and their relations to earthquakes." He commented that three earthquakes in an hour would be the warning that the "great one" was sure to happen within days. Another reporter came on to say that many people were not waiting for the final warning to vacate the island. The ferry service was reporting capacity loads outbound from the island, and airline ticket offices were answering extra requests about fares and schedules to Calgary and other points east. A call to the Empress and other hotels in Victoria revealed that hundreds of reservations had been canceled. One airline reported all flights to Calgary were booked full for the week ahead. The panic is beginning, Jamie thought. Where is it going to end? He went back to his computer and checked a hotel reservations Web page. Hotels and motels were filling in both Calgary and Edmonton.

A Seattle TV station was featuring the earthquake news. It was snowing on Snoqualmie Pass, but the road was open and there was a steady stream of eastbound traffic clogging the highway. Snow had closed Steven's Pass. The only other road open out of western Washington was up the Columbia River from Portland. That highway was reporting heavy traffic eastbound and very little westbound. The evacuation of the western seaboard was underway. A steam vent had opened on the side of Mt. Rainier

8

near the summit and it was feared that if it got bigger, melting snow would create a flood problem down the mountain. The steam vent could be a warning of a major eruption, the announcer said.

* * *

Jamie was born in Victoria, British Columbia, to John and Hilda Morgan. John was a mechanic in a garage in Victoria. Later, the family moved to the remote village of Campbell River where John set up his own garage. Because of his skill with cars, his honesty and his dependability, he quickly became successful. Finding it difficult to get fast service on parts, he developed an extensive parts department. Because John was free with advice, loaned shop tools and sold the required parts, the parts department rapidly grew to outstrip the garage in profits, and he started adding heavy-duty truck and equipment parts to service the logging and mining industry, which provided much of the employment in the area.

Jamie grew up with grease under his fingernails. At ten, he had become a valuable helper in the garage and was learning about parts. Enthralled with the floatplanes that operated out of the lagoon at the mouth of the Campbell River, he resolved to become a pilot. He cadged an occasional ride on a plane delivering parts to remote areas, and by the time he was twelve he was becoming proficient in handling the aircraft. Pilots appeared to enjoy giving him instructions and letting him fly from the copilot's seat.

Later, with the parts department getting out of hand, John decided to start a separate business and handle a wider line of auto and industrial parts and supplies. He rented a building next to the garage and incorporated Campbell River Auto Parts. When it was pointed out to John that the acronym resulting from the name might not be suitable, John refused to change it. "My customers are all full of it anyway," he said. "It might help them to remember where to buy their auto parts."

Jamie, at his parent's insistence, finished school and immediately started full time in the parts store. The next year he talked his dad into sending him to Vancouver for pilot training. Already partly proficient as a pilot, he went through ground school in record time and passed his flight test. After some arm-twisting, he convinced his father that a Piper Super Cub on floats that had come up for sale would be a good investment for CRAP. Within months Jamie was one of the youngest pilots active in the

9

Campbell River area. The plane was a financial success, cutting down on the costs and speeding the delivery of parts to the logging camps. A year later, they bought a Beaver, increasing load capacity and speed. The demand for lumber was increasing, resulting in a boom in the forest industry. New equipment was hard to get. Parts to keep the old stuff going were stretching the company to the breaking point. John sold the garage and went full time supervising the three men working in the parts store. Jamie was busy on the phone, tracking down parts, new or used, and flying the Beaver into the remote camps on deliveries. Running out of space, the company moved into their own quarters in a new building built for them on Sixteenth Avenue.

The next year, life changed for Jamie Morgan. A dynamic 18-year-old, Julie Paterson came to work for the company as cashier and bookkeeper. The petite blond hit Jamie like a ton of bricks. Julie became even more important than flying and auto parts in Jamie's life. Two years later, they were married. The young couple took one week from business for a honeymoon, flying the Beaver up the Inland Passage to Juneau, Alaska.

* * *

When Jamie got out of bed Thursday morning, the *Times Colonist*, one of the province's daily papers, was on the doorstep. The front page was devoted to earthquake news and the various predictions of Dr. Wolfgang. A quake with a reported Richter scale of five was recorded off the mouth of Juan de Fuca Straight and rattled Victoria and Port Angeles, but caused little damage. Swarms of small quakes were occurring around Mt. Baker and were being felt in Bellingham, Washington. The newspaper was doing little to stem the panic. The news seemed aimed at getting people more shook up. Can't the nitwits see what they are doing? Jamie thought. All they're interested in is selling papers.

* * *

Friday morning found Jamie at a small café on Shoppers Row for the coffee meeting that was a regular event for a group of Campbell Riverites. A large table at the back of the room was fully occupied. Jamie grabbed a chair from another table and squeezed into a corner space.

"Welcome to the Friday morning conference on earth-quakes," quipped Carl Smith, the bank manager from down the street.

"Thanks," Jamie replied as Marie, the effervescent young owner of the café, reached over his shoulder to place a cup of her famous coffee in front of him.

"I hear you got yourself in the doghouse with our good president," said George Brooks, the chief locksmith for the local security company.

"Not much," replied Jamie. "He called me this morning to say that I'd be the speaker for next week's meeting,"

"How come?" asked retired banker Keith Shaw.

"After the meeting Wednesday, Roger, in his polite way, chewed on my butt a little. I told him I thought Wolfgang was a fraud and I would like to be on the program next week to talk about him."

"What have you found out?" asked Keith.

"I'm not sure yet. I'm in the process of researching it. I think I'll be able to prove that Wolfgang is a fake. If he has the college degrees he claims, he probably bought them for a few dollars. There are companies advertising on the Internet that will provide any kind of degree you want."

"But he sounded pretty knowledgeable," Carl Smith said. "He seemed to know what he was talking about."

"Yes, he sounded good. But I spent yesterday afternoon surfing the 'Net. It's all there, except his predictions. There's no doubt that one day there will be a major quake, but no scientist has ever been able to predict when. Most agree that it will be sometime in the next 600 years. And as to it being so severe, that's unlikely. I could find no indication that there's ever been an earthquake anywhere as severe as Wolfgang is predicting. I'll take my chances right here. Besides, if everyone chooses to leave at once, how are they going to get off the Island? The ferry service would require many days to move the 750,000 residents across the straits. Another thing—the small shakes we've been getting could be a godsend. They could be relieving the stresses that are building up along the plates so that the big one won't occur at all or at least be less severe if it does."

"I wonder how long it would take to get everyone off the Island," George Brooks put in. "Did you do any research on that, Jamie?"

"I'm not sure, but I'm guessing it could be as much as two weeks. If you did succeed in getting off the island, what are you going to do? With the traffic generated, the lower mainland roads to the east cannot possible handle the load. There would be no accommodations available. The weather this time of year is certainly not good for camping out. It might even be impossible to get gas for your car. Thousands will be on the mainland without transportation. What are they going to do? I'll take a chance on the earthquake."

"Hey, you've convinced us," said Ken Wilson. "But what can we do to stop it?"

"I don't know if it can be stopped, but I think we should try. Talk to all your family and friends and anyone else you can corner. If we can't stop this insanity, those of us left on the island will get together and see what we can do. It might be possible to stop it. All we can do is try. Are you all with me?"

Everyone agreed.

"OK! Let's get on it. I'll have a good talk prepared for next Wednesday. We'll hope we can do some good." Jamie got up and strode from the restaurant. He'd spend the rest of the week trying to de-panic the populace. He was discouraged by his lack of success. Most people, if they listened to him at all, did not seem to absorb much of what he said. Many were making plans, getting ready and preparing to leave during the next few days. Many had already left, waiting long hours to get their turn on the ferries.

* * *

Sunday morning Jamie had a bad case of the blues. What little he had slept had produced a succession of horror dreams, cars speeding down the highways recklessly, crowding and crashing into each other. Drivers all seemed intent on getting to their destination ahead of everyone else. Seriously injured people were crawling out of smashed vehicles, calling for help. No one stopped for them. Everyone had turned into a mob of maniacs, obsessed by their desire to get away from the promised quake.

Jamie sat hunched at the kitchen table, his hands trembling from lack of rest. God, how he missed Julie. If he had had her by his side, this ordeal would be much easier.

Jamie's marriage to Julie had been a great success. They went to work together, worked all day in the same business and went home together. They cooked together and took care of the house together.

Julie had spotted the house for sale and insisted Jamie go with her to look at it. It was new, located on the edge of the bluff overlooking the expanse of Discovery Passage and Georgia Strait. It was love at first sight for both of them. The young couple brought Jamie's parents to look at it. The house was ideal for them, John and Hilda agreed. The next day John went to the bank with Jamie and signed a security for the mortgage. John advanced the money for the down payment, and a week later they were moving in. It was nip and tuck for a while, but Julie was ingenious. She created furniture from boxes draped with odds and ends of cloth. The thrift store proved to be a source for pots and pans and chipped dishes for nickels and dimes. They had a few things of their own and managed to make do.

Things went well for the company, and Jamie was taken in as a partner. They soon managed some better furniture, and the house became a joy to the couple. The view of the ocean, with its ever-changing pallet of blues and greens and grays, sometimes dappled with whitecaps, never ceased to enthrall them. Their happiness was complete, only marred by their inability to start a baby, regardless of their constant attempts. Julie was unable to conceive. They finally decided they were not destined to have children, and they became even closer to one another.

Jamie continued to fly parts deliveries up and down the coast, sometimes feeling his way through bad weather, flying only a few feet above the water. His extensive knowledge of the inlets and passages gave the confidence he needed to get the job done.

Then a series of disasters struck. The Beaver crashed while Jamie was attempting a landing on a rough stretch of water in front of a logging camp on an exposed stretch of Johnston Strait. Jamie did not see the log floating in a trough between the waves until it was too late. One float caught the log, and the plane flipped. Jamie managed to get out of the plane before it sank in 30 feet of water. He was able to swim ashore, with little injury except a badly bruised ego. The plane was salvaged and sent to the shop for repairs.

Julie and his folks insisted that he had flown enough. When the plane came out of the shop, they hired a young pilot to do the flying. He was a professional, but inexperienced in the ways of the coast. A week later, the Beaver crashed into the side of a mountain, the plane demolished and the pilot killed. Again, Jamie gave in to the admonishments of his father and Julie, and the firm started making their deliveries by commercial carriers. Several small airlines were operating in the area that the company serviced. Soon after, disaster struck again. John collapsed in the back room of the store and was rushed to the hospital where he died the same day of a massive heart attack.

Jamie was now half owner of the company with his mother. With his extensive experience in the business, he had no problem in taking over full control. Two years later, his mother died, and Jamie and Julie became sole owners of CRAP.

Ten years later the couple decided it was time to retire while they were young enough to enjoy it. The sale of CRAP provided them with enough resources to live comfortably and have money enough to travel to far parts of the world. They had been dreaming of faraway places for years, and it was time to fulfill their dreams. But it was not to be. A few months into retirement, as they were preparing for their first trip, Julie complained of intense abdominal pains. Rushed to the hospital, the doctors could find nothing wrong. Transferred to Victoria for additional tests, she was diagnosed with liver cancer and given just months to live. She died a month later. A year had now gone by, and Jamie was still not reconciled to his loss.

Chapter 3

Jamie entered the meeting room with a fair amount of trepidation. He had no idea how he would be received. He was expected. President Roger had sent an e-mail to all members who were on-line announcing that he would be on the program. He had also phoned many of them to try to defuse fears that he knew were building.

Roger Burkham raised his hands for attention. "Please stand for..."

A rumbling sound interrupted him. It seemed to go on for a long time, but was probably no more than five or ten seconds. Then the shaking began, followed by a rolling motion reminiscent of a boat on ocean swells.

Jamie shouted for attention. "Calm! Calm down. Don't run. Stay where you are. You are safest right here."

A man and his wife near the back of the room slipped out the side door as the balance of the crowd broke into wild chatter as the quake subsided. Roger waited a moment for the bedlam to subside before giving the bell a blow with the mallet. "Please stand for "O Canada." "

The salads were history and people had started halfheartedly on the fine lunch the hotel had provided. They seemed much more interested in expressing their sensations of the trembling earth that they had experienced. A definite aura of fear pervaded the room.

It was less than 15 minutes after the last tremor had struck when it was repeated with more vigor. A waitress in the middle of the room with a tray of glasses filled with milk was caught off balance, and the tray crashed to the floor. Milk spattered in all directions, splashing shoes and pants legs. As the shock wore off, men started dabbing at their lower extremities with napkins, and helpers came from the kitchen to clean up the mess. The edginess of the crowd could be felt.

Roger was having a difficult time keeping the meeting under control. In desperation, he gave the bell another terrific blow, and the room quieted down. "We're going to get on with the program. You all know Jamie Morgan. He is going to speak to you about the results of his investigation about last week's speaker. Jamie, it's all yours."

Jamie took his place at the lectern. "President Roger, fellow Rotarians, guests. I know that the news that has been coming over the media the last few weeks has been disturbing, and the speech you heard here last week increased your unease.

"It's true. There's probability of a major earthquake somewhere along the West Coast of North America during the next 600 years. I'd like to emphasize—I said during the next 600 years. That is the consensus of the scientific community. Six hundred years is a long time.

"Not one reputable geological scientist has ever made a prediction of when that quake will happen. They all agree that no science available today would make such a prediction possible. The 600 years is only a probability. That could be next week, or stretch out to 1200 years or 2000 years. No one knows.

"And if the big one comes, there's no probability that it would create the destruction that last week's speaker described. There have been some horrific earthquakes during our recorded history, but nothing that severe. Among the severe quakes in modern times was the San Francisco earthquake in 1906. On the Richter scale, it was a magnitude of 7.9. Although it was high on the scale, the majority of the loss of life was caused by the inferno that swept the demolished buildings after the quake. A more severe quake occurred in Alaska in 1964. It is now believed that the Alaska quake reached 9.2 on the Richter scale. The tsunami, or tidal wave, that demolished much of the fishing village of Valdez, Alaska, did the worst damage. The same wave severely damaged Crescent City on the north coast of California, killing several people and plowed up the Alberni Canal to wreck much of Port Alberni.

"As for these earthquakes that we've experienced most recently, they could be a blessing in disguise. They could serve as a safety valve, releasing tension in small increments, rather than one big bang. If the fault slips a little at a time, there's less likelihood of a great slippage. A series of small quakes could easily delay the occurrence of the big one for hundreds of years.

"As to our friend who spoke to you last week, I don't believe that he's the qualified scientist that he claims to be. I was unable to find any record of the educational institutions from which he claims degrees. I did find offerings of degrees for sale that don't require the attendance at any institution. If you say you have the knowledge, they will issue the degree—for money. Anyone can find them on the Internet.

"I have no idea what the so-called Dr. Wolfgang hopes to accomplish with his..."

Number three quake was stronger than the previous two. Lights flickered, but stayed on. Dead silence prevailed for a minute, and then as the shaking subsided, utter pandemonium broke out. There were screams and curses as people tried to get out the door. People were on the floor, screaming, as the mob trampled over the top of them. Jamie pounded viciously on the bell and yelled at the top of his voice, but to no avail.

The mob was out, and the room was silent. A scattering of people remained in their chairs. A man, appearing seriously injured, was staggering around in circles, trying to find the door. A woman sprawled in the middle of the doorway, skirt above her thighs, blood pouring from her neck.

Jamie was aghast.

"Sit still, everyone, and calm down. Someone near the door, see if you can help the woman in the doorway. She may be seriously injured."

Dr. Ron McIvor, giving his wife Marguerite a tap on the shoulder, got up and made his way to the injured woman. Marguerite, a nurse, followed him. It was a scant minute before Dr. McIvor got to his feet and turned to the room.

"I'm sorry," he said, "but she's dying. There's nothing I can do to save her. Her carotid artery has been ruptured, probably by someone stepping on her neck. She's already almost totally bled out. It's too late to do anything for her."

People had started to talk, but were shocked into silence by Ron's announcement.

"Ron," Jamie spoke into the mike, "could you check on the man that was staggering around back there? He went into the property room."

Dr. Ron, followed by Marguerite, entered the room where the club stored its various supplies. It seemed a long time, but was probably not more than a minute before the doctor came back.

"Another death," he reported. "It's Sid Evans. He's dead. Probably his chest was crushed by the crowd. I believe the lady is his wife, Diana."

A gasp of disbelief emanated from the group as they absorbed the enormity of the tragedy.

Jamie spoke again from the lectern. "If I could have had a few more minutes to explain things a little more, maybe this could have been prevented."

"I doubt it," replied Dr. Ron. "These people weren't listening. They were set for panic. It's unbelievable what fear can do to people."

"What do we do now?" asked President Roger. He sat in his chair as if stunned. "Shouldn't we call 9-1-1?"

"No use," called out George Brooks, holding up his cell phone. "There's no answer."

"If they are still functioning, they are probably too busy to answer," said Dr. Ron. "I doubt if they're functioning, if the panic we saw here is universal."

Jamie came forward and spoke without the mike. "We have about 30 people here. It looks as though we are a tiny nucleus of sanity in a world gone insane. If we had a panic like this in this setting, with a group of relatively intelligent people, what's happening in the rest of the area? Anyway, let's stay quiet here and consider what we are going to do."

Constable Pat Draper stood at one side of the group with a cell phone at his ear. "I've got in touch with Emma at home, and she is OK and holding fast. I've been unable to reach my office or any other phone contact. I'm going out to my car and see if I can raise anyone on the police frequencies."

Jamie looked around the room. Everyone was quiet, accepting his leadership without question. "Dr. Ron," he asked, "would you get some help and move the dead lady into the property room with the other corpse? We'll decide what to do about them later. I'm going to see if there is anyone left in the kitchen."

The scene in the kitchen was chaotic. Pots, pans and some food had crashed to the floor. A storage cupboard had spilled contents across the aisle. Three frightened people huddled at a table in the corner of the room. Two of the serving girls and the assistant chef seemed glad to see him. He knew the girls as regulars on the hotel staff. Meg Sanderson was a sprightly young brunette, and Sarah Harris, an older woman, had worked at the hotel for years. The chef, Ted Parks, was a young man who had recently joined the staff. Jamie motioned to them. "Come out and join us in the dining room. There are a few of us left here, and we need everyone. This quake wasn't too bad, but the panic it caused is disastrous."

The three followed Jamie back to the dining room, where he introduced them to the others. Dr. Ron and George Brooks were coming out of the property room, and the body was gone from the doorway. The pool of blood in the doorway was extensive, staining the carpet inside the door and spreading on the tile in the hallway.

"Ted, a woman got injured in the door over there, and she lost a lot of blood." Jamie spoke to the chef. "Do you suppose you could clean up some of the worst of it, so it won't get tracked all over the place?"

Constable Pat came back into the room leading a young woman by the arm. The girl was crying. "I found this lady sitting on the curb in front of the post office." He reported. "Her car was smashed up in the parking lot, too damaged to operate. She says that a guy in a truck banged into her and took off without stopping. A lot of people were trying to get out at the same time. The lot is almost empty now. I don't know what's going on. I couldn't contact anyone on the radio. It seems as though all my guys have flown the coop, along with the entire town."

Rosie Coleman spoke up. "Jamie, what are we going to do now? You seem to be in charge. Where do we go from here?"

"Maybe we should choose a chairman, to keep things organized. We all need to work together to figure out where we're gong."

President Burkham spoke up. "I think Jamie is doing a fantastic job. He is keeping things calmed down extremely well. I propose that we elect him our leader, and we all pledge to give him our full support. All in favor?"

Raised hands showed universal support. The group was eager to have someone take complete charge.

"'I'll do the best I can," Jamie agreed. "But I'll need all of you helping as much as you are able. You must feel free to make suggestions. We have to work together. OK?"

Again, acceptance was unanimous.

The woman that Constable Pat had brought in from the parking lot requested, "Sir, what am I going to do? My car's wrecked, and I can't go anywhere."

"Where were you heading when you got hit?" Jamie asked.

"I was going home to grab a few things and try to be first on the ferry." She replied.

19

"Well, you're among friends here. I'd suggest you stay right here in the hotel and join the people here."

Jamie was quiet for a moment. People were watching him expectantly. Christ, he thought, what the hell have I got myself into here?

"Let's start out by designating the hotel here as our headquarters. I'll be here as much as possible to receive your reports. Mary Andrews, I'd like you to act as my secretary. Find some paper and start keeping notes as of now."

Mary left the room and returned almost instantly with a secretary's pad from the hotel office.

"Jamie," Dr. Ron spoke up. "I think I should get up to the hospital and see what's going on there."

"Good deal," Jamie replied. "Take Marguerite with you, and report back here at seven o'clock tonight. Maybe you could make arrangements to have the two bodies back there moved."

"Will do. I'll take a couple of people with me and see if we can find an ambulance and send them back to pick up the bodies. I'll put them in the hospital morgue. Who wants to help me?"

A couple of hands went up, and the group left the room.

Jamie continued to speak. "Keith Shaw, will you take charge of a survey to find as many people as we can, in order to see what we have left? Assign areas to be checked. Downtown. Ironwood Mall area. Dogwood on the hill. The various residential areas. Nobody should work alone. Check as many business places and offices as possible. Anyone you find, ask them to assemble here tonight at seven for a general meeting. I'll take George Brooks with me and check the Indian Reserve, and then we'll go out to the mill and the industrial park. We will also check the airport. All of you be careful. If everyone hasn't left town yet, they could be dangerous drivers. Don't get in their way. Hotel staff, be prepared to feed some people tonight if they want to stay here. Also, assign them rooms to stay in. Don't try any fancy cooking. Be ready to get something on the grill if needed. Remember. Everyone back here at seven. Earlier, if you wish to eat here. Thanks. Let's go."

* * *

With George Brooks, Jamie left the Seaview Inn. It was almost three o'clock and a fine rain was falling with fog and low visibility. Only a few cars were in the parking lot. Jamie and

20

George went to his decrepit 1980 Chevrolet pickup, a holdover from his days as operator manager of CRAP, and made their way to the Indian Reserve.

The first house they came to in the reserve, a large two-story modern structure, belonged to Charlie Johnson, a hereditary chief of the Campbell River Indian Tribe. Jamie pulled into the driveway and parked behind a new looking pickup. Together, they went up the walk and rang the doorbell. Jamie had known the big Indian for many years. Charlie himself opened the door.

"Hey, Jamie," the chief greeted them. "It's good to see you. What brings you out on a day like this?"

"You must know about the earthquake panic that is going on," replied Jamie. "I'm glad to see that you haven't succumbed to fear and taken off like a scared rabbit as most of the town has."

"Nah! This old injun doesn't scare easy. But most of my people have gone. I talked the best I could, but they just had the shit scared out of them by that idiot on TV, and I couldn't talk any sense into them. What's going on?"

"Well, we have a few people left in town. I'm trying to round them all up for a meeting tonight. Would you get all the people you have left here on the reserve or any that might be living off the reserve, and get them to the meeting at the hotel at seven tonight? We need everybody. I don't think there are many left in town."

"OK. I'll be there."

Jamie and George left to drive to the pulp and paper mill north of town. They found the mill deserted, as was the adjoining lumber mill. Farther north, the industrial park showed no sign of life. Returning south, they followed the main highway to the airport. The terminal was open, but no one was in the ticket offices for either of the two airlines that operated out of the field. The fog was dense, precluding the possibility of any activity. They returned by way of South Island Highway and arrived back at the inn about five PM.

Mary Andrews was busy on the computer in the hotel office transcribing her notes of what had happened. "I had a little trouble with this strange computer, but I seem to have it under control now," she reported.

"You want to go home for dinner, or what are your plans?" Jamie asked.

"No. I think I will stay here and get ready for the meeting tonight. Nothing much for me to go home for. Ted and the girls are getting things under control here. I think they will be able to feed any that show up tonight."

Jamie turned to George. "Go home to Emily and have dinner. Or come back here for dinner. Whatever you do, bring Emily along, so she can know what's going on. Just be here at seven."

Arriving home, Jamie had trouble warding off the depression that he had fought intermittently since Julie's death. He had shared his life with her so completely, that even after a year, he was still having trouble adjusting. Entering the empty, cold house, Jamie turned the thermostat up and switched on the TV.

The news channel was all about the exodus from the island and the coast. The ferry lots were filled with hundreds of cars. The ferry service had announced their schedules had been abandoned. The boats would run all through the night if they were able to keep crews on duty to operate them. They had been operating extra sailings all week trying to keep up with the demand, and crews were getting tired. The ferries were going to the mainland loaded to capacity and returning empty. Numerous wrecks had been reported on approach roads to the ferries. There appeared to be no police control and ambulances were unavailable; hospital emergency rooms were abandoned. Only a few dedicated newsmen and women were still working.

Jamie turned off the TV. It was too depressing. How could a society of educated and intelligent people be caught up in total panic? He thought about fixing some dinner, but unable to face eating alone, decided to go back to the hotel and see what was available.

He walked into the Seaview dining room at six o'clock and found a number of people enjoying huge plates of spaghetti and sauce. Ted had done himself proud, with plenty of food for everyone. The girl that had had her car wrecked on the parking lot was helping serve.

Before seven, Jamie joined others from the dining room to move to the meeting room. More than fifty people were already there. He moved to the lectern that was still in place from the noon Rotary meeting and turned the speakers on. The room grew quiet, waiting for him to speak.

"Welcome, friends, to what is left of Campbell River. The folks that were here at noon asked me to serve as chairman of this group for the time being. I will continue until other arrangements can be made.

"I am utterly appalled at the disaster that has struck us. I don't know really what kind of a disaster it can be classified as, but I guess the best thing to call it is a psychological phenomenon. It has been brought on entirely by the malfunction of the brains of masses of people, probably instigated by the ranting of a complete nut that was able to establish control of their thinking and create almost universal panic.

"There are not many of us left here, and I don't know what we are facing. Are the people that have stampeded going to come back and start over? I guess we'll have to wait and see. In the meantime, we have to protect ourselves, our property and, I guess, other people's property, to the best of our ability. We had better have some reports now. I'd like to call on Dr. Ron for the first report. What did you find at the hospital, Ron?"

"First off, we took care of the bodies..." He paused and looked questioningly at Jamie.

Jamie picked up for him. "For those of you who weren't here at noon, two people were killed during the stampede to get out of here after the last quake. I asked Ron to move the bodies from the hotel. Please go on, Ron."

"Yes Jamie, we picked up an ambulance at the station across the street from the hospital and took the bodies to the hospital morgue. We found two nurses trying to cope with everything in the hospital and having a tough time of it. I put Marguerite in charge there. Seven patients had died, most of them within days of death, anyway. We moved them into the morgue. Most of the patients in the hospital were removed by their families or had walked out on their own. The few left are so far advanced in their conditions that they will die within days. I am absolutely appalled that the hospital staff, the doctors and all the technicians would abandon their patients this way. The Sunshine Lodge has three patients left, and the two nurses in the hospital are trying to look after them, too. We need some volunteers to get up there and help Marguerite.

"We checked on Yuculta Lodge. Most of the patients there were removed by their families early this afternoon or during the past week. I don't know how those older people will cope with the trauma of this mass exodus. There are only five patients left there, and two dedicated women have stayed to care for them the best they can. Some help is desperately needed there, too. It's a sad picture I've painted for you, but that's the way it is. I need to get back up there now and help Marguerite cope with things. I would like some volunteers to help out up there."

"Any volunteers?" asked Jamie.

Seven hands went up.

"There're your volunteers, Ron. Please meet Ron in the lobby, and he will take it from there. All of you who can be here in the morning at nine o'clock, Ted will have pancakes and coffee available at seven."

Jamie resumed. "Now let's hear from Chief Charlie Johnson from the reserve."

Charlie stood and took the portable mike. He was an imposing man, six foot two and well over two hundred pounds, with an angular face and neatly trimmed salt and pepper hair. His voice was deep and well modulated.

"I have only eighteen people left on the reserve that I can find, out of about 300. I cannot possibly explain what possessed them all to leave. Some of them are cowards, but I think that's a small percentage. The white man's devil must have entered their brains. Anyway, we have 12 adults and six children we can account for. If you want what's left of the tribe with you, we are ready and willing."

"Of course we want you with us," responded Jamie. "We are all in this together. It doesn't matter about background. Thank you, Charlie."

Jamie continued his program. "Keith, what have you to report?"

Keith Shaw stood with notes in his hand. "It's not good, Jamie. Most business operations have been vacated. Many left their doors unlocked. Some doors weren't even closed. No one was around the service station here behind the hotel, but the power was on and everything unlocked. I needed gas so I went ahead and filled." He shuffled through his notes and continued. "Ken Griffith found the manager and one employee in the food store at Mercroft. They promised to be here tonight. All in all, we found about a dozen people. All of them agreed to be here."

After some time of general discussion, Jamie ended the meeting.

"Be back here at nine o'clock in the morning," he requested. "If you want to stay here tonight, Sarah will find you a room. Ted has agreed to have hotcakes available from seven on. All of you do some thinking overnight and come up with some ideas about where we should go from here."

Chapter 4

Kelly, at the urging of her mother, had finished her lunch when the third quake shook the dilapidated mobile home the family was renting far up Quinsam Road. The fragile structure rattled and squeaked as though it was coming apart, then settled back in place with no apparent damage.

Kelly was ten years old, a gangling skinny kid, four foot nine inches tall and weighing a scant 70 pounds. Her blond hair hung below her shoulders. Her brilliant blue eyes seemed too large for the thin face.

"Gee," Kelly exclaimed. "That was a whing doozy! Does that make three in an hour?"

Grace, Kelly's mother, wrenched the sticky door open, shouting at the man they had been living with the past few months. "Joe! Get in here!"

Joe Drummond, still showing the effects of the previous night's binge, staggered through the door. "Christ, that was the third one in an hour. Guess it's time to get the hell off this island."

"Do we have to go?" demanded Kelly. "I'm just getting used to the school here. I don't want to move again."

"Never mind what you want, young lady," Grace screeched. "Get your butt in there and start packing."

"But I don't want to go. If you want to go, go ahead and leave me here."

"I don't give a good goddamn what you want to do. Get in that room of yours and put what you want to take along in a box. And do it quick."

"I won't go," Kelly screamed.

"We've had enough out of you, brat," Joe barked, "You're getting too damned independent for your own good. Do as your mother says, or I'll take a strap and whop that ass of yours raw. Now get! We're leaving here in thirty minutes." Turning to Grace, he ordered. "Get to packing right now. Take just what's most important. Everything has to fit in the pickup. Lucky the gas tank's full. Get going!"

Kelly stared in amazement at the two adults; then, tears streaming down her face, she scampered into her tiny bedroom, locking the door behind her. Opening the closet, she got out her warmest coat and a pair of rubber boots. The one window was over the bed, and she climbed up and slid it open. Wriggling and twisting, she managed to get her feet through first, and dropping to the ground, she ran into the forest behind their lot. Picking her way through the tall trees, she made her way to her special hideout. Two trees had fallen close together, and a heavy growth of brush over them had created a sheltered den about three feet high. Kelly had dragged an old piece of plastic tarp and a worn saddle blanket she found in the shed and created a reasonably dry place where she could curl up in complete privacy.

Joe Drummond was the sixth man her mother had taken up with since her father deserted them four years before. She had never been in one school for more than six months. Drummond had picked Grace up in a bar in Calgary, and brought them to Vancouver Island three months ago. The rundown mobile home was the only thing they could find that was within the limited budget of their combined welfare checks after deducting beer and cigarette money.

Back in the house, Grace was cramming things into boxes and suitcases, and Joe was carting them out to the old truck with the homemade canopy over the back. The truck filled up rapidly. Joe yanked the blankets off their bed and stuffed them into gaps in the load.

Coming back into the house, he yelled, "Where's the brat? Get her out here so we can get going!"

Her mother tried the door and found it locked. "Kelly, open this door and get out here." She pounded on the door with no response.

Joe added his voice to the ruckus. "Open this door right now or I'll bust it open."

When there was no answer, Joe backed up, raised his over-sized boot and kicked. The door flew open to reveal the empty room and open window.

"The little bitch climbed out the window and ran away. Think you can find her?" he demanded.

"She plays a lot back there in the woods," Grace said. "I'll go and see if I can find her."

"If you can't," Drummond said. "We'll have to leave her. I'm not going to stay on this island for any snot-nosed kid. I'll give you 10 minutes, so you better find her fast."

Kelly's mother ran to the edge of the forest, yelling at the top of her voice. "Kelleeey, where are you? I know you're hiding in there some place. Get out here right away, or we'll go and leave you."

Kelly huddled deeper under her old blanket and ignored the shouts.

Drummond came to join Grace and added his voice. Kelly winced at the sounds, but remained still. After about 10 minutes, the shouting stopped, and shortly after, Kelly heard the old pickup rattle to life and fade into the distance.

I wonder if they really did leave me. Maybe Joe has gone, and her mother would be waiting in the house. Kelly pulled the blanket up around her neck and settled down. Soon she dozed off and dreamed of a life without Joe, a life where her mother became a beautiful lady who never yelled at her, but treated her as an adult. When she woke up, she was stiff with chill, and it was starting to get dark. Crawling out of her hiding spot, she made her way toward the house.

Kelly approached the house cautiously, not knowing what to expect. No lights were on. Rounding to the front of the house, she found the spot ordinarily occupied by Joe's truck empty. Had they really gone off and left her? She slipped up on the front porch and pushed open the door. It seemed stiffer than usual, and she wondered if the quake had made it that way. Inside, the house was quiet. Turning on the light revealed a cluttered room, and she realized most of the family possessions had been removed. Only the original decrepit furniture that had been in the house remained, along with odds and ends of little value.

Rushing to her own little bedroom, Kelly found everything as she had left it, except for the broken door. The window was still open. She crawled up on the bed and closed it. A chill had taken over the room. She went back to the living room and turned up the thermostat. The propane furnace came to life and warmth flowed into the room.

Her mother had really abandoned her. She was alone. She thought about turning on the television, but it was gone, along with the radio. She realized that she had eaten little lunch, and the pangs of hunger started making themselves felt. She found a can of tuna fish overlooked in the back of a cupboard. The can opener was gone from its place on the counter. Rummaging in drawers, she found an old-fashioned one. With a great deal of difficulty, she managed to get the can partially open. With no tableware left, she found a Popsicle stick among odds and ends of trash in another drawer. Using it as a spoon, she gobbled down the can of tuna and felt a little better.

Kelly didn't know what time it was, but it was dark outside. She wondered if there was anyone else in the neighborhood. The people down the road seemed friendly. Maybe she could go and ask them what was going on. Shrugging into her coat, she headed down the dark street. The neighbor's house seemed dark and deserted, but she approached it anyway and knocked on the front door. Nobody answered, and for the first time, she began to feel fear. Perhaps everyone was gone. Hurriedly, she stumbled back up the dark road to her home.

What can girl do, who is left all alone? She had no TV to watch and no radio to listen to, and no food in the house. Maybe she could call someone on the telephone. In the front of the phone book she found the number for the police department. There was a dial tone, so she dialed the number, but there was no answer, even after a long wait.

Drying the tears from her eyes, Kelly went to her bedroom. Digging in her closet behind some boxes, she pulled out a paper bag, which contained her hoard of cash. Dumping the contents on the bed, she carefully counted. There was one five-dollar bill, five two-dollar coins, a dollar and eight quarters, making a total of $18. She didn't count the small change. She made up her mind. In the morning she would walk downtown. If she was careful, she should be able to buy enough food to last a few days.

There was nothing to do in the lonesome house, so maybe she had just as well go to bed and sleep. Pulling off her Levi's, she hung them up so the dampness from her afternoon in the forest hideout could dry out. The rest of her clothes followed. Naked, she reached in the closet for her ragged old pajamas. They were getting too small for her and were not comfortable. With a shrug of distaste, she tossed them in the corner. Her mother wasn't here to object, so she would sleep in the nude. Going to the living room, she turned the thermostat down, shut the lights off and returned to her room. With the lights out, she crawled into her bed and pulled the covers up around her neck.

Dawn was breaking when Kelly woke up from a night of dreams in which she was alone in the world and running from a variety of strange animals. Gritting her teeth against the fears, she huddled under the blankets for a few minutes, deciding what the best course of action for the day was.

Crawling from the warmth of the bed, Kelly hurried to the bathroom. Sitting on the stool, she made her plans. She would shower, wash her hair and wear the best clothes she had. Wherever she ended up, she would look nice. With her hair dried and brushed, she decided on clothes. She selected a top that was warm and in fair condition. The jeans she had worn the day before were the best she had. She found clean socks without holes and covered them with her best shoes. She was ready to go.

When she opened the door and stepped out onto the porch, the sun was just peeking through the trees. It was a clear and beautiful day. The rain and fog were gone. Still a little fearful, but determined, she started down the road.

Chapter 5

Arriving home about 10 PM, Jamie turned the TV on to see the latest news. It was not encouraging. The announcer looked tired and bedraggled. He was reporting on the exodus from the island that had gone on all week but accelerated greatly after the three quakes during the noon hour. All ferries were running at maximum capacity, and making turnarounds as fast as possible. The rail barges that plied between Nanaimo and Vancouver were hauling cars, but they were able to accommodate less vehicles and their turnaround time was slower than the ferries. The passenger catamaran sailing between Nanaimo and the inner harbor at Vancouver was running all out, taking capacity loads to the mainland. No estimate had been made of how many vehicles were lined up at the various ferry terminals, but the lines reached far back on the approach roads. Airlines were also running at capacity, putting on extra flights, utilizing all aircraft and pilots available. The bad weather added to the difficulties of the refugees.

Turning to a Seattle station, the news was the same as it had been earlier in the evening. The highways were jammed bumper to bumper and had become one-way roads. There appeared to be no police control of any kind. Stalled vehicles were unceremoniously shoved off the road.

Jamie went to bed about eleven, but was unable to sleep. At three in the morning, he crawled out of his rumpled bed and turned on the TV again. The same announcer was still on duty, looking even more worn and frustrated than he had looked earlier. He was not reading from a prompting board, now, but appeared to be freewheeling. "There is less and less information coming in, and none of it is good news. Most of our field crews have ceased reporting. I can report, however, that the Coho, sailing to Port Angeles, has left on its third trip tonight with a full load of cars and passengers. I assume that these people are hoping to be able to drive from Port Angeles by way of Tacoma, and make their way eastward. I don't know how far they can get that way, as all roads are reported to be..."

The reporter stopped, an uncertain look on his face, then slumped forward face down on the table. The picture bobbed erratically for a few seconds, then the camera pointed downward, showing the floor, and remained stationary in that position.

What happened? Jamie was puzzled. His first thought was that the announcer had fainted from fatigue. But what happened to the cameraman? Both of them should not pass out at once, unless some unusual phenomena had affected them simultaneously.

He started surfing stations. The other Victoria Station was off the air. One Vancouver station was on, but the camera showed an empty desk, with no movement of any kind.

Jamie switched to a Seattle station and found the screen blank. Another station was active, but showing a movie. Another station was on; the camera was focused on a desk, with no announcer behind it. Deeply puzzled, he picked up the phone and dialed a friend's number in Alberta. The phone rang, but there was no answer. He tried the operator; again, no answer. Perturbed, he sat for a few minutes, pondering the situation. He could come up with no logical solution. Picking up the phone again he dialed Roger Burkham. After several rings, a sleepy sounding Roger answered.

"Sorry to wake you up," Jamie said, "But something is going on that I'm not able to understand. Would you turn on your TV? Try channel six."

Roger responded shortly. "The station is on, broadcasting a picture that looks like a tile floor. There's no movement."

"I was watching it a few minutes ago. I couldn't sleep, so I got up and turned it on. The announcer was talking about the traffic pileup and everyone trying to get off the island. Then, he stopped and keeled over face down on the desk. The camera bobbled a little and shifted to the picture of the floor. There was no other action. All other stations I tried are the same. If they are on, there is no action, except one that was running a movie that was probably automated. I tried several eastern stations with the same results. Something has affected the TV stations, and communications seem to be nonexistent outside our own area. I have no idea what's going on."

"I don't either, but it sure as hell sounds scary. Maybe we're the only ones left in the world, and there doesn't seem to be very many of us. What are we going to do?" Roger sounded on the verge of panic.

"I don't think we can do anything right now," Jamie said. "I'm going to try to get a couple of hours sleep, and then start checking this out in the morning. Maybe we'll have some answers by the time everyone shows up at nine. I suggest that you do the same."

"I don't know if I can sleep after this, but I'll give it a try. But first, I'll try phoning my daughter in Ontario. She should be up and around by now." The phone went dead.

Jamie returned to bed and, surprisingly, went to sleep almost immediately. When he awakened, it was starting to get light. He got up and went to the kitchen where he was able to see out. The storm was over and a cloudless day promised. A faint edging of light was showing over the mountains on the mainland.

He tried the TV again. The same picture was showing on the Victoria station. He gave up and then showered and shaved. It was a little after seven when he was ready to go. Going out to his truck, he changed his mind. He would take the car today. He had bought the big luxury car for Julie, and since her death had left it in the garage, seldom using it. But today, maybe it would be like a part of Julie with him to help with the problems he was facing. As he backed the car out of the garage, he thought of the old couple that lived in the little cabin west of town, off Gold River Road. Maybe he had better check on them. He had time before he had to be downtown. He found the cabin empty, and the car was gone.

Starting back to town, he saw a figure trudging along the shoulder of the highway. Coasting up alongside, he saw that it was a girl, probably a preteen. Rolling the window down, he called, "Want a ride?"

Stopping and looking at him carefully, she replied. "My mom said I should never accept rides with a strange man." Her voice was clear and positive.

"I'm not a strange man," Jamie said, "I'm like a grandfather. It's a ways to town yet, and it's cold out here. Besides, I don't think any other rides are likely to be coming along this morning. You'd better get in. I'm safe to ride with."

The girl approached the car hesitantly. Jamie judged she was about four feet nine, with shoulder-length blond hair, slender to the point of being skinny, a narrow but attractive face. "What has happened to everyone?" she asked. "Did they all run away because they were scared of an earthquake?"

"Something like that," Jamie replied. "But there are still a few of us left. I'll bet you're hungry. Get in and we'll be able to have some breakfast. It's being prepared especially for those of us that are left."

"I am hungry," she conceded, "and a little bit cold. My name is Kelly. What's yours?"

"I'm Jamie. Are you all alone? What happened to your parents?"

"When the three earthquakes happened in less than an hour, they got scared and left."

"How come they left without you?"

"They wanted me to go, but I wanted to stay here. I kept arguing about it until Joe, he's my mom's latest boyfriend, said that if I didn't get in my room and get packed, he'd whop my ass raw. He would, too. I went in my room and locked the door. Then I crawled out the window, ran, and hid in my favorite hidey-hole out in the woods. I heard them hollering for me, but I wouldn't answer. After awhile I heard the truck start up and drive away. I stayed there until dark and then went home. They took almost everything. I found a can of tuna for supper."

"How old are you, Kelly?" Jamie asked, opening the car door for her. She hesitantly got in.

"I'm ten."

"You lived here long?"

"We came here about three months ago. Joe lost his job in Calgary, and we came out here because Joe said it was easier to get welfare here. I don't think Joe really wants to work if he can get welfare."

"How long has your mother been living with Joe?"

"I guess 'bout six months. The man we were living with before went off and left us. Mom went to a bar, got drunk and brought Joe home with her. He moved in and stayed."

"I take it you don't like Joe," Jamie said.

"I don't like him at all. He gets drunk all the time. He's mean to my mom and me both. I'm glad he's gone. Do you have a family, Jamie?"

"No," Jamie replied. "My wife died last year. We didn't have any children, so I live all alone."

"Maybe I could be your little girl. I could keep house for you and cook and things like that. I don't think you would be mean to me."

"No, I wouldn't be mean to you, but I don't think that would be a good idea. If Julie were still alive, I'd take you in a minute. I

34

think you're a nice girl that deserves a home. But we'll find someone for you to live with. Don't worry about that."

"I know what you're thinking," Kelly said. "It wouldn't be proper for a girl to live with a man alone. But if I were your daughter, it'd be OK, wouldn't it?"

"That's right, but you're not my daughter."

"We could pretend that I was. That would make it all right."

They were entering the hotel parking lot. "Let's see what comes up. We'll work something out," Jamie assured her.

It was past eight o'clock, and the hotel dining room was crowded. The three girls were already serving plates of hotcakes and sausages. Jamie spotted Mary Andrews sitting at a table alone.

"Morning Mary," Jamie said. "I'd like you to meet Kelly. Kelly, this is Mary. I picked Kelly up making her way downtown from somewhere up on Quinsam Road. She's been left all alone. May we join you?"

"Of course," Mary replied. "Who would abandon a sweet little girl like this?"

"My mom and Joe don't think I'm a sweet little girl," Kelly said.

Meg Sanderson approached their table. "I imagine you all want breakfast? And coffee? And how about a glass of milk for the young lady?"

"Yes please," Kelly said.

"So what are your plans, Kelly?" Mary asked.

"I don't have any yet. I'd like to keep house for Jamie and be his little girl. But he doesn't think that would be proper."

"Oh fiddle," Mary replied. "Jamie is alone, and he needs someone to make a home for him."

The waitress approached with three plates stacked with pancakes and sausage. Kelly's eyes bugged as a plate was set before her, and she lost no time in pouring syrup over the pancakes and digging in. Jamie realized he was hungry too. The three all fell silent as they tucked in.

"It's near nine o'clock, so I better get in the meeting room and be ready for whatever is coming today," Jamie said. "Kelly, will you hang out with Mary today? I might be rather busy. Mary, would you continue as secretary and make some record of what goes on? You two finish your breakfast and then come on in. Kelly can sit beside you during the meeting."

In the meeting room, the crowd was already assembling. Roger Burkham approached and drew Jamie to one side. "I couldn't get anyone on the phone anywhere in the eastern part of the country. Also, there seems to be no radio, as well as no TV. What do you think has happened?"

"I have no idea."

"Do we want to tell people about it?" Roger asked. "It might start another panic."

"We had just as well get everyone alerted. We're all in this together, and we have to make decisions together."

"You're the boss, Jamie."

Jamie moved to the podium and rapped for order. Mary and Kelly took seats to his left. The crowd obviously in a state of agitation gradually settled down.

"Good morning!" Jamie greeted them. "It's nice to see the sun shining for a change. I hope you've all had a good night's sleep, because we've a long day ahead of us. Some of you may have noticed that we have no TV or radio functioning this morning. Also, although phone lines seem to be working, no one anywhere outside our own area is answering them. I have no idea what has happened."

Everyone started talking at once.

"There's no use in asking questions, because I can't answer them. We have to find out the answers for ourselves. The worst prognosis is that everyone in North America, or possibly, even in the world, is dead or in some way incapable of functioning. This seems utterly impossible, but it is a possibility we must face. If that is true, we find ourselves, for reasons I cannot comprehend, living in a small community completely reliant on our own initiative. Does anyone have any ideas about what could have happened?"

There was complete silence in the room as people realized the enormity of the situation in which they were all involved.

"Sir!" A man stood at the back of the room.

"Go ahead," Jamie responded. The middle-aged man was a stranger to Jamie.

"My name is Chuck Marshal. I don't know what happened, but we have to accept things as they are. I'm a dairyman by profession and worked at an experimental farm at Black Creek for years. I have a good friend that operates a dairy down in the Comox Valley. I'd like to go down there and see if he has left, too.

36

I tried to call him this morning, but there was no answer. If he's gone, and the cows aren't being milked, they'll dry up pretty fast. It could be worth our while to keep that herd producing."

"That sounds great, Mr. Marshal. I'm glad someone here is being practical. Take someone to help you and report back here tonight. Regular time, seven o'clock."

"I'll take my wife and son," Marshal replied. "They're also experienced with cows."

"Keith Shaw," Jamie continued, "would you continue your survey to find more people that might still be around? Only today, head out of town and look at other communities. Check on Gold River and Tahsis. Send a team to Sayward and Kelsey Bay. We should also look as far north as Port Hardy if there is time today. You might send a crew up there and let them stay overnight. Split people up into small teams to cover every area that you can. Also, send people south to Comox, Courtenay and Cumberland. I don't think you should go farther south than that today. Everyone should gas up their cars. The Esso Station behind the hotel is unlocked, and you can serve yourselves. Dr. Ron. What's the situation at the hospital?"

Ron McIvor stood to reply. "It's not good, Jamie. We had two more deaths of old people during the night. The hospital morgue is getting full. We have to do something soon. I'll get you a better report this evening."

"Thanks Ron. If you have recommendations, I'd like to hear them this evening. Now, the rest of you get busy around Campbell River, here. Check out your own neighborhoods thoroughly. Go to every house and knock on doors. There could be more abandoned children—like Kelly here. I found Kelly walking down the road this morning. Her parents had gone off and left her to fend for herself. I think their loss is our gain. I don't know how anyone can abandon a girl like her.

"I know that many of you are in a condition of extreme shock. You're worried about family and friends all across the country. But let's face it; you may never see them again. You must rally around, and think about the present. We all need each other, and all of you have something to contribute.

"Now, there's another thing that I would like you to think about. You've designated me as your leader, but I can't do the job alone. We need a council, or a group of some kind, to work with me. So come back here tonight prepared with some ideas.

"I'd like George Brooks to work with me again today. George, I have some special ideas to use your particular capabilities. I'll meet you in the lobby in a few minutes."

Jamie shut off the microphone and turned to Mary. "I have a real job for you, Mary. We need a register of everyone here. I think we should plan on developing a form to fill out for every family, showing family members, professional or vocational capabilities and things like that. We need to know what we have to work with. Maybe you can start a database in the computer, providing we can keep computers operating."

Kelly spoke up. "Jamie, can I go with you?"

"No, little lady. You stay with Mary for today. Maybe you can help the staff here in the hotel."

"Can I go home with you tonight? Please don't leave me." Kelly appeared about to cry.

"You're not going to be abandoned again, sweetheart. I'll be back here to have dinner with you tonight. Now you stay with Mary today, and we will talk more tonight." Jamie turned away and made his way out to meet George Brooks.

George was waiting for him in the lobby, but before they could leave, Ted Parks approached them. "Mr. Jamie, I'm running low on some things in the kitchen. Is there any way to replenish our supplies?"

"The supermarket at the other end of the plaza should have plenty of everything. George, can you open it up for us?"

"Sure, let's take my truck. I may need some tools. Come on."

The three of them crowded into George's service truck and drove to the other end of the plaza. It only took George a few minutes to open the lock on the front door. Swinging the door wide, they walked in. Everything looked completely normal in the store.

"Take anything you need, Ted. We'd just as well use the fresh stuff before it spoils. Do you have any way of getting it to the hotel?"

"I have my pickup here. I'll manage fine. The girls will help me."

"You and the girls are doing a hell of a job, Ted. We all appreciate your efforts."

Jamie turned to George. "Let's take your truck, so we have your tools available."

"Where to?" George asked.

"The airport."

George put the truck in gear, and they headed along Island Highway.

"George?" Jamie asked. "You're a locksmith. Is there any lock you can't open without a key?"

"Not many," George replied. "There're a few, but they have to be tough."

"How about making keys, like ignition keys and things like that?"

"No problem. I make an impression of the lock and then cut a key to fit."

Jamie was silent on the rest of the drive to the airport. When they got there, he had George stop outside the office of a flying club. A Cessna 172 and a 152 two-seat trainer were tied down next to the building. The office door wasn't locked, and they walked in. Jamie opened the middle drawer of a desk and found keys tagged for the two planes.

"We're lucky today. You don't have to make any keys. They left them here for us. You want to go for an airplane ride?"

"Fine with me," George replied.

Selecting the keys for the four place Cessna, Jamie led the way out and unlocked the pilot's door. Trying to remember all the steps required, he started a preflight inspection. George watched carefully but made no comment. Jamie did a walk around of the plane, then, opening the engine cowling, he checked the oil, and drained a bit of gas from the fuel inspection bulb to check for water. A visual inspection of the fuel tanks showed both of them full.

"Everything seems to be in order," he reported to George. "I'm going to take it up for a spin. I haven't flown a plane for, I don't know how many, years. You wait here, and I'll be back in a few minutes, and then we will go for a little sightseeing trip."

Strapping himself into the pilot's seat and running a mental checklist to himself, Jamie continued his pre-start list. He found the trim tab and adjusted it to neutral. Set the gyrocompass to correspond with the magnetic. Altimeter set at field altitude. Toes forward on the rudders to engage the toe brakes. A shot of prime. Throttle cracked a notch. Engage the starter. The engine fired almost instantly.

Releasing the brakes and advancing the throttle, the bird moved smoothly forward. More throttle and they were moving down the taxiway. At the end of the runway, Jamie did a pre-takeoff check. Brakes on for a full power check, right and left magneto check, power back to idle, all gauges in the green. Without thinking, he spun the plane in a complete circle to check for other traffic and then realized that there was probably not an airplane in the sky anywhere. No traffic control, he thought, and no use for the array of radios in the dash.

Advancing the throttle slowly, he accelerated down the runway. Fifty knots an hour, then sixty. He eased back on the yoke. Seventy knots an hour and the wheels left the ground and the exhilaration of flight he had not experienced for many years gripped him. He eased the throttle back and adjusted the trim to climb at eighty knots per hour. At eight hundred feet, he swung the plane to the left a little, then to the right. His feel for an airplane was still there and his confidence grew.

He continued the climb to three thousand feet, then leveled off, adjusted the throttle to what he thought would be the best cruise setting. The air speed indicated 120 knots, and he did a number of turns to familiarize himself with the controls, then decided to try a stall.

Easing back on the throttle, Jamie held back on the yoke to maintain level flight. The speed came down to 100, then 80. At sixty knots indicated, the stall horn came on. He continued to hold back on the yoke. The stall came clean, with only a trace of shudder. As the nose dropped, he added power, holding straight ahead with the rudders. The recovery was quick, with only 500 feet of altitude lost. Satisfied that he was safe with the plane, he returned to the field to pick up George.

Leveling at 1500 feet, he followed the Island Highway south. There was no sign of traffic. Continuing south along the highway, they passed by Courtenay, then the Denman Island Junction. A few miles farther, they saw two cars on the shoulder of the road and then a big semitrailer overturned in the ditch.

"Let's land and take a look," Jamie said.

Continuing down the highway a short way, Jamie checked for power lines or other obstructions, then swung around to head north, throttled back and slowed to eighty knots. Throttling back more, he dropped the flaps and flared out to land. He was on a little fast, but had no problem, braking to a stop opposite the semi. Shutting the engine down, they climbed out and crossed the median to the truck. George climbed on the truck and looked in the window.

"The driver looks dead," he called back as he swung to the ground.

They walked about a hundred yards to the two cars. The first contained a man and a woman, slumped in the front seat, obviously dead. The other car had a couple with three kids in the back, all dead.

Walking back to the plane, George was the first to speak. "I wonder what happened to these people. What about everyone else? God, what are we going to do?"

"I don't know. We just have to do the best we can. We are going to have to make a lot of adjustments, but we'll do it. We have to work together. Let's get back to the River."

The little plane lifted off easily from the highway, and Jamie headed north. Past Courtenay, he swung east over Comox and then up the coast to Comox Canadian Armed Forces Base. He made a circle of the big airport, which government shared with civilian traffic. The field looked deserted.

"Let's land here and see if we can find out anything," Jamie said.

"OK," George agreed.

Jamie slid the plane onto the runway and taxied up to the Air Forces hangars. They got out and walked around. The hangars were unlocked, but there was no sign of anyone around. They continued on to the civilian terminal. A couple of West Coast Air twin-engine commuter planes were parked on the line along with a few light planes. The terminal buildings were empty.

"At least there are no dead people here," Jamie said. "It appears that whatever happened, it happened south of here."

Thirty minutes later, they were on the runway at the Campbell River Airport. Jamie taxied the plane to the fuel station and shut down. "Let's see if we can get gas," he said.

The gas pumps had padlocks on them.

"I'll go get the truck with tools and see about getting these locks off." George volunteered. A few minutes later, he parked the truck nearby and came over with a tool kit. He looked at the padlocks for a minute, and then produced a heavy hammer. Getting into a position that suited him, he swung the hammer for a sharp blow. The lock popped open.

Jamie tried the pump, but the power was off. A small building closeby looked favorable. It too was padlocked. George made short work of it as well. An electrical panel was inside with switches for the pumps. In no time the plane was refueled. Jamie taxied back to the original parking space and secured the plane. He returned the keys to the drawer where he had found them.

Mary greeted them when they entered the hotel. "I bet you guys haven't had any lunch. Let's see if we can get you a sandwich." She led the way into the kitchen.

Kelly was removing dishes from the big dishwasher. Seeing Jamie, she rushed to him and threw her arms around his waist. "Gosh," she said. "I'm glad to see you back."

"Kelly," Mary said, "these fellows haven't had any lunch. Do you suppose you could find them a sandwich?"

"I sure can," Kelly replied as she scampered back to the work counter.

"Let's sit down." Mary indicated a table in the corner. "Jamie, you've taken Kelly's heart by storm. She worried about you all day."

Their conversation was interrupted when Sarah Harris came with coffee. Kelly was right behind her with plates of oversized ham sandwiches. Both men were hungry, and they went to work on the food. Kelly returned to her chores with the dishwasher.

"Kelly's clothes look pretty rough," Jamie remarked. "Maybe we should take her up to her house and get some of her things for her."

"I thought the same," Mary said. "But she says these are the best she has."

"I guess we had better get her outfitted then," Jamie said. "George, before you go home, would you open up the Fields store?"

"No need. The doors aren't locked."

"OK. Mary, would you go with Kelly and me to pick out some clothes for her?"

"I've still got work to do getting ready for tonight," Mary said. "You'd just as well start getting used to being dad, and take her yourself."

"I'm headed for home," George said, getting up from the table. "See you tonight."

Chapter 6

Jamie walked over to where Kelly was emptying the dishwasher. "If you're through here, would you care to go for a walk with me? Grab your coat and come along."

Kelly dashed to a closet to retrieve her coat. "Where are we going?" she asked excitedly.

"You'll see," Jamie said, enjoying making a secret of it. Kelly grabbed him by the hand, almost running to keep up. It was only a short walk to a small department store. The door opened to Jamie's pull, and they entered. The lights were off, but enough light came through the front windows to see quite well.

"What are we doing here?" Kelly asked.

"We're going to see if we can find you some better clothes," Jamie told her. "Those you have don't look too good. First, how about taking off that coat?"

Kelly shrugged out of the coat and tossed it on the checkout counter.

"The coats are over there," she said, leading the way. "I've been here before, but we didn't have money to buy anything."

They shuffled through the rack of children's coats and found a jacket, semi-waterproofed with hood and removable fleece liner. Kelly tried it on. It fit perfectly, and she exclaimed joyfully at its quality.

"Now for some tops," Jamie told her. They found some that looked to be the right size. "You had better try some on," Jamie said. "There's a change room over there."

Ignoring him, Kelly shed the new coat and unceremoniously pulled her old top over her head. Jamie noted the thin frame. She definitely looked malnourished. He would have to rectify that. Pulling on the new top, Kelly spun around and threw up her arms. "How does it look?"

"It looks great, if you like it," Jamie told her.

"Can I really have it?"

"Yes, you can really have it. Pick out a couple more."

"Oh, thank you, thank you. I'd like the gray one and the white one."

"OK. Pick up your coat and bring them along. We need to find some better shoes, some new jeans and some underclothes and socks."

Twenty minutes later they left the store, Kelly lugging a duffel bag stuffed with the new outfits. They put the duffel bag in the trunk of Jamie's car and returned to the hotel.

Mary was coming out of the hotel office, and Kelly ran to her, threw her arms around her waist, then backed up and shrugged out of her coat.

"Look what Jamie got me," she exclaimed, "a whole new outfit. Two more tops, and another pair of jeans, and six panties. I've never in my life had so many wonderful clothes. Thank you Jamie. I love you."

"You really look great, kiddo," Mary said. "You deserve them."

* * *

Jamie took his place at the podium at seven o'clock. Mary had things well organized. The tables were moved out and chairs lined up to accommodate a larger crowd. Jamie estimated there must be 150 people in the room. Mary had placed a stack of registration forms beside him that she had prepared and printed on the computer. The microphone had been hooked up and turned on and a portable mike was on a stand in the center aisle. A bang with the gavel and the crowd fell quiet.

"I'll make the first report tonight," Jamie said. "Today, I discovered that, even after thirty years, I can still fly an airplane. George and I went to the airport, found a plane and went for a spin. We went south past Courtenay and past the Denman Island intersection. A few miles further we spotted two cars on the side of the road, then a big semi on its side in the ditch. We landed on the highway to take a look. The truck driver was dead, as were the people in the two cars. We took off and flew back over Courtenay and Comox. Everything was quiet there, with no evidence of death. We landed at Comox Air Base and looked around; we found nobody there and no dead people. We can assume that anyone beyond Denman turnoff is dead. We will fly farther south tomorrow and see if we can verify that. That, in a nutshell, is my report."

Roger Burkham stood and took the portable mike. "Jamie, do you really believe everyone south of there is dead?"

"It appears that way," Jamie said. "We will try to verify it tomorrow."

"Don't you think it could be dangerous to go down there? It might have been some kind of disease that killed those people." Roger seemed deeply concerned.

"I don't think so," Jamie replied. "It appears to have happened suddenly, like some kind of gas. People just seemed to have gone to sleep wherever they were. Anyway, we will chance it. We have to find out. Next report. I'll call on Keith Shaw."

Keith reported that he had sent teams out as requested. "They found about thirty people in a group in Comox, and some of them are in the room tonight. Ten people were left on the Indian Reserve out of Gold River. They will come over tomorrow. No one was in Tahsis. Two teams going to the north end of the island would stay over in Port Hardy and come back tomorrow. Charlie Johnson had taken a boat to Quadra Island. There are a few people on the island. They will check the whole island and report tomorrow."

"Is there a spokesman from the Comox group?" Jamie asked.

A man stood and someone passed the mike to him. "My name is Bob Elder. I'm president of the Comox Rotary Club. We have 32 people accounted for in Comox. We are not as well organized as you are here, and we would like to join your group for whatever you want to do. I've been talking to Keith Shaw, and we will get together and do what he says."

"Good," Jamie said. "Welcome to our group. We don't know where we're going yet, but we're glad to have you aboard."

"Chuck Marshal, what did you find on the dairy?"

"It was as we expected," Chuck reported. "The farm was abandoned. We rounded up the cows, and they were glad to be milked. If we milk once a day until we get organized better, they will hold out until we can get them back on a twice a day schedule. A young man on the farm next door saw us and came over. His folks had left, but he elected to stay. He has pigs, chickens and other animals. I told him to take the milk and feed it to his animals."

"Good work, Chuck. Now let's hear from Dr. Ron."

"We had two more deaths last night, and the morgue is full. We have to do something about the bodies. I would like to talk to you later about that."

"Thanks, Ron. We are getting more of an idea about how we stand, but there is still a long way to go. Now I want some help. I think we should elect, or appoint, a council to sit with me to form a more definitive leadership. Does anyone have any ideas on the subject?"

Roger Burkham stood. "I have a proposal to make. You are doing an outstanding job in running this show. You know who you would like to have working with you. I move that we authorize you to appoint a five or more person council, with you as the president."

"I'll second that motion." It was Constable Pat Draper.

"All in favor!"

Hands went up all over the room.

"All opposed!"

Nobody responded.

"Well, it looks as if I have the tiger by the tail. I'll do the best I can. Later, after we get better organized, we will hold a formal election. By that time you will know who the workers are, and may elect who you want."

"Now for the council. My first appointment will be Mary Andrews. She will serve on the council and act as secretary. Second, I would select Keith Shaw. Third, Dr. Ron, would you serve? Then, I would like to have Constable Draper and Charlie Johnson. Will all of you meet with me after this meeting? Also, would Bob Elder meet with us?"

"Now, one more thing. Mary has prepared a registration form. Mary will pass them out to you as you leave. Kelly, you may help her. Please fill them out and get them back to us as soon as possible. Would the new council members stay for a brief meeting? Meeting adjourned. Be here at nine in the morning. Good night."

Mary, with Kelly in tow, hurried to the door to hand out the census forms.

The crowd filtered out of the room, accepting the census forms as they went. The newly appointed council gathered around Jamie. Bob Elder came forward and held out his hand. The handshake was firm.

"Welcome to our group, Bob," Jamie exclaimed. "Have you surveyed your area completely?"

"Only Comox. It took us too long to recover from the shock. We still hadn't figured out that there was more going on than the

46

initial panic. I have assumed leadership of the group, but I'm sorry to say I don't have the capabilities that you have demonstrated. I'll subject our group to your leadership."

"How about serving on our council?" Jamie asked.

"If you think I can contribute something, I'll be glad to."

"OK. Let's call this meeting to order. This council has a tremendous load to carry for the foreseeable future. There are going to be an awful lot of difficult decisions to make. We will operate as a democratic group. All decisions will be approved by vote. Majority rules. I think we have a top group of intelligent people here, and I think we will be able to function efficiently. Now, for our first piece of business. Dr. Ron, you requested to talk to me after the meeting. Now you are on the council and can make your first presentation."

"I think this group has been subject to a hijacking. I never saw an election carried out so smoothly."

A chorus of laughing assent went around the table.

Ron continued, "That's the measure of a skillful leader. I think this council will go far. Now, my immediate problem is the growing number of bodies we are accumulating at the hospital. They must be moved or disposed of in some way."

"Don't they deserve a funeral of some kind?" Mary asked.

"None of them have relatives or family available," Ron replied. "Funerals are for the living. The dead do not care. I would recommend cremation. I think I can gather up enough manpower to handle it. Instructions for operating the crematorium up at the cemetery are posted on the wall. We have to learn to do things we have never done before. I think I can handle the project."

"Could we have a motion to approve Ron's request?" said Jamie.

The motion was made and approved unanimously.

"Keith, maybe you can work with Bob Elder, let him run some of the work down island."

"Good idea," Keith replied. "Ill put him in charge of surveys in the south end of our area."

"Good deal," said Jamie, "And how about a farm survey of all farming opportunities between here and Courtenay? We are going to have to live off the land in the future, and we need to locate as many people as possible on farms, to both feed themselves and produce food for those who don't grow things."

"We'll start on it right away," Keith promised.

47

"OK," Jamie replied. "I think we have all done enough for today. Let's go home and go to bed. I'm tired. Good night, everyone. Come on Kelly, let's go home."

"Miss Mary," Kelly exclaimed as she jumped up and grabbed Jamie's hand. "You said he would take me and you were right."

* * *

Kelly exclaimed in awe as Jamie pushed the button on his garage door opener and the door swung open, then closed when they drove inside. She had never seen a remote door opener before. She was further awed when they walked into the spacious and comfortable house and her own bedroom.

"Gosh! This is nice," Kelly cried. "Where's the bathroom?"

"Right through that door. You have your own. And there is a new toothbrush and toothpaste in the vanity drawer. Julie always kept it there in case we had guests that had forgotten theirs. Now it's past bedtime for both of us. Take a shower, if you want, or wait till morning. I always take my shower when I get up."

"Every morning?" Kelly questioned.

"Yep! Every morning."

With that, he gave her a quick hug and left the room.

* * *

Jamie was in the meeting room early and set up chairs on each side of the podium for council members. The crowd began to file in, and Jamie motioned the council members to join him at the head table. "From now on," he told them, "you will all share the hot seat with me."

There was a good crowd when Jamie called the meeting to order.

"We had a productive council meeting last night. We added another person to the council, Bob Elder, leader of the group in Comox." Jamie went on to review the results of the meeting.

"I am going to fly south on the island today," Jamie continued. "We'll go as far as Victoria if we have time, and try to determine what the situation is. I'll take George with me to ride shotgun and open any locks that need opening. You all know who the council members are now. If I am not available, bring your questions or concerns to any member of council. We are going to dispense with morning public meetings, but continue the evening meetings, at seven o'clock, until further notice. If you need groceries, the market at the end of the plaza and the store at Mercroft are open for self-service. Go in and help yourselves; there's no checkout. The perishables will not last, so they need to be used. This meeting is adjourned. See you tonight."

Chapter 7

Jamie sat on the side of the bed and tried to get his wits working. Why had he taken on the responsibility for leadership of a group of people that would have to establish a new community, disconnected from the world around them? What did he and his followers face in the future? At the moment, he was unable to grasp the enormity of the problem. Would he be able to cope with it? He sat for a moment, thinking, and his mind began to clear.

I guess I had better get going, Jamie thought. I can't solve our problems sitting here like a dunce. He staggered erect and headed for the bathroom.

Jamie was turning on the shower, when he realized that he had another problem; he had forgotten about Kelly. My God, I've taken on the job of caring for a 10-year-old female. I don't know anything about her, except that she is attractive and likable. I don't know anything about raising kids. What am I going to do with her?

Shutting off the shower, Jamie threw on a bathrobe and went to awaken his new full-time guest. Retrieving his sense of humor, he shook Kelly awake. "Rise and shine, sleeping beauty. You have thirty minutes to get showered and dressed."

"OK," Kelly mumbled. "I'll be ready."

Jamie had just entered the living room when Kelly came from her bedroom with her shoes in her hand "What are we going to do today, Jamie?"

"We'll go down to the hotel and have breakfast. You'll stay with Mary, and George and I will fly down toward Victoria and see what we can see."

"Can I go with you?" Kelly asked. "I've never been in an airplane. I wouldn't be any trouble, and I'd sure like to be with you."

"Not this time, Kelly. You'll have to stay at the hotel with Mary. As soon as I have time, I'll take you for a plane ride. Come on, it's time to go."

"Oh darn," Kelly exclaimed as she followed Jamie out of the house.

* * *

By nine o'clock, Jamie had the Cessna in the air with George beside him. It was a beautiful day with unlimited visibility. There's nothing like flying to make a person feel good and forget his problems, Jamie thought. In spite of all the problems, it was great to be in the air again. Forty-five minutes later, they were letting down over the Departure Bay Ferry Terminal at Nanaimo. There had been no sign of any activity on any of the roads they had flown over, except for the occasional vehicle in the ditch or stalled on the road. The ferry dock was empty but the parking lot was jammed with cars. Flying low over the lot, they were able to see people in the cars, with an occasional one slumped on the ground by an open door. Jamie pulled up and they headed on south to the Duke Point Terminal; it was the same there, with cars lined far back on the access road.

"My God," George spluttered. "There must be thousands of people dead around here."

"Yes," Jamie replied. "We'll probably never know how many there are. I'm not about to try to make a count. And later, after they all start to decay, it won't be a pleasant place to be. Let's take a look at Victoria."

They came in along the coast from the north. The ferry terminal at Sydney, the departure site for the route to Vancouver was similar to the other terminals. The parking lot was full with cars lined up on the approach road. Swinging to the nearby airport, they flew over the runway and could see no sign of activity on the field. A twin-engine commuter plane was near the end of the taxiway, off the pavement with its nose wheel collapsed, tail pointing in the air.

"Let's take a look," Jamie said, as he swung around and lined up for a landing. He landed close to the end of the runway and turned off on the taxiway to pass by the disabled plane. It was obvious what happened. The pilots were slumped in their seats in the cockpit, and the cabin had an almost full load of passengers. All appeared dead. The crew had been overcome while the plane was underway, had lost control and run off the taxiway.

Parking the plane in front of the terminal, they got out to look around. Doors were all unlocked, and no one was in evidence.

"I'll bet," George said, "that the last of the airport crew were leaving on that plane. That was a cleanup operation, but it was too late."

"Looks that way," Jamie agreed. "Is that a fuel truck parked over there by that hangar? Let's take a look."

It was a large semi with compartments for 100-octane gas and jet fuel.

"If we can figure out how to operate this critter," Jamie commented, "let's top our fuel tanks. I always prefer to fly on the top half."

Fortunately, the keys were in it, and after some confusion, they managed to figure out the system, and filled the tanks.

Jamie didn't bother to return to the runway, but took off from the taxiway and headed south to Victoria. They made a circle over downtown and flew low past the legislature building and over the harbor. No sign of activity was apparent anywhere. Climbing to about 800 feet, he flew up Douglas Street and swung west along the multi-lane highway leading out of the city.

"Hey, look," George exclaimed. "I believe there are a couple people down there walking along the road."

The two people were waving frantically.

Jamie swung the plane around and made another pass over them, waggling the wings, advising that he had seen them. Straightening out down the highway, he looked for wires or other obstructions. There looked to be a fair distance between a power line and an overpass that was clear, so he turned back and put down, coasting under the overpass to stop near the two. Shutting down the motor, he waited for them to approach. The two, apparently women, came running to the plane.

Both women were talking excitedly, and it was hard to make sense of what they were saying. One was young, good looking and slender. The other was middle aged and on the plump side.

"Hey, calm down," Jamie demanded. "One of you talk at a time. We can't understand you. Take it easy."

They both stopped talking. The older woman held her hand out, indicating to the younger one to keep still and let her do the talking. "I'm Hazel Evans, and this is my daughter, Sidney. We thought there was no one else left alive in the world. We didn't know what to do. We live maybe a mile from here. We started walking toward downtown, hoping to find someone. We saw the plane, and we were worried that you would not see us. We didn't think you would land here. Thank you for stopping."

"Slow up. Take it easy," Jamie requested. "Relax and tell us what happened."

"Let me talk, Mom," Sidney requested. "My husband, Carl, and I have not been getting along for some time. He beat me up and threatened to kill me, and when I tried to leave him, he really got violent. Wednesday morning was the worst. He dragged me into the car and drove over to Mom's house. We got to Mom's before the series of earthquakes. That really touched him off. He said we had to get off the island immediately. We refused to go, so he left alone. About an hour later he called on the phone. He said he knew Mom had a lot of money in the house, that we should get it and he would be back to pick us up soon, that he had a gun and if we didn't cooperate he'd kill us both. There's an old bomb shelter under the house; been there ever since the folks bought the house, that Carl didn't know about, so we locked ourselves in the shelter. We heard him crashing around in the house, shouting and swearing. He stayed around till about midnight, and then we heard the car start and drive away. We went to sleep and woke up about three o'clock. There was a funny smell, and we got a little dizzy and sick. After a while we felt better and slept till late in the morning. When we came out, everything was still; no TV or radio and no one answered the phone. We stayed home till this morning, and then we decided to walk toward town. It's really scary to be all alone."

"You were lucky," Jamie said. "Apparently some kind of gas or poison killed everyone. You didn't get a full dose because you were in the shelter. We are from the north part of the island, and for some reason we were not affected. There are a few of us up there still alive. We were trying to find anyone else who survived and trying to learn what happened."

"What are we going to do?" demanded Sidney.

"We suggest that you get in the back seat of that airplane and go to Campbell River with us," Jamie told her.

"But we don't know anyone in Campbell River."

"You don't know anyone here, either," Jamie said. "There isn't anyone left here for you to know."

Hazel spoke up. "We'll have to go back to the house and get some things, and some money."

"You can get what you need in Campbell River. And as for money, it's the most useless stuff in the world right now. You don't need it. We don't have time to go to your house; get in and let's go."

"I'm scared to death of small airplanes," Hazel said.

"Mom, you'll just have to control your fear," Sidney said. "I'm scared too, but I'm going to get in that airplane and you are too. Let's go."

Jamie climbed out in a long arc and headed east. "We have lots of fuel; let's swing over Vancouver and see how things look over there." Jamie continued to climb as they passed over the shore and the San Juan Islands were showing up ahead.

"Looks like a ferry boat down there against that island," George commented.

"Yeah," Jamie agreed. "Maybe we better go down and take a look at it."

The ferry was aground, its bow up on shore and the stern down from the outgoing tide. It appeared to be fully loaded, but showed no sign of movement onboard.

"They must have been hit while they were underway," George speculated.

"Looks that way," Jamie agreed, adding throttle and starting to climb again.

A short time later they were over Tsawwassen Ferry Terminal. Two ferries were docked, but there was no sign of life. Cars on the departure lanes were not moving. Continuing on, they picked up Highway 10 and followed it east. The westbound lanes were empty, but a steady string of cars were in the eastbound lanes, none moving. Many were in the ditch; some overturned. Some cars had rear-ended the ones stopped ahead of them. It was the same story they had seen elsewhere. The drivers had apparently been stricken suddenly.

"Look at that mountain," George exclaimed.

"That's Mt. Baker," Jamie responded. The mountain stood out like a lighthouse in the brilliant afternoon sunshine. What was unusual was the cloud forming over the summit. It was growing, expanding in all directions, like a giant rapidly expanding mushroom.

"It's a volcano," Jamie marveled. "The damn thing is blowing up. They've been reporting activity around it for weeks. Guess it finally decided to blow. Wow!"

"Are we in any danger?" asked Hazel.

"I don't think so," replied Jamie. "We are at least 50 miles away, and there is little wind. Nevertheless, it's time to head for home. It's going to take an hour or more to get there." He added

54

throttle and started climbing. "We'll pass over Vancouver on the way." They could see no movement in or around the city.

* * *

It was after three o'clock when Jamie made his way into the hotel and introduced the two women to Mary. Mary agreed to find Sarah and have her get the two settled in the hotel and then went to find some lunch for Jamie and George. A few minutes later they were sitting in the kitchen with a bottle of beer and a sandwich.

"Jamie, you need to take Kelly back to her old place so she can get some things that she needs," Mary told him. "I think she has some personal stuff she would like to have."

"OK," Jamie said. "As soon as I get through with this sandwich. We have some time to spare before evening. You come with us."

A half hour later, the three of them were in front of the dilapidated mobile home that Kelly had lived in.

"My God," Mary exclaimed, "do people live in a hovel like this?"

They walked through the door and stood dismayed at the conditions of the house. It was filthy dirty and had a bad odor.

"Come in my bedroom and I'll get what I need," Kelly said.

The bedroom was almost too small for the three of them to get into. There was a built-in single bunk, a small dresser and a closet without a door. The walls were of warped paneling, some of it cracking and peeling. Mildew showed on the corners of the ceiling.

"There is not much that I want," Kelly reported. "Just some books and a box of my own special things." Opening the top drawer of the dresser, Kelly pulled out a shoebox and set it on top of the dresser, followed by half a dozen worn looking books.

"That wasn't a nice place I lived in, was it?" Kelly asked as she headed for the car.

"I hope you never have to live in a place like that again," Jamie said.

Chapter 8

The evening meeting was well underway, and Jamie had completed the account of his flight to Victoria, when a question came from the floor.

"What caused all of these deaths?"

"Dr. Ron, do you want to handle that question?" Jamie said.

"It's impossible to answer that question with any certainty, but from what Jamie has told me, it was probably some sort of a very quick acting gas. That's only a guess."

"Shouldn't you pick up one of those bodies and do an autopsy?" The man suggested.

"Sir," Ron replied, "I am only a general practice physician. I am not a forensic scientist. I do not have the skill or the equipment to do such an autopsy."

"But, Doctor..."

"Let's move on," Jamie interrupted him. "We have no way of knowing what killed those people. We probably will never know. We are going to have to live with a lot of ifs, maybes and whys.

"Now to get on with things. Keith Shaw and Bob Elder have conducted a brief, preliminary survey of farmland available to us. It appears that most of the viable farms are in the Comox Valley within six or eight kilometers from Courtenay-Comox. Probably we'll make that area the center of our new community, because farming is going to be the most important part of our economy in the future. The council is going to go down tomorrow as a group to further examine the idea, also the non-farming residential situation."

A lady stood in the middle of the room, and Jamie recognized her with a motion of his hand. "Do you mean that you are going to recommend that we all give up our homes in Campbell River and move to Courtenay?" she demanded.

"That's a possibility," Jamie told her, "but no decisions have been made yet. We intend to have that answer for you tomorrow night."

"What's the big hurry?" she asked.

"The big hurry is that we must get people settled on these farms at once. Most of the places have livestock, and it's important that the stock be taken care of. On top of that, spring is coming. The ground needs to be prepared and planted. We must not tarry.

"Now, to everyone who thinks they would like to have a farm. We'll probably start some type of selection process tomorrow night. If you would like to go down in the valley tomorrow and look around and maybe get an idea of what place you would like, then make a second and third choice. Be here for sure tomorrow. If you need gas, the pumps are open at the Esso Station. See you all at seven, tomorrow evening."

* * *

It was another sunny morning when Keith Shaw pulled the van he had liberated from the Ford Dealership up facing the pickup truck parked on Ryan Road. Bob Elder and Joe Gardner were studying a map spread out on the hood of the truck. They both turned and waved a welcome as the balance of the council piled out of the van to join them. After a flurry of introductions, Joe took charge.

"As you know," Joe said, "I own a farm down here. Farming has been a major interest in my life. I've learned everything I can about farming in the valley, and if you have any questions, just ask.

"There is one thing we need to do," Joe went on. "We have to mark places already occupied and continue to mark places that are allotted to new owners. Perhaps it would be a good idea to get a bunch of spray cans of orange paint and mark places as they become off limits. I'm sure we can find the paint at the building supply store up Ryan Road. Chuck Marshal is on a dairy that he has taken charge of. He should be left there, and he said a young neighbor was hanging on."

"Can you suggest a place we can turn into temporary head-quarters?" Jamie asked.

"The Tsolum school is about as central as any place," Joe replied. "And I'm sure George can open it easy enough."

"OK, George," Jamie ordered. "Would you go on up and get it opened and we'll be right along."

"Jamie," Kelly demanded, "can I go with George? I'd like to see him open a lock."

"Curiosity can be fatal to cats, young lady," Jamie said.

57

George spoke up. "Sure, let her come, Jamie. I'll teach her to pick locks."

"Oh, thanks George." Kelly was bubbling over with enthusiasm as she bounced into the service truck.

* * *

George had the school unlocked, and Joe decided the most important thing to start was to get the occupied places marked. They loaded into the van and, with George and his new apprentice trailing along in the service truck, made Chuck Marshal's dairy farm the first stop. They visited with Chuck for a few minutes, and then sprayed large Xs on both gateposts. They found Chuck's young neighbor and explained what was going on. His name was Frank Eberly; he was 22 years old, had grown up on the place and didn't want to leave it under any circumstances. He was very upset that his parents had fled and were probably dead now. He showed them around the farm, with its neat house, small barn, chicken coops and pigsty. "I can live off of this place with no trouble at all," he said, "Especially if I can trade eggs and pork and maybe some produce for some other essentials that I can't raise here."

"You are the sort of person we need in our new community," Jamie told him, shaking hands in preparation to leave.

At his own farm, Joe introduced them to his wife, Ronda, a sturdy-looking attractive dark-skinned black-haired woman with almost oriental features and their 10-year-old daughter, Susie, and 12-year-old Bruce.

The farm, 80 acres of mostly meadowland, was neat and prosperous looking. The house was quite modern, and the barn and other outbuildings were painted and in good repair. Joe told them he raised a few beef cattle, had two milk cows, all the eggs they could use and plenty of garden produce and fruit. A structural engineer by profession, Joe had given up full-time employment to do consulting on a part-time basis. He was ready to go full time on the farm, which was his true love.

They spent the rest of the morning driving around the valley. George cut the chains off of several gates, and unlocked a number of houses. By noon they were back in the schoolhouse conference room. George and Joe, along with Mary and Kelly, took the van up the highway two miles to the Mercroft store to see if they could get something for lunch. They were back in a short time with milk and soft drinks, an assortment of cold cuts, bread and a few other things. They found the school cafeteria open, and Mary and Kelly soon had sandwiches ready for everyone.

"I want you all to realize," Jamie told them as they started eating, "that a few days from now, this milk in the stores will be spoiled, the cold meats unsafe to eat and the bread so stale and dry that it would be useless. We're going to have to adapt to a different life. It scares me a bit, but I am greatly reassured by the people we have here, especially Kelly. If we can all catch some of her enthusiasm and zest for life, we cannot help but be successful in our new venture."

"I'll drink to that," Mary spoke up. "Kelly has an effervescence about her that can't help but have a favorable influence on all who come in contact with her. Here's to Kelly."

Lunch finished, they spent an hour discussing how to dole out the farm properties, and finally settled on a form of raffle. Mary said that she could get it ready for the evening meeting, but she needed to get back to Campbell River and get to work on it. Kelly volunteered to help her, and Mary accepted.

Back at the hotel, Mary and Kelly went to work in the office, and Jamie left the hotel and walked down the mall to Fields Department Store to try his hand at shopping for a young girl. Luckily, he remembered the sizes that Kelly had selected on their first shopping trip. He filled a couple of shopping bags, putting them in the trunk of his car, and returned to the hotel to help Mary prepare for the meeting.

* * *

The meeting room was full when Jamie and Mary got there with Kelly tagging along.

"Good evening," Jamie spoke loudly to gain attention. "We're going to get started immediately, as we have a lot to do tonight. Your entire council spent today in the Comox Valley looking over the farmland situation. I think this is one of the finest little farming valleys in Canada. Most of it is bottomland, situated along the Tsolum River. We all seem to agree that we should center our farming activities in this area and to make the Tsolum Primary School headquarters for the time being. This is, of course, providing that you people approve of our program. Are there any questions?"

"How do you propose to assign these farms?" asked a man from the back.

"Mary, here, has designed a lottery that I believe is the fairest possible way," Jamie said. "Everyone will have an equal chance."

"Will we have ownership of the farms?" It was the same man. Jamie did not know him.

"Yes. Bob Elder has agreed to check the area assessment office for legal descriptions, former owners, and so forth. When that is done, sometime down the road, we intend to set up our own system, and you would become the registered owner of your plot of land. You would have full control of it."

"What if the original owner comes back?"

"We would, in all good conscience, have to give him back his land. But I can't see much possibility of that happening. You're not putting out any money on this, so you could return to your original place and you'd be no worse off."

"I don't think it's right to just take over people's property..."

A man stood in the back of the room, waving for attention. "Mr. President! Mr. President!" Jamie recognized Ken Griffith, an employee of a local fish farm.

"Yes Ken," Jamie answered.

"Mr. President, we can chew this thing over all night and nothing will be gained. Let's get on with the business at hand. I would like to make a motion that we accept the plan that council has proposed and get on with it."

The motion was seconded and hands went up all over the room in approval.

"Mr. President." It was a lady that Jamie did not know. "Before we go on, could I ask one question?"

"Go ahead, please," Jamie responded.

"You're making plans for these people, but nothing has been said about those of us who would be impossible farmers. Are we going to move somewhere?"

"Good question. We've talked about it but haven't come to a definite conclusion. We still have some more research to do before we can bring you an answer. It's essential that we get these farm folk settled, and then we'll come up with recommendations for the rest of you. OK?"

The woman nodded her agreement.

"We're going to work out of the Tsolum School tomorrow. Three properties are already occupied, and orange crosses are sprayed on the gate or mailboxes to mark them. Those are off limits, of course. Number one will be the first person out. You'll be given a can of orange spray paint, and you go make your selection. When you have decided, spray a mark in a prominent place and the place is yours. Return to the school, turn in your spray can and report what property you've chosen. Find a street number, name or something to identify it. We'll probably send out two or three people at a time and hope there isn't too much conflict."

* * *

Arriving home that night, Jamie got the packages from Fields and followed Kelly into the house. In the living room, Kelly plunked down on the couch with a big sigh of relief.

"Golly, I'm tired," she exclaimed.

"So am I," Jamie said, "but I have something for you before you go to bed." He placed the packages on the couch beside her.

Kelly forgot her tiredness as she opened bags and dumped the contents on the couch.

"Wow!" she stood and held one of the nightgowns up in front of her, then traded it for the other one. "They're beautiful. I've never had anything so nice. And a nice robe. And bubble bath and bath powder." She marveled over the treasures. "Jamie, you're so good to me. How did I ever get so lucky to find a dad like you?" She ran and threw her arms around his neck. "I love you, Jamie."

Gathering up her new treasures, she dashed for her bedroom. In a minute she was back, wearing the blue nightie and carrying the bathrobe. She threw the robe on the couch and twirled around to model the gown. The color was perfect for her and the fit good. It reached to mid calf and was loose enough to give her some room to grow.

"It feels wonderful," she exclaimed. "How does it look, Jamie?"

"A lovely gown on a lovely lady," Jamie told her.

She put on the robe and belted it around the waist. "And this will keep me warm. Thanks a thousand times."

"OK," Jamie told her. "You better get off to bed, now. We have to be down at the school at eight in the morning."

Chapter 9

When the van with Jamie and his executive team pulled into the Tsolum School parking lot at 7:45 AM, they found an old model large car waiting for them. Teresa Blunt climbed out of the car and came striding across the lot to meet them. At first glance she looked like a man, with work boots, well-worn blue jeans and a slouch hat. Probably 5 foot, 10 inches, with broad shoulders and a weathered face, she definitely could pass for a farmer or other outdoor man. Closer inspection showed a blue work shirt stretched over full breasts, long blond hair tied in ponytail and piercing blue eyes.

"Good morning, Mr. Jamie," she said, handing over a spray can of orange paint. "We've got our place marked, and we're ready to go farming."

"Good for you," Jamie replied. "Anything you need to know?"

"Only if it's OK for us to move in right away. The boys are anxious to get started. There's a lot to do to get that place in shape. Thanks for taking charge and getting everybody settled. I'd like you to meet my sons."

The three young men came ambling across the lot. All were powerful looking men, six-foot plus with blond hair that matched that of their mother.

"Boys, this is President Jamie. Sorry Jamie, I don't know your last name."

"Jamie's good enough. May I call you Teresa?"

"Call me anything you like, just so you smile when you do it. This first big fellow here is Nils. He's 22. The next one is Leif, 20. And this skinny one here that's not grown yet is Lars, almost 19. Between them there's close to 600 pounds of Scandinavian beef that's ready to work."

Jamie shook hands with the three. Their hands were all work-hardened; their grips crushingly firm.

"Your hands feel like you're all used to hard work. What have you been doing?"

"Working a wood lot up toward Kelsey Bay," Teresa answered. "Their dad worked it for years until he died a couple of years ago, and the boys and I have kept on. We'd take out enough timber every year to make a good living and still have plenty of wood growing. Mostly hand work, so they're in good condition. But it doesn't look like there'll be much demand for raw logs now, so we jumped at the chance to take a farm. We'll make a living on it come hell or high water. Only thing to make it perfect is to get some wives to keep these fellows calmed down."

"Well, I'd lay odds that you'll make a success of it," replied Jamie. "As for wives, first appearances indicate that there's a surplus of women in our colony. It's just up to you fellows to run them down. Go in the office and tell Mary where your place is, then you can get to work on it. Good luck."

As the Blunts left, a minivan with a family of five pulled in. The three kids, appearing from seven to twelve in age, rushed to where Charlie Johnson was waiting and threw themselves into the arms of the delighted man.

"Hi, Granddad," they all shouted at once.

"Jamie," Charlie beckoned for him to come over. "This is part of my family. This young one is Jane. The next one is Richard, and this little beauty is Phyllis. She's almost 14 and thinks she's all grown up. And this is my son, Garry, and his wife, Annie."

Jamie shook hands with the tall young man and the short sturdy looking copper-skinned wife.

"I've number nine," Garry said, "and I don't think anyone else will claim it. It's farther away on the other side of the river at the end of a road. We found it yesterday morning and stayed there all day and nobody came near."

"Something special about the place?" Jamie asked.

"It's pretty much a horse ranch. There's a bunch of horses, both saddle and work. I've been talking to Dad, and he agrees with me that there's a good future for horses here. We'll eventually be out of power equipment, and horses are the answer. Besides, the whole family's horse crazy. We already have five. The place will raise enough hay; there's some good pasture, a fine garden spot, and a couple of milk cows. We'll do fine on it."

"All right," Jamie told him, "I'll give you a paint can. Go ahead and mark it. Then come back here and register it. That's a fine looking family you have, Charlie. You should be proud of them."

"I am," the big chief replied. "Annie's a bright woman and hard working. All of the kids have been getting top grades in school and have had no troubles because they're Indian. Which reminds me, what are we going to do about school? We need to educate our young people."

"We must open a school as soon as possible. I think we've some teachers among us. As soon as we get organized, we should make it a priority. How about you take on that project, along with seeing your people are integrated into our society?"

"I'm not very well educated to take on that job." Charlie sounded doubtful. "Didn't even get through high school. But if you think I can do it, I'll give it a try."

"I think you're pretty well self-educated, Charlie," Jamie said. "And you can draft people to help you. You'll do fine."

More cars were lining up, and Keith Shaw was handing out paint cans. Mary was busy in the office with registration.

Joe Gardner drove in with another man in the car. They got out and approached Jamie.

"Jamie, meet Andy Blankenship," Joe said. "Andy's an electrical engineer retired from B. C. Hydro. He was in charge of the generating plants on the Puntledge River and at Elk Falls. He has some ideas about keeping electrical service going for us."

Jamie shook hands with the newcomer. "I've been puzzling my mind about that," he said. "We can sure do with some expertise on it."

"I've been thinking about it quite a bit myself," Andy replied. "The most important thing's to get us disconnected from the provincial grid. If something went down anywhere on the mainland, it could shut us down and we'd have a hard time getting back up again. I can down rate the generators to furnish the amount of power we need. We should keep shutting lines down until we're just serving our own area. The fewer hot lines we have, the less danger we have of failure, and the better chance we have of making repairs. I need a man or two to help me, and I can handle it."

"Sounds good," Jamie told him. "Let's go in the office and see if Mary has an electrician registered on her census."

When they asked Mary, she thought a minute. "I remember typing a census form for a man that said he was a heavy-duty electrician. I can't remember his name, but I think I can find it. Maybe Kelly can do it. Kelly, can you go through the census forms and find one that says heavy-duty electrician in the profession blank?"

"Sure, I'll find it," Kelly replied. She picked up the forms, went to the table in the conference room, and started looking at them one by one.

"Here it is," Kelly shouted. "Found it right away."

The man was listed as Dave Jorgensen, heavy-duty electrician. He was single, 39 years old, and had been working for a firm that built power lines and installed switching equipment. Jamie gave the information to Andy and asked him to contact him as soon as possible.

"Sounds like that might be your man," Jamie said.

"Fine," Andy replied. "In the meantime, I'll study some things out and see if I can get us disconnected from the mainland grid. There's a substation south of here. I might be able to shut it down from there. Would it be all right if I shut down the whole south island at the same time?"

"Sure," Jamie said. "The power has to go down south of here sooner or later. It had might as well be sooner. I can't think of any reason to keep it going."

"I'll try to shut off the main grid, and let the rest go a few days, just in case."

The end of the day found 23 properties assigned to new tenants, all marked and recorded in Mary's register with the best available descriptions and locations. It was late, and all were tired by the time they got back to the hotel. Ted and his staff were prepared for them with bowls of hot chili beans.

Chapter 10

Jamie and Kelly were home by eight-thirty, relaxing in the living room.

"Gee, I wish we had TV," Kelly said. "There isn't much to do with no TV or radio. Do you suppose we'll ever have them again?"

"It's unlikely," Jamie told her. "Unless we find that some part of the world was not affected by whatever killed everyone. We'll have to find other ways to entertain ourselves. We can play games, or we can do a lot of reading. The libraries are still here, so there are thousands of books to read. And maybe we have people among us that can write new ones, if we can learn how to make paper to print them on. There're many things that we're going to have to learn because there are so few of us. We could spend a lifetime learning how to do the things that we've never learned before, because someone else knew how and did them for us. Then there's plain old conversation among friends and family to pass the time with."

"But what do we talk about?"

"There're lots of things to talk about," Jamie said. "Like you. We haven't had much time to talk since I found you, so I don't know much about your previous life."

"But I don't know what to tell you," complained Kelly. "I don't know what you are interested in."

"I'm interested in everything and anything about your life. I want to know about your schools, places you lived, friends you had. It will take us weeks to get around to all of your history."

"Maybe you won't want me around if I tell you too much about the bad things that have happened to me."

"Hey, sweetheart, I'm stuck with you now. Whatever happened to you in the past is over with. We are going to live for the future and hope that it is good to us. That's mostly up to us. We have to try to make the best lives possible for ourselves. You have the right attitude for that. You have to keep that attitude up and force it on me. Don't let me get down in the dumps. Now, to start with, I'd like to know about your schooling. Did you get good grades?"

"I'll show you." Kelly came back with the shoebox containing her personal belongings. Rummaging in the box, she came up with several cards. "I have all of my report cards from all of the schools I went to since the third grade. Here's the last one from Calgary. I only went to that school for three months."

Jamie took the card and looked at it. She had straight A's on all subjects. A note on the back of the card read, "Kelly is an outstanding student. I hate to lose her from my class. She is eager to learn, well disciplined and has a charming personality."

"This one is from Lethbridge. I was only there two months. I wasn't there long enough to get grades."

The teacher's note on the card read, "Kelly was not here for the full term; therefore, grades have not been computed. Nevertheless, she completed all work assigned in an excellent manner and final grades are sure to have been tops. She is a pleasure to work with."

"This one is from Medicine Hat. I was there for seven months and finished the fourth grade. I had a man teacher, Mr. Harrison. He taught me a lot of things besides the regular subjects. He said it was fun to work with a kid who wanted to learn everything. I always wanted to learn more than the other kids did." Again, grades were straight A's.

"You like school a lot, don't you, Kelly?" Jamie asked.

"School is lots of fun. I don't know why some kids hate it so much. It's fun to learn new things. There's so much to learn, and I don't think I'll ever learn all that I'd like to. This card is from Moose Jaw. I went there for most of the third grade."

Jamie scrutinized the third-grade report card. Like the others, all grades were tops. "Excellent student, but a bit precocious," read the teacher's note.

"You never stayed in one place long," Jamie said. "How come you moved so much?"

"Mom never seemed to be able to keep a man for very long. After my real dad left, she took up with one man after the other. They didn't stay long. Mom would get drunk; they'd take off, and she would find another. None of them were nice. Some of them were really mean."

"How old were you when your real dad left?"

"I guess 'bout five. It was before I started school."

"Did you like your real dad?"

"Yes. I guess I loved him. He was good to me most of the time, except when he and Mom got in a fight. Then sometimes he'd yell at me too. But most of the time he was OK. Sometimes he bought me presents, and a couple of times he took me to movies. His name was Ralph Brooks, and he worked in the oil fields mostly. We moved around a lot because he never seemed to have a steady job. Then, after he left, Mom got a job as a waitress, and we lived in one spot for about a year. That was the best time I had. I went to the first grade for the full year. But Mom lost her job, and we had to go on relief. Mom started drinking more and then she started bringing men home. Sometimes they stayed overnight. I didn't like that very well. I told Mom I didn't like it, but she said that's the only way she could get money for us to live on. I won't ever do that. I think it's bad."

"Yes," Jamie said. "It is bad and I hope that you never get to where you have to do those sorts of things."

"I never will. I'd do anything rather than that. I know what they did. I could hear them in the bedroom. Sometimes they talked awful."

"OK, girl!" Jamie said. "It's bed time. See how fast the time goes when you get started talking. We have to do a lot of talking from now on. We won't miss the TV at all."

"Gee, Jamie, you're fun to be around. I like talking to you. I really do love you very much. Good night." She gave Jamie a big hug and went to her bedroom.

"Good night sweetie," Jamie called after her.

For a long time, he sat still, mulling over the things he had learned about his protégé. How had she survived such a life and managed to retain such high ethical standards? She was more than highly intelligent. Somehow, she had gained a sense of propriety and morality that seemed impossible in one so young. How Julie would have enjoyed her. She was exactly the kind of daughter that he could envision Julie having. I sure have a lot to live up to, now, he thought. This kid is going to change my life. I hope I can do her justice.

Chapter 11

With the second day of farm allocations getting under way, Jamie met with Dave Jorgenson, the heavy-duty electrician, and the rest of the council. After introductions, he turned the floor over to Andy Blankenship.

"As I told you yesterday, I was in charge of Puntledge and Elk Falls plants. There are several generators at each plant. Any one of those generators will furnish all the power I can see needed. These generators can be set to adjust themselves to the amount of power being called for. If a generator goes down for any reason, another will pick up the load automatically. If one plant is cut off line, it will shut itself down and the other plant will take over. I know how to manage all of that. There are plenty of spare parts on hand, and it will be a long time before we can wear out all of those generators, if we take care of them. Where I need help is with the transmission lines and switching. I hope, Dave, that you can help."

"I've been working on power lines, along with substations and other switching facilities, for the last 10 years," Dave said. "I know how to build and repair lines. I think we can work together and keep a system going here OK. Only thing is, if we have a bad storm and get many trees down, it might take us a few days to get things going again. People should be prepared for some delays in service."

"It sounds like you two are a godsend to us," Jamie said. "Where do you want to start?"

"I think the first priority," Andy said, "is to get the north end of the island disconnected. I've already shut off our connection to the mainland grid. The area north of Campbell River to Sayward is always a problem every time there's a bad storm. Trees fall on the line and knock it out. Quadra Island's connected too. We'll try to locate the proper switches and get it cut off today. Also Gold River."

"OK," Jamie replied. "Keep us informed. Now what do you think about local power?"

"As soon as you decide where everyone is going to live," answered Andy, "we should start redesigning our distribution system to take care of only the areas that are important to us."

"The council will be deciding that by tomorrow night's general meeting, if possible."

"In the meantime," said Andy, "we'll get back to Campbell River today and get the north end shut off. I think I can find diagrams of all transmission lines and switches, and I'm sure Dave can interpret them without any trouble. Do you want us back down here tomorrow?"

"Yep," Jamie told him. "We should get all of the farms allotted before noon tomorrow, and the council can get together and try to decide where we want to locate the rest of the people. We may well need your input for that. Let's meet here tomorrow noon."

* * *

After lunch, the entire council, along with Andy Blankenship and Dave Jorgenson, gathered in the conference room. Kelly found a chair and sat in a corner behind Jamie.

Jamie brought the meeting to order.

"This afternoon we have to decide what to do about locating the rest of our population. I think we should be in as small an area as possible. There was not much choice about where to locate the farmers. I think we made the right choice. Most of them are happy with the choice we made. Everyone got a good farm with equipment and livestock. Mary's lottery worked out well. Fortunately, there were more than enough places to go around, and there is still room for more, if needed. There are 55 farms occupied. Mary, do you have any idea how many people are on those 55 places?"

"Yes," Mary responded, pulling a sheet of paper from a folder. "I know exactly. There are 52 couples and three single people. That means there are 107 adults. Those 52 couples have 130 dependants. One single person has three dependants. That makes a total of 240 people. You notice, I say dependants rather than children. The one single person has three boys, who could actually be classed as adults, but they are registered on one census form as a family."

"That would be Teresa Blunt," Jamie said. "I have a hunch that family will be branching out soon. Those big boys are not going to stay single long, if they can find a female to hook up with. What about the people left?"

"Most of the people left are more senior. Their families are mostly grown up. There are a few exceptions, like Jamie here who is starting a new family. There are 56 couples registered with 12 dependants and 15 singles with three dependants, for a total of 142 people. That makes a total population of 382 registered so far. I think there may be more people to register, especially among the native group."

"Charlie," Jamie asked, "do you think that some of your people may not have registered?"

"It's probable," he replied. "Some of them were reluctant to fill out papers. I'll get after them and twist their tails. Also, Mary, I'd like a list of the children by age so that we can start thinking about school for them."

"I can have that for you soon, Charlie," Mary responded.

"You've done a terrific job, Mary," Jamie said. "That means we need 71 houses for non-farmers to live. Where are we going to find them? I'm open for comments, now."

"About six or eight square blocks in either Comox or Courtenay would provide that many houses," commented Keith Shaw.

"There's one fallacy with that," said Bob Elder. "Those houses would all be hooked up to city sewers and water lines, plus most of them are on gas heat. That means there is city infrastructure to maintain. I doubt that we are capable of doing that. And we will probably not have gas for long."

"I had an idea," Jamie said, "but you've shot that down. I was thinking that maybe we should establish around the marina and the hospital, in case we wanted a fishing industry. But that doesn't seem like a good idea now. You must have something else in mind, Bob."

"Yes, I do. You have stated that you want people as close together as possible. You go about two kilometers north of Courtenay, and you run out of city water and sewer. Like the farms, most houses have their own wells, or are on small community systems. Sewers are all septic tanks, and there's not much gas service. I'm sure we can find more than 71 houses you need within a kilometer or two of the school, which could continue to be our civic center. We could establish a small satellite village at the marina, possibly in float houses, if we have some people that want to live on the water. There are two or three float houses there now. Their sewage goes in the bay."

"What about water and hydro?" Jamie asked.

"There's an old well near the head of the dock," Bob reported. "It has been closed down for years. The city tested it not long ago. The water was good and flowed enough to service up to 20 homes. There didn't seem much use for it, so the city capped it. The well is shallow. We could stick a pump on it and run a line down to connect with the present lines on the dock. I don't think that would be too much problem. As for hydro, maybe Andy or Dave can answer that."

Andy answered. "I think we could probably trace out a line to get power down there. It might take awhile to do it. It's just a matter of sorting out a routing on wires already hung and cutting off all side connections."

"Jamie, I'd like a word on that," chimed in Charlie Johnson.

"Go ahead, Charlie."

"I think I may have two or three, maybe more, native families that have not registered and would fit well down there. They came from a fishing village on an island north of Port Hardy. They have never done much, except fish. They have been threatening to go back to their island and go it on their own. I'll see to it that they are registered and take them down to have a look at the situation. It would be a great benefit to them, as well as us. They are really a primitive bunch, no education and no social graces. They may be a little difficult to integrate."

"Good deal, Charlie. We'll leave that up to you. Now, let's hear from Dr. Ron. What about hospital and health care?"

"I have an answer to that," Ron reported. "Some rich guy from the states bought ten acres about a kilometer from the school. It's up on a hill east of here. He built a big lodge to entertain his stateside friends. The house has ten bedrooms, and I could convert it to a clinic and hospital that would be more than adequate for us. He also built three smaller houses for staff. Marguerite and I could take one of those houses, and we could reserve the other two for additional staff if needed. We could move the patients still alive in Campbell River down to Comox Hospital until we could get that place ready. We can move what equipment we can use from one of the present hospitals."

"One other thing," Jamie said. "How about the Armed Service Base? What facilities are out there?"

"I can answer that," Bob responded. "There is a trunk electric line to the base. They have their own sewer and water systems for facilities on the field."

72

"That's good. It sounds like we have a good grip on things. Does anyone have anything to add at this time? We can flesh out as we go."

All agreed the plan was right.

"OK," said Jamie. "I'll see you all tonight in Campbell River for our last, I hope, meeting there. Come along, Kelly, let's go."

Kelly grabbed his hand, and they headed out the door.

As they got in the car, Kelly asked, "Are we going to have to move out of our beautiful home to one down here? I don't like that."

"I don't either," Jamie agreed. "I've lived in that house many years, most of them with Julie. We'll find a nice house down here, I'm sure. Fasten your seat belt, and we'll get going."

They drove around some of the side roads to get an idea of the houses available.

"There's one up on that hill that looks nice," Kelly said. "Could we go look at it?"

"There's not much use, because if we don't draw a low number, someone else may pick it before we have a chance."

"Please, Jamie, could we just look anyway?"

Jamie backed the car up and turned into the long driveway that ended in a circle in front of a wide porch that extended across the entire front of the house. Getting out, Kelly dashed up the steps, tried the front door and found it locked.

"Let's try the back door," Jamie suggested.

Kelly tore around the house at a run. Jamie, following, found her at the back porch facing a large dog. The dog stood rigidly at attention, its tail stiff, hair bristling on his back. Kelly looked paralyzed.

"Hello, dog," Jamie spoke in a mild voice. The dog shifted his eyes in Jamie's direction, but made no move. "You look like a Golden Lab, and Labs aren't mean dogs." The hair on the animal's back settled a little. "I know you're guarding your master's property, but he's gone and we are here." There was a slight twitch at the end of the tail, and the hair settled along the back and then settled a little more.

"Kelly, stand still," Jamie continued, in the same soothing voice. "Don't move. He'll be OK in a minute. Come on, dog, come over here and talk to us. You're a nice dog, and we are friends. Come on, be our friend."

The dog visibly relaxed, and the tail began to wag slightly.

"That's a good dog," Jamie continued. "Here's a girl that wants to be friends. Come on and show her you are a friend. Stay still, Kelly, hold your hand out, palm down—easy, gently—that's it."

The dog took a pace forward, then another.

"Don't be nervous, Kelly," Jamie instructed. "He's not going to bite. Give him time to come to you. Come on dog. Come to Kelly."

The soothing voice was having its effect. The dog moved forward slowly until he was close to the girl.

"Kelly, move your hand toward his nose. Slowly."

The hand inched forward, until inches from the dog's nose; Kelly could go no farther. The dog stretched forward, sniffed at the hand, and then extended a wet tongue for a sloppy lick, and the tail began to wag furiously. With a squeal of delight, Kelly started petting the dog's head as it moved forward to lean against her thigh. The friendship between the girl and dog was immediate. Jamie came forward, and the dog accepted him too.

On the porch, Jamie found a large empty bowl, obviously for the dog. A water bowl was also dry. The owners had apparently left food and water, but the supply was now exhausted. He went on to try the back door and found it locked.

"Kelly," Jamie called. "This door's locked too. Do you have your lock pick outfit?"

"It's in my bag in the car," she replied. Returning in a flash, she went to work on the door. The big dog watched her with interest. The first pick didn't work. The second one did, and she threw the door open in triumph. The dog crowded into the house ahead of them. Inside, they found the kitchen modern and immaculately clean. The appliances looked to be new. A counter separated the kitchen from a large dining-living combination. A stone fireplace with a modern steel insert dominated the end of the room. Broad windows looked out over the valley. A master bedroom with its own bath was off one end of the room, and two bedrooms with shared bath were on the other end of the house. Kelly was ecstatic. The dog followed them around as they surveyed the house, occasionally rubbing up against Kelly. Back in the kitchen, Jamie found a bag of dog food under the kitchen sink and poured some in the dog dish on the back porch. Kelly brought the water dish to the sink and filled it with water. The dog lapped eagerly at the water and took a few bites of food.

Obviously, the food had not been out for too long, but he was getting thirsty.

Kelly took another quick look around the house. "It's almost as nice as your house, Jamie. Do you think we can have it?"

"Let's go, youngster. There's a lot to do. If I get a low enough draw number, we might get it. If not, we'll have to settle for something else."

Kelly locked the back door. "Maybe if someone comes ahead of us and can't get in, they might go to another house," she reasoned.

The big dog followed them as they returned to the car. Kelly opened the car door to get in, and the dog jumped in ahead of her. "Hey, Jamie, he wants to go with us. Can we take him? I've never had a dog, and this one sure is nice. Please, Jamie, can we have him?"

"Here, you doggone Dawg, get out of there. If you're going to ride in this car, you've got to take the back seat." Dawg obediently got out of the front seat and sprang into the back.

"OK, Dawg," Jamie commanded. "Don't go slobbering down my neck."

"We can't keep calling him dog," Kelly said. "We need to give him a name."

"I said Dawg, not dog. That's Dawg, not dog. D-A-W-G. That's a good enough name until we come up with a better one."

Chapter 12

Jamie wondered if it would cause a problem bringing Dawg into the hotel. But Dawg took the situation into his own hands. With the dignity befitting royalty, he stalked into the dining room with Kelly and took his place at her side as she sat. Dawg had no regard whatsoever for any anti-dog rules. It was his right to be there, and he demonstrated that right with complete aplomb. Sarah Harris took it in stride as she approached the table to serve big plates of boiled ham and beans.

"Is this your dog, Kelly?" Sarah asked.

"Yes," Kelly answered. "I've always wanted a dog but never thought I'd be lucky enough to have one."

"What's his name?" Sarah asked.

"Dawg," Kelly replied.

"Dog. He must have some name other than dog."

"Not dog, Dawg. You know. Dawwwg," Kelly drawled.

"Oh, I see," Sarah responded. "Dawg. I guess that's as good a name as any."

Dawg wagged his tail in acknowledgment.

* * *

Jamie made his way into the meeting room to bring people up to date.

"First thing," he started out, "Everyone who wanted farms has been settled in the Comox Valley. Not all places have been allotted, so if any of you change your minds and want a farm, there are still a number close to the Tsolum School, which we'll be using as headquarters.

"Your council has spent a lot of time deciding on where the non-farmers should locate. We've found close to a hundred small acreage places in the same neighborhood that appear to be ideal for our settlement."

"Mr. President!" A woman was standing up waving her arm. "Do you mean you expect us to leave our nice homes here in Campbell River to live in some shack in the country? Well, I, for one, am not going to do it."

"Lady, would you give us your name so that Mary can get your objections down for the minutes?"

"It doesn't make any goddamn difference what my name is. I'm not going to be forced to do something I don't want to do."

Jamie held his cool. "We're not going to force you to do anything. The people will have an opportunity to vote approval or not."

The woman sat solidly back in her seat.

A man stood. "I'm Bufford Granger. I'm very sorry, but my wife has been drinking. I'll take care of her." He took the woman firmly by the elbow to escort her out.

"OK," Jamie said. "Let's get back to work. Now, I'd like Bob Elder to tell you why we are recommending the rural area."

Bob stood. "Thanks Jamie. I was president of the Comox Rotary Club, and have been active in civic affairs for many years. I'm familiar with the costs of maintaining infrastructure in an urban setting. The utilities in the Comox/Courtenay area are designed to serve 30 to 50 thousand people. Our little group is less than 500. There is no way we can keep a big sewer or water system working. And there is no way we can downsize it to fit our needs. We'd have to start installing septic systems and drilling wells. That's not practical. We are fortunate in having a good number of rural homes on small plots of land, from one quarter acre to five or ten acres. These places have septic systems and wells installed. As we have heard before from Andy and Dave, the power system can probably be maintained indefinitely. Most houses in the area have electric or wood heat. There's lots of wood available. When you're selecting a house, be sure it is not dependent on propane or natural gas for heat. If you do, be prepared to change in the near future. That's the gist of my report. Thank you."

Jamie came back to the lectern. "Are there any questions, before we put this proposal to vote?"

"Yes," a lady stood. "My name is Rosie Coleman. A number of people have asked me if you had considered the Cowichan Valley instead of Comox. There is a lot of good farmland there, and the climate may be milder."

"Yes Rosie, we did. But everything, or most things, at least, are dead there. Cattle and horses are spread across the fields. They would have to be disposed of, a Herculean job, and new livestock imported from the North Island. Health hazards from decaying carcasses would be a serious hazard."

Teresa Blunt stood, hand raised. "Mr. President, I move we get on with the selection lottery."

"Second," shouted Ken Wilson.

"All in favor?"

Hands went up all over the room.

"Against?"

There was no response.

"OK," Jamie continued. "We'll go ahead with the lottery."

* * *

The next morning at the hotel Meg Sanderson brought them plates of pancakes, then sat down at their table and hesitantly began to speak. "Mr. Jamie, I drew a number last night, but I really don't need a house of my own."

"How come?" Jamie asked her.

Blushing furiously, she answered. "Well, you see, Ted and I, we get along so well working together, that we decided we'd get married, and we only need one house. We want to get married as soon as possible. But how do we do it now? There're no preachers around."

"I'll talk to the council and see what they say. There are no civil authorities around to do it. On ships, the captain can perform marriages. Maybe I can be classed as a captain and marry people. Someone has to do it. See me when you get down to the valley."

"Oh, I knew that you would have an answer." She threw her arms around his neck and kissed him on the cheek. "We are sort of old fashioned, and we want to sleep in our new home tonight."

* * *

Jamie, the last person to draw in the lottery, had drawn number one, so he and Kelly went early to mark their selection. Kelly was ecstatic at getting her choice. Meeting later with his group, he informed them of the problem with the young couple.

Pat Draper had the answer. "I move that we designate Jamie to serve as Justice, or Judge, in addition to his duties as President, along with all of the powers ordinarily associated with those positions as we have known them in the past."

"Second," said Bob Elder.

"That sounds good to me," Keith Shaw said, looking for approval from the group. They all nodded.

Ted and Meg showed up at the school before noon.

"When do you want to get married?" Jamie asked them.

"You mean you have found someone who will marry us?" Meg demanded.

"I sure have. The council has designated me judge or something like that and given me the power to marry people. When do you want to do it?"

"I think it would be nice if we could get married in our new house," Meg replied. "What do you think, Ted?"

"That would be great," Ted agreed. "How about at two this afternoon?"

"Sounds OK to me. I'll get it set up. You'd better have a bridesmaid and best man selected."

"Mary," Meg requested, "would you be my bridesmaid?"

"I'd be delighted," Mary replied.

"Who can I get for best man?"

"Here comes the Blunt family," Jamie said. "I'll bet that one of the boys would do it." He made introductions all around.

"Sure," Teresa responded. "One of these hellions will handle it. I don't know which one. I might have to do some arm-twisting. They are all sort of antisocial. You said two o'clock. We'll be here. Say, the boys don't have much dress-up clothes. Is that all right?"

"Sure. Clean jeans are fine. Be here at the school before two," Jamie requested. "If they have their new house secured, they'll be married there. Otherwise it will be here."

The group assembled in the front yard of the little house. Jamie stepped up on the front porch and faced the assembly.

"Let's make this an outdoor wedding. The weather is fine, so we had as well enjoy the view. Is that agreeable to the newlyweds to be?"

Ted and Meg expressed their approval.

"Now, we want the bride and groom to stand right here at the head of the steps. Mary, you stand beside Meg, and which one of you Scandahoovians is going to stand with Ted?"

The two older brothers pushed Lars to the front, and a scared and bewildered looking young man stumbled up to his place beside Ted.

Jamie moved to face them at the foot of the steps. "Now, let's proceed with this very important ceremony." Pausing for a minute, he put on a stentorian voice. "By the powers bestowed upon me by the Supreme Council of the State of New Island, I have been empowered to act as Justice of the Peace, Judge of the Courts, and Marriage Commissioner for said State of New Island." Another pause, then in his normal voice, he continued. "After the council appointed me to these positions this morning, I realized that our state doesn't have a name. To make any decree legal it has to be issued by the legal representatives of a state, or other legal entity. With no opportunity for consultation with others, I selected a name for our country. In that we are making a new start here, in a world that is new to us, why not call our country New Island? With my newly endowed powers of Judge of the Courts, I decree that the name be adopted.

"Now, as marriage commissioner, I'll continue. Do you, Meg and Ted, understand the commitments you are about to undertake?"

"We do," they said in unison.

"Do you, Ted Parks, take this woman to be your lawful wife, to honor and protect, through sickness and in health, until death do you part?"

"I do," Ted's voice was loud and clear.

"Do you, Meg Sanderson, take this man to be your lawful husband, to honor and protect, through sickness and in health, until death do you part?"

"I do," Meg's voice was equally clear.

"Ted and Meg, I now pronounce you husband and wife. You may kiss the bride."

Jamie stepped back as the young couple embraced and kissed, and then broke apart to come down the steps.

Meg threw her arms around Jamie's neck. "That was short and simple and wonderful. How can I ever thank you enough?"

Ted extended his hand for a shake. "I really thank you, Sir. It was very important to me to have this done properly. How can I ever repay you?"

"You can both repay me by honoring the commitment that you have made," Jamie told them.

After a round of congratulations, handshakes and kisses, Ted spoke up. "I have a couple of bottles of wine in the house. Would you all come in and drink to us?"

Inside, Jamie took it on himself to propose a toast to the happy couple.

Chapter 13

"This is the first meeting of our new community in its new location." Jamie was standing at the front of the Tsolum School's gymnasium, facing a crowd consisting of the majority of the people, as far as he knew, that were still alive on earth.

"It seems impossible that it is only a few weeks ago that the triple earthquakes set off the final phases of the panic that has changed our lives forever. In that short time, we have managed to relocate all of our people to an area where it will be much more practical to maintain the highest standard of living possible under the new conditions.

"We have 397 people registered on our present census forms, of which 382 are located within two or three kilometers of this building, which we have preempted as our community headquarters. Another 15 people have chosen to live in float houses at the Comox Marina. They chose to live there because they have been making their living off of the sea, and wish to continue doing so.

"We chose this area to settle in because it provides some of the best farmland on the island, and farming is going to be the essential part of our subsistence. We have to raise most of our food. The balance will come from the sea and the forests around us. I can see no problem with availability of food.

"The only problem is that the food will be somewhat different from what we have been accustomed to in the past. There will be no tropical fruits, such as oranges and bananas. We will run out of sugar and will have to learn how to manufacture our own. We will have to raise our own grain and mill our own flour. We have much to learn.

"We think that we will be able to keep electricity flowing to our homes, but that is not a sure thing. Also, when we have the inevitable breakdowns in electric service, it could well take days instead of hours to get it functioning again. You must be prepared to do without sometimes. Therefore, you should always have drinking water on hand to last a few days, and it would be a good idea to build old-fashioned outhouses, because your indoor toilets will not function without electrical power.

"About transportation. You've been using your automobiles as you wish since the panic began. When we use up the motor fuel stored on the island, we may not be able to replace it. Also, fuel can go bad if it is stored too long. We may well have to revert to more primitive modes of transportation. That is one of the reasons we wanted everyone grouped as close together as possible. You are all within walking distance of this center.

"There'll be a school established as soon as possible, here in this building. Charlie Johnson is in charge of setting up a school. We will concentrate initially on the three R's: reading, writing and 'rithmetic. We'll extend it beyond that point as soon as we can. It is absolutely imperative that we give our young people as much education as possible.

"We'll set up a medium of exchange in the near future. A simple barter system is not too practical. Your council is working on possibilities. That will be under the direction of Keith Shaw and Carl Smith, both experienced bankers.

"We had an emergency that required us to take immediate action to set up some civil service. A young couple came to me with a request to be married. They wanted it right away, so they could move into their new home as husband and wife. As you know, there are no preachers left on the island. I think they were all in the forefront of the scramble to get away. I called an emergency meeting of the council, and they solved the problem by appointing me as judge, justice of the peace and marriage commissioner. Any of those offices would enable me to perform a marriage ceremony, legal in our new country. I married the couple that afternoon, but at that time I realized we had missed an important item. To be an official of a country, that country must have a name. We didn't have one. On impulse, I decided that we would call our country New Island. We are new, so old names do not fit. We are starting a new life, so why not New Island? If you disapprove of the name, we'll have to change it. The newlyweds are Ted Parks, and Meg Sanderson, who spent much time providing us with food at the hotel in Campbell River. Stand up Ted and Meg, and let the people see the first newly wedded couple on New Island."

Ted and Meg stood and were met with a round of applause and continued calls of congratulations.

Jamie continued, "That proves that life is going on in a normal way on New Island. People are getting married, and I'm sure that, in due course, people will be having babies. I'm sure that Ted and Meg are doing what they can to insure that that happens."

More applause and whistles from the floor.

"I have covered most of what has been accomplished in the very short time we have been going. Now is the time for questions or comments. I or members of the council will try to answer your questions or concerns."

A hand went up at the rear of the room. "Why can't we use regular Canadian money as a medium of exchange?"

"There is too much of it floating around, and it could get out of control, resulting in extreme inflation. One suggestion, however, that we are looking at, is to use Canadian hard coins— dollars and two dollars—in connection with an extreme deflation of goods and services prices. For instance, if we started with a devaluation of 90%, wages that have been $10 an hour would now go for a dollar an hour. A candy bar would sell for a dime and a dozen eggs for 20 cents. There's not enough loose change wandering around to have any substantial effect. We can find enough coinage to get us going. Does that answer your question?"

"Good enough," was the response.

"What about health services?"

"Dr. Ron. Would you take that question?"

Ron took the floor. "We have a new 10-bed hospital, less than a kilometer from here, almost ready to go. It will be operational within a week. I am the only doctor available, but with less than 400 population, I will have fewer people to care for than I am accustomed to. My wife is a registered nurse and has a good knowledge of pharmaceuticals."

"Dr. Ron, will this be a self-pay facility or a community service one?"

"That's up to the rest of the council. I am responsible for the medical operation, not how it's paid for. For the time being, at least, it's available to anyone needing it."

"Any other questions?"

Teresa Blunt was standing with her hand up.

"Go ahead, Teresa," Jamie requested.

"First, I'd like to make a statement. I think that you and your council are doing an outstanding job getting this community put together. Without your leadership, we would have been scattered around like a bunch of chickens with a hawk flying over them, crying over the terrible losses of families and friends. Most of us probably would not have survived for long. You pulled us together, gave us a kick in the butt and now we have a chance for a reasonable life. I think this group owes you a vote of confidence and a pledge to cooperate every way possible. How about it, folks?"

There was no doubt about the response. The crowd was on their feet, clapping, whistling and shouting at the top of their voices.

"Jamie, are you going to continue to hold these meetings at regular intervals?" Teresa continued.

"We'll hold council meetings at least once a week, or as often as needed. We've been meeting every day so far. As far as general meetings, that's up to the people. We should have them once a week for a while, then perhaps once a month."

"I would like to suggest," Teresa said, "that we continue having them once a week, either Saturday or Sunday, and combine them with a social event. We could have potluck dinners, or something of that nature, to give us a chance to get to know each other, then have your business meeting afterwards. Does that sound like a good idea?'

There was an immediate response from the group. "Sounds great." "I'll help." "Tell us what to do."

Jamie waved for silence. "It looks like you hit the jackpot, Teresa. I appoint you as our social director, with Rosie Coleman and Annie Johnson to help you out. Would you people prefer Saturday or Sunday for your regular meeting and social event? All in favor of Saturday?" A few hands went up. "How about Sunday?" Without question, Sunday was in order.

"OK," Jamie continued, "we will meet a week from tomorrow at four PM for a potluck dinner and social, with the general meeting at seven."

Teresa came forward. "Hi, everybody. I think you all know who I am by now. I've made a bit of noise now and then. Anyway, my name is Teresa Blunt. Would my two helpers that Jamie volunteered come up here so we can get acquainted?"

Rosie Coleman came briskly up the aisle. Annie Johnson had to be given a shove by her family before she came reluctantly forward.

Teresa continued. "I know you're Rosie; you've been up front before, so this bashful beauty has to be Annie."

The three women held a brief conference. Teresa turned back to the audience to give instructions for the next week's event.

Chapter 14

Jamie and Kelly had finished cleaning up after breakfast when a horn announced the presence of a car in the front driveway. Kelly rushed to see who it was and returned escorting Mary Andrews. Mary hadn't been in the house before, and Kelly took her on a tour. Mary was properly impressed, and Kelly was pleased. Completing the tour, the two returned to the living room.

"So, boss man," Mary asked, "What did you have in mind for today?"

"I want to bring the little airplane down from Campbell River, so I wondered if you would come along and drive the car back to Comox base. We'll take my car. We should be all finished up before noon."

"Can I come too?" Kelly asked. "And how about Dawg?"

"Ask Mary," Jamie replied. "She's the one that has to put up with both of you."

"Sure," Mary said. "The more, the merrier."

Thirty minutes later, Jamie parked the car alongside the Cessna at Campbell River Airport.

"Is that your plane?" Kelly asked.

"That's it," replied Jamie. "Come along and you can look at it. Leave Dawg in the car."

As Kelly and Mary looked at the plane, Jamie retrieved the keys. Under the close observation of the two females, he made his preflight walk around. Turning to Mary, he asked. "Do you suppose you and Dawg can get the car back to Comox if Kelly rides with me?"

Kelly was jumping up and down, squealing with excitement. "You said you would take me up someday, but I didn't think you really meant it."

"Hey kid," Mary exclaimed, "if Jamie says he will do something, he means it and will follow through."

Jamie opened the passenger door. "OK, throttle down a bit and get in here." He helped with her seat belt and went around, taking his place in the pilot's seat.

"We'll be in front of the big hangars on the air base." He called to Mary. "The gates are open; you can drive in. See you there."

The engine started promptly, and a few minutes later they were off the ground and headed southeast. Jamie did a few steep turns and an approach to a stall to see what the reaction would be from his passenger. Kelly was flushed with excitement, but showed no sign of fear.

"You're not afraid?" Jamie asked.

"No, of course not," Kelly responded. "With you driving, there's nothing to be afraid of, is there?"

Back at the house, Kelly, still walking on cloud nine, got the ground beef and buns that had been thawing in the refrigerator and, with Mary helping, started preparing hamburger sandwiches for lunch.

* * *

They had finished cleaning up after lunch when a pickup came up the drive. It was Charlie Johnson, and Jamie invited him in to see the house. Kelly, with her usual exuberance, conducted the tour.

"Nice wigwam," concluded Charlie. "You made a good pick."

"Kelly made the pick," Jamie told him.

"What's a wigwam?" Kelly questioned.

"A wigwam was an Indian house. It is shaped like an ice cream cone turned upside down. It was made of poles lashed together at the top, covered with hides. A vent in the top let out the smoke from the cookfire. Many of the tribes, especially the inland ones, moved around a lot and the wigwam, or teepee, was easy to take down and set up at a new campsite."

Kelly had listened attentively. "Yeah, I think it's a nice wigwam. Only it wouldn't be easy to move."

"Well," Charlie asked, "who's going with me to visit the wild bunch down on the docks?"

"What do you mean, 'wild bunch'?" Kelly demanded.

"They haven't been around people much, and they get scared real easy, especially the kids. They haven't had much school, and they don't talk very well. I've had a hard time getting them to come to meetings or anything."

"I'd like to go meet them," Kelly said. "Maybe I could get them to come and get to know us. They'd find out we won't hurt them."

"If Kelly can't bring them out of their shells, nobody can," Mary said. "Let's go!"

Jamie brought the car around, and Dawg crowded into the back seat with Mary and Kelly.

As they drove toward the docks, Charlie told them something of the group they were going to meet. "There are three couples plus grandma, who looks as old as the hills. She came to the coast from some tribe in the interior 80 or 90 years ago. She's a medicine woman, a dreamer. She knows all about native cures for everything and mixes up medicines from plants and roots and bark and chants or sings to make sick people well. Sometimes it works, too. She brought a baby with her, a woods colt, I guess, caught from a white man. She got kicked out of her tribe because of the baby."

Kelly interrupted. "What's a woods colt?"

Charlie was stumped as to how to answer, and Mary came to his rescue.

"A woods colt is a baby that was born to a girl that wasn't married. The dad isn't around. It's an illegitimate baby."

"Oh, I see," Kelly said. "That shouldn't happen, should it?"

"No, it shouldn't," Mary agreed. "But sometimes it does."

"Anyway," Charlie continued, "she brought the kid, a little girl, with her and wound up with one of the tribes here on the coast. The little girl grew up and married a local man. They had a girl baby, and the mother died during birth. The father was killed in a fight with another tribe. Grandma raised the baby, who married a man from Kingcome Inlet. You'll meet that couple today. They have grandkids and great-grandkids here."

Jamie pulled the car onto the parking lot at the head of the Comox dock and stopped close to three girls, Kelly's age bracket, that were playing some kind of a game marked out with chalk on the blacktop. They were neat looking youngsters, with jet-black hair and coppery skin. They stopped their play to look apprehensively at the newcomers, obviously ready to flee. Charlie spoke to them, from the rolled down window, in their native tongue, and they seemed to relax a little. Kelly got out of the car and, followed by Dawg, approached the trio.

"My name is Kelly," she said. "And this is Dawg. What game are you playing?"

The three started chattering in barely understandable English, and Dawg was in the middle of it, sniffing hands and rubbing against legs.

"Looks like Kelly and Dawg saved the day," Charlie said. "Let's go and see if we can talk to the older people."

Charlie led the way out onto the dock where the float houses were moored. An old woman sitting cross-legged on the deck of the first house struggled to her feet as they approached. As Charlie had said, she looked as old as the hills. The skin of her face was walnut colored, wrinkled and shriveled like an over dried prune. Her lips sunk in over toothless gums, and deep sunken eyes peered through slits in folds of skin. Wisps of stringy gray hair escaped from under her shawl.

Charlie spoke to her in her native dialect and then introduced them. "Jamie and Mary, this is Little Bird. Jamie is the chief of our tribe of combined Indian and White people, and Mary is his scribe. They come here as friends and hope that you will honor them with your friendship."

Little Bird studied them for a minute, and then spoke clearly in English. "Who is the girl child playing with my children?"

"That is Kelly," Jamie answered. "When the land shook and people ran away, Kelly was left behind. I have taken her as my own daughter. She gives me much pleasure."

"And the yellow dog?" Little Bird asked.

"That's Dawg," Jamie answered. "He was also left behind and is a part of my household now. He is friendly and has great regard for children."

"Hmm. You take in stray kids and animals all the time?"

"Only those two," Jamie replied. "That's as many as I can handle."

"That's not true," Charlie told her. "Jamie has taken many hundreds of us in and is treating us as family and is directing us in making a new life here. Only a great chief can lead people as he is leading us. He leads us with kindness and compassion that is the measure of success and is only possible with the greatest of great chiefs."

Little Bird drew herself more erect, stretching to attain the scant five feet remaining of her aged frame. Her glittering black eyes surveyed Jamie from head to toe, and then settled to meet his eyes with a directness that he found hard to meet. Holding out her hand that appeared to be not much more than a bundle of bones, she accepted Jamie's shake with a grip that surprised him. "I will accept you as my chief, and chief of my family. I will follow you as long as these battered old legs can carry me, and pledge that my family will also follow you. Come and meet the others." With surprising agility, she stepped from the float-house deck to the dock and led the way to the second house. Opening the door to the living area, she waved them in. Nine people were in the room, evidently expecting them.

Little Bird took center stage in the middle of the room. "My people, this is our great Chief, Jamie. The lady is his scribe, Mary. And you know Chief Charlie." Waving to an elderly couple seated in the corner of the room, she continued, "This is my granddaughter, Mountain Flower. You can call her Julia. By her side is her husband, Johnie Jacob. This lady is Julia's daughter, Blue Mountain, or Angela, and her man, Robert Dick. The young buck is Johnie Dick and his woman, Marie. The three girls are sisters of Johnie. The oldest is Francis, then Marjorie, and the young one is Bonnie, or Sweet Grass. Sweet Grass is learning to be a medicine woman, and she can already make great medicine and dream some. The kids out on the parking lot belong to Johnie and Marie."

Jamie shook hands all around, ending up with Sweet Grass. He judged her to be not more than 20 years old, about five foot two, with an athletic build that still had all the curves in the right places. "So you will be a medicine woman and a dreamer?"

"If the Great Spirit wills it," she replied, accepting and holding eye contact. Her eyes were large and black as ebony, with an unbelievable intensity. "Little Bird has been teaching me for eight seasons."

Little Bird chimed in. "She will be a great medicine woman if this old person lives long enough to teach her."

"I am sure she will be," Jamie responded, "if she is being taught by such an expert as Little Bird. I hope that all of you will become a part of our tribe and enter into our community activities, and let us have access to your expertise in areas which the modern white man has little knowledge."

"I have already pledged our support," Little Bird said. "They will all go along with what I say."

Jamie turned to Mary. "Do we have census forms for these people?"

"Yes, but they are not complete," Mary replied.

Jamie turned to Little Bird. "Mary will help in getting your registrations filled out properly. We need good records of all our people, and the white man does not have good memories as the Indians do, so we need to write it down in order that we do not forget."

"Sweet Grass can tell her everything she needs. Why don't you take the lady to your house where it is more peaceful and help her fill out the papers?"

As the two women left the room, Charlie spoke up. "We are going to start a school soon, so that our children will be able to write and read and count. I know that the three girls out front should go, but what about others of you?"

"I'd love to go school," said Francis. "But I'm 25 years old and too old to go to school."

"You're never too old," Jamie said. "You need to have at least a basic education. You older girls can help take care of the younger children and be a great help to the teachers. We don't want you to be left behind at any time because of a lack of knowledge. We want you all to have equal opportunity in our new society, and education will insure that."

"Chief Jamie is right," said Little Bird. "I think you should all go. I would go myself if I were a few years younger."

"It's settled," said Charlie. "I'll let you know when we start and arrange to have a van pick you up on school days."

"I hope all of you will come to our potluck dinner next Sunday," Jamie said, "and attend our general meeting. We we'll go now."

"You like crab?" Johnie Jacob asked Jamie.

"Sure do," Jamie responded.

"We give you some for dinner," Johnie said. Going to a rope tied to the dock rail, he pulled up a wire holding cage, which held several live crabs. "How many can you use?"

Mary was approaching, having finished her work with Sweet Grass. "Will you have crab dinner with us tonight, Mary?" Jamie asked.

"Yeah, sounds good."

"What about you, Charlie?"

"No thanks, Johnie gave us crab yesterday."

"Three will be fine," Jamie said, turning to Johnie.

Johnie selected three of the biggest crabs and flipped them on their backs on the dock. "Do you want them cleaned?" he asked.

Jamie nodded his assent. Deftly catching the struggling crabs one by one, he cracked their under shells against a corner of the dock, killing them. Pulling the top shell off and breaking the crabs into two sections, he left the sets of legs connected and clean. One of the women brought a container, bagged the crabs and handed them to Jamie. After a round of handshakes, Jamie led his entourage back to the parking lot.

* * *

The council met that evening in Jamie's living room.

Jamie brought up the first order of business. "We need to elect a vice president for this organization. If something happens to me, someone needs to be able to take over as president without a lot of fuss. Does anyone have any ideas?"

After a long silence, Pat Draper spoke up. "You have been working closely with all of us, Jamie. I'm sure that you have a preference."

"I'm trying not to impose my will on the council," Jamie told them. "Any one of you could take over and run things as well as I do. I'd like to have as much democracy here as possible."

"That's fine," Keith Saw said. "But we would still like to have your preference expressed. If we don't approve, we can call for additional nominations and vote on it."

"All right, if that's the way you want it. Mary Andrews has been able to absorb all of the details of every part of our operation and has an outstanding ability to get to the crux of any situation. I would like to nominate her as vice president. Are there any other nominations?"

"I move the nominations be closed," said Keith Shaw.

The motion was seconded, and the vote was unanimous.

"Mary," Jamie said, "you have been elected vice president of New Island. Will you accept the position? That will be in addition to your duties as secretary."

"I'm flabbergasted," Mary replied. "Yes, I'll accept and do the best I can. I hope nothing happens that I have to take your place. That's impossible."

"That's settled," Jamie said. "Now for my own report. I found a nice Cessna 206 out at the air base. I want to check it out, and if it is in good condition, I'll use it for the exploration I want to start on the mainland. It will carry more weight and is faster, with longer range. I'll carry a small generator and an electric pump that

I can pump gasoline into the plane with. I'll map out fuel stops as we go, and never extend more than 50% of our range without finding a fuel stop that we can use. We need to find out if there are any more live people kicking around somewhere."

Mary spoke up. "It seems to me there is a lot of risk involved in this kind of program."

"The risk is minimal," Jamie replied. "The greatest danger is from the decaying corpses. I'll have Dr. Ron brief me on how to stay healthy. Water could be a problem, so we will carry water with us. More reason for the larger plane. Now, if there is nothing else, we'll close this meeting and meet again Sunday afternoon at three. That will give us an hour before the big party starts at four and the general meeting at seven."

Chapter 15

Monday was bright and sunny after a week of typical Island weather, overcast and rainy. Jamie had sat up till midnight reading the logbook and operation manual for the Cessna 206 and felt as if he had a fair idea of the operation of the plane. Along with Dawg and Kelly, he headed for the airport to have a closer look at the craft. George Brooks' work truck was parked by the hangar when they arrived. They opened the hangar doors wide to let the sunshine in.

Jamie spent some time checking the plane from end to end. When he was satisfied, he told the others to stand back while he started it up. He found a pre-start checklist, as well as a pre-takeoff list, in the cockpit, and with that to guide him, he had no trouble starting the engine. Taxiing out of the hangar to the main ramp, he shut the engine down. The others came running.

"Are you going to fly it?" Kelly demanded.

"Yes," Jamie replied. "I'm satisfied with it. I am going to take it up and be sure everything is OK, then I'll take all of you for a ride."

"Why can't we go with you now?" asked Kelly.

"Because it's not good judgment to take passengers on a test flight," Jamie told her. "Stay here and I'll be back soon."

The takeoff was uneventful, and Jamie was pleased with the short run and the climb rate. The engine was smooth and everything operated perfectly. In less than 15 minutes, Jamie was satisfied with the condition of the plane and that he would have no trouble with it.

Back on the ramp, Jamie loaded George in the passenger seat, Kelly in the middle seats, and Dawg in the back seat with a leash that he tied to a cargo ring.

"Why are you tying Dawg up?" Kelly demanded.

"This is probably Dawg's first trip in an airplane," Jamie told her. "If he gets excited, I don't want him jumping all over the place. If he is OK, we won't have to tie him in the future."

The plane broke ground smoothly. The extra three passengers seemed to have little effect on the performance. Dawg sat on the seat looking out the window until they were airborne, and then laid down and went to sleep.

Jamie climbed the plane to the southeast and leveled off at 6500 feet, adjusting the engine controls to cruise and trimmed the airplane to fly hands off. "How about," he asked the others, "if we nip over to Vancouver International and see what conditions are there?"

George and Kelly agreed, Kelly with her usual enthusiasm. Forty minutes later, they were taxiing up to the South Terminal, where short haul airlines, charter and private planes usually operated. A small office building displayed the sign of an aviation fuel label, and Jamie parked the plane in front of it. They opened the doors to the unmistakable odor of decay.

"Wow," Kelly exclaimed. "It smells like there is something dead around here."

"There is," Jamie replied. "That's the smell of dead people. Probably anywhere you go on the mainland now, you would find that same odor."

George had the office door open in short order. Inside, Jamie found the keys to the fuel truck hanging on a nail. The keys fit and the engine started readily. The tank had compartments for 100-octane gas and jet fuel. They left the keys in the truck. Back in the plane, they taxied across the field to the main terminal and located the fueling facility where a large semi fuel truck was parked. They stopped close to it and shut down. When they opened the doors, the odor was much worse.

"Let's check that truck and get out of here fast," Jamie said.

They found keys in the truck, and the engine started with no problem. "Looks like we can get all the fuel we need in the foreseeable future here," Jamie said. "Let's get out of here and get some clean air."

Back in the air, they headed east to Abbotsford and found a comparable situation. An operable fuel truck, apparently ready to go, except for ignition keys, was parked by the fuel office. Jamie and George walked to the office, and George tried the door. It opened; George looked in and staggered back. "God," he exclaimed. "That's terrible."

Jamie took George's place at the door. A corpse was slumped over a desk, bloated out of all proportions, with swarms of flies buzzing around it. The stench was overpowering. Jamie, holding a handkerchief over his face, moved quickly into the room. He found the truck keys in a basket, inches from the dead man's hand. Beating a hasty retreat, he closed the door behind him. George was at the corner of the building, vomiting. Jamie tried the keys in the truck. They fit, and he left them in the ignition. Back at the plane, a pale-faced George was already in his seat. They were soon back on the field at Comox.

They climbed from their seats, reveling in the fresh smelling air of New Island. Jamie opened the cargo door and untied Dawg's leash. The big dog jumped to the ground and circled the plane, sniffing each wheel, and was about to raise his leg for the conventional ritual. Jamie saw what was coming and yelled, "Dawg, no!" Dawg looked over his shoulder, acknowledged Jamie's objection with a twitch of his tail, and trotted deliberately across the tarmac to the corner of the hangar where a fire hydrant was conveniently placed. Looking back at Jamie to see if there were any further objections, he wasted little time in giving the hydrant a good soaking.

They were getting ready to push the plane into the hangar when the quake hit. With a roaring sound like a freight train coming, the ground rolled in a waving motion that was hard to stand up to. Kelly wound up on the tarmac on her rump with an astonished look on her face. The plane bounced and swayed on its spring suspension. The metal skin of the hangar cracked and snapped as the building twisted and shook. Gulls flew squawking into the air, and Dawg jumped up and down and barked. The shaking seemed to go on for minutes, but Jamie estimated it was probably no more than 30 seconds.

Kelly was the first to recover. Springing to her feet, she exclaimed. "Wow. That was a ding blasted whoperroo."

"I guess that describes it as well as anything," Jamie agreed. "Let's get the plane inside and go and see if everyone is OK."

Chapter 16

Mary Andrews was in her garden when the quake hit.

A tall fir tree with a snag top had caught her attention. The tree, at the edge of the garden, dominated the grove that backed it up. The tree didn't look healthy, and she decided it would have to come out.

Wandering aimlessly around the plot, she stopped in the middle to survey the tree again. The snag top of the tree appeared to be moving. With her gaze transfixed by the treetop, she became aware of a rumbling sound. The ground began to heave and roll like waves in the ocean. My God, she thought, we're having an earthquake. She tried to run, but the heaving ground made movement impossible and she fell to her face, realizing that the tree was falling towards her.

She tried to scramble away, but before she could make any progress, a green sea of branches engulfed her. There was a snapping sound as the dead top broke loose and a flash of lightning like fire as the snag fell across the power line, forcing wires together to short out the system. Mary was flat on her face, her arms outstretched, unable to move. She was being pressed face first into the soft soil of the garden, her body wracked by pain. Her first thought was: am I dying? Am I already dead?

She realized quickly that she was not dead, but she could be dying. If she were dying, she would like to get it over with and be relieved of the pain that seemed to be invading every part of her body. She tried to move, but she was pinned solidly by a multitude of branches, with the main trunk of the tree above her back. The branches were supporting the trunk, keeping her from being crushed. She was completely immobilized, with only her fingertips and toes able to move. That was good, she realized. If her fingers and toes were movable, her back wasn't broken. But it didn't matter much. If someone didn't find her, she would die here, and she didn't want to die when living was getting good again. Another spasm of pain swept through her body, and she lapsed into unconsciousness.

* * *

Mary Bromley was born in Toronto and lived there until she was six, when her father was killed in a car accident. Her mother took the meager amount of insurance money and moved them to Vancouver, where she was able to make a living for the two of them as a hairdresser. Mary graduated from high school and went to secretarial school for a year. She was 19 when she met John Andrews, a forestry student at the University of British Columbia, and promptly fell in love. John was about to graduate from the university, and the couple decided that a life together was their destiny. With the blessings of Mary's mother, they were married the day after John graduated.

John got a job with a firm that did contract timber cruising and land surveying and was assigned to the Campbell River office. The couple bought a home on Peterson Road and settled down to raise a family, but a family was not in the cards for them. John's sperm count was virtually nil, probably because of a bout with mumps when he was 18.

Mary went to work in a woman's clothing store, one of a chain of 350 across Canada, as a salesperson and was successful from the beginning. Her thin figure enabled her to wear the current fashions to advantage, and her outgoing personality made sales a breeze for her. When the manager of the store was promoted to head office, Mary was given her job.

With John gone for long periods on jobs far in the mountains, Mary found time hanging heavy on her hands. She enrolled in night school and rounded out her business education with courses in bookkeeping and computers. She found that she was particularly adapted to the computer world and enjoyed the challenge of learning the new technology. As the years went by she became bored with the job in the clothing store. While she carried the title of store manager, there was little real management involved. The head office controlled everything, and she was obliged to blindly operate strictly by the book.

Mary was ready to resign her job when John came home from a trip complaining of severe pains in his chest and shortness of breath. Fearing a heart problem, Mary rushed him to the doctor. His heart was fine, but x-rays showed a massive tumor in his chest. A biopsy showed that the tumor was cancerous. It had invaded both lungs and was inoperable. Six months later he was dead, and Mary's world seemed to have ended. She couldn't conceive of living without the companionship and love of the man that had been an integral part of her life for 20 years.

* * *

Mary felt like she was emerging from a sea of dense fog. Then the pain took hold of her, clearing her mind and she remembered what had happened. She heard a roaring overhead, and she thought another earthquake was coming. Then she realized that it sounded more like an airplane and wondered if Jamie was looking for her from the air. She opened her mouth to scream for help, but no scream came, and she found herself choking on a mouthful of garden soil. The sound of the plane came back again and seemed closer, then faded away. She tried to move, but her efforts made the pain worse. She became conscious of a feeling of wetness around the area of her groin. Oh my God, I've peed my pants. With that, she faded back into unconsciousness.

Chapter 17

Back at the Tsolum School, Jamie learned there was a power outage. Andy Blankenship and Dave Jorgenson were there ahead of them. Andy reported that a circuit breaker had blown at the main switching yard, which indicated that there was probably a short in the local system, likely caused by a falling tree. Also, the Elk Falls plant had gone off-line. The Puntledge unit was supplying power. The changeover had been automatic and worked, as it should.

"The first priority," reported Andy, "is to find the problem."

"We will have to follow the lines and check them visually," said Dave. "That may take awhile. Too bad we don't have cell phones available so we could keep in touch. That way we could all go in different directions."

"Would it help to use the plane?" Jamie asked. "The 172 is ready to go, and we can fly slow enough to see any major problem."

"That would be great," Dave said. "If you and Andy want to go fly the lines, I'll go get the line truck and bring it here. If you find anything, come give us a buzz and fly in the direction of the trouble. I'll get in the truck and follow."

* * *

Minutes later Jamie had the Cessna in the air, and Andy was giving directions on where to go. "We'll start at the switch yard and fly up Dove Creek Road, then back down and go up Headquarters Road. That's where the tallest timber is. We'll have to zigzag back and forth to cover the sidelines. I'll direct you as we go."

Jamie eased the plane down to about 150 feet as they started their search. He flew to the left of the lines so that Andy would have a good view out of the passenger window. "Can you see OK from this height?" he asked.

In less than 30 minutes, they had covered the area west of the river and the Central Valley. They swung back around and started along Old Island Highway, passing over the school. Just up the road, Andy spoke up.

"There it is, I think." The downed tree and the snag hanging in the wires were readily visible from the air.

Jamie swung in a wide circle and came back past the school headed north. He surged the engine and swung into another circle. Dave had obviously understood their directions. The line truck was already moving up the highway, followed by a couple of cars.

In minutes, Jamie had the plane on the ground and taxied it into the hangar. Ten minutes later, they were at the school, picking up Kelly and Dawg. Jamie was worried. It seemed to him the downed tree was on Mary Andrews' property. A minute later, his worries were justified.

Dave had the line truck ready with the outriggers set to stabilize it. A couple of cars were parked nearby, and several men were watching as, with chain saw in hand, he worked the levers to raise the crane, riding the box on the end of the boom. Getting in position, he started the saw. One cut was enough. He lopped the end off the snag. The rest of it flipped over and plunged to the ground. The wires swayed and settled to their normal positions. They had been held tightly together, wedged between the main trunk of the snag and a branch growing at a 45-degree angle.

Jamie parked the car in the space in front of Mary's house, and Kelly and Dawg were out in a flash, rushing to the front door. In seconds, Kelly was back out the door, screaming, "Jamie! Mary isn't here, but her car is. Where is she?"

Jamie had a sick feeling in the pit of his stomach as he turned towards the tree. "Maybe she's out for a walk," he said.

They started toward the tree, Dawg dashing in front of them. The dog sniffed at the edge of the tangle of foliage, backed up, barked a couple of times and then plunged into the mass of limbs. It was too dense, and the big dog backed out, looking for another way in.

"She's in there," Kelly screamed. Dropping to her belly, with hands out in front, she started crawling snake-like into the tangle.

"No," Jamie yelled. "Stay out of there." It was no use. Kelly had already disappeared into the tangle of limbs with Dawg trying his best to follow her.

Dave came down from his perch and rushed over to join Andy. "Probably a coon in there. That would attract the dog. They better watch out. Coons can be dangerous."

Kelly's voice came from the depth of the tree. "I found her. She's here. I think she's alive, but she's hurt bad. There's a lot of blood."

"OK!" Jamie called. "Come back out. We'll get her out of there as fast as possible."

Dawg appeared first, backing out of the brush. Then Kelly came wriggling like a snake, feet first. She stopped, tangled in a branch, and Dawg grabbed her pants leg and began to tug, trying to help her.

"No, Dawg, no," Kelly yelled. "You'll pull my pants off."

Dawg let go, and Jamie reached in, found the branch that was holding Kelly, and managed to lift it enough for the girl to wriggle out. Jamie couldn't believe what he saw. Kelly's face and arms were covered by scratches, one on her arm weeping blood. Her hair was a tangled mess, full of the dead fir needles and small twigs from near the center of the tree. Her shirt was torn, and tree trash and garden soil covered her clothing.

"How did she look?" Jamie demanded. "Is the tree crushing her bad?"

"No," Kelly replied, her voice trembling. "The tree is a couple of inches above her back. But the limbs are pressing her down. They're pressing on her awful hard. We got to get her out of there quick."

Dave was returning from the truck with the chain saw. "We'll have to cut our way in there. Got to go slow. We don't want to destabilize the tree and have it settle down on her."

Jamie took command. "Someone go up to the hospital and get Dr. Ron. Have him bring the ambulance. The rest of us will pull the brush back as Dave cuts it loose. Move carefully. Take your time. We have to do this right."

It was ten minutes before enough limbs were cut off to get a glimpse of the victim. Jamie heard the sound of a vehicle and saw the ambulance coming at high speed. With a spray of gravel, the vehicle stopped feet away, and Dr. Ron, accompanied by a nurse, piled out. Ron fell on his knees trying to get close to Mary. He could reach her head and neck and felt for a pulse. It was there, but not as strong as he would like. He felt around her head, and his hand came away bloody. Backing out, he reported. "She's alive, but I don't know how bad she is hurt. She's lost some blood. We have to get her out of there as soon as possible and get her to the hospital where we can take proper care of her."

Dave was coming back from the truck with a big hydraulic jack. "I'll cut some more brush out to the right of her there and try to get this jack under the tree. If we can take the weight of the tree off of those branches that are holding it up, maybe we can cut the ones that are holding her."

Dave made quick work of getting a space cleared to the tree trunk about three feet from Mary. Going back to the truck, he got a couple of pieces of plank. Shoving them in place between a pair of down projecting limbs, he established a base for the jack on the soft garden soil. Inserting the handle, he began to pump; the jack took hold, and the tree rose perceptibly.

"Now I'm going to cut the limbs off the top side of the trunk and work over to the other side and clear out some space there so that we can see conditions there. I'd like to cut the tree in two here, but I'm afraid it might cause settling, or something. I can't take a chance."

A few minutes later, Dave was able to step over the tree and work from the opposite side. He started clearing back towards Mary. It wasn't long until they had cleared enough space for Dr. Ron to get across the tree and kneel beside his patient. "I can slide my hand between her back and the tree," he reported. "She is being held down only by these big branches that are bent down over her. Let's see if we can raise the tree a little more?"

"Slow and easy," Dave ordered, as Andy started working the jack handle. The tree moved slowly upward. With two inches gained, Dave ordered a stop and they cleaned trash and small limbs out from around Mary. Dave got in with his hands and started feeling for the branches that were holding her down.

"There're only a couple of big branches that are holding her," he reported. "Bring me some blocks from the woodpile. Raise the tree another couple of inches." Andy worked the jack, and others brought armloads of stove wood. Dave directed them as they built piers to support the tree should it settle again. They lifted the tree another two inches. Ron reported that there was now six inches of clearance between Mary's back and the tree.

"Now if we can get these big limbs cut out, we're home free." Dave said. "This is going to be tricky, so hold your breath." The chain saw came to life, and working only inches from Mary's body, Dave started nibbling at the limb. A little at a time, he cut a notch in the two-inch thick branch, until it started to bend at the cut. Then going to the opposite side, he cut slowly into the limb, until it parted. Grabbing the cut end, Dave lifted up on it and called for Andy to hold it. Andy took hold of it and lifted while Dave cut it off at the surface of the soil in which it had buried itself. A few minutes later, the other big limb was removed. Dave held the saw flat against the underside of the log and zipped off the few small branches that remained.

"I believe we have it now," Dave called. "I think she's clear. It's up to you now, Ron."

Dr. Ron moved in and ran his hands around her body. "Let's see if we can move her now. I need about four people to help."

A backboard, brought from the ambulance, was eased under Mary, and she was slowly drawn into the clear. A minute later she was in the ambulance and headed to the hospital. Jamie and Kelly followed close behind.

Ron began his examination as Jamie and the nurse wheeled the ambulance gurney into the operating room. Ron's wife, Marguerite, arrived on the scene to help.

"We have to get these clothes off of her," Ron said. "I think most of her injuries are on her back. That's where the blood appears to be coming from."

Marguerite got out scissors, and she and the nurse began clipping away at Mary's clothing. While this was going on, Ron was examining her head. "She has some bad cuts to her scalp that are still bleeding," he reported. "Scalp wounds bleed badly because of the concentration of blood vessels there. Let me take a listen to her chest." Moving the stethoscope over her upper body, he continued talking. "Her lungs sound all right. I can't hear anything to indicate internal injury. Let's get her turned over onto the operating table, and we can get a look at her back."

With the gurney close against the operating table, they carefully rolled Mary's body onto the table, leaving the bloody clothing behind. Several puncture wounds showed on her back, some of them oozing blood. A thumb-thick length of dead limb protruded from the right upper thigh, and a bulge in the muscle showed the depth of its penetration. Blood was seeping from around the penetration point. Ron was having a hard time examining the head wounds. Mary's thick hair was matted with drying blood and masses of dead needles and bird droppings.

"We have to get this hair off before we can do anything with these head wounds," Ron said.

Kelly piped up, "Are you going to cut all her hair off?"

"Afraid we'll have to," Ron answered. "Those wounds have to be cleaned and dressed."

"Kelly," Marguerite spoke up, "you had better go and wait in the lobby. This is no place for little girls."

"No," Kelly responded. "Mary is like my sister. I want to be with her. I'll help. I can stand some blood."

"Let her stay," Ron said. "But she's incredibly dirty. Get her washed up and a cap and gown on her."

The nurse led Kelly to a scrub sink. "Wash your hands and arms with lots of soap." Taking a washcloth, the nurse swabbed Kelly's face and pulled a cap over her head, tucking her hair up inside it. "Let's get into this." The nurse held a surgical gown, and Kelly pushed her arms through the sleeves. It was much too large, but the nurse pulled the ties around in front and snagged them tightly. With latex gloves on her hands, she was ready to assist.

"All right," the nurse said. "Help me with the hair. Hold it up and away as much as you can so that I can get down close to the skin with the scissors." Quickly, she started snipping away as Kelly held the mass of tangled hair aside.

Ron examined the wound in the thigh with the piece of limb protruding from it. "I have to cut that out, so we can clean up the wound. It's hard to say what that stick has brought in there with it."

Taking a scalpel from the tray beside him, he made a clean incision so he could remove the piece of wood. He held it up in triumph. "That's a nasty son of a gun. Let's get that wound cleaned and stitched." As Marguerite kept the blood swabbed away, he dusted the wound with antibiotic powder and started pulling it closed with sutures.

"There, that's that," the nurse said as she made the last snip, and Kelly was left holding the entire mass of Mary's hair. It was so badly tangled and sticky with blood and debris that it held together like a mat. Kelly dropped it in the waste can on top of Mary's clothing. The nurse continued working, cleaning Mary's scalp in preparation for stitching and dressing.

Ron spoke to the nurse, "Help Marguerite get those back wounds cleaned up, and I'll start stitching these head cuts. Kelly, you can help." The longest head wound was gapping wide and oozing blood. "I want you to hold the sides of this cut together with your thumb and forefinger while I get the stitches in."

Kelly, with surprisingly steady fingers, pulled the skin in place and held it as Ron inserted the sutures. When he was through, he had nine stitches holding the wound together. He put a dressing on the wound and went on to the next one, which required five stitches.

With the head taken care of, Ron went on to the back. A couple of the punctures were so deep that he deemed it advisable to cut them open to be sure they were clean, and placed stitches to close them. The rest of the scratches and cuts were cleaned and dressed. With a sigh of relief, he finished. "Let's get her in bed. She seems to be doing fine. I think she'll come to most anytime. Jamie, you'd better take Kelly home and get her cleaned up. We wouldn't want Mary to see her in the shape she's in."

* * *

By the time Jamie and Kelly got back to the hospital the patient was awake, but not aware of her surroundings. Dr. Ron was still there, and Dave Jorgenson was sitting in a chair by her bed.

"I had to come and see if she was all right," Dave explained, his face suffused by a blush. "I've sort of taken a liking to this little gal."

"She's worth liking," Ron told him. "We have to be sure she recovers OK. She had quite an ordeal under that tree, but she's going to be fine. She has some cracked ribs, which are causing her a lot of discomfort. I've given her a shot to ease the pain, so she's pretty much out of it right now. There's nothing we can do about the ribs. They will heal themselves. We have to watch all the cuts she has and be sure no infections show up. There must have been a lot of birds making that tree their home. Bird droppings were all mixed in with the other stuff that got into those cuts, and that makes a perfect breeding ground for strange bugs. If all goes well, she can go home in a few days. All of you had just as well go home and get some rest. Hopefully, tomorrow, she will be able to talk to you and thank all of you for the efforts you made to get her out of that mess."

Chapter 18

Kelly was eager to get to the hospital to see how Mary was doing, but Jamie made her wait until they had finished their breakfast. As they were entering the lobby, they met Dave Jorgenson coming out.

"Good morning Dave," Jamie greeted him. "Have you been to see Mary?"

"Yes," Dave answered. "I came early because Andy and I are going to Campbell River to check up on the Elk Falls power plant. I was anxious about how she was coming. But she's doing fine."

"Seems you're developing a special interest in her," Jamie remarked.

Dave blushed furiously. "Well, yes, I am. But I don't want to push it if you're interested yourself."

"Hey," Jamie told him, "I think the world of that girl, but not in the matrimonial way. Besides, I'm much too old for her. She needs a young man like you that will be around for a long time."

Kelly spoke up. "Dave, are you going to marry her?"

Dave's blush grew deeper. "I could consider it real easy, but I haven't talked to her about it."

"Well," Kelly told him, "you'd better. Someone else might ask her. I think you're a real nice guy, and if she's going to marry someone I think it should be you."

"Thanks, young lady," Dave answered. "I've got to get going or Andy will think I'm lost. Take care of our lady."

Jamie and Kelly found Mary sitting up in bed. She was pale, and her closely clipped head with its dressings was a shock to her visitors. Kelly ran to her and threw her arms around her.

"Go easy," Mary cautioned her. "Don't squeeze the fruit. My cracked ribs can't stand much."

"How do you feel?" asked Jamie.

"Like a tree fell on me," Mary replied. "But I'm going to be all right. Ron says I can probably go home tomorrow, providing I come in to see him every morning."

"Will you be able to take care of yourself alone that soon?" Jamie worried.

"Oh, yes," Mary replied. "I've already been up walking around. I just have to be careful not to move too sudden or take a deep breath. If I do, I'm apt to say words I shouldn't."

"I'll come and stay with you and take care of you," Kelly said. "I can cook and keep house and everything, and I'd love to help you—if Jamie will let me."

"Sounds like a great idea," Jamie agreed.

"Sounds good to me, too," Mary agreed. "Just promise not to make me laugh too often. It hurts like hell when I do. Jamie, would you take Kelly to the house and let her find some clothes for me? I don't have anything here. I think a skirt and blouse would be easier than jeans to get on. Everything is in my closet and dresser."

"Will do," Jamie agreed. "We'll pick them up and be back this afternoon sometime. Take care of yourself. Come on Kelly, let's go and let this lady get some rest."

* * *

That evening Jamie and Kelly returned to the hospital to find Mary and Dave sitting in the luxurious lobby that had been the living room of the lodge that Dr. Ron had converted to a health center. Mary, her cropped head covered by a colorful scarf and dressed in a short skirt and bright blouse, looked extraordinarily well. Color had come back to her face and little showed of her ordeal except for a bruise on her forehead and scratches on her arms. Kelly had picked well for clothing and possibly Dave's company was contributing to her bright appearance.

"You're looking great," Jamie told her. "Good to see you up and coming along."

"Ron says I can go home in the morning, so I'll take you up on your offer to give me a ride. Also, I think it would be great if Kelly stays with me a few days. With her help, I will get along fine."

"OK," Jamie agreed. "We'll be here in the morning to pick you up."

* * *

As Jamie pulled up to the hospital, Mary came out to meet them. She walked gingerly, being careful not to move too fast.

Jamie opened the car door for her and told Kelly to get in the back with Dawg. Carefully, Mary fitted herself into the seat.

"I still have a few sore spots," she said. "Besides my cracked ribs, my thigh is awfully sore. Ron said he took a chunk of wood out the size of a broomstick."

"The way I heard it," Jamie said, "it was more the size of a baseball bat."

"Awe, Jamie," Kelly interposed. "You're exaggerating things. It wasn't near that big. I watched him cut it out. He took a knife, cut right down the whole length of it, picked it out with his fingers, and held it up for us to see. It was about three-inches long."

"You mean you were there watching me get patched up?" Mary demanded.

"Yeah, I helped, too." Kelly bragged. "I held the big cuts on your head together while Dr. Ron sewed them up. I think I'd like to be a doctor when I grow up."

"What a girl," Mary said. "The way you go at things, I think you can be anything you want to be when you grow up."

* * *

Jamie found the house an empty void without the lively company of his adopted daughter, so he spent his time getting better acquainted with the people of New Island. He found it a revelation. While they grieved deeply for lost relatives and friends, most of them were happy with their plight, realizing that they were perhaps a privileged few to have avoided the disaster that had overtaken the world. They had accepted that they were members of an extremely small society that had to depend on each other to survive, and were looking forward to making their little world a good place to live. They realized that they would have to forgo many of the luxuries that they had enjoyed in the past and would have to work hard to survive, but they were confident in their abilities. Jamie came away from his first day of visitations with a loaf of fresh bread and a jar of honey and a feeling that New Island was on the way to permanent survival.

Stopping by Mary's house on his way home, Jamie found Dave and Kelly preparing dinner. Mary was enthroned on a chair, giving directions, and promptly invited Jamie to join them. Jamie brought in the bread and honey to add to the feast of baked ham and mashed potatoes that were in progress. It turned out to be an enjoyable evening, although Mary was showing signs of fatigue by the time dinner was over, and she was shipped off to bed.

* * *

Jamie found Charlie Johnson sitting on his front steps when he arrived home.

"Hi," Charlie greeted him. "Figured you would be along soon, so I waited for you. I've come up with a problem that I need to talk to you about."

"Come on in. Hope your problem isn't serious. Anyway, let's hear it."

"I have a native family just showed up from the Gold River Reserve. A white fellow that has been living with them convinced them that they should stay in Gold River rather than move over here. The parents are both half-white and were well employed in Gold River. After a time of being the only people in the whole area, they decided that that wasn't such a good idea. They showed up at my place this morning. We scouted around, and I located them on a vacant farm not too far from my place. All was well until I asked for census registration. The mother filled out the forms for the family; they have two teenage girls and a boy, 14. One of the girls has an illegitimate baby. But when I asked the guy that is trailing along with them to register, he refused. He is arrogant, almost combative in his attitude. Said he wasn't going to grub in the dirt and shovel cow shit on any farm. What should we do about this character?"

After some thought, Jamie answered. "I think this is a matter for the council to consider. Let's call a special meeting for Friday evening. Get the family there and we'll welcome them to New Island. Your young outlaw should be there, too. Can you take care of getting them there and I'll notify the rest of the council tomorrow?"

"Sounds good to me," Charlie agreed. "I was willing to go on my own getting the family located, but I didn't know what to do about this guy. This kind of problem can be touchy."

"I agree," Jamie responded. "We all need to work together on something like this."

Chapter 19

Most of the council, including a fast recovering Mary, was seated at the conference table when Charlie Johnson escorted the newcomers into the room, followed by Constable Pat Draper with a reluctant young man in handcuffs. Charlie introduced Walter and Natalie Jim, and Pat introduced his captive as Lorne (Billie) Bolten, from Vancouver. With everyone seated, Jamie took the floor.

"Walter and Natalie," Jamie said, "I'd like to welcome you and your family to New Island. I hope that you will find your association with us to be a valuable one with a wealth of companionship, friendship and love. I'm sure that everyone will make you welcome. Now, things are going on here that I don't understand. Would you bring us up to date on what's going on?"

Walter spoke up, "Mr. President, I would like to fill you in on what's happened. This young man came to Gold River before the big earthquake scare to visit our neighbors. He had become a friend of their son at some affair in Vancouver. The son was away, but Billie stayed with the family anyway, and started sparking our girls. My son, Wallace, and I were planning a hunting trip upcountry, and we invited Billie along. While we were out in the woods, the three quakes came along, and we hurried home. The family he was staying with had joined the panic and left, and he stayed on with us. Charlie showed up and invited us all to Campbell River. Billie talked and talked and finally convinced us that we should stay there. Nevertheless, we soon realized that we were on the wrong track and, with him protesting all the way, came on over here. After Charlie found us a farm to work and live on, Billie raised hell. I told him if he was going to stay with us, he had to change his ways and get in and work with the rest of us. He refused. I told him he couldn't stay with us anymore. He refused to leave, so I went and told Charlie. Charlie got Mr. Draper and when Billie refused to cooperate, Mr. Draper put handcuffs on him and brought him along."

"Thank you, Wallace," Jamie said. "Now let's hear from Mr. Bolten. Billie, what do you have to say for yourself?"

"I don't have anything to say," the captive replied. "This is all a crock of bull, and I'm not going to have anything to do with it."

Jamie, speaking in a mild voice, said, "Billie, if you're going to live in this community, you're going to have to change your attitude. You must register for our census in order to reap any of the benefits that come from our association. You must leave the Jim household, and we will find you a place of your own to live. In order to be eligible for a piece of property, you must register. There is no other way you can stay here."

"You mean you'll kick me out of the community?" Billie demanded. "You have no right to do that. I demand a lawyer. That's my right. You have to get me a lawyer."

"Sorry," Jamie told him. "We don't have any lawyers in this community. This council is the law here. We make the law, and you'll obey it or leave."

"Where do you expect me to go? They say there is nothing but dead people anywhere else."

"Maybe," Jamie replied, "dead people are the only kind you can get along with. What is the wish of the council on this matter?"

There was silence for a minute, as everyone considered the problem.

Bob Elder spoke up, "I don't see much chance of making a good citizen out of this outlaw. A person who refuses to get along has no right to live in a community like this. Therefore, I think the only solution is to banish him from New Island. I so move."

"I'll second that motion," said Keith Shaw.

"It has been moved and seconded that Mr. Bolten be banished from New Island. Is there any comment?"

Billie rose from his seat, struggling with the handcuffs. "You have no right to do that. What will I do out in the woods all alone?" He went into a fit of cursing all those who would vote for such treatment.

Jamie spoke firmly. "That's enough, Mr. Bolten. Shut up and sit down."

"Up yours," the youth responded and continued his tirade.

"Pat," Jamie asked, "will you remove the prisoner from the room?"

Pat grabbed Billie by the shoulder and propelled him through the door, shouting over his shoulder as he left, "I'll vote yes on that motion."

"Walter and Natalie," Jamie asked, "do you have anything to say on the subject?"

"No," Natalie replied, "I'll certainly be glad to get rid of him. He's nothing but trouble."

"You have my OK," Walter agreed.

"All in favor?" Jamie asked. The vote was unanimous.

Jamie went to the door. Pat had the prisoner sitting on a bench at the end of the hall.

"Pat, would you return the prisoner to the court to hear his sentence?"

Pat brought the youth back to stand at the front of the room.

Jamie stood and faced the prisoner. "Billie Bolten, by the unanimous vote of the Council of New Island, you have been banished from this community for a minimum of three years. If, after that time, you have seen fit to mend your ways, you may return to the community on a probationary basis, probation to be for the rest of your life. Do you understand the sentence?"

"Fuck you," was the reply.

"Pat, can you carry out the sentence?" Jamie asked.

"I sure can," Pat affirmed. "But I'd like someone to go with me so that, in case I have to shoot him, I have a witness."

Charlie Johnson and Bob Elder both volunteered.

"OK," Jamie told them. "I'll leave it up to you three to carry out the sentence."

"I have a set of leg irons I'll use to keep him under control for tonight," Pat said. "In the morning, we'll decide where to dump him. Maybe we should get him off the island entirely. What do you think about that?"

"We can take the airplane and move him anyplace you think would be good," Jamie volunteered. "Providing we have a landing strip there."

"Hey," Pat said. "That's the best idea yet. Do you have room for all four of us to go?"

"Sure, we have a six-place airplane. Have him at the field at nine in the morning. I'll have the plane ready."

"It's a date," Pat agreed. "We'll be there."

* * *

Jamie had the Cessna 206 rolled out on the tarmac, fueled and inspected, when Pat Draper, Charlie Johnson and Bob Elder arrived with the prisoner.

"Where do you want to take this character?" Jamie asked.

"We discussed a number of places, but came to the conclusion that somewhere on the mainland was best."

"Get him out here," Jamie requested. "And let's ask him."

Pat and Charlie dragged the recalcitrant prisoner out of the car and stood him up on the tarmac.

"Where would you like to go, Mr. Bolten?" Jamie asked. "We can take you to Powell River, or some place in the Vancouver area. What's your choice?"

"I don't want to go anywhere," Bolten whined. "You have no right to do this. If you do, I'll get a gun and come back here and shoot the whole damned bunch of you, and run this place the way it should be run"

"That's enough," Jamie said. "Get him loaded up. Put the prisoner in the center right-hand seat. Charlie, you take the back seat behind him and watch him carefully. Pat, you sit beside him, and Bob can take the copilot's seat. Let's get going."

"I don't want to go," the prisoner yelled. "I'm afraid of airplanes. They're dangerous. It might crash and kill us all."

"Shut up and get in that plane," Pat commanded. "I've had about enough of your guff. I'd very much like an excuse to shoot you, and much more of this crap and I'll have the excuse." Pulling his handgun from the holster on his belt, he held the muzzle against Bolten's neck. "Now straighten up and behave."

"Charlie," Jamie said, "you get in the back seat, and then Pat can put the prisoner in the seat in front of you."

Charlie fitted himself into the back seat, and Bolten, not liking the pressure of the gun on his neck, climbed into his place.

"Bob," Jamie directed, "fasten his seat belt. Charlie, get him by the collar and hang on to him till Pat gets in on the other side. OK, Bob, you get in the front. Everybody in place and seat belts fastened?"

Pat handed his gun to Charlie. "I don't trust this character. If he makes a move, don't hesitate. Shoot him. Careful, the safety is off."

Forty minutes later, Jamie settled the plane onto the Boundary Bay Airport, a small field about 25 miles southeast of Vancouver International, and parked at the outer end of the runway.

Pat got out and came around to the passenger door. Bob got out of the front, and Pat prepared to help Bolten. "Christ," he exploded. "He's pissed his pants and pissed all over the airplane." Roughly, he jerked Bolten from the plane.

By then, Charlie was out to help. Jamie got a towel from the baggage compartment and mopped up the urine from the floor. The other three marched the prisoner to the airport fence, where Pat unlocked the leg irons and handcuffs. Taking his gun back from Charlie, he directed the prisoner to grip the top wire of the fence with both hands.

"Now stay right where you are until the plane is gone. Don't move or I'll start shooting."

A few minutes later, the plane airborne, Jamie circled back over the airport. Bolten was still hanging on to the fence. It was an easy flight back to Comox.

Chapter 20

Billie Bolten felt like his hands were frozen to the wires of the fence. He was conscious of a chill from the breeze blowing off the bay around his urine-soaked pants. Straining to look over his shoulder, he could see that the airplane was coming back over the airport, but it was still climbing. Only then did he pry his fingers loose from the fence wires and turn around to survey his situation.

Clenching his fists in the air and shaking them at the disappearing aircraft, he shouted incoherently, "You bastards, you can't get away with this. I'm coming back to the Island and kill you all. Then I'll show those hicks how a country should be run."

Billie started walking towards the airport buildings, keeping alert for the possible signs of the airplane returning. That cop, he reflected, was a mean bastard, worse than the other two characters that had hauled him away to dump him on this God-forsaken spot. He did not doubt that the cop would have shot him if he had even half an excuse. Flying in that flimsy machine had terrified him more than anything in his life had before. His fear on takeoff had been so severe that he had dribbled a little piss in his pants, but by gritting his teeth, he had managed to turn it off. But the landing was another thing. As the plane approached the ground, he was sure that it was going to crash. He lost all control of his bladder, and the urine had gushed out of him soaking his pants all the way to his shoe tops. He would get even with those characters, if he ever got a chance, and he would make that chance.

Billie's feet were starting to hurt by the time he had traversed the half-mile to the other end of the field. There was no evidence of life anywhere, and he made his way out the entrance to the street beyond. He found a bus stop, but then realized that there would be no bus. He hadn't been able to believe the story that all life was gone on the mainland, but it was starting to look like the story was true. He walked a ways along the road, wondering how he was going to get to the city.

Then a solution presented itself. There, by the side of the road, an older style small bungalow had a deserted look. In the driveway beside it, an eighties-model Chevrolet pickup was parked. Billie figured that, if no one was around, he could break into the truck and hot-wire it, and it would serve to get him into the city. Cautiously, he approached the house, and then with everything still looking deserted, he worked up enough nerve to walk up on the porch and bang on the front door. There was no answer, and his confidence returned. He went to the pickup and tried the door, but it was locked. Maybe if he broke into the house, he could find the keys to the truck and save having to hot-wire it. The back door did not look too substantial, so he decided to try the trick he had seen in a number of movies. Stepping back a couple of paces, he lunged forward, planting his foot just below the doorknob. The door shuddered, but held firm. The third try and the door popped open. His whole body hurt from the strain.

Stepping into the kitchen, Billie looked around. He thought there might be something to eat in the refrigerator, and a cold beer would really go good. Opening the door, the odor of spoiling food greeted him, and he closed it hurriedly. The power had been off for some time here, he realized. He found the keys to the pickup in the top drawer of a cabinet.

The truck was a little slow to start, but sounded OK when he got it going. The gas gauge showed the tank half full. He had a little problem with the stick shift, but finally managed to get going. Finding his way to an interchange that got him onto highway 99, he headed towards downtown Vancouver. The multilane highway, ordinarily very busy, was without moving traffic. Cars were stopped along the shoulder, some of them in the traffic lanes. When he stopped to look closely, he found that they contained decomposing bodies.

Billie was becoming more and more frightened and depressed as he realized that he was probably alone in the city. He found his way to his mother's apartment on 11th Street. Fearful of what he would find, Billie approached the apartment. His key worked in the lock, and he hesitantly entered. There was no sign of life as he went through the rooms. Again, he found only spoiled food in the refrigerator. Most of his mother's belongings were still in place, but there was evidence of some hasty packing, and a suitcase she kept under the bed was gone.

Absence of his mother was of no particular concern to Billie. She was not there to lecture him about being gone so long, and ask questions about the truck he was driving. He could get along without her abrasive presence. He was hungry, and thought of going for a hamburger, then realized that there was little likelihood of finding a place open. Looking through cupboards, he found a can of beans, but the electric can opener on the counter wouldn't work. Grumbling in frustration, he got out a butcher knife and hacked the can open, then ate the beans direct from the can with a spoon.

Wandering into his own room, Billie changed into clean, dry pants. Going back outdoors, he started walking the area. The smell of death pervaded everything. Down on Broadway, he found street people dead, wrapped in their blankets in doorways and alleys. He was totally alone in a city that ordinarily contained millions of people. Cars scattered along the street had bodies in them, and the smell was nauseating.

Billie missed his old gang. If the Smarts were here, he'd be able to cope with the conditions the city was in. Billie had worked his way to the top of the Smarts by acting and talking tough. One did not have to fight to be boss. He just had to act tougher than the others, and with a few supporters, it was easy to maintain control. The Smarts had been a good gang and had provided a good lifestyle for their members. For the most part, they had succeeded in keeping out of jail, and were gaining control of more territory under Billie's leadership. When he got back to the island and got rid of the tough acting cop and the sanctimonious fool that called himself President, he could make his leadership abilities evident to the rest of the population and take over control. He would just have to act tougher than he ever had before.

There were girls on the island. Billie was sure that they would fall for his tough-guy character. The two Indian girls in the family he had thrown in with at Gold River were falling for his charms. He was sure that he would have had them in bed in another couple of days, probably both at once. He did not like Indians, but he had noticed a number of white girls in the group on the island.

Yes, he reflected, it would be best if he got back to the island. He was 22 years old, with seven years in the Smarts gang, the last two as leader. He had the knowledge and experience necessary to take over the group of hicks in the community that they called New Island.

Chapter 21

Jamie was at the airport when George arrived.

"Jamie," George greeted him, "there's something I have to talk to you about. Emily is getting very unhappy about me flying with you. In fact, she's very insistent that I stop. And I don't relish seeing and smelling more dead people. I promised her that I would make this flight, then no more, unless it was a real emergency. I'm sorry, but that's the way it is. Someone else who enjoys flying more than I do can do a better job for you than I can."

"That's OK, George," Jamie told him. "I've had a feeling you were a little on the reluctant side, but I needed your locksmith capabilities so badly that I ignored it. Do you suppose you could train someone else in a reasonably short time?"

"Well," George replied, "it takes awhile, but I'll sure do the best I can. I hate to let you down this way, but I can't help it."

"OK, fellow," Jamie said. "I'll find someone else to fly with me. And we'll just have to carry a hammer and pry bar to take care of the locks until you can get someone else trained. You still OK to go on this trip?"

"Yes, I want to go this time, finish out this last trip."

A few minutes later, they were in the air headed south.

"I think," Jamie explained, "we'll take a little jaunt over to Port Angeles and then south along Highway 101 down towards Grays Harbor and back by way of Olympia and Seattle. We should be back fairly early. Sound all right to you?"

"Whatever you say," George agreed.

Jamie leveled the plane at 3000 feet and set up cruise power. "I'm going to stay at this altitude," he told George. "Better chance to see something, if there is anything to see. Watch for smoke, or movement, or anything that might indicate life."

An hour later, they were passing Victoria, moving out over the Strait of Juan de Fuca.

George, looking to the right and forward, suddenly straightened, coming alert. "My God, is that a boat down there?"

Jamie craned his neck to see, turning the plane to the right, dropping the nose and pulling the throttle back. "It looks like a submarine," he exclaimed. Rapidly, they drew closer, losing altitude. At 1000 feet, they passed over the sub and started a long circle for a closer look. There were men on the deck, waving frantically. Jamie turned the radio, so far unused, to the emergency frequency and picked up the mike. "Submarine, submarine," he spoke slowly. "This is aircraft circling overhead. Do you read?" Hesitating a minute, he repeated the message. "Submarine, this is aircraft overhead on 121.5. Do you read?"

"Aircraft overhead. We read you loud and clear. This is nuclear submarine Denver, bound for our base at Bangor, just north of Bremerton. Who are you and where are you from?"

Jamie set the plane in an easy circle at reduced power, maintaining his 1000-foot altitude. "I am Jamie Morgan, President of the Council of New Island, about halfway up Vancouver Island, near Comox. We have a group of about 400 people who, for some reason, have survived the catastrophe that seems to have overtaken the entire world. As far as we can determine, there is no one alive at your base in Bremerton. I think that your vessel would be able to dock at Comox. We would be happy to have you and your crew join our little community. We are setting it up to be self-sufficient with the hope of building a new society for the future. Over."

"Mr. Morgan, this is Patrick Holden, Commander of the submarine Denver. You are the first voice we have heard since we left Southeast Asia. We encountered two merchant vessels on the high seas, both of which we boarded. No one was alive on either. We touched at several islands and found everyone dead. One island was spared, and two-thirds of our crew elected to stay there and live off the land. The rest of us chose to come on home to see if anything is left. I think we should continue to our Bangor base to see what goes on there. Over."

"Commander, I appreciate your desire to see if anything is left at Bangor. However, if you wish to come to Comox and dock there, I'll take you in the plane to Bremerton tomorrow. This would get your crew on land a good deal sooner and may save them from some severe trauma. I'm sure you must have charts onboard that show Comox Harbor."

"My navigator has just signaled that he has the chart, and he can put us in the harbor sometime this afternoon. All the crew around me here seems to be in favor of your offer. We will proceed to Comox at once."

"That is good, Sir. We will return home at once and prepare for your arrival. How many crew do you have that we will need to find accommodations for?"

"There are only 42 of us onboard. We can continue to live onboard temporarily, but it would be nice to get our feet on solid land again. We are easy to get along with, so don't go to too much trouble for us."

"We will be on the dock to meet you this afternoon. Have a safe voyage. Looking forward to meeting you."

Jamie swung the plane onto a course for home. Looking back, he saw the submarine changing course for the trip up the strait. Turning to George, he remarked, "So much for our exploration trip south of the border. This trip will turn out easy for you."

"That suits me fine," George replied. "It's quite amazing to come on that sub the way we did. A half-hour later or earlier and we would have missed them. You might have some very valuable people off that sub. Most men who qualify for the submarine service are very capable people and well educated."

* * *

A shout from the outer dock announced the submarine was in sight. Jamie asked Little Bird to come along to welcome the newcomers. The boat appeared monstrous to the people on the dock. It approached slowly, a man in the conning tower giving instructions to guide it. Gradually, as the boat slowed, the bow came around and the stern edged toward the dock. Men appeared on deck with mooring lines, as with hardly a bump, the huge vessel came to rest against the dock.

As a gangplank extended from the boat to the dock, a tall gray-haired man in Navy blues stepped on it and approached. Jamie moved forward to meet him. He noted the three gold bars on his shoulder that designated a rank of Commander.

Jamie extended his hand, "Commander Holden, I presume."

"Yes Sir." His handshake was firm and positive. "And you must be Mr. Morgan."

"Yes Sir, but I prefer to be called Jamie."

"And I am Patrick, or Pat, to my friends. Your island looks like a beautiful place to live."

"Yes, it is," Jamie told him. "But what you see here is mostly abandoned. Our community is a few kilometers from here. Only one extended family lives here, in the float houses over there. Come, I would like you to meet our most respected elder. Commander Holden, this is Little Bird, our much esteemed Medicine Woman and Dreamer."

Holden extended his hand to meet the firm grip of Little Bird. She looked up at him, her glittering black eyes surveying him minutely.

"I do not understand the title Commander, but I assume it means you are the Chief of the monster boat tied to our dock. Welcome to our island, Chief."

"Yes, Commander is just another word for chief, used by the United States Navy. I can tell by his voice that Chief Jamie has a great deal of respect for the great Medicine Woman. I am very proud to meet you and hope that our association will be beneficial and enjoyable to both of us. I would be honored to be addressed as Chief. Chief Patrick."

"Thank you, Chief Patrick. I hope you are as great a chief as the other chiefs we have; Chief Jamie is the greatest. He gathered the people together into one tribe and leads them with the skill of a great leader. And here is Chief Charlie. He is Chief of the local Indian Tribes, but now sits on the council of the great Chief Jamie."

Charlie stepped forward and shook hands with Patrick. "I think, Sir, that you can invite your crew to come on land, and we will start getting things organized."

Patrick shouted a command, and the crew filed down the gangplank to line up on the dock at attention. Taking Little Bird by the arm, he escorted her on an inspection of the troops. On return, he snapped to attention and shouted. "At ease, gentlemen." The sailors relaxed their rigid stance, but still maintained a tight formation.

"Lieutenant Commander Cameron," Patrick commanded. "Please step forward and meet the great Medicine Woman, Little Bird. And this gentleman is Chief Jamie, in command of the local garrison, and Chief Charlie, a member of his council. These are our hosts on New Island. Folks, this is Lieutenant Commander Barry Cameron. He is my second in command."

With handshakes out of the way, Jamie turned to Patrick. "We have two buses on the parking lot to transfer your people to our headquarters where we have a dinner planned. If you can turn command of your men over to someone else, I would like you and Barry to ride with me. That will give us a chance to get acquainted a little better."

"That sounds great," Patrick responded, "But there is one more man I would like to bring along, with your permission. I think you will find him interesting."

"Of course," Jamie responded. "Bring him along."

Patrick turned to face his men. "Lieutenant Veary, will you come forward?"

A small black man, not more then five foot eight, very slender, with short cropped hair and smooth dark skin, stepped briskly forward and saluted. His eyes looked oversized behind extremely thick lenses.

"At ease, Lieutenant," Patrick said. "I think your saluting days may soon be over. Come meet our hosts."

With introductions over, Patrick explained. "Brian, you and Barry and I are going to ride with Jamie. The rest will follow by bus." Turning to the line of troops, he called out. "Lieutenant Portman, will you take charge, please, and get the men loaded on the two buses on the parking lot. We are going to have dinner with our hosts."

A cheer went up from the men as Lieutenant Portman formed them into two columns to march to the parking lot.

Jamie turned to Charlie. "Invite Little Bird to the dinner, if she will come." Motioning to his guests, he led them off the dock ahead of the sailors.

In the car, Commander Pat was in the front seat with Jamie and the other two officers were in the back. "The reason I wanted to bring Brian along was to let you meet him," Pat said to Jamie. "Brian is a mechanical engineer, one of the sharpest I have ever met. He can repair anything, or if it is not repairable, he'll build a new one. His greatest desire is to fly airplanes, which the Navy will not let him do because of poor eyesight. When he saw you flying overhead, and heard your story, he got very excited. He thought that there might be a chance for him to at least ride in a small plane if we stayed here."

Jamie turned to Brian. "Brian, you may be the answer to my prayers. The man who has been flying with me is scared of airplanes and wants to quit. I've been pushing him to keep flying because he is a locksmith and is very valuable in some circumstances. If you stay here, I'll ask you to become my copilot, mechanic and engineering consultant."

"Chief Jamie," Brian exulted, "I am your man. I'm not a licensed pilot, but I can fly and I'd like to learn more. I can't pass the required medical exams because of my eyes, but I can see well enough to do most things. And I am a locksmith, along with being licensed as an aircraft engine and airframe mechanic, including propjet. If you have a shop, I can do most any kind of mechanical or machine work. My mind is made up. With Commander Pat's permission, I would like to join your community."

"You have my permission," Pat told him. "I think that it is likely that we will all stay here. Right now, I can't see anything to prevent us. After Jamie takes us to have a look at our base tomorrow, we'll be able to decide."

* * *

The three officers were waiting when Jamie arrived the next morning.

At the airfield, Brian Veary followed Jamie as he inspected the airplane, paying close attention to what he did. When the inspection was finished, Jamie ordered the men aboard.

"You take the copilot's seat," Patrick told Brian. "You had just as well start getting used to your new job."

With the plane established in a climb configuration, Jamie glanced at Brian. "Ready to take it?" he asked.

With his feet on the rudders and hands on the yoke and black face glowing with pleasure, Brian responded, "I have it, Sir."

"OK," Jamie told him. "Level off for cruise at six thousand. Maintain the heading we are on." Turning to the men in the seat behind, he asked, "How do you like our little bird?"

"Brian seems happy with it," Pat replied, "so that makes it OK with me."

Brian asked a few questions as he leveled at altitude. "What is cruise power, what RPMs?" He had little trouble in getting the plane properly trimmed.

An hour later, Jamie took the controls and started the letdown to Bangor. They flew over the base at 1000 feet, and then returned at 500 feet. There was no show of life anywhere.

"It looks very discouraging, but I would still like to land and go to the Commander's office."

"Will do," Jamie responded.

The small Silverdale field, with a 2500-foot runway was only a few miles south of the base. Jamie slipped the plane onto the runway and taxied along a line of parked planes and small hangars. The only car visible was an older model Ford sedan parked by one of the hangars.

"There's the only transportation I can see," Jamie said as he parked near the car.

"Let's take a look," Brian said. "I can hot-wire it if I have to, if such an act is permissible."

"I don't think the owner will object."

Brian tried the driver's door and found it unlocked. He looked inside, reached up and pulled down the visor, then lifted the floor mat. The keys were under the mat. Sliding into the seat, he pumped the gas pedal, and then tried the starter. The engine caught, stuttered a time or two, and settled down to a contented purr. Jamie called to the other two, and they got in the car and were on their way. Brian knew the area, and in ten minutes time they were entering the gates of Bangor Submarine Base. There was no sign of a guard.

"Let's go to headquarters," Patrick requested. "I'd like to see if the old man's office is open and see if any records were left."

Brian parked the car in front of an office building, and Patrick got out. "Come along, all of you," he requested. "I don't know what I'm going to find, and I'd like some company finding it." He led the way into the building and down the hall to a corner office marked Admiral Jacob Masterson. The door was unlocked, and Patrick led the way into the outer office, then on into the open inner office. The room was light and airy, with pictures of famous Navy ships and submarines decorating the paneled walls. A big desk sat facing the windows looking out over the parade grounds. Patrick walked behind the desk and picked a sheet of paper from the middle of an otherwise clean surface. He looked at the paper for a minute, and then read aloud.

I am shocked beyond belief at the evaporation of my command. The nattering of an inane imbecile started a panic that I was unable to control. Then, the occurrence of three rather moderate earthquakes finished off the debacle. Everyone was gone within hours. This is the most heart-breaking thing that could ever happen to a Navy Officer, to see his command break and run like a bunch of scared rats. I thought we had the finest Navy in the world that would stand and fight against any odds. I was wrong.

Admiral Jacob Masterson

Patrick put the letter down and stared out the window for several minutes before turning to the others to speak. "What a way for a great Navy man to end his career. My experience has been rough, but nothing to compare to this. Let's go and see if he may be home."

Patrick gave Brian directions as they drove to the officers' housing area and parked in front of a modern house set in the middle of an unmowed lawn. "If you people will wait for me, I think I'll handle this alone."

He climbed out of the car and strode up the walk. The front door was unlocked, and he walked in. In only a short time, he was back in the car, his face pale and drawn. "He was in an easy chair in the living room, a part bottle of Scotch on a table beside him. He is bloated and getting mighty ripe. The smell is not pleasant. Let's get back to the plane and go home."

Jamie noted that he said "home."

* * *

They touched down on Comox Base in early afternoon, and things looked different. The two buses were parked alongside the barracks building, and a number of cars were in front. Some men were pitching a ball back and forth. Jamie thought that it was good to see some activity on the base.

After putting the plane away, they went to the mess hall, where they found a group of men drinking coffee, among them Lieutenants Cameron and Portman. Patrick told them briefly what they had found.

"So I assume that we will be staying here," Barry Cameron said.

"If Chief Jamie will allow us," Patrick said.

"You are more than welcome," Jamie told him. "I think you should get your men together as soon as possible so that we can tell them what the situation is. I'd like to explain what will be expected of them so that they can make up their own minds about staying with us."

"I don't think they have much choice," Barry said. "Have you fellows had any lunch? I didn't think so. Brian, can you go see if the cook can shake up some sandwiches? In the meantime, I believe that everyone is on base. I'll see if we can get them together right away to hear the news. I think they are all anxious to hear."

126

A few minutes later an orderly came in from the kitchen with a tray of sandwiches and a pot of coffee with coffee mugs. As they started eating, a loudspeaker blared out. "All personnel. All personnel. Please muster in front of the mess hall in 15 minutes."

Jamie stood on the front porch of the mess hall beside Patrick, overlooking the group of men standing in formal ranks at attention.

"Gentlemen, at ease," Patrick commanded. "It looks like the United States Navy is a thing of the past. The base at Bangor was totally abandoned. We found a note written by Admiral Masterson in which he expressed his dismay at what had happened. The Navy personnel apparently joined the civilian population in the general panic after listening to the so-called scientific expert that predicted an earthquake that would destroy the entire west coast and most of them deserted and ran. When the three earthquakes happened within one hour, the rest of them left. We found Commander Masterson dead from the gas or poison that apparently killed most of the people in the world. As of now, you are released from any obligations to the Navy. I am accepting Chief Jamie's offer to stay here. The rest of you may do as you see fit. Thank you for being a great Navy Crew. I will never forget you. Now, Chief Jamie will speak to you."

"It was difficult," Jamie started, "to witness the disappointment in your commander's face when he verified what he already expected to find. A great institution had dissolved in a few short days, defeated by a terrible panic that gripped the entire country. But it is over, and we must look to the future. Most of us in New Island are in the same boat as you fellows. We have lost family and friends in an unbelievable catastrophe. We are starting over with the aim of establishing a new society from scratch. We hope that it will be a better society than that which we lived in during the past. In spite of the hardships we are bound to experience, we are making a good start towards that society. We welcome all of you to join us.

"We haven't established much in the way of laws as yet. That will come as needed. Everyone is registered as a citizen of New Island. We will expect you fellows to do the same.

"We will get you settled as soon as possible. In the meantime, you may stay here on the base. There will be a potluck dinner at the school gymnasium next Sunday at four PM, followed by a general meeting. I hope you will all be there to meet your new neighbors.

"Now, it is up to you. You may stay, or go, although, for the life of me, I don't know where you would go. Any questions?"

Lieutenant Commander Cameron stepped forward. "Chief Jamie, I think I can speak for most of our men. Your offer is wonderful, and we have little choice but to accept it." Turning to face the men, he continued, "While Commander Holden has released you from any obligation to the Navy, I would like to remind you that you are still Navy trained and disciplined. I hope that you will show that training in your conduct here. I will still act as your leader here on the base until you find yourselves places in the community. Let's show these wonderful people what true Navy people are like. Now, what are your wishes? Do you want to become part of the New Island Nation?"

There was a period of silence, and then a man in the rear ranks threw his hat in the air and let out a war whoop that would give credit to any Indian Brave. The rest joined in, and there was complete pandemonium. Then men started pushing forward, eager to shake hands personally with Jamie.

Chapter 22

Jamie and Kelly picked the Dick girls up at the dock and got to the school early for the regular Sunday council meeting. Kelly herded her charges off to a classroom for some extra tutoring. Jamie found Mary in the office working on the computer. Mary looked little the worse for her recent encounter with a falling tree, except for her bald head that was just showing a covering of fuzz. He noticed a particular air of ebullience that surprised him. She was literally aglow, as if an inner fire was lighting up her face.

"Hey," Jamie exclaimed, "you look like something special is happening in your life. Tell me about it."

"I didn't know that it showed that much. But I am very happy. I hope you approve."

"If it makes you look the way you're looking right now, I have to approve."

"Dave just left a few minutes ago. He asked me to marry him, and I said yes. When John died, I didn't think I could ever fall in love again, but I have. I'm as excited as a teenager."

"Congratulations. I think Dave is a fine man, and I heartily approve. The main thing I'm interested in is your happiness, and I think marriage is the ideal thing. When is it going to happen?"

"Soon, I hope," Mary said. "We haven't had much time to make plans, but I think it has been coming on for some time. We seem to get along so very well, and we have many common interests. Most of all, I would like to have a baby, and I am almost too old. I always wanted children, but John was unable to be a father. Now I want to try again. Do you think that is sensible?"

"It's not only sensible, it's wonderful," Jamie exclaimed. "You had better get married right away and get this major project off the ground. I would be honored to tie the knot. And I'll volunteer Kelly to be bridesmaid if you can tolerate anyone so young."

"Kelly may be young, but she shows an unbelievable maturity. I wouldn't have anyone else."

"Have you considered where you will live?" Jamie asked.

"Yes. We'll live at Dave's place. He has a larger house, more land, a milk cow, and a flock of chickens that are laying eggs. And he has a mamma pig that is grossly pregnant. I think she is going to have at least a dozen piglets. I'm all excited about learning to be a farmer's wife, and working with the animals and everything. If I can just get pregnant myself, that will top off everything. I don't want to be like that mama pig, though. One will be enough for me."

Jamie looked at his watch. "I think it's about time to get into the boardroom for the meeting. Can we announce the good news to the rest of the council?"

"We can announce it to the world, if you want," Mary responded. "I'm so happy and excited that I'd like everyone to know."

The council was gathering in the boardroom as Mary and Jamie took their places at the table.

Charlie Johnson sat down across from Mary and stared at her for a minute. "Hey, gal, you look like the cat that swallowed the canary. What have you been up to?"

Jamie spoke up. "As the first item on the agenda for this meeting, I have a special announcement to make. Mary not only looks like she swallowed a canary, but possibly a turkey gobbler as well. She just told me that she is engaged to marry Dave Jorgenson. I would like to put it on record that the entire board concurs in offering their congratulations and the best of wishes. All in favor?"

Hands went up around the table, and a babble of conversation broke out. Congratulations were offered by all.

Keith Shaw spoke up. "I hope you're not going to quit your position as secretary and vice president of the council?"

"Never," Mary replied. "I have never been so happy with a job in my life. I feel like I'm doing something worthwhile. It's a terrible thing to say, but I'm almost glad that that crazy seismologist came along and scared everybody away. We have our own little world now, and in spite of all that we have given up, I think we will have something better than we ever had before."

"I'm just about inclined to agree with you," Charlie Johnson said. "I think we have a wonderful and caring group of people that will make a New World better than the old one was. I'm glad to be a part of the leadership of it."

"OK!" Jamie spoke out. "Let's get down to business. We'll start with reports from the council members."

* * *

130

With the social part of the afternoon over, it was time for the general meeting. Jamie called the meeting to order, then gave a general report summarizing the reports of the various council members at the afternoon meeting. With that out of the way, he went on to tell about the events leading to spotting the submarine in Juan de Fuca Strait and the results of that discovery.

"Now I have something special for you. You have all been wondering what caused the death of most of the people of the world. A possible answer will be passed on to you today. This is a theory only, but it makes sense. To tell you about it, I present Commander Patrick Holden, of the nuclear submarine Denver. Commander, the floor is yours."

Commander Holden stepped confidently to the podium. Out of uniform, he was dressed in blue jeans and a western-style shirt. He surveyed the crowd before him for a minute and then spoke in a voice that one would expect from the commander of a submarine.

"I may be able to shed some light on the puzzle of what happened a few weeks ago to change your lives so drastically. Please understand that I am not sure about this, but the theory that I am going to present to you makes more sense than any other idea that I can come up with.

"During early February the Denver was on patrol in the Tasman Sea when I was called to attend a conference in Sydney, Australia, with a group of intelligence agents from the U.S. and Australia. This group had gathered information that China was developing a new chemical weapon at a facility in Xinjiang Province in the far west regions of the country. This weapon was supposedly a gas that was held under very high pressure as a liquid. When released from this pressure, it expanded rapidly and rose through the air to high altitudes where it could possibly spread around the world in a few days. After a time in the high altitude environment, possibly due to the action of solar rays or the ozone layer, its composition changed and it became heavier and settled to earth where it was fatal to most air-breathing organisms. It settled out very rapidly and lost its toxicity on contact with the ground. The report was that the Chinese had learned how to manufacture the product but had still not learned how to control it. They had made a large amount of it and were holding it in pressure tanks at their compound in the Xinjaing desert. The

131

authorities were extremely concerned, and a vast effort was being launched to try and learn what was going on.

"I was instructed to proceed to Suva, on the island of Viti Lavu in the Fiji Islands, to pick up a crew of Navy SEALs that would be flown in there. We were to leave part of our crew at Sydney to make room for the SEALs. They would have instructions on where to go for a possible insertion onto the China Coast.

"We left 12 of our crew on extended leave and sailed immediately. Due to a severe storm over the Coral Sea, we ran due west and then north through the South Fiji Basin, running submerged to avoid the rough water. Two days later we surfaced off Suva to find that the world had fallen apart. There was nothing but dead people in Suva. We broke radio silence and tried to raise someone. There was no answer, until our radioman picked up a weak signal from a small island in the Vanuatu Group, about 700 miles east of Suva across the North Fiji Basin.

"We arrived there to be greeted by a frantic chief. Their island had less than a thousand people. One hundred of their young men had gone to Port Vila to take temporary jobs on an airport expansion project. Then, overnight, all radio communications had been lost. Some men went out fishing about twenty miles south of the island and found a group of ten fishing boats with all of their crews dead. They visited a neighboring island, and it was the same there. Everyone dead.

"We had to conclude that, with our sophisticated communications system, that this disaster had overtaken the world. For some reason, this one little island was missed. The chief invited us to take our hated nuclear sub out, sink it and make our home on the island. They were very self-sufficient, with fish in the sea and a plentiful supply of fruit and vegetables on the land. With a hundred of their men gone, a new infusion of males would be highly welcome. I presented the chief's offer to the crew, with my permission to take him up on the offer. Eighty of my seamen elected to stay on the island. The appeal of the laidback lifestyle on the tropical island, along with a surplus of beautiful women, was a major enticement. Most of them were single men without important attachments at home. Forty-two of us, all officers and higher rated non-commissioned officers, many with wives and children at home, decided to stay on the boat and return immediately to our base in Bremerton. We encountered two freighters on our way, which we boarded. They were lifeless. Then, coming down the strait south of Victoria, your President Jamie spotted us. You know the rest of the story.

"The only conclusion that I can make is that, somehow, those tanks blew up and the gas got away from the Chinese scientists that had developed it. That may not be the true story, but I doubt if we will ever know. There probably are other people alive in the world, and maybe, sooner or later, we will make contact with them. In the meantime you are on the way to building a new society here that I hope will never be interested in developing poison gas or nuclear submarines. I thank you all for making it possible for me and my crew to become a part of your group."

Dead quiet pervaded the room for several minutes. Teresa Blunt stood. "Commander Holden, you have obviously left us speechless. It seems impossible that the desire to control, to dominate, could lead to the development of such a weapon. I almost hope that you could be proven wrong and that this terrible event was caused by natural causes rather than the struggle for power by human beings. However, your conclusions are almost surely right, and on behalf of my fellows in New Island, I thank you for your presentation."

Jamie returned to the podium and thanked Patrick for a reasonable sounding explanation of the disaster, then called on Teresa again. "Are we going to meet the same way next Sunday?"

"Yes. We are all having a lot of fun out of these parties. Only next Sunday, I'd like to suggest that we come at two o'clock and see if we can't get a little baseball going. I think we can develop our own league here and have a lot of fun and fellowship out of it. How many of you would like to take a try at it?"

The idea was accepted with enthusiasm.

Chapter 23

Jamie and Kelly arrived home after the wedding of Mary Andrews and Dave Jorgenson to find Brian Veary sitting in his truck in the front driveway. "I thought you'd be home soon, so I waited," Brian reported. "Something that I think is important came up and I wanted to get the information to you as soon as possible."

"Come inside where it is warmer and tell me about it," Jamie requested.

Settled in comfortable chairs in the living room, with Kelly preparing coffee for them, Brian was quick to get on with his report.

"We have a radioman from the sub, Stan Bowman, who knows more about radio than anyone I have ever known. He's fiddling with radio equipment all the time. He brought a bunch of stuff out of the sub, and he found a lot more in the communications section here on the base. He set up a scanner that would monitor all possible frequencies and lock on to any signal that came up. The scanner got a lock this afternoon. The signal is weak, but he thinks that whoever was sending it was trying to attract attention. He rigged up a direction finder, and it is almost due east of us, probably over the mountains. He doesn't have any idea how far, but it probably is anywhere between 100 and 300 miles. Because of the high mountains in that direction, it's hard to pin down."

Jamie thought about it for a minute, and then asked, "What do you propose we do about it?"

"It might be worthwhile to try to trace it down with the airplane."

"I doubt if the radios in the plane would be suitable for a mission like that."

"No, they wouldn't. But Stan says he can install enough equipment in the plane to do the job. He has volunteered to work as long as necessary overnight to get the stuff in. I will help him to be sure he doesn't do anything to interfere with the operational safety of the plane, and he will go with us to operate the equipment."

"Is there room in the plane for the gear?" Jamie asked. "And what about weight?"

"We've considered all that. By taking out the center seats, we can get all the gear installed and have room in the back seat for Stan to handle it all and be strapped in his seat most of the time. We'll have to install some antennas, probably on the cabin roof. We can do that without interfering with the integrity of the plane, and we can fix it all back as it was after we are through."

"And you can have it ready to go in the morning, and still have enough energy left to go tomorrow?"

"We should be able to do the job in four or five hours so there will still be time to get some rest."

"OK," Jamie said. "It all sounds good to me. Here comes the coffee."

"I'll take time for a quick one and be on my way. Stan will be excited to have your approval."

* * *

Jamie reached the airport early. Both Brian and Stan were there and had the airplane rolled out and ready to go. The weather was favorable with a high overcast. Jamie got out charts, and they decided to plan on Kelowna for the first stop, unless they were able to intercept radio signals sooner and determine a different destination. Kelowna was almost due east and about 250 miles away. Looking at the plane, Jamie was amazed at the work that had been accomplished. The center seats had been removed and a rack made of aluminum angles bolted to the floor. An array of black boxes, radios and gauges had been installed, all looking very professional. A pair of antennas had been installed on the cabin roof and another one on the belly.

They were on their way shortly after nine o'clock, and 40 minutes later they passed over the town of Squamish located at the head of Howe Inlet. The snow-covered mountains of the park were a spectacular sight off to their left. Stan, in the back seat, wearing earphones, was intent on his dials. They were passing over the famous Hell's Canyon of the Frazer River when Stan came to life. "Hey, I've got a signal," he called out. "Hold on a minute. It's fairly strong and coming from somewhere around 110 degrees. It's just a steady warbling sort of sound, but it is definitely being broadcast."

"Let's continue on this heading for a while," Jamie requested, "and you may get a better reading."

Twenty minutes later, another call came from Stan. "The signal is getting stronger, and the direction dial is swinging steadily towards the south. I'm now getting a reading of about 140 degrees which would put us in the vicinity of Penticton, if the signal is coming from a populated area."

"Turning right to 140 degrees by the gyro compass," Jamie reported. "And I'll start letting down. We have about 100 miles to go."

The plane picked up speed as Jamie trimmed the nose down. As the altitude lessened, the air become turbulent and the plane began to bounce. Jamie looked back to see Stan tightening his seat belt. "Are you OK back there?" he called.

"Yeah, I'm fine," Stan replied. "But I'm sure glad I listened to Brian and secured all this gear good and solid. The signal is getting stronger and the bearing is the same."

Brian reported that he could see Lake Okanogan, and the town was at the south end of the lake. Jamie picked up the airport a short distance south of town. He continued his descent and leveled off at 1000 feet above the ground. Above the airport, Stan reported that the signal direction had reversed itself and must be coming from the city. Jamie circled back over the city, continued north a short distance and turned back to head south over Highway 97. He made another circle over a residential area and dropped to 500 feet, slowing to 100 miles per hour. Suddenly, from the corner of his eye, he caught movement on the ground and banked the plane steeply. Someone in the middle of a street was waving a white cloth. Jamie waggled the plane wings to indicate he understood the signal and continued to circle. The man ran to the driveway and got into a station wagon. Backing into the street, he headed south towards the airport. Jamie swung the plane around and passed the car. The man was leaning out the window and pointing towards the airport. Jamie got the message and headed in the same direction. By the time Jamie had landed and taxied to the ramp, the car was coming through the airport gate. Skidding to halt a short distance from the plane, the man got out and ran towards them, arriving almost before Jamie could get the engine shut down and the door open to greet him.

The man, an outdoor kind of type, looking about thirty, with dark hair and a ruddy complexion, almost knocked Jamie off his feet has he hurled himself forward and threw his arms around him. Stuttering and stammering in an effort to talk, he finally settled down, released Jamie from the bear hug and started getting words organized. "Who are you? God, I'm glad to see someone. Where are you from?"

"Slow up and settle down," Jamie requested. "I'm Jamie Morgan."

Stan and Brian were coming around the plane.

"And this is Stan Bowman and Brian Veary. We are from the coast, on Vancouver Island. Stan here picked up your radio signal yesterday, and we came today to trace it down. We have a community of more than 400 people that were spared by the disaster that hit the world last month. Now, who are you and how many people do you have around here?"

"I am Archie Summers, and there are six of us here. Everyone else is dead. We were spelunking in a deep cave, and when we came out, the world had changed. Can you help us? We're getting desperate."

"Well," Jamie responded, "let's get the rest of your people together, and we will see what we can work out. We have to talk it over and see what the alternatives are."

"OK," Archie replied. "There are six of us, and we are all living in one house. Come on, and I'll take you there. They are going to be as glad to see you as I was. Let's go."

At the house, Archie made introductions. His wife, Jane, was an athletic looking 30-year-old. Jane's sister, Susan, appeared younger, but also physically fit. Harold Evans, a little older, probably near 40, tall and beanpole thin and his wife, Rhonda, a short blond on the plump side and Rhonda's sister, Klari, also blond but taller and leaner.

"We moved into this house because it has three bedrooms and we could all live in one place," explained Archie. "Somehow, it seemed important for all of us to be close, considering that we are the only people in the entire valley, as near as we know. This house was empty, the owners gone to Europe on vacation. It was furnished, so it suited us fine. We had all lived in other parts of the valley before."

"The odor of death isn't too bad here," Jamie commented. "How do you account for that?"

Harold Evans answered. "There were a number of houses empty. Those that had bodies in them, we cleared them out and hauled them to a vacant lot. I found a backhoe, dug a trench and buried them. We cleaned up for several blocks around us, but the odor is still bad at times. It depends some on the weather."

"Who's responsible for the radio signal?" Jamie asked.

"I am," Archie responded. "I have had some training as a radio engineer and have worked in radio stations a bit. I went to a local station and set up a transmitter to operate around the clock on a low frequency commonly used. I monitored it three times a day for recorded responses. The station has a generator that keeps things going when the power goes off. We had power for some time, but it all went off last week. We still have natural gas flowing, but I expect it will stop soon. I kept hoping that someone would hear the signal and respond, but I had about given up any hope."

Jane Summers questioned. "What's it like on Vancouver Island? Do you have someone who is in control of the settlement? Are you organized, or anything?"

"Yes," Jamie told them. "We have set up a simple form of government. We have a council of which I am president. The council works together well, and the people seem to be happy with our work. Most of the people are settled on farms in the Comox Valley, and the rest have individual homes. Everyone in the community has their own place. We are all close together, and we have meetings once a week. We are trying hard to develop a community that will grow and give us all a chance to lead the best possible lifestyle."

"Could we come and join you?"

"Yes," Jamie replied. "We would welcome you. We just have to figure out how to get you there."

"Maybe we could drive over," Archie speculated. "I think we could find a van that would hold us all. We could drive to Vancouver in one day."

"I'm not sure the roads are open," Jamie told them. "There are an awful lot of vehicles stopped on the roads where people were caught by the gas. They just folded up and went in the ditch or stopped in the middle of the road. The road could be blocked anywhere. And snow over some of the passes is possible. I think flying is the best choice. I suggest that we go home, get the gear out of the airplane so it can haul a full passenger load and come back to pick you up. Another idea. We could take one of you with us, and I could come back alone and take the other five and only have to make one trip."

After more discussion, it was decided that they would follow the last suggestion. The weather was starting to look bad, and it was decided that they would wait till the next day to take off. They would go to the airport, fuel the plane, and tie it down in case the wind came up.

Back at the house, the aroma of roast beef greeted them. The women were preparing dinner for all of them. Archie suggested that the three men bunk in the house next door. He had extra gasoline lanterns that they could use for light.

The next morning the storm was still raging. After a breakfast of pancakes with bacon and eggs, there was nothing to do but wait for the storm to abate. Susan and Stan decided they 'needed some fresh air' and bundled up in rain gear to go for a walk. They were gone for a full two hours and returned looking exhilarated, faces flushed and eyes bright.

By two o'clock the weather was looking more favorable, and Jamie decided they could take a look at it. With no weather reports available, he would have to play it by ear.

"Who's going with us this trip?" Jamie asked.

"I am," Susan reported, without hesitation. "I've already got my bag packed."

"I hope it's not too big," Jamie said.

"No, it's just a few things to get me by for a day or two," she replied. "Stan said I could get what I needed over there."

With the group together, Jamie told them his plans. "It's possible that we can't get through today. If that happens, we will return here and buzz the house. If we do get through, I'll be back tomorrow to pick up the rest of you, weather permitting. Weather not permitting, I'll come as soon as possible. It could be days or weeks. Good weather here doesn't mean good weather on the coast. So if I don't show, be patient. Pack only a small bag each. We don't have much baggage capacity with a full passenger load. Now, if you'll get us out to the airport, we'll be off."

They were off the ground at three o'clock. In the air, they could get a better look at the mountains to the west.

"Things don't look too good in that direction," Jamie told Brian. "Let's go north and see if we can follow Highway 97C across to Merritt. If that doesn't work, we can go on up to the Shuswup Lake and follow the Thompson River down to the Frazer."

The air was fairly good along the lake, but when they turned off to follow the highway, the turbulence become extreme again. Jamie turned back and flew north along the lake to its head where Highway 97 crossed the river towards Kamloops. He had been able to gain altitude until he was just under the clouds at 4000 feet above sea level. There appeared to be clear air over the hilltops as far as he could see, so he decided to brave the turbulence and plow through. "Hang on," he told his passengers. "It's going to be rough for a while." It was extremely rough, but the Cessna handled it in good form. Thirty minutes later, they were out into the Thompson River Valley and following the river down to Kamloops. The air, although still bouncy, was much better.

"We can stop in Kamloops and spend the night," Jamie told his passengers, "or we can go on down the river. An hour should put us out into the lower Frazer Valley; then it's an easy jaunt home. What's your choice?"

Stan called from the back seat. "I've got a gal here that is a little scared, but she's settling down now. We're game for going on if you can keep on manhandling this critter."

"Same with me," Brian assented. "Let's keep on."

The trip down the river was exciting to the passengers. To Jamie it was much like the flying he had done in earlier days, delivering parts up and down the coast. Most of the time he managed to stay at least 500 feet above the river. It got really exciting for the passengers as they penetrated Hell's Gate Canyon. Stan afterwards claimed that the wing tips were scratching the cliffs on each side of the gorge, and the wheels were hitting the tops of the waves making the boiling turbulence of the water even more spectacular. When Stan told the story, Susan always verified it. She was in the seat beside him and was even more frightened than he was.

Through the canyon, the river widened out, and they had more room. Nevertheless, the clouds became denser overhead, and forced them to stay close to the water. As they passed Hope, it began to rain and Jamie realized that they had a strong tailwind. A typical coastal southeaster was blowing, and the rain was getting heavier. As they left the mountains and started out over the lower Frazer Valley, Jamie was able to relax.

Visibility was good enough for him to follow the river with no difficulty, and maintain altitude enough to not have to worry about wires or towers. With the speed of the tailwind boosting them along, they were soon out over the Strait of Georgia and thirty minutes later were over the base. Jamie made a circle over the valley and back across the docks to let everyone know that they were home. They had barely got out of the plane and got the kinks stretched out of their limbs when the side door of the hangar flew open and Kelly erupted through it like a cyclone.

"Hey, I'm glad your home," she yelled as she threw herself at Jamie. Jamie picked her up, swung her around and set her on the floor again. "I'm glad to be home," he told her.

Charlie Johnson followed her through the door. "I was visiting at the Dicks when she heard your plane. I think that if I hadn't agreed to bring her here, she'd have sprouted wings and flown herself."

Jamie introduced the newcomers and briefed them on the results of their trip.

"Did you have a good flight home?" Charlie asked.

"We got here, so I guess it was good." Susan exclaimed. "But I've never been so scared in my life. I've never been in a small plane before, and we flew down a canyon right over the river and it was so rough that I thought the plane was sure to come apart."

"My hand is still numb," Stan said, "from her squeezing it so hard. She was really hanging on. That Jamie is some pilot. I don't think anyone else could have brought us down that canyon like he did."

"That was Hell's Gate Canyon, which is really spectacular. But it wasn't that bad. I've flown worse here on the coast. The air turbulence made it seem worse than it really was. Do you fellows think you could have the bird ready to go back in the morning, get the gear out and the seats in? Leave the antennas in place. I know the rest of the group would like to get out of there, and if weather permits, I'd like to go get them."

"No problem," Brian told him. "We will have it ready to go."

"Jamie," Kelly said, "there was a bunch of small earthquakes this afternoon, then when the storm got bad, there was a nasty smell. It wasn't like the dead-people smell. It was more like rotten eggs."

"Hmm," Jamie mused. "Sounds like it could be from Mount Baker. Remember when we flew to Vancouver the first time; we saw the mountain erupting. Volcanoes sometimes smell that way. It's sulfur and other gases coming out of it. I don't think it's anything to worry about. We are in a direct line to get fumes from it when a southeaster blows. We could get some ash too. Let's get out of here and get some supper. Susan, you stay with Kelly and me until we get organized."

* * *

The next morning the storm was gone, and the air was clear with a bright sun. Jamie arrived at the airport to find Brian and Stan putting the final touches on the aircraft.

A few minutes later, Jamie was in the air, climbing to 10,000 feet. As he swung over Vancouver, Mount Baker became visible to the southeast. A plume of smoke was issuing from the top of the peak, and Jamie felt his analysis of the odors experienced the day before was verified. As he left the city behind, he set a direct course for Penticton. The flight over the mountains was spectacular. Snow covered all higher elevations. Sun and shadows provided a view that could be likened to a giant artist's canvas etched in minute detail. A day like this was the real reward of flying in a small plane. All too soon, he was letting down for Penticton. Flying over the town, he circled once and went in for a landing. He had hardly arrived on the ramp when Archie was there to greet him.

"It's great to see you again," Archie told him as they shook hands. "We were worried about you as the storm got worse after you left. We were all delighted and relieved when we heard you fly over. The girls are fixing lunch, let's get going."

A few minutes later they were sitting down to an early lunch, with the whole group showing a high degree of excitement. By noon, Jamie had them all loaded in the refueled plane and ready to go. The weather continued to cooperate, and before two o'clock, they were circling over the valley to announce their arrival.

Chapter 24

Jamie Morgan looked over the largest crowd yet in a New Island general meeting. The population of the little community was growing. There were now 459 people registered as citizens of the new country, and most of them were in the hall waiting for him to speak.

"Good evening, Citizens of New Island." There was a burst of applause from the audience, then silence again. "This has been a busy week for the leadership of our community. Probably you have heard of the events that have taken place, but I'll review them to be sure you are up to date.

"Our council vice president and secretary, Mary Andrews, is no longer Mary Andrews. As of last Monday, she is Mary Jorgenson. She and Dave were married Monday evening. The couple is going to live on Dave's farm on Township Road. Mary will continue her position with the council, and Dave will work the farm and spend part time helping Andy Blankenship keep our electrical system in order. Mary and Dave stand up and be recognized."

The applause was thunderous as the embarrassed couple stood. Jamie held up his hands for silence, and the room was quiet again.

"One of our new citizens from the submarine Denver is an outstanding radio technician. Stan Bowman loves to tinker with radios. Monday, he was fooling around with some of his equipment when he picked up a radio signal from somewhere east of here. Obviously, there were live people behind the signal. Stan went to Brian with it, and Brian brought it to me Monday evening. The two men suggested they equip the airplane with some more radio gear, including a direction finder, and see if we could track it down. They installed the gear in the plane, and we left Tuesday morning and wound up in Penticton, in the Okanagan, where we found six people alive. They were exploring a cave and were deep underground when disaster struck. Many of you have met them, but I'd like to introduce them for the benefit of those who haven't. Archie and Jane Summers, please stand; Jane's sister, Susan Bailey; Harold Evans and Rhonda, and Rhonda's sister, Klari Hayes. Please welcome these newcomers to our community."

There was another round of applause. Jamie held his arms high in acceptance and was turning to leave the podium when the shot rang out. There was utter silence, as Jamie staggered back and fell to the floor. Pat Draper was the first to respond. As he sprung from his chair and turned towards Jamie, the second shot exploded and Pat spun around with blood spurting from his left shoulder. Disregarding the wound, Pat snatched his handgun from its holster and squeezed off two shots over the heads of the crowd. A window partially open at the far end of the hall shattered, and a scream resounded through the room. Several men near the window rushed to see what was there, only to observe a shadowy figure disappear across the road.

Doctor Ron was kneeling at Jamie's side as Doctor Bill Weaver, medical officer off the submarine Denver, elbowed his way through the crowd to help.

Charlie Johnson jumped on the platform and shouted for silence. "That had to be Billie Bolten," he shouted to the crowd. "That's the guy we took off the island a couple of weeks ago. He threatened to come back and kill Jamie and Pat. We have to catch him before he shoots anyone else. I know there are several Indians here that are excellent woodsmen and trackers. I want all of you that are qualified in the woods to join me as soon as possible. Bring your guns and be prepared to stay out until we catch him."

Pat was returning from the window, holding his shoulder. "I caught a glimpse of him at the window before he hit me. I got off two rounds at him as he shot through the open part of the window. I missed with one shot and hit the glass, but the other shot may have made contact. I'm afraid I can't help much, but get some men out there and look for tracks under the window, and look for blood. Don't let the crowd trample around until you've had a chance to look at it."

Doctor Ron stood. "Jamie is hit badly in the chest area. We have to get him to the hospital as soon as possible where we have a better chance to help him. Grab one of those folding tables to use as a stretcher, and we'll load him in a pickup rather than wait to get the ambulance. You come along Pat, so we can take care of you, too."

Minutes later they were on the way. It was a sad and frightened group that gradually broke up and headed for home, not knowing if their leader was dead or alive.

Chapter 25

It felt like he had been hit in the chest with a sledgehammer. He was down on the floor and not sure how he got there. He wanted to get up, but somehow, there seemed no way he could do it. Jamie was only partially conscious. The pain was getting worse. It felt like a hot iron burning its way through his body. He recognized the voice of Doctor Ron, but what he was saying was garbled. He was being moved onto a flat surface that several men picked up and carried away, sliding him into the bed of a pickup. He wanted to ask what had happened, but words would not come. Then he was on a table under bright lights, and someone was cutting his shirt to remove it from his body. Then total darkness.

* * *

The lobby of the little hospital was jammed with people. Mary sat on a lounge with her arm around Kelly. Big tears were flowing down the girl's cheeks to drip off her chin, but no sound came from her. She had promised Mary that she would be brave, and she was trying her best. She could control the sobs that she wanted to release, but she had no control over the tears. Jamie was the greatest thing that had ever entered Kelly's life, and she was unable to conceive of what life would be without him. Please, please don't let him die.

Pat Draper emerged from the operating room. His shirt was off, and a bandage went around his chest and over his shoulder. His left arm was in a sling. He looked pale, but appeared determined to carry on. He picked up his jacket from where it was hanging on a coat rack and examined it carefully before draping it over his shoulder.

"It's sort of bloody," Pat said, "but it will have to do until I can get home. My shirt is totally ruined."

"Shouldn't Emma take you home?" Mary asked.

"No," Pat replied. "I'm all right. The bullet went all the way through and didn't do any serious damage. I'll just be sore for a few days. I don't want to leave until I find out how Jamie is. He doesn't look good. I hope I hit that bastard, and I hope he's hurting bad."

All of the council members were there except for Charlie Johnson. The big Indian was organizing the hunt for the shooter. Commander Patrick Holden from the submarine Denver was there, along with Brian Veary and Stan Bowman. Teresa Blunt had arrived with Commander Pat.

Doctor Ron entered the room and everyone looked at him expectantly. "I'm sorry, but the news is not good. The bullet hit a rib, which splintered into his lung. The bullet was smashed by its encounter with the rib, plowed a nasty hole, and lodged against another rib in his back. We are going to operate to get the bullet out and repair as much damage as possible. He has lost a lot of blood, and we need to give him transfusions if we can find people with the right kind of blood. His blood is type A, Rh positive. That is the most common blood type. If any of you have that blood type, you can help. If you don't know your blood type, the nurse can take a sample and type it."

Every hand in the room went up, including Pat Draper. Two knew that they had the right type, and the rest were willing to be tested.

"You're out Pat," Ron said. "You don't have any blood to spare after what you have lost tonight. I'd suggest that you let Emma take you home and put you to bed. You can do more good getting rested up and in condition to help run down that nut." Emma took Pat by the good arm and marched him from the room.

Ron continued. "Those of you, who know your blood type and it doesn't match, had as well go home. It's going to be several hours before we finish up and have an opportunity to assess Jamie's chances. Those who are a match, we'll probably use you soon, so stay around. The nurse will type the rest of you as soon as she can." Turning away, he returned to the operating room.

A nurse came out and asked for the two who knew they had the right blood type. Bob Elder and Pat Holden followed her from the room. Time passed slowly for the people waiting. There was little conversation. Then the nurse returned. She had set up a station for blood testing in the old dining room and asked that they take turns coming in for the test. Mary was the first in line, and Kelly was with her.

"Are you sure you want to be tested, young lady?" the nurse asked. "You're young to be a blood donor."

"If my blood's OK, I want to give it," Kelly told her. "Jamie is by far the most important thing in my life. I have to help, if I can. Can I go first, Mary?"

"Go ahead, youngster," Mary told her. "I know how you feel."

Kelly jumped up and down in excitement when she learned that her blood was a match. Mary was also a match, as were Brian Veary and Teresa Blunt.

Doctor Ron came back to the lobby. Splotches of blood covered his hospital scrubs. "We have Pat Holden hooked up for a direct transfusion while we continue to operate. Bob Elder will follow. That will be enough for tonight. The rest of you should go on home, get some rest, and come back in the morning to see if we need more."

"Let me take Bob's place," Kelly demanded. "I want my blood to help Jamie get well."

"No, dear girl," Ron told her. "It's already one o'clock in the morning. Go get some sleep, eat a good breakfast and get back here in the morning. If we need more, I promise you will be first."

Kelly looked disappointed as Mary dragged her from the room. "You're going home with me, and I promise to get us both back here early in the morning. Let's go."

* * *

Thirty minutes after the shooting, twelve men and a woman plus Dawg were gathered in the school boardroom. All of them had backpacks and had guns except Bonnie (Sweet Grass) Dick. Bonnie had a long knife in a scabbard at her waist and a small pack on her back. She was dressed completely in black and her face covered with charcoal dust. Charlie Johnson started organizing the group.

"It's almost impossible to track in the dark, but if anyone can, it's Johnie Jacob. He looks older than the mountains, but he still gets around good and has keen eyesight. He will lead the tracking, helped by Robert and Johnie Dick and Sweet Grass. This young woman has the best night vision of anyone I have ever known, and she can move through the forest with no sound. She has the ears of a fox and can detect the slightest sound that anyone else would miss.

"The rest of us will establish roadblocks to the north and south in case he tries to leave the area. There are only two roads in each direction, and you should pick a spot that can't be bypassed on other roads. I don't think he could have got out yet. He probably left his car some ways away, and he is wounded. I found blood under the window from which he shot. I brought Dawg along. I don't know if he can track or not, but he and Bonnie get along well, and she is going to take him with her. Let's get on our way."

The three Indian men and Bonnie went to the window where the shooter had been. The three men held back, and Bonnie and Dawg moved up. Bonnie talked in undertones to Dawg, and Dawg started sniffing the ground. He uttered a low growl and tugged on the leash. Bonnie and Dawg disappeared into the night. The three men followed at a discreet distance. Dawg kept his nose to the ground and pulled gently on the leash. The two moved like ghosts through the night, making no discernible sounds. They crossed the road and headed up the hillside to the east, through a field, then entered dense second growth forest. The canopy shut out what skylight there was, but the girl and the dog continued. A little way into the forest, Dawg stopped and Bonnie could feel him stiffen. He sniffed at a downed log that impeded their progress, but stood still. Bonnie made a slight chirping bird noise, and the three men closed up. Johnie Jacob came forward and produced a small hooded flashlight. The top of the log was barkless, about two feet off the ground. Johnie moved the light over it until he spotted a brown stain. They all crowded close to look, but made no sound. Johnie turned the light off. Bonnie urged the dog over the log, and the two again ghosted into the forest.

They came out of the forest onto a gravel road. Dawg coursed back and forth for a minute, then tugged on his leash to go east on the road. Bonnie lengthened her stride, and the two went along the road at a faster pace. The three men followed at a distance. Twenty minutes later and a half-mile down the road, Dawg stopped, sniffed the ground around him and turned back. Bonnie let him lead and zigzagged along the road for perhaps fifty feet, sniffing carefully. Stopping again, he moved to the side of the road and started back, sniffing at the overhanging brush and grass. Again, he stopped, then plunged into the undergrowth and moved positively forward. An hour passed and Dawg still led them through the forest. Another hour and Bonnie stopped, and her birdcall brought the others forward. The four Indians, with Dawg in their midst, huddled together for a whispered conference.

"He is lost," Bonnie told them. "He is going in circles. We are not far from where we entered this patch of timber."

"Are you sure?" asked Johnie Dick, the youngest and least experienced of the three Indian men.

"She's sure," responded Johnie Jacob, Bonnie's grandfather. "She started woods training when she was a toddler, with Little Bird. Twenty years ago Little Bird was still young and agile and could get through the forest like a wolf ghost. Little Bird, besides knowing all the plants and animals, knew how to find her way in the densest woods without any moon to guide her. Sweet Grass is right. I knew some time ago we were going in circles."

"Are you sure the dog is really tracking him, or is he leading us on a wild goose chase?"

"He is tracking," Old Johnie replied. "I have felt signs of his going. He breaks brush and stumbles over logs. We are on his trail. I could follow it myself, but the dog is much faster. He is one smart animal, equal to the wolf or the fox. We are on the trail."

Another hour went by, and the group was still following Dawg through the tangled forest. The sky had cleared, and some moonlight was filtering through the trees. Dawg slowed and Bonnie put her hand on his back. She could feel the hair rising along his spine. Slowly, they moved forward. A low, rumbling growl erupted from Dawg's throat, and suddenly he bounded forward, jerking the leash from Bonnie's hand. She plunged after him, barely able to see him in the faint glow of the moon. With a vicious snarl, the dog launched himself through the air. A scream split the air, and a gunshot sounded. Dawg was on the fugitive. Another gunshot sounded, and Bonnie, fearful for Dawg, plunged into the melee of dog and man. She saw the moon reflect off the gun, which was pointed at Dawg, and Bonnie, knife in hand, swung at the gun hand. The knife slashed across the knuckles, and, screaming, the fugitive dropped the gun. By then, the three men had joined the fray, and the fugitive was soon subdued.

Robert Dick produced a flashlight from his pack, and Johnie tied the man's hands behind his back with a leather thong he had in his pocket. Rolling the man over, they turned the light on his face. It was, as expected, Billie Bolten. Face white with fright, the side of his head bloodied by the loss of the top of his ear; the fugitive was a pitiful sight. Bonnie was hanging on to Dawg, trying to calm him. Dawg was not in the mood to be calmed down. The ordinarily gentle animal had turned into a snarling monster.

"Keep him away from me," Billie begged. "He'll kill me if you let him loose. Please keep him away. He has already bitten me twice. Please don't let him bite me again."

Bonnie was stroking the dog trying to calm him when she felt blood on his shoulder. Calling for the light, she found a deep gash across the shoulder where the first shot fired by Billie had grazed the dog. Taking a small bag out of her backpack, Bonnie removed a couple of containers. They both contained natural medicines obtained from forest plants. The first was a liquid that she poured over the wound, and then wiped it with a cloth. Dawg flinched as the medicine burned like fire, but held his ground. The second container held an ointment that Bonnie applied liberally to the wound. Talking steadily to him, Bonnie finally convinced him to calm down, and he lay down on his belly at the girl's feet.

"Let's get out of here," Johnie Dick said. "I'm ready to go home and have some breakfast." He helped the prisoner to his feet and searched him, taking the knife from his belt and dropping it in his backpack. "Does anyone know the way out of here?"

"I do," Bonnie replied. "We are not nearly as far as it seems. We have to go west and north to come out on the road."

"That's if you know which way is west or north," Johnie replied. "I'll bet no one has a compass."

"Don't need one," Old Johnie shot back. "If Sweet Grass can't lead us out of here, I can. But I have every confidence in this girl. She knows exactly where she is and how to get out. Lead off, Sweetie."

Sweet Grass and Dawg led the way, with the prisoner between two of the men. Old Johnie brought up the rear. A half-hour later they came out on a road. Bonnie turned right on the road for a short distance before plunging into the forest again. This was more open, and progress was much easier. A short distance into this forest and they came on a fence and open pastureland. Bonnie crawled through the fence and stood by until the others were through. It was downhill now, and they came on a barn and some other outbuildings.

"Shall we see if anyone lives here?" Bonnie asked.

"Do we have far to go?" Johnie asked. "If not, let's keep going and not bother anyone."

Bonnie led the way and came out on a road. Confidently, she turned right. It was getting light. Dawn was on the way. The road curved downward, past small farms, and shortly exited onto the

150

highway. Bonnie turned right on the highway, and in a few minutes they were at the school.

"What are we going to do with this punk?" Johnie asked.

"Let's take him back to the dock," Robert said. "We can tie him up and keep him safe until we hand him over to the council."

They were loading the prisoner into a car when Charlie Johnson pulled in from making his rounds of the roadblocks. Charlie was elated to find them there with the fugitive. "Let's go wake up Pat Draper and get his leg irons and handcuffs. I'll feel better with this guy well secured."

A half-hour later, Charlie was back with Pat, who had insisted on coming along, in spite of his wound. Pat supervised the shackling of the prisoner, and Bonnie got out her medicine kit and cleaned up his torn ear and the gash across the back of his hand, which was still bleeding. Billie screamed in agony as the liquid disinfectant poured over his wounds. The ointment calmed him down, but he was still blubbering.

"He's a real crybaby," Charlie commented.

Emma Draper arrived to check on her husband, demanding that he come home at once. Pat resisted forcefully. "I'm in charge of this guy, and I'm going to see to it that he is retained for trial. You can stay with me if you wish, but I'm not going home until we get some more people here. These people have been out all night, and it is time for them to go home and get some rest. For the time being, we'll lock him in the janitor's closet, but I'm staying here to make sure he stays locked up."

Defeated, Emma headed for the kitchen to make coffee. Charlie left to pull in his roadblocks. Bonnie elected to stay with Emma and Pat until more help arrived, and the three men headed back to the dock.

* * *

Dave, Mary and Kelly arrived at the hospital at seven AM. Mary had gotten Kelly up early and insisted that she eat a good breakfast. Dr. Bill Weaver greeted them in the lobby.

"I'm glad you're here," Doctor Bill told them. "I sent Ron home for some rest. He was about done in. I'm younger and more able to go without sleep than he is. Jamie is holding on, but we need some more blood in him. Ron said he had promised the young lady here that she would be first up. Are you ready?"

"I'm ready," Kelly spoke stoutly.

"All right, let's go. I'll take you next, Mary. It may be a half-hour or so. Just sit down here and rest."

In the operating room, Kelly was shocked at the look of Jamie. He was pale and breathing shallowly. Dr. Bill placed her on a table beside Jamie and prepared the apparatus to transfer blood directly from Kelly to Jamie.

"I have to put this needle into a vein in your arm, so expect a little pain. After the needle is in, you will not feel much. Ready?"

"I'm ready," Kelly said.

Kelly winced as the needle penetrated, but she settled down and watched with interest as her blood started flowing through the clear plastic tube.

"Relax as much as possible." The doctor told her. "We are going to take about a pint of your blood, which you can spare with no difficulty. It will mean a lot to Jamie. It will take about a half-hour."

The time went by quickly for Kelly, and Mary replaced her on the table. In the lobby, a nurse brought Kelly a cup of hot cocoa and a cookie. Now the time dragged by slowly. Dave tried to cheer her up, but Kelly was not much in the mood for conversation. Mary had finished her stint on the table and was drinking coffee when Sweet Grass ushered Little Bird into the lobby.

Kelly ran to Sweet Grass and threw her arms around her. "Golly," she said. "I'm glad to see you. They said that they were making up an Indian crew to try to track the shooter. Did they have any luck?"

"We caught him early this morning, and he is in irons waiting for the council to decide what to do with him," Bonnie told her.

Little Bird spoke up in a firm voice. "You mean you and Dawg caught him. This young woman has proved that all my efforts in teaching her to get along in the forest were worthwhile. She and that yellow dog of yours tracked all night through the bush to catch him."

"You and Dawg were all alone?" Kelly asked.

"No," Little Bird said. "The three men were with her, but it was her and the dog that did the work."

"Dawg did most of it," Bonnie insisted. "He is a wonderful tracker. He stayed on the trail through very rough going, and then attacked the guy when we came up on him. He was wonderful."

Dr. Bill entered the room at that time, and Bonnie approached him instantly. "Dr. Bill, Dawg got wounded last night. A bullet grazed his shoulder. I have medicated it with nature's best, but I think that it should have some stitches. I could do it, but I would rather you would. Could you? He's out in the car, and I could bring him in right now."

"Sure, bring him in," the doctor replied.

Bonnie went to get Dawg, closely followed by a concerned Kelly. "Is he hurt bad?" Kelly demanded.

"You can see for yourself," Bonnie told her as she opened the door and Dawg jumped out to welcome his mistress. Kelly didn't like the looks of the four-inch gash on Dawg's shoulder, but after seeing the cuts on Mary's head sewed up by Dr. Ron, she was less concerned. Back in the lobby, Dr. Bill took a quick look and agreed that it needed to be stitched.

"What did you medicate it with?" Bill asked.

"It's natural medicines that Little Bird taught me to make. They work well. I put a liquid on it to sterilize it and an ointment on it to make it heal. If you would put some stitches in it to close it so it won't make a bad scar, that's all it needs."

"I think I should clean it up before stitching it," Bill said.

Little Bird joined in. "No, leave it the way it is," she ordered forcefully. "Sweet Grass knows what she's doing. If you don't want to do it, give us some equipment and I'll sew it up."

Bill studied the old woman for a minute and replied. "You are the famous medicine woman they told me about. I'll bow to you. Let's get him on the table, and we'll get him stitched up. Should we give him some anesthetic?"

"No," Little Bird replied. "I don't like anesthetics. They are bad poison. Kelly and I will talk to him, and he will be all right."

They stood Dawg on the table, and Kelly took him by the muzzle and leaned her face against him. Little Bird put her face close to his ear and started a slow, monotonous chant in her native tongue. Dawg, stiff at first, visibly relaxed, and his tail wagged. The doctor approached with his needle and pulled the wound together, forcing the needle through the tough hide. Dawg winced slightly, but made no sound and did not move as the stitching continued. Finished, the doctor stepped back. Dawg jumped down from the table and followed Kelly from the room. The doctor, with an amazed look on his face, watched them go.

Chapter 26

Jamie was in a semiconscious state. He realized he had been hurt, but he could not remember how. The pain in his chest was incessant. He wished it would stop for a while. He drifted into dreams. A girl and a big dog were moving through a vague area of darkness. The dog was on a leash, and the girl followed. They were barely discernible in the dark fog that surrounded them. Then the dog was charging forward with the girl plunging after him. There was a scream and a gunshot, and the dream faded away. Then he was aware of someone on a bed beside him. He thought it was Kelly. Tubes attached her arm to his arm. What was Kelly doing here? Again, he faded into unconsciousness.

* * *

Kelly and Mary retained a vigil for all of Monday until Dr. Ron came back on duty and insisted that they go home and rest. Jamie was being cared for. The two doctors were alternating shifts. One of them was at Jamie's bedside at all times.

They were back at the hospital first thing Tuesday morning. Jamie was showing no improvement. The day dragged interminably. Many people came by to inquire about Jamie, but no one was allowed in his room except Kelly and Mary. Again, Dr. Ron insisted they go home for the night.

Wednesday morning, they were waiting in the lobby while Jamie was being cleaned up and having a bed change when Charlie Johnson came into the room.

"Mary, I'm glad to see you. We are going to have a council meeting this evening, and we need you there. You are the vice president, and you have to take Jamie's place until he is able to be back."

"I don't know," Mary replied. "I'm so upset that I don't know if I can really do any good."

"Jamie would want you to. He believed in your capabilities to do the job, or he wouldn't have proposed you for it. He would expect you to carry on with running the community. All of us on the council are depending on you for leadership."

"All right," Mary conceded. "I'll do the best I can. I'll be there."

Mary was already in the boardroom when the other members of the council arrived. All were present, including Dr. Ron and Pat, looking better, but his arm still in a sling. Mary called the meeting to order.

"I know that there are some concerns that caused you to request this meeting," Mary started out. "And I should have known what they were and called this meeting myself. Nevertheless, with Jamie in desperate condition, and Kelly distraught, I have not been thinking about much except my responsibilities to them. Please bear with me and tell me what we need to do tonight."

Pat Draper took the lead. "We have Billie Bolten under arrest, and we need to make a decision on what to do with him."

"Where are you holding him?" Mary asked. "Is he in a secure location? Who is taking care of him?"

"We have him in handcuffs and leg irons," Pat told her. "I'm keeping him in a shed at my place. I have a log chain padlocked to his leg irons and locked around a tree outside the door. Yes, he is being treated humanely. I knew you would ask that. I have provided him with a pad to sleep on and a pot to use as needed. Emma has been serving him regular meals, the same food we eat ourselves. He is secure and cared for—better than he deserves."

"Let me hear what all of you think. We need to talk this out and not make any rash decisions."

"That's why we wanted you here," Charlie Johnson said. "We knew you would be a tempering factor on those of us that might go off half-cocked and do something we could be sorry for afterwards. Most of us would like to execute him without any further ado, but that may not be the right way to go."

"No, that would not be right," Mary told them. "Jamie is trying hard to build a stable, honest and ethical society here. I agree with his ideas, as I am sure all of you do. In our new society, no one should be executed without due process. I'm not sure that anyone should be executed at all."

"Due process?" Keith Shaw asked. "That means a trial and a lawyer to represent him and a judge to monitor the trial and a jury to decide guilty or not guilty. How do we do all that?"

"All those problems can be overcome," said Bob Elder. "We have no lawyers, but we can find someone to represent him, possibly even better than a lawyer. I'd suggest Commander Pat

Holden. He is experienced in a lot of lines; he is capable, and I think he would do the job well. As for the judge, Jamie has been appointed as a judge, and Mary is his designated replacement in case he isn't able. Mary is well qualified to be judge. She is honest and compassionate and has all the attributes necessary in a judge. I'm not sure we need a jury. Many cases are tried with a judge only."

"Whew!" exclaimed Mary. "That's an awful responsibility to hand a girl, or a man, who is totally inexperienced. I think Patrick would be better qualified to be judge, and you can find someone else to represent the accused."

The discussion went on for some time, and many pros and cons were discussed. They agreed that a fair trial had to be held.

Mary stopped the discussion. "We've done a lot of talking. Now it's time to make a decision. We have to settle on something. Someone come up with a motion, please."

"I move that we approve the first proposal that Bob made," said Charlie Johnson.

"I'll second that motion," called Dr. Ron.

"Question?" Mary asked. There was no answer. "All in favor?"

The vote was unanimous.

"All right," Mary said, "when are we going to have this trial? I'd sure like to wait till Jamie got better and could handle it. What's the possibility of that, Ron?"

"Not good," Dr. Ron replied. "Jamie is very sick. He is going downhill, and neither Bill nor I have any ideas on how to stop his decline. If we don't think of something, he'll be dead inside the week."

Charlie Johnson spoke up. "We can't wait long for a trial. We have no suitable jail to hold him in, and his care is too much of a problem. We must get it over with promptly. I would suggest the general meeting this Sunday. We can have the input of the public then, and it might be easier to make a decision. And as for Jamie, I have a suggestion I'd like to make as soon as this trial business is decided."

After a short discussion, it was decided that the trial would be held Sunday, and Bob Elder was appointed to make arrangements and to notify as many people as possible on what was happening. If Patrick agreed to represent the defendant, he should see him beforehand to prepare his case.

"All right," Mary concluded. "That's settled. Now you had something, Charlie?"

"Yes," Charlie said. "It regards Jamie. I know that we have topnotch modern medical doctors trying to help him, but they are not, by Ron's admission, having much luck. I would like to bring Little Bird in and see if she can do anything. Maybe she can't, but a lot of people have a lot of faith in her. What do you think, Ron?"

Ron studied the question for a minute. "A few weeks ago, I would have jumped up and down and hollered like hell at any such suggestion. But since I have been here in the valley and talked to the woman some, and heard how much she is admired and trusted by her people, I don't know. She was in the hospital Monday when Bill sewed up Kelly's dog, who had a bullet wound in his shoulder. Sweet Grass had medicated the wound earlier, and Little Bird would not allow Bill to do any cleaning, or anything. 'Just sew it up,' she demanded in no uncertain terms. She wouldn't even let Bill use anything to deaden the pain while he sewed. Kelly held the dog's muzzle, and the old woman chanted in his ear. The dog hardly flinched. I saw him this afternoon, and the wound is healing perfectly. Let me talk it over with Bill tonight, and if Jamie isn't any better in the morning, I'd be inclined to say give her try."

"I'll go see her tonight," Charlie answered, "and have her there first thing in the morning. I'm sure that you will say yes and want to get started as early as possible. Agreed?"

"Agreed," Ron said. "I'm sure that I will say yes."

* * *

Mary and Kelly were at the hospital, when Charlie escorted Little Bird into the lobby, followed by Sweet Grass and grandparents, Johnie and Julia (Mountain Flower) Jacob.

Kelly ran to Sweet Grass and hugged her. "They say that Little Bird and you are going to treat Jamie. I'm glad. He's going to die if you don't do something to make him well. I know you can do it."

Both doctors had entered the room and heard what Kelly said.

"Thanks for your vote of confidence, young lady," Ron said. "But I guess I have to agree with you. We are losing rather than gaining. I only hope that they have success." Turning to Little Bird, he continued. "I am told that you are a great medicine woman. If you can help our patient, I will agree that you are not

157

only a great medicine woman, but also a great doctor, and that you are equal to or better than the modern ones such as Dr. Bill, and I. Come with us and see the patient."

The old lady stumped into the sick room behind the doctors. Sweet Grass followed, carrying the medicine bag. Little Bird stood for a long moment, looking down at the patient. Then she sniffed loudly.

"Open the window," she demanded. "There are bad smells in here. There is much poison in the air."

Dr. Bill threw the window open.

"That is better," she conceded. Bending over the patient, she stripped the covers down to his waist. The wound was freshly dressed, but already blood had soaked through to stain it. She spoke to Sweet Grass in her native tongue, and the girl opened the bag and brought out a glass jar filled with a dark-colored ointment. Little Bird pulled the dressing loose on one side and lifted it to expose the wound. Leaning over, she sniffed at the wound. Again, she spoke to the girl, and after rummaging in the bag, Sweet Grass handed her a bottle.

"The wound is full of poison. My nose, old as it is, can smell it. I need some cloth."

Dr. Bill hurried from the room, and a nurse came in with a handful of washcloths.

Little Bird took one of the cloths, poured liquid from the bottle on it and began cleaning the wound. With the cloth covered with blood and pus, she took another and swabbed until she was satisfied. She reached for the jar, unscrewed the lid and dug her fingers into the almost black looking paste. The smell of the ointment was foul beyond description, and both doctors looked doubtfully at her as she spread it over the wound. "Now, a clean dressing," she requested. The doctors hurried to oblige.

"The smell is very bad," she told them. "But it will draw the poison from the wound. Now, we need to get him into a sweat lodge to sweat the poison from his body. I will have my people prepare the lodge in the backyard. Then, while he sweats, I will sing the old songs to the spirits, and that will help draw the poison out. Sweet Grass will help me."

She stumped from the room and gave rapid orders to the old Indian couple who were waiting, and they left with Charlie to follow her instructions.

An hour later, Charlie drove his pickup into the backyard of the hospital, followed by a van with the adult members of the Jacob and Dick families. On the truck were an assortment of long willow stems, a number of round boulders, a supply of firewood, some plastic tarps and sheets of clear plastic, buckets, a shovel and other tools.

The Indians got to work. They dug a fire pit and lighted a fire in it. When it was going well, they piled rocks in the center of the fire. In the meantime, the willow sticks were bent to form arches and the ends shoved into the ground. Other lengths of willow were tied to the arches with cord until they had a framework about six feet long, four feet wide and four feet high. A shallow pit was dug to one side near the center. The frame was covered with tarps and plastic, the sides weighted down with rocks, leaving flaps that could be opened at the ends.

They brought Jamie out on a gurney. Charlie had found a narrow door, covered by several folded blankets that doubled for a stretcher. They moved Jamie onto the stretcher and maneuvered into the sweat room. He was nude, except for a towel across his groin. Using a shovel, Johnie Jacob moved hot rocks from the fire to the pit in the sweat lodge. A bucket of water was set alongside it. Little Bird and Sweet Grass were wearing ankle-length robes of colorful cloth, and Little Bird carried a skin bag. The two women slipped out of their long robes and entered the sweat lodge completely nude, where they sat cross-legged on each side of the hot rocks facing Jamie on his pad. Little Bird pulled a tin cup from her bag and dipped water from the pail to pour over the stones. The rocks sizzled, and a cloud of steam immediately filled the lodge. Reaching in the bag again, Little Bird brought a handful of dried grass and leaves, which she dropped into the pail. More water increased the steam. Little Bird began a chant in the native tongue, and Sweet Grass joined in.

Sweat appeared on the patient's naked torso and on the bodies of the women. Little Bird dipped her hand in the pail, pulled out some of the grass and sprinkled it over the hot rocks. They sizzled, and an acrid smoke swirled around the lodge. The chanting continued as Little Bird poured more water over the rocks and sprinkled more grass.

* * *

Jamie was aware that something was changing. He felt himself lifted from the bed to the gurney and then to the stretcher. He wondered if he was dreaming. He was in a fog; the fog was hot, and there was a peculiar smell that seemed to penetrate his being. He tried to breathe deeper to get the odor into his lungs. Somehow, he knew that he should inhale it. Then he became aware of the chanting, in some language that he did not understand. He turned his head to see the source of the chant. An incredibly old looking woman sat cross-legged on a pad, lips in the wrinkled face sunk over toothless gums. Arms like sticks and only a sheath of sagging skin covering the bone. The elbows were larger than the arms, and the hands looked too big for the arms that supported them. Breasts, flat as pancakes, dried and lifeless looking, sagged to her navel. Streams of perspiration trickled down her naked body.

He became aware of the girl. She was the extreme opposite of the oldster. Long black hair cascaded over her shoulders. Breasts were firm and high, with a trickle of sweat running between them. Skin was like burnished copper, and the arms were well rounded, yet muscular. She was beautiful.

This must be a dream. The chanting continued, and he drifted off.

The camp was beside a small river. Cottonwood trees and thorn apple bushes grew along the stream. To the east of the river were open grassland hills and flats. West of the stream, wooded foothills led up to mountains. Several teepees were in the camp by the river; horses grazed nearby. Three women came from one of the lodges. Two were old, and one was young and beautiful. They all carried digging irons and buckskin bags swung from their shoulders. Up on the plateau, not far from camp, they started harvesting bitterroots, a favorite food with the Kootenai tribe. Only during the early summer before the plants bloomed were the roots edible. A rosette of green short-stemmed leaves grew flat on the ground. Later, brilliant pink flowers would mark the site. The women started digging the roots. The digging iron was about 30 inches long with a tee bar at the top. The bottom of the iron bent in a gentle curve to the sharpened tip. The point of the iron, pushed into the ground beside the plant, penetrated under the root. Bending back on the iron lifted the plant from the ground. The central root stem was two- to three-inches long and feeder roots radiated from it. A red skin that peeled off readily covered the white-fleshed roots. The name of the plant came from the red kernel imbedded in the center of the taproot. The kernel was extremely bitter and must be removed before the roots were cooked or dried.

It was like a movie, some parts vague and foggy and others brilliantly clear. Three horsemen approached the women, who looked up uneasily. They appeared to be cowboys, probably connected to the settlers that were moving into the country. The women turned towards camp, but one of the men spurred forward and stopped them. Another, appearing very young, swung his foot over the neck of his horse and slid to the ground singling out the young woman to approach. The other cowboy slid his carbine from the saddle boot and held it up in one hand, his finger bent through the trigger guard. In minutes, it was over. There was no way she could resist. The man climbed back on his horse, and they rode away to the east.

Jamie became partially aware, the chanting had stopped and a man was shoveling new stones into the pit. Jamie could feel the heat radiating from them. The chanting started over, and he drifted off again as the steam enveloped him.

The dreams resumed. Now, the same young woman was in a council of elders. Dissension was evident in the lodge. The girl was distressed, but the old chief was firm as he pronounced an ultimatum. Then it was dawn, and the three original women were emerging from a lodge. One of the older women was giving instructions to the girl, who carried a baby on a papoose board on her back and a large deer hide bag in one hand. The woman passed over a sheaf of bills, white man's money, and the girl tucked them away in a pocket, turned her back and strode purposefully away towards the west. The two watched as the girl climbed the bluffs and disappeared from view.

Jamie kept up with the girl as she walked across a large grassy flat. He recognized the place where the women were digging bitterroots, which seemed like the year before. She continued across the flats and climbed over a range of low jumbled hills. On the last hill, she paused to stare into the rising sun at the open valley ahead of her, the first part of it a barren stretch of white alkali. Sitting for a time, she removed the baby from the pack board and allowed it to nurse.

She had crossed the barren area and was following a rough wagon road through a flat valley between low ranges of forested hills. Round rocks and gravel littered the floor of the valley, as if it had been a riverbed. Then, the sun was at her back and, drooping with fatigue, the girl was standing at the crest of a hill and staring at a vast lake ahead of her. It was perhaps three miles down a long grassy slope to the lake. Some wooden buildings and several Indian lodges were located on the meadow near the shore. The sun was setting as the girl approached a lodge and was welcomed in.

It was morning, and the girl was boarding a steamship. Then it was evening, and the Indian girl was getting off the ship and boarding a train. The dream faded into nothingness, and he was semiconscious again. He was back in his hospital bed and wondering if everything was a dream. He was sleepy and decided it didn't matter if he could sleep.

* * *

Jamie woke to see sun streaming through the window. It seemed as though he was in a hospital room. Marguerite McIvor was sitting by his bed, reading a book. Ron came in. "Good morning Marg—how's our patient this morning?"

"He slept like a baby all night, and his temperature is almost down to normal this morning, and his pulse is normal. I think he is a lot better."

"I'll be damned," the doctor said. "That old shaman really knew what she was doing."

"I'd be careful whom I called a shaman, dear," Marg told her husband. "You might be one yourself."

"Well," Ron replied. "I sure as hell have to give her credit. She sure put herself into it with all her heart. She and that great-great-granddaughter spent the whole day in that sweat lodge with him, sweating as hard as he did, and chanting all the time."

Jamie had listened long enough. "Good morning, you two." His voice was weak, but clear. "I gather that Little Bird and Sweet Grass gave me some old-fashioned medicine women treatment. What happened to me? Have I been sick?"

"You don't remember being shot?" Ron asked. "Billie Bolten got a bullet through your chest from a window in the gym. You have been very sick. We thought we were going to lose you. Charlie Johnson asked us to let Little Bird try. We were desperate, so we agreed. She had you in a sweat lodge all day yesterday. She poured medicine down you and put the most evil smelling salve I have ever come across on your wound. Now, it looks like you're going to recover. Are you ready for breakfast?"

162

"I'm ready," Jamie replied. "What day is it?"

"It's Friday." Ron told him. "You've been out of it since Sunday. There's going to be a lot of people glad to see you coming around."

A nurse brought a tray with milk and juice and a dish of oatmeal mush, and Jamie dived in. He ate most of it before fatigue overcame him, and he laid back and went to sleep. Visitors came, but Ron would let no one in the room except Little Bird and Sweet Grass. The old medicine woman sniffed the air and approved. She lifted the blanket and inspected the dressing. Lifting a corner of the dressing, she saw that the wound appeared dry. Opening her medicine bag, she brought out a bottle of medicine. "When he wakes up," she instructed, "give him a half cup of this. He will not like it, but tell him I said to drink it. Give him some every three or four hours. I'll be back tonight."

True to her word, Little Bird was at the hospital early in the evening. Jamie was still sputtering from the last draught of medicine that the nurse had insisted he drink. It was the third dose of the day, and Jamie thought it tasted worse than the first. Jamie was looking better, but pale and weak.

Seeing Little Bird in the room, he muttered, "That medicine is the worst tasting stuff I have ever had in my mouth. Is it true that you ordered them to give it to me?"

"It is true," the old woman responded. "I told them to tell you that I ordered that you have it every three or four hours. Those orders will continue until I say otherwise. The great white doctors have turned your care over to me, and I will be your doctor until you are well."

"How long will that be?" Jamie asked.

"I am not sure," Little Bird replied. "But it will probably be at least a week. You have been very sick. The Great Spirit had his arms around you and was ready to carry you off when I intervened. It took much good medicine, many hours sweating, and much chanting by Sweet Grass and this old woman to pull you back. You have lost much strength, and it will take time and care to get it back."

Jamie did not hear the end of Little Bird's speech. He was sleeping soundly.

* * *

"How is Jamie?" was the first thing Mary heard as she and Kelly entered the boardroom for the Sunday afternoon council meeting.

"Dr. Ron let Kelly and me in to see him for the first time this morning. He only allowed us to stay about ten minutes. To me, he appeared very weak, but in good spirits. Dr. Ron can probably give you a better medical report than I can. Ron?"

"He is still weak, but I think he is out of the woods and will make a full recovery. I have to give full credit to Little Bird and Sweet Grass. Bill and I had about given up all hope. That old medicine woman has more medical power than a whole regiment of modern doctors. We might have been more successful if we had had the facilities of a modern hospital with all of the science that has been available, up until disaster overtook us. Bill and I are reasonably proficient physicians, but we are small town when it comes to what was the up-to-date science that was being practiced. I'm afraid that that is one of the things we will have to do without for the foreseeable future. Don't downgrade the natural medicines. The unfortunate thing is that Little Bird cannot possibly be with us for long. I have no idea how old she is, but she has to be over a hundred. The fortunate thing is that young Sweet Grass has been tutoring under the old lady for many years. We must give Sweet Grass all the support that we possibly can, for we need her sorely. As for Jamie, I think he may be out of the hospital in a week, but he must be given a good deal of time to regain his strength."

Mary sat for a minute, listening to the sounds of the baseball game going on outside. She was overwhelmed with the enormity of the task that was before her. It was bad enough to be left in charge of the counsel and the colony, but to have to take over under adverse conditions was beyond her conception. Gritting her teeth and throwing back her shoulders, she resolved to go on.

"What is the next order of business?" She asked.

"I guess there is only one order of business that is important at this time," replied Bob Elder. "We have to settle this trial business. Decisions have to be made in accordance with what comes out of the trial. I have asked Roger Burkham to act as prosecuting attorney, and he has reviewed everything we know about the case. Pat Holden will defend Mr. Bolten. Pat has interviewed the defendant several times and will do a good job in defense. I don't think any of it will change things. The man is guilty. The big problem is going to be the sentencing. That is where we should be having a jury, and not put the burden on one person. Sentence should be either death or life in prison."

"But if the man is insane," countered Mary, "do we have the right to put him to death? As a rule, modern society has frowned on the death penalty, and especially in the case of the mentally unsound. Constable Pat, is it possible to keep him imprisoned if he is found not guilty due to insanity?"

"Yes, it's possible," Pat conceded, "but not too practical. It would be a real burden on us to set up a jail and take care of him from now on out. But, like it or not, if that is what the community wants, I'll manage the problem OK."

"I have no doubt about that," Mary told him. "I know it would be best if we could get rid of him, but I cannot, in my own mind, condone murder of a mentally incapacitated person. Is there any way we can let the members of the community make the decision? I think I could live with that a lot easier."

"I don't see why not," Bob Elder replied. "We are not bound here by the laws of the past, but have the privilege of creating our own laws to suit the needs of our citizens. We could pass a new law right now that requires the imposition of a death or a life sentence to be approved by a 75 percent majority vote of the citizens present in the courtroom. In fact, I'll put that in the form of a motion."

Mary turned to Kelly, sitting at her side, "Kelly, could you write notes on this so that we can have a record of it for the future?"

"I'm already making notes 'cause I knew you didn't have time to. But could I have the motion repeated, so I can be sure it is right?"

Bob repeated his motion as Kelly scribbled madly. Kelly read the motion back, and Bob approved it.

"You have all heard the motion," Mary said. "Does someone wish to second it?"

Ron McIvor seconded the motion, and it was passed unanimously.

"Thank you, gentlemen," Mary told them. "The trial will start at 7 PM this evening. If it can't be finished tonight, we will continue it over for another day. I'll be trying hard in the meantime to get prepared for it. This meeting is adjourned."

Chapter 27

The gymnasium had been set up to simulate a courtroom. The judge's bench, a table, was at the rear of the stage with a chair for the witness alongside. A chair for the secretary of the court was on the other side. Forward and to the sides were tables and chairs for the prosecutor and defense. The audience filled most of the hall.

Constable Pat Draper ushered the defendant into the room and seated him, facing the bench, at the defendant's table. Pat Holden took his place beside the defendant, and Roger Burkham sat at the prosecutor's table.

Pat moved to the center and called out. "All please rise for the Honorable Justice Mary Jorgenson."

With everyone on their feet, Mary entered and took her seat at the bench, and Pat moved to the side of the stage to remain on guard.

Mary faced the audience, as Pat motioned them to be seated, with a feeling of trepidation that she did her best not to display. Adjusting the microphone in front of her, she spoke with as much authority as she could command. "This court is meeting to consider the case of the State of New Island against the accused, Billie Bolten, on two charges of attempted murder. Will the defendant please rise?"

Pat Holden urged the defendant to his feet to face the judge.

"How does the defendant plead?" Mary asked.

"Not guilty." The voice of the defendant was tremulous and barely audible.

"Let the record show that the defendant pleads not guilty," Mary instructed. "A judge only, who will be deciding the guilt or innocence of the defendant, will try this case. A jury consisting of the entire adult membership of the State of New Island present at this trial will decide the fate of the defendant if he is found guilty. Is the prosecution ready to present his case?"

Roger Burkham stood. "I am, Your Honor."

"Please proceed," Mary told him.

Roger Burkham moved to the center of the stage and faced the jury. "I intend to show that the defendant, one Billie Bolten, did plan with forethought and deliberation, to murder Jamie

Morgan, President of our country, and Constable Pat Draper, a member of the council and the officer in charge of law enforcement of our country. I will prove that the defendant threatened to come back to the island and shoot the two men a full two weeks earlier, while he was being deported off the island for a series of disturbances of the peace and threats of violence in our community. I will prove that he did, indeed, return to the island and, during a general meeting of the people of this community, did aim a handgun through that window at the far corner of this room and shoot President Morgan in the chest and Constable Pat in the shoulder. President Jamie was seriously wounded and only now, after a week, is judged to be out of danger of dying from his wounds. Thank you, Your Honor."

"Would the defense care to make a statement?"

"I would, Your Honor," Patrick Holden said. "I will attempt to show that the defendant is unable to judge right from wrong, that he does not understand the seriousness of what he has done and that he is basically unfit to defend himself against the charges. I have interviewed the defendant extensively, and he is convinced that he was doing the right thing by attempting to kill Jamie and Pat. He feels that if they were out of the way he could take over New Island as a dictator and that everyone here would fall in line and do his bidding. I do not consider it necessary to go through an extensive trial as the defendant has admitted that he is guilty of the charges made against him. Therefore, I would recommend that Your Honor find him not guilty of the charges by reason of insanity."

"Would the prosecution like to respond to the defense?"

"Yes, Your Honor. The defendant may be to some extent mentally deficient, but he is certainly able to lay elaborate plans to carry out his objectives. He was absolutely cold-blooded in his planning, and shows no remorse for his actions. He has only expressed remorse in that he did not succeed. I think he should be found guilty of attempted murder and sentenced accordingly. He is a menace to society, and he cannot be released to do further harm."

"Does the defense have anything further to add? You have admitted to the defendant's guilt, even though the defendant has pleaded not guilty."

"Yes, Your Honor, it is true that he pleaded not guilty. But he has admitted to me that he did the shooting and why. The why is so bizarre that I cannot plead anything but insanity for this man; there is no use subjecting us all to an extensive trial to get at the same results."

"Mr. Burkham, do you have anything further to add?"

"No, Your Honor. The prosecution rests."

"Mr. Holden?"

"The defense rests, Your Honor."

Mary sat for several minutes, thinking of the decision she had to make. "I admit that the defendant could in some ways be judged to be insane. Nevertheless, he has shown an extensive ability to reason and plan his actions. Insane, or sane, he is a menace to our society and must not be allowed to continue his freedom to plan further crimes. The council of New Island considers attempted murder the same as murder. The intent was there, so the defendant should suffer the same consequences. A person found guilty of murder, or the attempt thereof, must be sentenced to either death or life imprisonment. The judge hearing the trial can decide whether the defendant is guilty, or not guilty. The jury, in this case, all of the adult registered citizens of New Island who are present at this trial will decide which sentence to impose on the defendant. I find you, Billie Bolten, guilty of attempted murder.

"Now, my instructions to the jury." Mary paused again to gather her thoughts. "I know that some of you will favor imposition of the death penalty while others of you are dead set against killing a human being, regardless of the reason. Over all, most civilized countries of the world have passed laws against the death penalty, considering it barbaric and inhumane. In making your decision, you should consider the consequences of your actions either way. As a civilized group of caring, compassionate human beings, can you condone murdering another human being? On the other hand, if you choose life in prison, you should consider the burden that maintaining the subject for the rest of his life will impose on our society. Constable Draper assures me that he can arrange to keep the subject imprisoned, but it will result in a substantial financial burden on our community. The decision must be by a margin of 75 percent for whichever sentence you impose.

"I would suggest that all of you that are not qualified to vote, that is, the people under sixteen years of age or anyone not registered, leave the room. The principals in the trial, including myself, will adjourn to the boardroom. I would suggest that you elect a jury foreperson to act as chair in your deliberations. If you are not able to make a decision tonight, you may carry over till tomorrow morning and reconvene to continue your deliberations. Court is adjourned until you call us back."

Mary led the way out of the courtroom, and the principals gathered in the boardroom. The young people leaving the room gathered in some of the classrooms down the hall. Billie Bolten started ranting about not being treated with respect. Pat Draper snapped the cuffs and leg irons on him and locked him in the janitor's closet. Someone brought a pot of coffee from the kitchen, and the group sat silently, finding little to talk about while they waited. More than an hour went by before Constable Draper called them back to the court.

Mary resumed her seat at the judge's table, and the others took their designated spots. Pat brought the prisoner in to sit at the defense table. The room was quiet.

"Has the jury reached a verdict?" Mary asked.

Teresa Blunt stood. "Yes, we have, Your Honor."

"What is the sentence?"

"There are 123 people here qualified to vote. They have voted 118 in favor of the death penalty to be carried out by firing squad as soon as possible, under the direction of Constable Draper. The vote was by secret ballot. There were three votes for life imprisonment, and two did not vote."

"I wish to thank the jury," Mary said, "for doing a job that has to be unpleasant in the extreme. People like you are going to make New Island a fine place for all of us to live. The jury is excused. Constable Draper will see to it that the sentence is carried out at the earliest possible time. Court is adjourned. The council will meet in the boardroom immediately."

Constable Draper dragged the prisoner, crying like a baby, to the janitor closet, where he locked him up before joining the others in the boardroom. The council was all there and with them Dave Jorgenson, Kelly and Pat Holden.

"How did I do?" Mary asked.

"You did a great job," Bob Elder exclaimed. "You were superb."

A murmur of assent went around the table.

"Now I have the hot seat," Constable Pat spoke up. "I have said many times that I would like to shoot that bastard, but now that I have the authority to do it, I don't in the least feel good about it. The poor guy doesn't have any semblance of a brain in his head, and I feel sorry for him. Mary, you have the power as judge and President of this country to change the sentence—to commute to life imprisonment—if you choose. What do you think about it?"

"The jury made its decision, and I should not care to override them. But the thought is tempting. Have you made any plans for the execution?"

"No, I haven't," Pat answered. "I'll need at least a day to make arrangements. I have to find at least five men to form the firing squad; I need five rifles of the same caliber, plus live and blank ammunition. Only one gun has a live round in it, and the rest are blanks. That way no one knows who fired the fatal shot."

"I can help you with the guns," Pat Holden spoke up. "There are some regular army rifles in the armory at the base, and I am sure there is plenty of blank ammo. They use it to fire salutes, so there are no stray bullets flying around. I can probably get you the men to serve also. Military people are trained to handle disagreeable situations, such as this."

"That's a big help," Pat Draper replied. "I'll leave that up to you. We will plan on doing the deed Tuesday morning. Mary, you have up to 10 seconds before I give the command to fire to commute the sentence."

"If I thought there was the remotest possibility that the guy could be redeemed in any way and allowed back into society, I would commute in a second. But there is too much chance that he would be nothing but trouble from now on out."

"I agree." Pat conceded. "But that still doesn't make it any more enjoyable. Nevertheless, it's my job, and I'll do it. Bob, can you help me drag him back to my place and get him chained up in his shed? He resists all the way."

Pat and Bob left the room, and the others were preparing to leave when Bob charged back in. "Dr. Ron," he exclaimed, "come quick. The prisoner has passed out."

The doctor hurried from the room, followed by the rest of them. The man was crumpled up inside the door to the janitor closet. The smell of human excrement was overpowering. Pat and Bob pulled him into the hallway and stretched him out on the floor. The doctor kneeled beside him, feeling at the side of his neck for a pulse.

"He is dead, probably from a heart attack."

"A heart attack in someone so young?" Mary asked. "Is that possible?"

"Yes. It happens occasionally under cases of extreme stress, such as fear. They get so shook up that the heart gives out on them. I am sure it was a case of cardiac arrest. His bowels emptied, and that is another sign of extreme stress, or fear. I can do an autopsy on him, if you wish, but it won't really accomplish much. We are well rid of him. I think everyone will be relieved that we didn't have to kill him. I'll arrange to have the body cremated tomorrow."

Chapter 28

Jamie was sitting up in bed finishing his breakfast when Mary and Kelly entered the room. Kelly rushed to Jamie and gave him a hug. "Golly," she exclaimed, "you are looking a lot better this morning. I'm really glad. Are you feeling better?"

"Yes," Jamie replied. "I'm feeling a lot better. But the doctors will not let me out of bed yet. They say it will be at least a week before I can go home. Mary, Dr. Ron tells me that you are the accomplished judge, that you conducted the hearing with an expertise that he would expect from a professional."

"I'm sure that he is exaggerating a great deal. I didn't do nearly as well as you would have, and I was so scared that it is a wonder that I got through it without blowing it to smithereens."

"I doubt," Jamie told her, "that I could have done any better. I knew you were capable and that was the reason I suggested you for the job. Anyway, congratulations on your accomplishment. You did the right thing in loading the responsibility for the death sentence onto the public. It is fortunate that the guy died before we had to kill him. None of us can be criticized for being bloodthirsty. How about you, Kelly, haven't you missed enough school over this?"

"Mary is going to take me to school right away; we wanted to see you first. School will be a lot easier knowing that you are getting better."

* * *

Jamie was sitting in an easy chair in the lobby reading a book when Charlie Johnson brought Little Bird into the room.

Jamie looked at Little Bird. "I'm glad to see you, honorable medicine woman. I've been trying to get the doctors to let me go home, but they say they won't release me until you say it is OK. I want to get out of here. I have much to do."

"The doctors are right," the old lady replied. "They have given me complete charge of your treatment, and they will let you out when I have determined, in conference with them, that you are in proper condition to get out. If we let you out too soon, you will overdo and land back in here again. Maybe Sunday you can go home."

"That's another three whole days," Jamie grumbled.

"Don't act like a little boy. That is the trouble with men; they are all alike. They think that they are infallible."

"I guess it's you that is infallible. The doctors tell me that I was about dead when you took over. For that, I wish to thank you. I have some memories of a lot of dreaming. Somehow, I seem to think it was connected to the chanting that you and Sweet Grass carried on for hours and hours. And some of those dreams seemed like they had something to do with you."

"You are more astute than most patients I have chanted over," Little Bird told him. "Among pleas to the spirit world to save you for some future time, I sang the story of my life."

"Will you tell me that story in English, so that I can understand it? I am deeply interested in how you became a great medicine woman and how you have lived so long."

"If you stay here and take your medicine as I have instructed, I will tell you the story on Saturday morning. Then, if everything goes as I expect it will, I will let you go home on Sunday, and soon after, you can go flying in that airplane again." Little Bird turned and hobbled from the room, followed by Charlie Johnson.

"I have to go, too," Kelly said. Giving Jamie a hug and a kiss, she followed Mary from the room.

* * *

It was Saturday morning, and Jamie had relished his breakfast more than any day yet. They had served him, for the first time, ham and eggs and a stack of toast, which he polished off in record time and was almost ready to ask for more. Life was starting to look desirable again.

Now, after a short walk around the grounds, he was seated in an easy chair in the lobby when Charlie Johnson escorted Little Bird into the room. He pulled a chair close to Jamie for Little Bird and left, saying that he would be back to pick her up later.

Jamie studied the old woman for a few minutes before speaking. "So you are, as promised, going to tell me the story of your life that you sang to me while I was sick."

"I only tell the story of my life to special people. You are a very special person, so I will tell you the story. It is only by the will of the Great Spirit that I have lived so long, and he will be unable to keep this worn-out body functioning for much longer. Perhaps I have fulfilled my final duty to the people that are left in the world by saving your life to go on serving them. I will be able to cross the great divide knowing that I have earned any reward that the Great Spirit of the beyond has granted me.

"I am not sure what year I was born, but it was before the turn of the last century, sometime around 1895. My father was a chief of the Kootenai Tribe, and my mother was of the Kalispel people. Both tribes are part of the Salish Nations of the northwest United States and southern Canada.

"My mother was a great medicine woman of her time. She knew all of the plants that cure sickness and heal wounds. She was able to sing to the spirits and bring help from the greatest of all spirits. She could sing dreams and take medicine to make herself dream of the past and the future. She started teaching me the art of being a healer when I was very young. I worked with her in gathering plants and preparing the potions and ointments that were the tools of her trade.

"The Kootenai and the Kalispel people were greatly inter-mixed by marriage, and all were of the great Ktunaxa Nation. They lived in a large area of the Kootenai River and the Tobacco Plains in what is now Canada and Montana and Idaho. The tribes were nomadic and moved around much. After the white man formed the great Flathead Indian Reservation, many of the Kootenai people joined the Salish people that lived on the reservation and formed the Salish Kootenai Federation. The Flathead tribe had long ago been absorbed by the other tribes in the area and ceased to exist as an independent tribe.

"My mother was unable to read or write. She thought that the knowledge of the white man's language and knowing how to put that language on paper would be of great benefit, so she sent me to the Catholic School at St. Ignatius to learn. I lived at the school during several winters, became proficient in English and learned to write it on paper.

"Although the Kootenai people lived on the reservation for most of the time, they still moved around a lot. My tribe always went to the Little Bitterroot River for the harvest of the bitterroot plants during the month of June. That is where my life was destined to change.

"We had set up our lodges on the banks of the Little Bitter-root River. It was shortly after the reservation opened to homesteading by the white man. The white man's government had decided that there was more land on the reservation than the

174

Indians needed, and many white men were looking for land. There was a great rush, and all open land was gobbled up. Some of the white men who came were not nice men, as we found out.

"My mother and my aunt and I went out to dig bitterroots. We had just started when three white men on horses came over the ridge on which we were digging. They stopped and talked among themselves, and then one of them, the youngest, got off his horse and approached me. I was going to run, but another pushed his horse ahead of us, and the other one pulled out his rifle and pointed it in an unfriendly way. I knew there was no use in resisting, so when the young man pushed me to the ground, I did not resist. If I had, all three of us would have probably been killed.

"The result of that encounter was that the white man had placed the seed of a baby in me, and the seed sprouted. I was promised to a prominent sub-chief of the tribe to become his bride during the next year. But when he found that I was carrying a white man's child, he no longer wanted me. The child, a girl, was born in the spring and was three months old when we arrived back in the Little Bitterroot camp. After a long conference with my father and elders of the tribe, the young man agreed to go ahead and accept me as his bride, but he would not take the child.

"I was called into the conference lodge and told of the decision. I must dispose of the baby. I was instructed to take her to the top of a nearby mountain and leave her. The coyotes would take care of her. I was very upset and decided to leave the tribe. I would not give up my baby to be eaten by coyotes. My mother and aunt helped me prepare and gave me instructions on where to go. They gave me white man's money that they had earned sewing deer hide gloves, moccasins and jackets for the white people.

"At dawn the next morning I left the camp. I walked all day, and at sunset, I arrived at a lodge of some people I knew on the shores of the great Flathead Lake. In the morning, a steamship stopped at the camp, and I boarded it and paid money for a ticket. The ship took me to the head of the lake where I boarded a train. That train took me to a connection with the much longer train that would take me all the way to the end of the continent at a city called Seattle. There I got on another steamship and finally arrived at an island far north where there were some people of the Salish Nation. They took me in and gave me a home.

"An old man there knew much about medicine. He taught me much of what I know today. My daughter, named Running Water, grew up to be a beautiful maiden. She married a man named Seal Hunter when she was about 15 years old. She died during the birth of her first child who was named Golden Spring. I took Golden Spring to raise. Seal Hunter was killed in an intertribal battle over fishing rights.

"Golden Spring married Big Knife, and they had a daughter who was named Mountain Flower. Golden Spring and Big Knife both died of smallpox. But Mountain Flower survived, and again I had a girl child to raise. Mountain Flower, whom you know as Julia, grew up to marry Johnie Jacob. You know Johnie. Julia and Johnie had a daughter named Blue Mountain whom you know as Angela. Angela married Robert Dick. Their first child, Johnie, broke the long string of daughters. Three girls, Francis, Marjorie and Bonnie, or Sweet Grass, followed Johnie Dick.

"The year Sweet Grass was born, my family left the village where we had been living and moved to a more remote island. The tiny harbor would accommodate small boats only, so we were more isolated than ever. We were very self-sufficient. We lived there until Chief Charlie talked us into coming here. I am glad we took his advice. We were in Port Hardy for supplies when Charlie ran into us.

"Sweet Grass is the first of the long line of children to show any sign of having the inner strength to become a medicine woman. I have been training her as fast as I can, and she shows great promise. I only hope that I can live long enough to pass on most of the knowledge I have gained over all of these generations. Your young lady Kelly shows the same sort of promise that Sweet Grass has shown. I hope that you will not object to her becoming a medicine woman. She is needed to carry on the work. I would hate to see the world lose the abilities of medicine women who are guided by the Great Spirit.

"Now you have heard the story of my life in a short version. But it is about all that I am capable of telling you at the present time. I find that my abilities to concentrate are limited. I know that I shall not be too long for this world. I probably have lived far longer than I deserve. I hope that I have been able to be of use during the extended period that I have been allowed by the Great Spirit beyond the sky."

With a sigh, the old woman settled back in her chair. She was obviously suffering from extreme fatigue.

"Thank you for sharing your life with me," Jamie said. "Now I understand some of the dreams I had during the time that I was unconscious of the world around me. I thank you with all my heart for the efforts you extended in my behalf. I assure you that if Kelly shows the capabilities of becoming a medicine woman, that I will give her my full support. I can think of no better way for her to serve our nation."

Chapter 29

After a boring morning and a lonely lunch, and back on the front porch, Jamie was delighted to see Brian Veary, accompanied by Stan Bowman, enter the driveway. Jamie sent Brian to the kitchen for beer, and they pulled up chairs on each side of Jamie to enjoy the view and the beer. Jamie knew that they had something in mind besides a visit, but he waited for it to come out. Finally, with the beer about finished, Brain spoke up.

"Stan has some ideas he has approached me with. I think they are good ideas, so we decided to run them by you. Do you feel up to listening? I know that you have been ordered to rest."

"My old and badly used body may require rest, but my brain is still in pretty good condition. I can use it without working my body. Stan, let's hear what you have on your mind."

"Well, Sir, as you know, I am sort of a radio and electronics freak. I like to play with stuff all the time, and over the years, I've learned a bit. I've been experimenting and found out I can connect with at least two satellite birds that are positioned over the northwest part of North America. I have been able to send a signal to a satellite with one radio and receive an answer with another radio. I think I can set up a radio in your airplane that I can hear at home while you are gone, and you can receive an answer from us. It would be great if we could maintain communications with you when you were out on your exploration sorties."

"You mean," asked Jamie, "that regardless of distance, or mountains, or any terrain, that we could make contact with you?"

"Yes," Stan replied. "As long as the radio works and the satellite stays up, we should be able to talk. The satellites are supposed to keep operating for at least five years and probably much longer. I am in contact with two; if one goes haywire, the other should work. And there are other birds up there, if I can find them. We should be able to maintain communications anywhere over North America as long as the birds keep working."

"Sounds wonderful, Stan," Jamie said. "How soon can you have a system working?"

"I have it working now. I just have to install a radio in your plane and have you fly off somewhere and test it."

"OK, guy. Get going on it. You can remove some of the radios that are in the plane that we have no use for. Brian knows which ones we can as well dispense with. Let me know when you have it ready."

"I'll probably have it ready for testing tomorrow," Stan told him.

"Then we will test it tomorrow," Jamie told him.

"But you are supposed to be resting all week," Brian objected. "We'll all be in the deep stuff if you don't follow orders."

"Hey, I can rest sitting in an airplane just as much as I can sitting in this chair, and enjoy it a lot more. We'll test it as soon as you are ready."

"OK, I'll get right on it," Stan told him. "But there is one more thing that I would like to try. There is a radio relay tower over close to the airport. I believe that I can activate it and set up a cell phone system here in the valley that would give us a communications system here that could be very useful. I think I can put a cell phone in every house in the valley, if I can find enough phones. We should be able to find the phones OK."

"Gosh damn," Jamie exclaimed. "What are you going to come up with next? Do some work on it, as soon as you finish this other project, and I'll take it to the council next meeting. I'm sure they would be delighted with the idea."

* * *

The earthquakes started at around six the next morning. The first one woke Jamie and was strong enough to rattle dishes in the cupboards and sway the draperies. A few minutes later, another shake was less severe, but gained one's attention. Jamie went about his regular morning routine and was joined by Kelly who commented on the "jiggling" of the ground. By the time breakfast was over, several more "jiggles" occurred, and they had lost track of the number.

Jamie insisted on taking Kelly to school, and he stayed there until all of the students had arrived. No one seemed too concerned about the swarm of earthquakes; they had become routine during the past weeks.

Midmorning came, and Jamie was getting restless. The last tremor had occurred about 9:30 and was hardly noticeable. Jamie could contain himself no longer, and got in the car and drove to the airport. He found both Brian and Stan working on the airplane.

Stan had finished hooking up the new radio installation. He had installed headphones for both pilots with attached microphones controlled from buttons he had taped to the control yokes.

"It looks like a professional setup," Jamie complimented him.

"With the noise of the airplane, earphones make it much easier to understand if transmission gets shaky. I have also installed a VHF set in my office, which I will leave tuned to 121.5 so that you can talk to me on that frequency if you wish. Of course, VHF is line of sight, so you are out of range if you are behind a mountain. But it should work for local contact. The satellite system is set on one frequency, so we don't have to fuss around when we are trying to make contact."

"It sure looks as though you have all the bases covered," Jamie told him. "But do you plan on manning your station all the time?"

"I'll be available all the time when you are in the air. I have a cot in my office. I can sleep there if necessary. Also, I'm going to see if I can get the instrument landing system working. Then you could find your way in if you got caught in bad weather. I already have a switch on my desk with which I can turn the runway lights on. With the GPS system working, you can find your way almost anywhere. Of course, the GPS depends on the satellites that control it. But as long as they stay up, your system should work."

"Man, you sure make life a lot easier for us. When do you want to test your system?"

"I'm ready anytime," Stan replied as they walked out of the hangar door. "Hey, look at that funny cloud over there."

A plume of smoke was towering high over the mountains to the east, reaching a high altitude in the still air before drifting off to the northeast.

"What do you suppose that is?" asked Brian. "Looks big to be a fire."

"Just a minute," Jamie told them, as he went to the plane and came back with a chart. "Looks like a volcano eruption to me. It's about over Mount Garibaldi. Garibaldi is an extinct volcano that last erupted about 10,000 years ago. That could explain the swarm of earthquakes we had this morning. We know Mount Hood has come to life, and Garibaldi is in the same chain with Hood and Rainier, and the other mountains down the Cascade chain. Let's take the plane and get a look, and check out the radios at the same time."

"OK," Brian replied, as he hooked the tow bar to the nose gear of the plane to guide it out to the ramp.

"I'll get back to my office," Stan said. "It's in that building over there, on the second floor with big windows looking over the field. It was an auxiliary tower and was wired the same as the tower. I'll be monitoring you."

Jamie went through his pre-start checklist and started the engine. Checking to be sure the switch was turned to the VHF radio, he keyed the mike button and spoke, "Comox, this is Cessna CFRK, ready to taxi for takeoff."

The reply came back loud and clear. "Cessna CFRK, cleared to taxi and cleared for takeoff. Jamie, I believe this radio setup is going to work very well. We'll try it again when you are farther away."

"Roger, Stan. We are on our way." Jamie shoved the throttle in and started his takeoff run.

Thirty minutes later they were level at nine thousand feet and north of Mount Donaldson. From here, they had a good view of Garibaldi. A huge column of smoke was billowing straight up as far as they could see. Garibaldi was in full eruption. Brian was reporting to Stan, trying to explain the vastness of the eruption, when Stan interrupted. "We have another earthquake here. It's a strong one with a jarring feeling."

There was a sudden ballooning at the base of the column of smoke, a huge bulge at the point where it issued from the mountain. It was a dark gray color and climbed rapidly up the smoke column.

"Golly," Jamie exclaimed. "That's what caused the earthquake. There was an explosion in the mountain that sent that huge gust of smoke upward. The earthquakes and the volcano are definitely connected. We saw it. It happened at the same time that Stan felt it on the ground. That bulging cloud is probably full of ash from an explosion inside the mountain. That baby is really cooking."

They were getting close enough now to see more details. Several steam vents had opened on the side of the mountain, and a lava flow was edging down a defile from the summit. The air was getting turbulent with updrafts sucking air into the ascending column of hot smoky air. Jamie decided they had gotten close enough and swung the plane to the south and started descending towards Howe Sound.

"Stan," he requested, "let's switch to the satellite system. VHF is getting scratchy, and we'll be behind a mountain here in a minute or two. We are descending towards Squamish at the head of Howe Sound."

"Changing over," Stan responded. There was a pause, then, "Now transmitting on satellite system. How do you read?"

"Loud and clear, Stan. We'll go on down behind the mountains towards Horse Shoe Bay and see if we can keep contact."

With the air smoothed out as they got away from the influence of the volcano, Jamie trimmed the plane for a high-speed letdown. They were soon past Squamish at 2000 feet, and Brian was still in contact with Stan. It was obvious that the satellite system was working well. Jamie hoped it would work equally well over long distance. Feeling exhilarated with the sensation of flight and the performance of this fine aircraft, Jamie figured that flying was doing him more good than rest at home would do. His recovery was coming along well. A half-hour later, they were back at the airport, and Jamie was congratulating Stan on his radio work.

"Nothing to it," explained Stan. "All the equipment was here. It was only a matter of hooking it up properly. To me, that is fun."

* * *

Jamie entered the boardroom Sunday afternoon at the regular time to find the entire council there ahead of him. They rose to their feet in a noisy ovation, as Jamie took his place at the head of the table. Mary was the first to speak.

"Welcome back, Jamie. We have missed you very much."

"It's good to be back," Jamie told them. "But from what I hear you got along well without me. Kelly has brought me up to date on what you have been doing, and I feel extra good about the progress our little community is making on its way to becoming a successful country.

"Now, I have some information to report. You all probably know that Brian and I had a look at Mount Garibaldi and the volcanic eruption that is taking place there. We have positive evidence that at least part of the quakes we have been experiencing is coming from there. While we were within a few miles of the mountain, Stan reported by radio that you had had a good tremor here. At the same time, a huge blob of gray smoke billowed out of the mountain. It was obvious that a substantial explosion had occurred in the mountain.

"The best thing about the flight is that we got to test out our new radio capabilities with the aircraft. Stan is a real genius with electronics, and he has figured out how to use the satellites that are in position to relay radio signals. We can talk to each other from behind mountains and over long distances. It will be valuable when we start exploring farther and farther away from home base. Also, he has our VHF working well for local communications. He is operating sort of a radio central base at the field."

"You mean," Mary asked, "that you intend to keep up exploration and go farther afield with the airplane? Why do you want to keep that up? It's too dangerous."

"Yes, I intend to keep it up. Who knows what's out there until we go and look. With our new radio capabilities, I hope that we can stay in contact with home base at all times. That will increase safety a great deal."

"But that won't do much good," Bob Elder interceded. "We would know that you were in trouble somewhere, but it would be difficult to mount a rescue attempt. We need some other pilots, besides you. How about Brian?"

"Brian can fly well, but he still needs some experience. He'll get that experience flying with me, and I need his help. I intend to start training a couple of more pilots right away if I can find anyone that is willing. I'll ask at the general meeting tonight."

"But," Mary said, "that will take time. Will you stay on the ground in the meantime?"

"No. I can't promise that. It will take a couple of months to get new pilots ready to fly cross-country. I'll push them as fast as I can. But in the meantime, Brian and I must keep on exploring. We will stay close to home in the northwest part of the continent. Our plane is in excellent condition, and Brian keeps it that way. There is little danger involved.

"Now, there is one more thing to tell you about. Stan has an idea that he can rig up a cell phone system for the valley. The tower is in the right position to cover all of our territory, and he thinks he can modify the switching equipment to handle up to a hundred or more phones. We could provide a phone for every house. We have to locate the phones, but that shouldn't be a problem."

"Sounds like a great idea," Bob Elder said. "We are sure lucky to have that young man in our community. We could ask everyone that might have a phone hanging around to turn them in. Then I think we could scour the electronic stores around the island and find a lot of new ones. I think we should tell him to go ahead with it."

"I've already told him to go ahead," Jamie said. "I'll run it by the people at a general meeting soon. I'm sure that they will all be thrilled with the idea. Now, I think it's time for potluck."

Chapter 30

When Jamie arrived at the airport on Monday morning, the two men who had volunteered to take flight training were there already, talking to Brian and Stan. They introduced themselves as Randy Earheart and Kevin Gomez. Randy was a slight blond youth, about five-seven, and not more than 140 pounds. Kevin was about the same height, but stocky build with a dark, swarthy complexion. Jamie guessed him at about 165 pounds with muscular arms and broad shoulders. Both of them had worked in the navigation section in the submarine and were familiar with reading charts and plotting courses, which gave them a start towards being pilots. Randy had taken flight lessons before he joined the Navy. They looked like good candidates for flight training.

"There's a Cessna 152 up at the Campbell River Airport that would be good for primary training," Jamie said. "Maybe we should go up and get it. It wouldn't take long."

"I saw a nice one over at the little field in Courtenay," Brian said. "It looked like a nice little bird, and it is close. We could go and look at it."

"Sounds like a good idea," Jamie responded. "Let's go. Stan, you stay here and monitor VHF, and the rest of us will go and check it out. A southeaster could be coming up; we better get at it before a storm hits us."

Fifteen minutes later the four of them were surveying the plane. It was tied down under a shade port and was locked. A sturdy looking wooden locker at the back of the port had a padlock on the door. Brian had little trouble in getting the lock off and the door opened. Inside were a small workbench and some tools. A set of keys hung on a nail over the bench.

"We are in luck," Brian exclaimed. "I could get into the plane and make a key for it, but it would take some time. If this fits, we're in good shape."

Jamie took the keys and unlocked the cabin. The ignition key fit. He led the prospective pilots on a thorough walk-around inspection, checked the gas and oil, and drained some gas from the sight glass, explaining everything as he went.

"Let's see if it will start," Jamie said, climbing into the pilot's seat. He looked the instrument panel over, located the trim tab control and gave the engine two shots of prime with the priming pump. "Clear," he called and turned the starter switch. The prop made a quarter turn and stopped. "Damn, the battery is down. Brian, do you know how to prop an engine?"

"No," Brian responded. "I never have."

"OK," Jamie said. "You get in here, and I'll swing the prop. Just follow my instructions, responding verbally to each command. Crack the throttle a little bit."

Jamie walked to the front of the plane and stood aside. "Brakes on," he called.

"Brakes on," Brian responded.

"Switch off."

"Switch off."

Jamie pulled the prop over a few times and stood back. "Switch on," he called.

Grasping the end of the prop, which pointed towards the ground with his left hand, he gave it a quick pull as he stepped away to the right. The engine fired, sputtered and settled into a rough idle.

Jamie pulled the chocks from in front of the wheels, told the other fellows to take the car back and climbed into the right-hand seat.

"Let's go," he told Brian. "It's all yours."

"You sure you want me to fly this thing?" Brian asked. "This wind is really coming up."

"You'd as well get used to some wind. It catches you every now and then. Taxi to the end of the runway and do a pre-takeoff check." Picking up the radio mike, he checked that the radio was on 121.5 and spoke to Stan. "Stan, this is Jamie. Do you read?"

"Loud and clear," Stan responded. "The wind is really coming up here. Are you on the way?"

"Taxiing for takeoff. Will call you in a minute."

Brian turned the plane into the wind at the end of the runway and shoved the throttle in to read 2400 RPMs. The motor sounded rough. He turned the switch to the left magneto, and the motor nearly died. Switching to the right mag, it ran fairly well.

"This motor needs some tuning up. The left bank sounds like most of the plugs are misfiring. Do you think we should go?"

"It's only a three-minute flight. If we can get up to a couple of thousand feet, we can glide to either field. If we can get it home, you can work on it a lot easier."

"OK," Brian said, "here goes." Lining up on the runway, he shoved the throttle in.

"Give her full power for takeoff, then throttle back to 2400," Jamie instructed. "Rotate at 60 and climb out at 2200."

"Can't get more than 2300," Brian exclaimed. "But, by God we are flying."

The wind had picked up more and was gusting. Brian handled it OK and swung in the direction of the home field.

Jamie picked up the mike. "Stan, we are in the air and headed home. It's extremely turbulent, and we have a sick engine, but we should be there in about two minutes. We will approach from the northwest."

"Understand," Stan replied. "I'll be watching for you. The wind is getting really strong here. Heavy gusts to 50 knots. Be careful. That little bird could get blown away."

"Roger, we are lining up for the runway now. Get out, open the hangar door, and stand by to help us get it inside."

Turning to Brian, Jamie said, "I'll take the landing. It isn't very good conditions for a training landing."

"It's all yours," Brian responded calmly.

The little plane was all over the place as Jamie brought it over the fence, maintaining almost cruise power. The landing was rough but controlled. Stan was waiting in front of the hangar, with the door open. Jamie taxied into the hangar and kept the engine running until the door was closed.

"That engine sounds terrible," Stan exclaimed. "This is awful weather for flying a sick airplane."

Randy and Kevin burst through the side door.

"It's really getting nasty out there." Kevin told them. "There's tree branches blowing across the road, and the gusts almost knocked the car off the road. Does this happen often here?"

"No," Jamie replied. "But occasionally we get a tough one from the southeast. This seems an unusually bad one. I think I better get back in the valley and check things out." He was turning away when the earthquake hit, the first jolt almost knocking him off his feet. The sheet metal on the hangar snapped and popped, adding to the noise already being generated by the storm. The planes bounced up and down on their springs. The shaking continued for what seemed like minutes, but probably was no more than 30 seconds.

"Wow," Brian exclaimed. "That was a bad one. Is it as bad as the original one that started the panic?"

"Somewhat worse," Jamie replied. "Now I know I better get back to the valley. Brian, if you want to check that engine over, we'll start flying tomorrow, weather permitting. If you have time, start teaching these fellows some of the fundamentals of what makes an airplane fly. Weather permitting, I'll be here at nine in the morning."

* * *

Jamie made the school his first stop. He was worried about Kelly and the others. He found Charlie Johnson there ahead of him. Charlie was taking his responsibility for the school extremely seriously, Jamie reflected. The kids were all OK, but frightened. The teachers were keeping things under excellent control.

The two men were entering the fourth classroom when another quake hit. Jamie was amazed at the speed with which the kids popped under desks or tables. The teacher had them well trained. A bookcase toppled over, and books went skittering across the floor. A window shattered and glass cascaded to the floor. The wind came through the broken window with gale force, scattering papers everywhere. The wind was bringing with it an overpowering smell of rotten eggs. Gradually the shaking stopped, and students came crawling out from their lairs, their faces pale with fright.

The teacher came out from under her own desk and shouted over the roar of the wind. "You kids did real well. You've really been learning the earthquake drill. You were really fast. Please remember what you did and do it the same way, next time. Hello, Mr. Jamie and Mr. Johnson. You got here just in time to join the earthquake drill."

Mary and Dave Jorgenson came running down the hall. "Is everything all right?" Mary exclaimed. "That quake almost knocked the car off the road."

Charlie came back from a quick survey of the rest of the rooms. "I believe that the only damage was in this room. We need to get that window covered. I think we can find some plywood in the shop room."

"I'll help you," Dave said. "Let's go."

The teacher came over to join them. "Hello Mary. Jamie, do you think we should send the kids home?"

"No," Jamie replied. "They are safer here than out on the roads alone. The parents will probably come for them if this doesn't stop soon. It's early in the day, yet. And, I must say, I was impressed with the reactions of the kids. Your earthquake drill was effective."

"Charlie suggested this a week or so ago, and we have all been practicing it at least once a day. All the rooms are doing well."

Charlie and Dave appeared outside the broken window, wrestling with a sheet of plywood that was proving recalcitrant in the wind. They finally manhandled it into place and a few nails secured it.

Jamie entered the next room down the hall, which was Kelly's room. Kelly waved at him from a corner where she was huddled with the three Dick girls, evidently giving them some special tutoring.

"Good afternoon," the teacher greeted him. "Did you cause that last earthquake? I believe it's the worst one we've had yet."

"Yep," Jamie replied. "I'm going all over the valley shaking things up. Don't you think I'm doing a good job of it?"

"Yes, you're doing a good job, but what about the smell? It's getting worse. Is the quake causing the odor?"

"No. The quake isn't causing the odor, but it might well be that the cause of the smell is what caused the quake. It appears that some of the quakes are triggered by the eruptions of volcanoes along the Cascade Range. We know that both Garibaldi and Baker are erupting, and I think the odor comes from the gas out of the volcanoes. The southeast storm is blowing towards us, and we'll probably keep smelling it until the storm blows over."

Charlie entered the room. "I think the wind is letting up, but look at this," he said, holding out his hand, palm up; a gray smudge covered the palm and fingers. "I wiped this off of a car in the lee of the building. I believe it is ash. Could ash be coming from the volcanoes?"

"I think it could well be," Jamie replied. "We saw a dark cloud erupt from Garibaldi that could be ash. This wind could bring it to us."

"Do you think there is any danger from it?"

"No," Jamie replied. "The ash from an eruption doesn't usually do any damage unless it gets too thick and smothers out crops. There doesn't seem to be much in the way of health records that show damage to humans unless they are close enough to be buried under the ash or smothered by it. I think we are far enough away to suffer little more than inconvenience and irritation. I'm surprised at the strength of the quakes that are coming from them. These quakes may not be related to the volcanoes. I think we are going to have an interesting summer."

A stronger gust of wind shook the building. The lights flickered and went out.

* * *

Mary and Dave were already in the boardroom when Jamie entered, followed by Charlie. Bob Elder arrived shortly after and then Andy Blankenship.

"The power outage is caused by a failure on the mainline coming down from Puntledge," Andy told them. "I don't know why Elk Falls didn't come on automatically. There must be trouble somewhere up there, too. This is one hell of a windstorm. Dave and I will take the big truck up towards Puntledge and see if we can locate the trouble. Jamie, this wind should slacken up in a while. Most storms wind down pretty fast. If it gets flyable, would you take a plane and survey the main line up to Campbell River?"

"I'll go right away," Jamie replied. "I'll take Brian along as an observer, and we will stay in contact with Stan at the airport by radio. If someone can go out there to act as a runner, messages can be relayed to you."

"Jamie, you can't fly in this storm," Mary exclaimed. "It's too dangerous. You'll have to wait till it gets better."

"I can fly in it," Jamie retorted. "I just can't get as close to the ground as I would like. Otherwise, the wind is no problem."

"Please be careful," Mary entreated as Jamie went out the door.

* * *

Jamie found Brian and Stan working on the 152.

"Brian," Jamie asked, "are you game for some flying in the wind?"

"Sure, I can take it if you can," Brian replied. "When do we go?"

"Right now," Jamie said. "Let's take the 172. Stan, will you monitor the radio? Someone will be here soon to run messages if there are any. I'll start the engine in here, and then Stan, if you will open the door for us, I'll taxi outside. Then you can shut the door."

As the plane moved through the door, the wind hit with full force, and Jamie shoved the yoke forward to keep the nose down. He glanced back and saw the door sliding shut and Stan running towards the radio room.

"I think we'll take off from right here," Jamie told Brian. "I don't like taxiing in wind this severe if I can help it. There is almost enough wind for a vertical takeoff right here. I'll move forward a bit to avoid any chance of being blown back into the hangar." He moved about halfway across the big ramp, set the brakes and did his pre-takeoff check. The airspeed indicator was showing 55 knots, which was almost enough for takeoff. Going to full power, he released the brakes, the plane moved forward a short distance and sprang into the air as he pulled the yoke back.

"Whew!" Stan exclaimed. "That was some takeoff."

Climbing straight ahead to 1000 feet, they were still almost directly over the ramp. Jamie leveled off and moved to cruise-power and they started moving forward over the ground. "We have at least 60 knots of wind," Jamie told Brian. "We can make about 60 knots ground speed heading into it. Check with Stan for the air speed."

"I'm showing 58 knots here," Stan reported. "You'd better be damned careful out there, or you'll wind up at Port Hardy. The visibility is going down fast here. I can hardly see the runway. There must have been a hell of a blowup in one of those volcanoes, and the ash is coming in on the wind. I think you should get back here while you can still see."

"Stan, we are over the main power line and following it north. We can see the lines fairly well from 800 feet. There are two lines on steel towers and one on wood poles. I'm indicating 60 knots, which is as slow as I can fly in this air, but we are making about 120 ground speed. The turbulence isn't as bad as I would expect with this wind speed. We have just crossed the highway at the Miracle Beach intersection, so we are east of the highway now.

Hey, I think we see the problem. There are two steel towers down. We'll turn back for a closer look."

Jamie added full power and had started a turn to the left when the engine spluttered and stopped.

"Damn," Jamie exclaimed. "We're going to have to put it in the bush. Keep Stan informed."

The stall horn was blowing, and Jamie dropped the nose and leveled the wings to maintain control. Brian seemed calm, as he relayed events to Stan. Jamie gingerly eased the plane into the wind and noted the air speed at 65. They were almost in the treetops when a tiny clearing showed in front of them. Jamie eased back on the yoke, and the wheels clipped the top of a tree as they came over the edge of the clearing, still a hundred feet above the ground. Jamie dropped the plane into a vicious sideslip and straightened only feet above a tangle of down trees and brush. They had little forward air speed, but the wind was less with tall trees all around, so the plane quit flying almost immediately. They hit hard in a three-point position, bounced over a stump, hit the ground again, just short of a downed tree. The tree caught the nose wheel, and the plane came gently to rest on its nose, tail pointed at the sky.

"Well," Jamie said, "I've made better landings."

"That was the best landing you have ever made," Brian said. Keying the mike, he spoke to Stan. "Stan, can you read?"

"I read," Stan replied, "but you are very garbled. Are you on the ground?"

"We're on the ground and OK, but this plane isn't going anywhere for a while. We are northeast of the highway and just west of the power line. I think we can walk out to the highway. It would help if you could send someone to pick us up. Understand?"

"Understand east of highway and west of power line, and you had passed the Miracle Beach intersection. I will get someone on the way pronto."

"We understand, Stan. We are leaving now to walk to the highway. Out."

Gingerly, they opened the doors, unfastened their seat harness and lowered themselves to the ground. They were in a small patch of swampland not more than a hundred feet in diameter. The going was hard until they got out of the swamp, but in the tall second growth timber, there was not too much ground cover and they made good time. Twenty minutes later they came out at the highway and only waited a few minutes until Stan pulled up in Jamie's car. Another ex-sailor was in the passenger seat. Jamie and Brian pulled the back doors open and settled in the seat.

"I'm sure glad to see you guys," Stan said. "I just about had a hemorrhage when that engine stopped. Brian was so good on the radio that it was just like I was there. It seems like a miracle that you were able to land and walk away from it."

"No, it wasn't a miracle," Brian told him. "It was some of the best damn flying I have ever seen or heard of. I'll ride with this pilot anytime."

It wasn't long until they were back at the schoolhouse, where a reception was waiting for them.

"So it's perfectly safe to go out in a storm in an airplane," Mary tied into him like a fishwife.

Kelly had flung her arms around him and was sobbing in relief. "Mary said you should never have gone out in this storm. I was scared to death. What if you had been killed?"

"Hey, you two," Jamie said emphatically. "Calm down. All's well that ends well. The storm wasn't the problem. The volcanic ash in the air was the problem. The engine ingested too much of it and gave up. We had to make an unscheduled landing, but it came out OK. We aren't hurt. The plane is bruised, but nothing serious. We can fix it if we can figure how to get it out of the bush."

Kelly still clung to him. "I don't like to be scared that way. Please be more careful."

"Hey, kid," Brian spoke up. "Don't worry about him being careful. He can handle anything that an airplane can throw at him. He's the best pilot in the world."

"It's nice to have a fan club," Jamie said. "Now, back to realities. Have you heard anything from Andy or Dave?"

Yes," Mary replied. "They have found the problem and will have a temporary cable laid around the break and should have the power on soon."

* * *

Tuesday morning, residents of New Island woke up to a day of sunshine. The windstorm was over, but a haze of ash in the air obscured the view of the mountains. Ash was everywhere. It pervaded every home. A thin layer of it covered the furniture, and it clung to draperies and carpets. Outside, drifts of ash had formed in the lee of fence posts and shrubbery. Everything that one touched left a gray smudge on the hands. New Island faced a massive cleanup.

At the airport, Jamie found his crew, including the two new pilot recruits on duty and busy sweeping out the hangar and cleaning the airplanes. He marveled at the dedication of these young men. With people like these, New Island was bound to succeed.

All four men gathered around him, obviously ready for whatever he had in store for them.

"Brian, is there enough of this ash in the air to create a problem with engines? I'm not particularly eager to teach forced landing until these fellows have had a little basic instruction."

"No," Brian replied. "It's not likely there is enough to cause a problem. I'll check filters after every flight to be sure. It's just that yesterday there was so much of it that the filter must have clogged and shut off air supply to the carburetor."

"OK, let's get the 152 out, and we will see what you two new fellows are made of. I'll take Randy up first to see what his initial training has accomplished. Then I'll take Kevin. Let's go, Randy."

When the morning was over, Jamie felt that he had the makings of a couple of good pilots.

The base mess hall was still open. The submarine cook was still serving a number of sailors who had not made a decision on where to settle. The five men gathered at the mess hall for lunch and a long discussion about the volcanic activities.

"I wonder," remarked Stan, "which volcano blew up. It seems, from the wind, that it must have been Mount Baker. With the way the wind was blowing, that would be the most likely. Could the ash travel that far?"

"I think it could," Jamie replied, "especially if the blowup occurred at the time the storm came up. Also, there was no rain with this windstorm, so the ash could travel farther. Wherever it was, there must have been an awful cloud of debris blown into the air."

"I'd sure like to take a look at it," Brian said. "It really would be something to see."

"Maybe we should take the 206 and investigate," Jamie remarked. "It's only about an hour away. We could take a look and be back here in a couple of hours, or three at the most. And that would give us a chance to test the satellite radio some more."

"Let's do it," Brian concurred. "If we can still talk to Stan from behind Mount Baker, we are in good shape for communications."

* * *

An hour later, Jamie and Brian were approaching Mount Baker, level at 10,000 feet, a little below the summit. A cloud of smoke and steam was towering high above the mountain. Jamie swung around the west shoulder of the mountain and headed east on the southern flank.

"Holy Christ," Brian swore. "Look at that."

The whole southeastern side of the mountain was a scene of unbelievable devastation. Rivers of mud and debris were moving down several channels toward Baker Lake, five or six miles away. The heat from the eruption, with pyroclastic materials from the interior of the mountain, had melted the snow and icecap. A deluge of water was carrying huge volumes of rock, mud and other debris towards the valley below.

As Brian kept up a running commentary to Stan, Jamie headed northeast, then turned back to the south and started a letdown towards the lake. There was little to see of the lake. Steam was rising from the surface, indicating the temperature of the inflow. The lake appeared to be little more than a mass of debris, moving southward towards the Baker Dam. The dam was invisible. It was either torn away or flooded over. Shannon Lake, which was formed by the Lower Baker Dam, appeared one with Baker Lake. They could see nothing of the Lower Baker Dam, as they flew over it at about 1000 feet above the ground. The town of Concrete was totally obliterated, and the Skagit River was a raging torrent. They followed on down the river to where it spread out over farmlands and inundated the Hamilton and Lyman areas. Burlington was heavily flooded, and most of Mount Vernon was underwater. The debris-laden river poured out over the delta lands and on into Skagit Bay, discoloring the ocean for miles.

Jamie swung the plane in a wide circle and started a climb on a northerly heading. At Bellingham, he let down again and flew low over the airport. As he looked back, he could see a huge plume of dust disturbed by the wash of the plane.

"God," Jamie said, "there must be inches of dust on that runway. We sure don't want to land there until it rains and settles that ash."

"I can't believe the destruction we saw back there." Brian seemed awestruck. "It's probably a good thing people that lived there died when they did. Their death would have been much harder in that flood. I'm glad we live in New Island."

An hour later, they were home. The two men said little on the trip home, each involved in his own thoughts. The power of nature on the rampage had left them unable to express themselves. They were still quiet, as they taxied the plane to the hangar and put it away. As they left the hangar, it started to rain.

"Thank God for small favors," Jamie said. "A good rain will wash away a lot of this ash and make life easier for all of us."

Chapter 31

Jamie sat in his chair, waiting for the assemblage of the people of New Island for the weekly general meeting, his mind running over the events of the past week. After the eventful Monday with its two substantial earthquakes and the windstorm that had dusted ash over the island plus his flight on Tuesday to investigate Mount Baker, the week had been uneventful. He had concentrated on training the two new pilots; Randy was flying solo, and Kevin would be soon. The crowd was settling down. It was time for him to speak.

Standing up, Jamie raised his arms, asking for attention. He got it immediately. "Welcome again to a general meeting of the residents of New Island. There have been a few interesting events since we were here a week ago. Probably many of you know about most of those events. Certainly, you all know about the two severe quakes we had on Monday and the extra severe windstorm that deposited volcanic ash over our community.

"That windstorm was vicious. Stan Bowman recorded gusts to 58 knots per hour. That's in the neighborhood of 100 kilometers per hour, and that is an extremely strong wind. It knocked out the power on both transmission lines to our community. Nevertheless, our power people, Andy and Dave, were able to make temporary repairs to the Puntledge line and get the juice back on before evening. Since then, they have repaired the mainline from Elk Falls and made permanent repairs to the Puntledge, so we are in good shape again. There was a lot of blow down, with trees blocking a number of roads, but they have all been cleared. Damage from the quakes was not extensive. A couple of old chimneys came down, and one punched a hole through the roof. Fortunately, no one was injured. Some masonry walls came down in the older part of Courtenay. But our wood frame buildings in the valley showed little effect. They will stand a much stronger quake than we have had so far.

"On Tuesday, Brian and I flew to Mount Baker. The mountain had had a major volcanic blowout. Brian was in radio contact with Stan and gave him a running commentary on what we observed. Stan recorded that commentary, and I am going to play it for you now. That will give you a much better picture of it than I could give you from memory. Here goes."

"Holy Christ, look at that." Brian's voice was loud and clear as he got his first look at the damage. His commentary graphically described the view below them and continued until they made their sweep over the mouth of the Skagit. The audience broke into spontaneous applause as the recording ended.

"I don't know who ordered the heavy rain we had over Tuesday night, but it sure was welcome. It not only settled our worries about drought in the valley, but it washed away most of the ash that had settled over us. The ash will do no damage to our soil. In fact, it is probably beneficial.

"Now, we ask the question. Did the earthquakes cause the volcanoes to erupt, or did the volcanoes cause the earthquakes? I am not sure, but I am sure that they are related. Nevertheless, after studying the information I had printed out from the Internet after the first quake and digging up some more in the library, I think that the earthquakes were caused by the slippage of the tectonic plates. Rather than one huge surge, they are slipping a little at a time. That is good for us, because it relieves the pressure gradually, rather than all at once. These quakes will probably continue for some time, until the plates have gained some semblance of equilibrium.

"I do think that the quakes have disturbed the mountains enough to cause the eruptions. They have probably been building up to it for hundreds or thousands of years and finally found an excuse to go active. Remember—Mount St. Helens blew up in 1990, and has shown recent activity. These mountains are all in the same chain up the Cascade Range.

"Now, I have another little demonstration I would like you all to experience."

Jamie pulled a small cell phone from his pocket and held it up for all to see. "As you can see, this is a cell phone. Now I am going to dial a number," he said, punching the keys of the phone.

A ringing sounded in the back of the room, and Stan Bowman pulled a phone from his pocket and answered.

"Stan, is that you?" Jamie asked.

"Yes Jamie, this is Stan. How can I help you?"

Jamie closed the phone and spoke to the group. "While Stan and I were just across the room, within talking distance, we were actually talking by way of a phone relay tower on the ridge between here and the airport. Our electronic genius here has figured out how to set up the switching system and activate the phones. He thinks that he can provide a phone for every family in the community. Nevertheless, it will take him some time to do it. How does that sound to you?"

There was a round of noisy applause.

"He is going to provide the first phones to the council and other people who have the greatest need of communications, and then go on as fast as possible with the rest of you. We are having trouble finding phones, so if you have a late model unit, bring it in. Stan will reprogram it and assign a number to you. We will put out a directory as soon as possible. You can leave your phones with Mary in the office.

"Now, for my final comments for tonight. I am in the process of training two new pilots. We have a good start. They will be backup, or rescue pilots. Stan has succeeded in getting a satellite radio system working, and we can communicate from the plane to Stan's office, we hope, from great distance. This will be invaluable as we start an extensive exploration program to find out conditions in other parts of the continent. I think this activity is vital. If there are other people alive out there, we need to get in contact with them, for both their benefit and ours. Exploration with the airplane has brought 56 people to our colony, much to our benefit."

"Jamie," Teresa Blunt was on her feet. "You have admitted that there could be many health dangers out there. Do you think it is good judgment for you to expose yourself this way?"

"Yes," Jamie admitted. "There are some dangers. Dr. Ron has provided us with lots of advice and help and emergency medications. We will carry our own water and food supply. We have water purification tablets if we run out of water. We will avoid contact with dead bodies as much as possible. I think we can keep the risk to a minimum. I feel it is necessary to take that risk."

"We are all concerned about you, Jamie, so please, for all our sakes, be careful."

"I will be, Teresa. Thanks for your concern. Now, if there is nothing else, let's end this meeting."

"One more thing," Teresa said. "Our next potluck will be a picnic. It will be in Charlie Johnson's cow pasture, which runs down to the river and is a nice place for a picnic. Charlie has agreed to move the cows to another pasture a few days ahead of time, so there will be no soft cow patties, only dry ones. There will be foot races, sack races, jumping and other activities. If the weather is bad, we will be back here for our usual. See you all there."

"Thanks Teresa," Jamie said. "Sounds wonderful. See you then. Goodbye, everyone."

Chapter 32

No one knew there was a cougar in the area. It was known that the big cats were on Vancouver Island, but none had been seen in the New Island community.

The picnic in Charlie Johnson's cow pasture was a huge success. There had been a couple hours of games and fun, and now Teresa was blowing a whistle and waving her arms to draw attention. It was time to eat.

Jamie joined the lines moving down the tables, filling plates to capacity. With a full plate, he found Kelly with the Dick girls and Little Bird sitting on both sides of an ancient downed tree, using it as a table. They welcomed him to the group and made room for him. The conversation was animated and more adult than he would have expected and time went fast. Dawg was with them and scrounged a few tasty bits from various members of the group, and then licked plates clean as they were emptied.

The women started picking up the dishes and cleaning up the mess. People moved away, scattering over the pasture, in groups of various sizes. Kelly and the Dick girls, joined by Fluorine Jim and Susie Gardner moved up the slope a ways and started playing a game. Dawg was in the center of the group, enjoying their attention.

Louise Jim with her three-month-old baby girl moved off to herself and sat cross-legged on the ground to nurse the baby. Louise, only 15 years old, was unmarried, but was showing a good deal of responsibility with the care of her baby. With an olfactory notice that the babies diaper needed changing, Louise removed the little girl from her breast and laid her on the ground beside her. Folding the blanket back, she removed the soiled diaper and stuffed it into a bag. Lifting the infant by the feet, she cleaned its bottom with a tissue, and then with the baby waving its feet in the air, she turned to get a fresh diaper from her carry bag.

With the group of girls some twenty yards up the hill, Dawg went stiff legged and started to growl. The hair came up on his back, and he was making little whimpering sounds between growls. Suddenly, he broke from the circle of girls and, barking furiously, started a mad dash towards Louise and the baby.

At the same instant the huge cat broke from the timberline and, in only a few giant leaps, snatched the baby in its jaws and headed for the protection of the trees. Dawg, digging up the turf with his feet in his effort to catch the cougar, was only feet behind the big cat. The cat, changing its mind about disappearing in the forest, opted for the safety of a high spot and went up the nearest tree, Dawg snapping viciously at its heels and trying his best to climb the tree after it.

Louise, screaming at the top of her voice, alerted the scattered crowd, and they all started converging on the site. The cougar reached the first branch in the maple tree, a dead limb about six inches in diameter that angled up at 45 degrees from the tree trunk. He wedged the crying baby in the V formed by the dead branch and clawed his way to a higher branch where he crouched, snarling and spitting at the dog barking at the foot of the tree.

"Get my baby," the girl screamed. "Help me. Someone get my baby."

Charlie Johnson, hearing the commotion from the barn where he was talking to some other men, ran into the pasture, immediately saw the situation and ran to the house for his rifle. Young Lars Blunt, followed by his brothers, came across the field, long legs eating up the distance, elbowing his way past anyone in the way. Women were crying hysterically, and men seemed unsure what action to take. Lars stopped a short distance from the tree, a maple about 24 inches in diameter. He could see the bare-bottom of the little girl, her body wedged in the crotch of the tree, a good 30 feet above the ground, the huge cat snarling a few feet above her. She had stopped crying.

Louise continued to scream. "Please, please help me. Someone help me get my baby."

Lars, his six-foot-four frame towering over the petite girl, grabbed her by the shoulder and shook her. "Shut up," he ordered. "We'll get your baby down. She'll be all right. I'll get her for you."

Louise grabbed him around the waist. "Please do," she begged. "I'll love you forever if you do. Please get her down."

Charlie Johnson appeared among the group, levering a shell into the chamber of the high-powered rifle he carried. "Everyone get back," he ordered. "I'll make short work of that varmint."

"Better not shoot," Dave Jorgenson told him. "The critter could fall on the baby and knock it out of the tree. And if you just wounded it, hard to say what would happen."

"You're right," Charlie responded. "But how are we going to get her down?"

"I'll get her down," Lars said as he pulled off his shoes and socks. "Gimme that rope." He snatched the jump rope some children had been using and knotted one end around his waist. "Brothers, give me your belts," he demanded.

The two older boys unbuckled their belts and pulled them free. Lars buckled one belt and hung it around his neck. With the other, he ran the belt through the buckle and slid the buckle down the leather until he had a small slip loop and tucked the belt under his own belt. He gathered up the rope and started towards the tree.

"Lars, what are you going to do?" screamed Teresa, gasping for breath as she staggered to a stop beside the boy. Patrick Holden caught up with Teresa and grabbed her hand.

"I'm going up there and get that baby," replied the boy.

"You might be the best damned tree climber in the world, but it is too dangerous with that monster up there. You can't do it. I will not let you."

"I think the boy knows what he is doing," Pat cautioned her. "I've heard your stories about his tree climbing. Let him go."

Lars turned to his brothers. "Leif, give me your knife," he demanded. The older brother pulled a six-inch hunting knife from its sheath and handed it to Lars. Lars slid the blade under his belt and stalked stolidly towards the tree. Wearing cutoff jeans, the boy's legs were bare. His longish blond hair was blowing in the breeze. He seemed unconcerned about what he was doing. At the foot of the tree, he passed the rope around the trunk, looped it through the rope around his waist and fastened a quick release knot. Pulling the knife from his belt, he cut the excess end from the rope, leaving about four feet to dangle.

His movements deliberate, he replaced the knife under his belt, faced up to the tree and flipped the loop of rope upward. Leaning back against the rope, he placed the arch of his right foot against the tree. With his leg stiff, he supported his body with the rope and moved the left foot to a position even with the right. A quick jerk of his body forward released the pressure on the rope and he flipped it upwards. Leaning back, he repeated the procedure and gradually moved up the tree.

Dr. Ron, arriving on the scene, quickly assessed the situation and grabbed his cell phone to contact Dr. Bill Weaver at the hospital. "Bill, get the ambulance over here immediately. We have the potential for serious injuries here in the next minute or two, and we could need the emergency equipment in the truck. Expedite!" He closed the phone, not waiting for an answer.

Lars was inching his way up the tree, deliberate in his actions, trying not to make a misstep that could cause him to fall. Halfway up, he paused and looked up at the snarling cat, less than 20 feet above him. The animal looked twice as big and twice as ferocious as it had from the ground. Going back to his own problem, that of getting safely up the tree, he proceeded cautiously to flip the rope and gain another step upwards. He chose to ignore the danger above him.

Charlie Johnson stood with the rifle at his shoulder, sight centered on what little showed of the animal's head. If he had to shoot, a headshot would be best, killing the cat instantly. A shot to the body inflicting less than an instant fatal wound could well increase the danger to the child and the rescuer.

Lars came within reach of the child, but she was wedged so solidly in the crotch of the tree that he could not get her loose without danger of injury. He had to get higher, so he could lift the child in order to free her. Another two steps upward and his head was level with the baby. Settling his body against the rope, he had both hands on the child, when the cat, hissing furiously, took a swipe at him, hitting the side of his head and throwing him off balance. A cat claw had slashed a long wound across the side of his head, and blood flowed down the side of his face.

Lars struggled to regain his footing on the tree, edged sideways to place himself in a better position. Pulling the hunting knife from his belt, he looked up at the glaring yellow eyes of the beast only feet away. He was not in a position to make the knife a viable choice, so he gripped the haft between his teeth and again reached for the child. This time, he was able to lift the baby high enough to release her from the grip of the tree and pull her down to his chest. Glimpsing another strike from the lethal paw, Lars ducked his head sideways, the claws of the beast passing through his hair. Removing the looped belt from his waist, he pulled the loop over the child's naked lower body and up to her chest, slipping the buckle down the leather to secure the belt snugly. Glancing up, he saw the cat changing position with the possibility

204

of another attack coming. Dropping the knife from his teeth, he replaced it with the strap holding the child, and grasping the ropes with both hands, flipped it free and let it fall, at the same instant releasing his grip with both feet. The feet came in contact with the tree at the same time the rope gripped the trunk, and Lars was three feet down the tree, narrowly escaping another swipe from the vicious claws. Looking up at the animal, he began inching his way down the tree, the baby dangling from the strap gripped between his teeth.

The sound of the ambulance, sirens screaming at the empty roads, notified that Dr. Weaver was on the way. Lars was still 20 feet from the ground when the rope hung up on the backside of the tree. Several tries failed to free it. Reaching forward, he let loose of the rope and gripped the tree with his hands. At the same time, his feet lost their grip on the tree, and he swung his lower body forward and gripped the trunk with his knees, still keeping his chest away from the tree far enough to protect the baby. Sliding downwards, the rough bark tore the skin from the inside of his thighs and knees. At 15 feet, he pushed himself from the tree and fell free, his knees bent to absorb the shock, his arms swinging in to grasp the child tightly to his chest. He hit the ground on both feet and allowed himself to roll backwards. Coming to rest on his back, he still had the baby securely clamped against his chest, the leather belt still gripped between his teeth.

A shot rang out and the cat tumbled from the tree. Charlie Johnson had found an opportunity for a headshot, and the beast was dead before it hit the ground. Dawg jerked away from Kelly's grip and bounded forward to attack the lifeless form. Kelly ran forward screaming at him to stop. Reluctantly, Dawg gave up his attack. There was no fight left in the critter.

Louise snatched the baby from Lars' grip and hugged her to her breast. Dr. Ron reached for the baby, and Louise reluctantly released the unconscious child. The ambulance was bouncing across the pasture and came to a halt feet away, Dr. Weaver piling out almost before the vehicle had stopped. Racing to the rear of the ambulance, he swung the doors open. "What do we have here?" He asked Ron.

"The baby is unconscious, but breathing OK. We need to get her to the hospital as soon as possible to see what we can do. And look at that young man over there. He's bleeding badly."

Ron shoved Louise into the ambulance and handed her the baby, then turned to follow Dr. Bill.

Assisted by Pat Holden and Teresa Blunt, Lars was getting shakily to his feet. Blood was still flowing down the side of his head and neck and soaking his shirt, and the insides of his legs were covered in blood.

"My God," Teresa exclaimed. "His legs look like hamburger."

The two doctors took a quick look. "We need him in the hospital, where we can patch him up," Dr. Ron told Teresa. "Don't worry about him."

"Don't worry about him, you say. He's my baby son. How can I help but worry about him?"

Ron turned to Pat Holden, who was holding her hand. "Follow us to the hospital. We have to get that baby there pronto. We can take care of both of them there."

With a doctor on each side, Lars walked to the ambulance and hoisted himself inside.

Louise looked at him. "Oh you poor man. You're bloody from one end to the other. My God."

"Don't worry about me," Lars told her. "We just have to worry about the baby."

"You saved her life, so I have to worry about you as well as her. I hope you both will be all right."

"I'm tough," Lars replied. "I'll be fine. The doctor just has to get this blood stopped. My God, how my legs hurt. I hope he'll have something to stop the pain."

"He will," Louise said reaching for his hand and squeezing it. She kept on squeezing, and Lars turned beet-red with embarrassment. Never before in his life had a girl held his hand.

The ambulance arrived at the hospital, and Louise, carrying her baby, followed Dr. Ron into an examination room. Laying the little girl on a table, he started his examination. She was breathing, and heartbeat and pulse were normal. She started kicking her feet, then opened her eyes and started to cry.

"She is OK," Dr. Ron told Louise. "Just some scratches where she was jammed into the fork of that tree and some bruises where the cat had hold of her shoulder. We'll put some disinfectant on them, and you can take her home. I'd like to see her tomorrow."

"Thank you, Doctor," Louise said, starting to cry.

"Hey, nothing to cry about. It all turned out well. We are very fortunate. If you want to thank someone, thank that brave young man that went up the tree and brought her down. And thank that big dog that chased the cougar up that tree. But for the dog, the cougar would have disappeared in the bush and that would have been that."

"There's lots to cry about," Louise blubbered. "I'm crying because my baby is safe. And I'm crying because of that wonderful man that saved her, and I'm crying because he is hurt so bad. He was so brave. And I'm crying because of Dawg who gave the alarm and made the cat go up the tree. I'm crying because there are so many wonderful people here, and they look after each other so much."

"I agree with all you say, except you should be laughing instead of crying. We live in a wonderful country, even though it does have some cougars."

In the other examination room, Dr. Weaver was cleaning the gash on Lars' head. His mother was watching closely, and Pat Holden was waiting in the background. Charlie Johnson came in with Little Bird and Sweet Grass, who was carrying Little Bird's medicine bag. Little Bird crowded up to look at the wound, and the doctor made way for her.

"That tiger claw likely had all kinds of bad bugs on it," Little Bird said. "We need to put the right medicine on it before you sew it up."

"Lars," the doctor said, "do you want Little Bird to use her natural medicine on you?"

"It worked on Mr. Jamie, didn't it?" Lars replied.

"Yes, it worked well on Jamie, but I also have some good medicine. It's up to you. Take your choice."

"Tell the lady to go ahead," Lars replied, "but I would like you to stitch it up."

Little Bird took the jar of evil smelling ointment and smeared it liberally on the wound, then held the edges of the gash together while Dr. Weaver stitched it.

"There, that should do it," the doctor said. "Took 17 stitches. That was quite a gash. Let's take a look at his legs. They sure need some cleaning up."

The insides of both the legs, from ankle to mid-thigh, were scraped and torn. Blood was oozing from small abrasions, and large areas of skin appeared badly damaged. Bits of bark and moss were embedded in the bloody mess.

"Do they hurt?" the doctor asked.

"They hurt real bad," the youth admitted.

"I have something that should relieve the pain while we clean up," Little Bird said.

"OK," said Dr. Weaver. "Let's try it."

Sweet Grass extracted a bottle from the medicine bag. With folded paper towels saturated with the contents of the bottle, she began patting the injured legs.

"Now we can wash with soap and water," Little Bird told them. "It should be much less painful now."

The cleanup took some time, as slivers and bark were embedded in the flesh, and some had to be picked out with tweezers. Lars flinched occasionally, but made no complaint. When they were finished, Little Bird selected another ointment from her collection and smeared it over the entire area of abraded skin.

"All right," said Little Bird, "I think you will be fine now. This will heal up fast. Best not to wear long pants for a few days. Keeping the area open to the air will make it heal faster. And some sandals would be best for your feet."

Chapter 33

After dropping Kelly at school, Jamie was at the airport at nine o'clock. He found Brian and Stan tinkering with the radios in the 206. They had installed satellite-navigation instruments mounted in the dash showing the compass heading, ground speed, distance and time to a predetermined point. By keying in the longitude and latitude of any point, the pilot could fly to that point with reference to the instruments on the panel.

"You fellows are making things too easy for us," Jamie told them. "Do you have enough gear to equip more planes?"

"Yes," Stan replied. "I can fix up three or four with what I have on hand. Then I would have to start scrounging from other airplanes or boats. I'm sure many boats have the gear, and commercial airplanes would have it onboard now. It has been available for some time."

"The other fellows are flying?" Jamie asked.

"Yes," Brian replied, "Randy is on a solo cross-country to Nanaimo, and Kevin is practicing landings at Campbell River. They are both due shortly. I think those two guys are both going to be good pilots. Anyway, they sure are trying hard."

* * *

Jamie headed back to the valley and stopped at the school. He found Mary, as usual, busy in the office.

"What are you up to now?" Jamie asked.

"I'm preparing a telephone directory. Stan is getting the phones ready fast, and I can get the directory done ahead of time. I've gone ahead and assigned numbers to those that we are going to provide phones to in the first round, and Stan will program the phones as he gets them ready. That way, we can provide the directory along with the phones. It should all be done this week."

Jamie sat quietly for minute, watching Mary work at the computer. Her blond hair had grown into an inch-long curly mass covering her head. Scars from the tree accident didn't show. She's a beautiful woman, Jamie reflected, but somehow, she has an extra aura about her this morning.

"You look like the cat that swallowed the canary," Jamie said. "What has you all aglow this morning?"

"I didn't realize that it showed, but I am really extra happy this morning. I'm pregnant. Here I am nearly 40 years old and never thought I would be blessed with children. But now, I'm on the way. Dr. Ron verified it this morning."

"Wonderful," Jamie exclaimed. "Congratulations. Nothing could please me more. Does Dave know?"

"Yes. We had suspected it for several days. I was more than a week late with my period, and I was always very regular. This morning I went to see Dr. Ron, and he verified it. I called Dave on his cell phone to let him know. He was so excited he could hardly talk. Both of us want children very badly. Dave had a family, but they were lost in the disaster, and he wants to start over. I've always wanted children, but regardless how we tried, it never happened. Now, it happened so quickly that I couldn't believe it. I think I must be the happiest woman in the world. For the life of me, I am unable to feel sorry for the way the world has turned out."

* * *

The council took their places for the regular Sunday afternoon meeting. Word had gone around that Mary was pregnant, and congratulations came from all of the members.

"Thanks for all of your support," Mary told them. "But I have other news for you. I'm not the only one pregnant. Meg Parks is going to have a baby too."

"Looks like we are on the right track here," Jamie said. "That's two more potential New Islanders within the year. That's what we need for the long term good of our country. Shall we call the meeting to order? I'll fill you in on what's been going on this past week.

"I've been working the butts off of both student pilots, and they are really coming along. Both of them are now qualified on the 172, and both have completed initial cross-country trips. I'm going to give them some rigorous training on short field landings in cow pastures and on roads, then get them qualified on the 206. We found another good looking 206 at Victoria Airport, and Brian and I went down and got it."

"You're developing quite an air force, it sounds like," interposed Bob Elder. "How many planes do you have now?"

"Our fleet is all Cessna," Jamie replied. "We have a 152, a 172, a 182 and two 206 six placers. That's five total. The 206 is the most useful for our long-range exploration work because of its greater capacity, better speed and longer range."

"What about the two airliners you have in the hangar?"

"I wasn't counting them," Jamie replied, "because we can't fly them yet. They are 36-passenger propjet Shorts 360s built in Ireland. We can't fly them yet, but Brian has been bugging me to learn. He knows all about propjets and thinks he can help me learn to fly them. In that I've never flown twin engines, I've been a little reluctant to try. Besides, we have no particular needs for larger planes at the present time. Now Brian wants to try to locate a single propjet Cessna Caravan. There are a number of them in use on short-haul air operations, especially in remote areas because of their short field capabilities. They carry eight passengers or a lot of freight. Brian thinks we might find one in Edmonton, as an operator there was using three of them. He found an article about it in an old aviation magazine. It would be easier for me to get used to turbo props on a single engine plane before I go to twins."

"You can learn to fly propjets without an instructor?" Bob asked.

"Flying the airplane is no different," Jamie replied. "I have to learn engine management, and Brian can teach me that. Then I just have to get in the airplane and fly it. I think we will make a trip to Calgary later this week. We'll probably go to Lethbridge and Edmonton on the way. It looks like the potluck crowd is gathering. Let's go see if there is enough to eat."

Chapter 34

Brian and Jamie spent the day preparing the 206 for a long cross-country flight. They checked the emergency supplies and prepared for a week of food and water. They weighed all of the gear and planned how best to load it, insuring proper weight and balance. They included sleeping bags and foam pads for sleeping on the ground and a portable gasoline stove for cooking. At the last minute, they decided to include a pup tent that would provide shelter for two. They were ready to go at 8 AM on Tuesday morning. Kelly would stay with Mary until they returned.

"You fly the first leg," Jamie told Brian. "We'll go through Stevens Pass along Highway 2 and land at Wenatchee for fuel."

They broke ground at 8:30, and Brian climbed to 8000 feet. Jamie manned the radio and made regular reports to Stan who had his recorder going to keep a record of the flight. Approaching Everett, Brian turned east and climbed to 10,000 feet. He was soon past the mountains and letting down for Wenatchee.

"Better monitor me close on this landing," he told Jamie. "This will be my first on a strange airport."

"Just remember what I have taught you. Keep some power on your approach. Use full flaps. As you come over the end of the runway, don't look down. Look at the far end of the runway. Gradually reduce power, bring the nose up, and feel for the runway."

Brian was calm and followed instructions. The landing was smooth as silk.

"A grease on," Jamie complimented him. "Nothing to it."

"But I sure used a lot of runway," Brian complained, turning onto a taxiway towards the main ramp.

"That's OK," Jamie told him. "You'll get better with experience."

They found the fueling station and had to use the generator to activate the pump. Brian made notes of the fuel situation in his logbook, and they prepared for the next leg of the flight to Spokane and continued on to Kalispell, Montana, where they ate a hasty lunch.

Jamie took the controls, and they flew over the spectacular mountains of Glacier National Park, marveling at the soaring spires of snow-capped rocks. With the Rocky Mountains behind them, they turned north and were soon crossing into Canada.

Brian, making regular reports to Stan, kept him posted on their location and route. The satellite radio system was working perfectly. The air was crystal clear and visibility unlimited. They continued north, edging a little west, with the mountains towering west of them and the open prairies stretching to the east. They were flying over rolling hills and a lot of open grassland.

"What's that up ahead?" exclaimed Jamie. They were close to an hour north of the border.

"Looks like smoke. I don't think there are any volcanoes here, are there?"

"It is smoke, I'm sure. And where there's smoke, there's fire. And where there's fire, it's likely there are men. This bears some looking into."

Jamie dropped the nose and started descending. As they came nearer, the smoke defined itself more clearly. It was billowing from behind a range of low, grass-covered hills. Jamie leveled the plane to clear the hills by a good 1000 feet. As they topped the hills, a valley opened before them. It was at least two miles wide and stretched in both directions for some distance. The fire was burning in a field of dry stubble, apparently set to remove the ground cover. To the right of the burning field were several other fields, fenced, some under cultivation and some apparently for pasture. Cattle grazed in one of the fields. In a further field, a group of buildings were visible. Jamie turned the plane toward them and flew over them, then started a long sweeping turn. Coming back towards the buildings, they could see several large houses, a couple of large barns and a gaggle of smaller buildings. People were running into the yards and waving at them. Jamie waggled the wings as he went over and started another turn.

The valley was divided down the center with the south half fenced and the north side open range. A little used road ran east and west along the fence. The road appeared to be only a track along the fence, with no ditches or grading. Turning back a mile to the west, Jamie dropped to 50 feet and flew back to the east, parallel to the track. It appeared reasonably smooth, and Jamie could see no obstructions that would prevent landing. A mile east of the buildings, Jamie pulled up and turned back for his approach. He touched down about a half mile from the buildings. A small rise bounced the plane into the air again, but Jamie eased it back to the ground and coasted to a halt at a gated entrance to the farm.

A tall, lean man wearing a broad brimmed black hat and black clothing opened the gate and came towards them. It was hard to determine his age. He had a full black beard that reached to mid-chest, but no mustache. He stopped a few feet away, surveying them critically, his eyes wandering from Jamie to Brian, lingering on the black man for an inordinate amount of time. Brian squirmed nervously under his gaze.

"Where did you men come from?" He demanded brusquely.

"We are from the coast," Jamie replied. "A small community named New Island on Vancouver Island, off the coast of British Columbia. We saw the smoke from your burning field and stopped to investigate."

"I have geography books and an atlas. I never heard of a place called New Island."

"You wouldn't," Jamie replied. "It is the new name given to a community of a few hundred people that survived the great catastrophe that appears to have destroyed most of the world. We are out exploring trying to find other people that may have survived."

"Why do you want to find them? Do you think they might have something that you want?"

"No, we are not interested in what they have. We have plenty of everything. We think that by finding other people that are still alive, and working with them to build a new civilization, we can build a new population for the world. Without cooperation of other groups that we may find, we will be hard pressed to build a new and viable world."

"How come this black man is with you? Are there other black people in your group?"

Jamie was hard pressed to hold his temper. "No, Brian is the only black man in our group, unfortunately. I wish there were others. We are dedicated to the premise that all people are created equal, regardless of the color of their skin. We are not concerned with race, or religion. We have no state religion. All of our people are free to believe as they wish, as long as it does not interfere with the welfare of the group as a whole."

"What will this black man do when he wants to find a woman?"

"If one of our girls wants to marry him, that is up to the two of them. I hope no one would object. We have a few native Indians in our community, some of them of mixed blood, some pure Indian. There is no discrimination. We are all equal, which is as it should be. In the future, with mixing the blood of all of our people, there will be no race distinctions. We will all be one race. Now, it is time for us to ask some questions. We have been interrogated in an unfriendly fashion. If you do not want us here, we will get in our airplane and be on our way. I'm sure that we will find more friendly people in the world."

The stranger was quiet for several minutes, his eyes floating from one to the other, and to the airplane. Finally, he spoke.

"I am sorry, Sirs. You took us by surprise. After the strange death apparently took everyone in the world, we assumed that we were God's chosen few, left here in our valley to rebuild the world. Then you strangers come in your flying machine, the first one ever to land in our valley. You totally disrupted my thought process, and I obviously did not present myself in a friendly way. I am sorry."

"I accept your apology, Sir," Jamie said, holding out his hand. "My name is Jamie Morgan. I'm President of our community. And this is my copilot and very capable assistant, Brian Veary."

"I am Job Navolsky, leader of our group." His grip was firm. He turned to shake Brian's hand. "Sir, I have never shaken the hand of a black man. We have always been led to believe the African races were inferior and to be avoided. Perhaps we were misled. Welcome to our community."

"That's all right, Sir," Brian said graciously. "It seems to be the heritage of the black races to be considered inferior. We are gradually convincing people that we are no different under the skin."

"As I said before, we were sure that we were God's chosen few. We are from Mennonite people that came here more than 80 years ago and bought two sections of land in this valley from the Canadian Government. We were satisfied that God destroyed the rest of the people and left us as his chosen ones to carry on his work in the world, building a new society under his dictates. Our faith was abruptly shattered when your strange machine come flying in, and a black man is considered equal to the white man that is in command. It makes me wonder."

215

"Mr. Navolsky," Jamie said, "there are many things to wonder about in the world. I am sure that we will never solve all of the puzzles. But we are firmly convinced that more people are left alive in the world, and it is our duty to find them and help them in any way possible. We have already found a number. We stumbled on a submarine with 42 crewmen aboard. Brian was one of her officers, and his expertise as a machinist and an aircraft mechanic has proven invaluable to us. We found six people in the Okanogan Valley that survived because they were exploring a cave deep underground. All of these people have joined our colony. We now have almost 500 people in New Island."

"Come, Sirs," Job said, "I am failing as a host. Dinner must be waiting for us. We all eat together in a central dining room. You will meet all of our people at mealtime." He turned and led the way to the gate. The group of people that had remained behind the gate turned and hurried ahead of them, disappearing into various buildings. Job led the way to a hall-like building and motioned them inside. The large room had three long tables set up for the meal.

"This is our communal dining room," Job said. "We all eat together here. The kitchen is through those doors at the back. The women work together preparing the meals." He took position behind a chair at the head of one table and motioned Jamie and Brian to seats on each side. "The men all eat at this table. The women share the center table, and the young people use the other table. Please be seated."

People started filing into the room, taking seats at their designated tables. The men's table filled up quickly, but no words were spoken. Nevertheless, they looked at the strangers with a good deal of curiosity. There was no sound, even from the children's table, except for the scuffling of feet and the scrape of chairs.

Job stood and spoke. "You are all aware that a couple of strangers have arrived in our community. One of them is a black man. I am sure you are wondering about him, given our heritage that assumed a black to be inferior and not welcomed by us. Nevertheless, his companion assures me that that is not the case where they came from. This man is well educated and was an officer in the United States Navy. While in our community, it is my command that he will be treated the same as any other guest. Now, it is my pleasure to introduce Mr. Jamie Morgan, President of the country of New Island, and his companion, Mr. Brian Veary. Please make them welcome. Now, we will eat."

The women hurried from the room and returned with dishes of plain, but nourishing looking food and set them on the tables, serving the men first. The dishes were passed hand to hand, and plates were quickly loaded. There was no conversation as the men ate. The meal was completed without a word being spoken other than the occasional request to pass a dish. Job pushed his empty plate to the side, and men down the table did likewise. The women and young people made short work of clearing the tables and disappeared into the kitchen, leaving the men alone.

Job rapped his knuckles on the table for attention. "Now, with all of us here, perhaps we can learn more about these strangers that have dropped out of the sky. Mr. Morgan, would you tell us something of your country and how you came to be here?"

There were 14 men seated at the table, ranging in apparent age from late teens to old. Bearded faces were impassive, showing no sign of interest.

"First off, I am known to my friends as Jamie. I hope that all of you here are my friends. There are so few people left in the world that there is no room for enemies. We are from the north part of Vancouver Island, which is off the coast of British Columbia. The Island is about 300 miles long, and the northern half of the island was free from the disaster that wiped out life over a large part of the globe. Most of the people on the island panicked when a disastrous earthquake was predicted and fled the island, only to die as they tried to escape over the mountains. A small group of us were left and started out to establish a new life for ourselves."

Jamie went on to outline the events that followed. He told of the establishment of their council as a governing body and their move to the Comox Valley because of the availability of farmland as they realized the need of growing their own food and otherwise becoming self-sufficient. He told of the arrival of the American Nuclear Submarine and the theory that the commander of the submarine had about the cause of the deaths. He told about the earthquakes and the volcanic eruptions and his own quest for more living people, which led him and Brian to see the cloud of smoke over the fields and discovery of the isolated community.

"Now, we are here and hope that we may become friends. It is obvious that our cultures are different, but that does not matter.

Culture and beliefs are the right of all people and not to be interfered with. In our culture, religion is the right of every person, but it is not a part of government. In the history of the world, religion and government have never blended well, so it is our belief that they be kept separate, neither to interfere with the other. If any or all of you would like to join us in our country, you will be welcome. I have given you a brief outline of our country and how we came to, as you put it, 'drop out of the sky' into your valley. Now, I would like to hear from Mr. Navolsky, or someone else, about something of your settlement here."

Job stood and leaned his hands on the table. "Thank you, Jamie, for your explanation. You may call me Job. All of us here go by first names among family and friends. We do not talk to others much. It is true that our cultures are different, but I believe that you are a good and honest man, so we may not be far apart. A small group of us, including my father, came here shortly after World War I. We wanted to establish a colony where we could continue the customs that we had grown up with in Pennsylvania. Many of our people were drifting away from the old customs. They were starting to drive trucks and accept other so-called modern conveniences that some of us thought would jeopardize our fundamental ideas. We did not break with our neighbors, though. We still maintain contact with them and arrange marriages with their young people and ours, to avoid the evils of inbreeding.

"Now, we must assume that they are no longer alive. At least we have not been able to establish any contact with them. We have been considering the feasibility of sending a delegation to check on them. But it would take many months to go that great distance and return.

"We are very self-sufficient here and can continue to live adequately off of our land. The other half of the valley is government land, so we can use it if we need to. We grow our own grains and have a mill to grind them into flour. We raise and preserve a large variety of vegetables and fruits. We have pigs, chickens and cattle to produce meat and milk and cheese. I do not think we would want to migrate to your country, wonderful as it sounds. Nevertheless, I am not averse to visiting and exchanging ideas and trading with your country. Perhaps our young people could find mates there. With our small numbers, we are in dire straits to prevent inbreeding. Trade would be of benefit to both of our communities. Perhaps we produce things here that would be of

218

value to you, and I am sure that you have things we could use, simple as our needs are.

"Now, the sun is down. Our people are accustomed to going to bed with the chickens and getting up with them, so I will excuse them. Perhaps you and I, and your associate, can continue our conversation for a while longer. Then I will show you to your room for the night."

The men all got up and left the room.

"You seem to be in absolute control of the people here," Jamie said. "Is that true?"

"It is true after a fashion, but the control is not absolute. The men all join in conferences and have a chance to say what they think. Nevertheless, the final decision is mine. I listen to their views and give them due consideration and consult with our God before I make up my mind. If I am too far out of line, they would make it known, and I would probably back down."

"Don't the women have any say?"

"The women have a say in matters of the house, otherwise, no."

"I can see where our cultures could be in a great deal of conflict. Our women are considered equal. They are entitled to vote on any subject that comes to a vote. I have a woman who serves on our council. She is also secretary to the council and serves as vice president. In my absence, she acts as president. Our women are enlightened and contribute much to our community. Also, we do not arrange marriages for our young people. There would be a war on our hands if we tried that."

"Perhaps your way of doing things has some merit. But in a small community, like ours, I do not think it would work. Our women are educated the same as men, sometimes more. They all get through the eighth grade at least and many go to high school. Nobody goes to college. We do not need higher education in our simple way of life here."

"Do you follow closely the Mennonite customs of your Pennsylvania heritage?" Jamie asked.

"No. We have diverged a great deal from our cousins. We change as we find it necessary to adapt to our own unique problems. We are isolated here, and we have little interchange with other people. Our children go to public high schools, but they spend so much time on the busses that there is little time for them to intermix with outsiders. And the other kids in school have a tendency to shun them because of their differences in dress and customs. They keep to themselves pretty much. They know that if they misbehave, they will be taken out of school. That is a big deterrent. For the most part, they are determined to get an education."

"Good for them. I am convinced that it is important for every child to get at least a rudimentary education."

Their conversation went on for another hour. Jamie told of their trip, locating fuel supplies for the aircraft, while at the same time looking for the possibilities of other human survivors. He told of their hopes of finding a larger jet turbine aircraft in Edmonton and their hopes to continue their exploration. He told of the developments in their own country, of their ability, at least for the time being, to have electricity and running water and indoor sanitary facilities. He explained their democratic style of government, in which anyone in the community had a right to be heard. He told of the diversity of their population, of the mixture of native Indians and people from many backgrounds, including two doctors, and people with many other useful skills.

"You make your country sound very enticing," Job said. "Perhaps I will come and visit it someday—with your permission."

"Come anytime you like," Jamie told him. "You, or any of your people, will always be welcome."

"But it is far away. How would we get there? It would take many days, and you are on an island. How far is it across the water?"

"We would take you in the airplane. It is less than four hours if we fly directly."

"How are you going to keep in contact with us? There is no mail service, no way of communicating."

Brian spoke up. "We can solve that problem, I think. We have radio communications with our base. We talked to them the last time after we landed this afternoon. We will contact them again in the morning before we leave."

"But how would we get a radio?"

"We have a radio expert that can set one up for you. We could bring him over here to take care of it."

"You would come all the way back here just for that? Are those little planes really safe to ride in? I hear about a lot of them crashing. I have never ridden in an airplane of any kind. We always traveled by train or bus."

"I think they are safe," Jamie told him. "You are as apt to be killed falling off of the barn or having a horse step on you. I'll take you up for a ride in the morning, if you wish."

"We will see," Job said. "In the morning, we will see."

Job showed them to their quarters. It was a room attached to an outbuilding, crude, but clean, with two beds. A small adjoining room had a washbasin and a bucket of water. Job pointed out the nearby outhouse.

"About daylight," Job said, "someone will bring you a bucket of hot water so you can wash and shave. We will have breakfast shortly after. Have a good night."

* * *

The beds were clean and reasonably comfortable and Jamie and Brian had a good night's rest. Roosters crowing served as an alarm clock, and they pried themselves from bed to find the promised bucket of hot water. With their morning chores completed, they headed out towards the dining building. Job met them at the door and led them to the same spot they had occupied the night before. The breakfast consisted of bowls of hot cereal with milk and honey and stacks of buttered toast with hot tea.

"I think I would like to accept your offer of a ride in your airplane," Job told them. "And two of my young men are eager for a ride, too, if there is room for them."

"Yes, I can take three of you up at one time. When would you like to go?"

"Right away," Job said. "We have much work to do and cannot spend too much time."

"That's fine," Jamie replied. "Brian, the back seats are filled up with gear, so I'll leave you on the ground. Let's go get the bird ready."

They headed out towards the front gate, followed by Job and two young men. Job watched them critically as they meticulously checked the plane. When everything was in order, Jamie turned to Job. "OK Sir. We are ready to go."

Job indicated the two men with him. "Jamie, this is Jacob and Joseph. Fellows, this is Mr. Jamie and Mr. Brian." The two men stepped forward and shook hands.

Jamie placed Jacob and Joseph in the middle seats and helped them secure their safety belts, then introduced Jacob to the right-hand seat in front. With himself belted in place, he started the plane and taxied up the road to the little rise that had bounced him into the air on his landing the night before. Turning around, he explained his pre-takeoff check to his passengers and started his run. The road was not as rough as he expected, and in the cool morning air they were airborne in a reasonable distance. His passengers were obviously extremely tense. Circling over the valley, he talked reassuringly to his passengers, and then headed east.

He could see that Job was relaxing and starting to pay attention to the country. Flying out over the narrow entrance to the valley, Jamie noted that the road on which they had landed continued in a straight line for several miles. A set of ranch buildings surrounded by trees occupied a corner adjoining a paved highway oriented north and south.

"That was our nearest neighbor," Job told him. "That is ten miles from our place. His land is east of that highway. I went over there recently and found several people dead. I tried to use their telephone. It rang, but no one answered. That is when I decided that the world must be dead. His stock was all dead, and there was a truck on the highway with a dead driver. I went home and told the others that we were alone in the world, and God must have saved us for a purpose. We came back, buried the people in the backyard and said a service for them. There is no one else for several miles in each direction."

Turning back to the west, Jamie flew over the home ranch and headed towards the hills visible at the head of the valley. The road appeared to peter out as it entered the foothills. Scattered timber and brush covered the rising terrain.

"That is government land," Job told him. "Nobody lives there. This road gives access to the area for hunters. Some of the sheep men rent summer grazing rights there, and sometimes there are several sheep camps in the area. We have a permit to cut fence posts and firewood there."

Jamie swung back to the west and started a letdown. "How do you like flying?" he asked.

"It is great," Jacob and Joseph said in unison. Jacob continued. "I was not nearly as scared as I thought I would be."

"It is much more satisfying than I expected," Job said. "I think I could easily get used to this mode of transport."

With no wind, Jamie made a straight-in approach. The plane bounced and shook as it rolled over some rutted areas and coasted to a halt at the gate. A crowd behind the gate watched them as they disembarked. The two younger men thanked Jamie and hurried to the gate, obviously eager to relate their experiences to their companions.

"Thank you very much, Jamie," Job said. "That was an experience that I shall not soon forget. I must admit that flying has some distinct possibilities as a mode of transportation. You are going on to Calgary now. Would you stop back by here on your way home? I would like to see you again before you leave the area."

"We will do that," Jamie replied. "I am not sure when. It could be two or three days or as early as this afternoon. As we leave, I would like to have Brian make a couple of practice landings on this road. He is not accustomed to landing on rough surfaces, and I would like him to get some experience."

"Of course," Job replied. "We will enjoy watching you. I assume he is not as experienced as you are?"

"No, but he is becoming proficient. He is the kind of person that can do anything he sets his mind to. Now, we will be on our way."

The two men shook hands, and Jacob turned to shake hands with Brian. "Please forgive me for the unfair remarks I made about black men last night. I have completely changed my attitude."

"Thank you, Sir," Brian replied. "And perhaps I have changed my mind about oddball religious sects. Maybe we have both learned something."

Turning to the plane, Brian discovered Jamie strapping himself into the right-hand seat. "You want me to fly out of here?" he asked.

"Yep, this is a perfect place for you to get some rough field experience. There is lots of room. You can make a couple of practice landings."

"OK," Brian said, as he strapped in and started the engine. "Is there anything special I should watch for?"

"No. Just be sure you stay as near the center of the road as possible. Hold the nose as high as possible. These tri-gear planes have a tendency to kick up rocks, which can chip the prop. If you hit a rough spot and bounce off the ground before you have flying speed, don't try to hold it off, let it settle back on the ground till you have good lift. Let her go!"

* * *

"There it is," Brian exclaimed. "Northern Air Transport. That's the outfit using Caravans. There's one parked alongside the hangar."

With the plane parked, they got out and walked towards the Caravan. It looked little different from their own Cessna 206, except for the elongated nose to accommodate the jet turbine engine and the extra 16 feet of wingspan. It had the same kind of spring landing gear that made the Cessna capable on rough fields, except the tread was wider. The plane was locked, so they walked around the hangar to a small, locked door with a sign above it proclaiming office. Brian went for his tool kit and soon had the door open. The office was a combination maintenance and dispatch office. They found keys for two planes, and logbooks and maintenance records for five, along with operations manuals.

The door leading to the hangar was unlocked, and they found another Caravan there. Unlatching the big hangar door, it took both of them to push it open and let some light in. Back in the office, they found the records for the two planes.

Sorting out the logbooks for the two planes, they found the one in the hangar was undergoing a 1500-hour check. The one parked outside had a hundred hours on a factory rebuilt engine.

"That looks like the one we want," Brian said. "Let's go take a look at it." Selecting the keys for the plane, he led the way outside and unlocked the cabin doors. With Jamie in the pilot's seat and Brian beside him, they started studying the controls, referring to the operating manual as they went. Brian was familiar with the engine and had worked on them. He was also reasonably familiar with all of the engine controls, and explained them in detail to Jamie. After three hours of concentration, Jamie felt he was beginning to understand the complexities of the airplane.

Finally, Brian put the manual aside and said, "Let's see if it will start. We might have to get the booster box for it after sitting here all this time. I saw one in the hangar. But these engines are easy to wind up, and normally the booster is not required. Go ahead and try it. Prop control to zero pitch. Try the starter switch."

Jamie turned the starter switch and held it. The engine started to turn, faster and faster, then, with a puff of smoke out of the ·exhaust, it fired and continued to accelerate. Jamie pulled back on the engine revolution control, and the engine settled into a high-pitched hum. The two men verbally checked the gauges until they were sure everything was in order.

"OK, let's move it out on the ramp," Brian said. Jamie gently moved the control to change the propeller blades to a positive pitch and continued until he felt the pull of the prop on the plane. He released the brakes, and the plane moved forward. Out on the main ramp, he stopped the plane and moved the prop into reverse position. The plane backed up. Back to forward and they were again moving forward. They continued to play with the plane. Jamie practiced ground control and then flew the plane. It was much like flying the smaller Cessna, except for more speed and faster climb. Stalls and steep turns were easy, and Jamie finished with several landings.

By now, it was getting late in the afternoon, and they decided to stay in Edmonton for the night. The airport seemed relatively free of the odors of death, so they decided to bunk in the hangar and make-do with their emergency foods that they had brought with them. Brian used the 206 radio to contact Stan and bring him up to date. They laid out the charts to plan for the next day, and decided that they would refuel both planes at Calgary, and then stop at the Mennonite colony. Although the Caravan was a good deal faster, Jamie decided to stay with Brian for the entire flight.

* * *

They were up early and got underway as soon as they had eaten a cold breakfast. Brian took off first, and Jamie followed as soon as Brian cleared the runway. The faster plane caught up with the 206, and Jamie established himself a hundred yards off Brian's wing and practiced his speed and engine control to maintain his position.

Leaving Calgary, Jamie called to Brian. "Can you find the ranch OK, if I go ahead?"

"No problem," Brian replied. "I have it set in the GPS system. But I won't use that unless I goof up. I want to be able to find my way without electronics, and use them only as a backup."

"Good thinking," Jamie said. "I'll keep in contact on 121.5. You can keep Stan up to date on our actions."

Forty minutes later, Jamie was touching down at the ranch. The big plane handled the rough road as well as the smaller Cessna. A large delegation was behind the gate to meet him. Job came through the gate and strode across the road to shake hands.

"You have a different plane? Where is your partner?" There was concern in Job's voice.

"He will be here in a few minutes," Jamie told him. "He is flying the plane we had here yesterday. We had hoped to find this plane in Edmonton, and we did. We are taking it back to New Island to add to our fleet. It is larger and faster and will carry a much larger load."

"That is interesting," Job said. "We had a meeting last night with our entire group participating. I tried to explain what all you had told me, but I think I was inadequate. I agreed to another full meeting when you returned, if you would consent. They heard the plane come in, so they will be gathering in the dining hall now. Will you talk to all of us and answer questions?"

"I'll be glad to. Here comes Brian now."

A minute later, Brian had parked alongside the Caravan. Jamie told him of the request for a meeting, and they followed Job to the meeting room. The chairs had been rearranged in several rows to face one table at which Job seated Jamie and Brian on either side of his own chair. When the crowd was settled down, he stood and introduced Jamie and Brian.

"Now the meeting is yours, Jamie," he said as he sat back in his chair.

Jamie stood and looked at the group. Most members of the colony were in the room.

"Hello, friends," Jamie began. "I hope that I may address you as friends. There are so few people in the world now that it is essential for all of us to be friends. We must consider all our equals and treat all the same."

Jamie went on to repeat, essentially, the speech he had made to the men on their first night. He placed more emphasis on equality of women and of dark skinned or different looking races.

In conclusion, he said, "Any of you, male or female, are welcome to come to our country for a visit, or as permanent residents. We will furnish transportation. It is only about four hours by airplane. Now, I would like you to hear a few words from my companion. Brian is a brilliant machinist and aircraft mechanic. He came to us from the United States Submarine Denver, where he was an officer. Brian!"

Brian stood and faced the crowd. "I'm not used to speaking to a group. But I would like to tell you about one thing. What President Jamie has told you about equality in New Island is true. I have suffered, as a black man, a good deal of discrimination. But I was accepted into the Navy as equal to all others and attained the rank of Lieutenant. I was proud of that. When Jamie invited what was left of our crew to join the group, who was attempting to start a new life in New Island, I was happy to accept; I am treated the same as if my skin was white. And women have absolute equality with men. They vote, and they are listened to if they wish to say something. I think you people here could benefit from some equality. I am sorry to be critical, but after the treatment I suffered when I was growing up, I can't help it. Please excuse me."

Job stood again. "I guess that we have been criticized thoroughly. I have to admit we probably deserve it. It is hard to change the beliefs that have been ingrained in us from the time we were born, but perhaps it is time to entertain the possibilities of change and start working toward it. I felt a sense of rebellion in many of you during last night's meeting. But this change cannot come all at once. We will have to work at it over a time.

"I promised last night that I would make a visit to New Island, and that, if President Jamie permits, I would take one or more with me. I will ask that he bring us back here within a week. So, Jamie, how many can you accommodate, now that you have two planes?"

"We can take eight passengers, plus baggage, in the larger plane. I would use that plane to bring you back here within a week, weather permitting. I would like to have at least one or two women included."

"I think I want to keep the group down to about four or five. I promised the two young fellows who rode with you yesterday that they would get first chance. Now, are there any of the ladies that would like to go?"

A lithesome looking girl in a front seat bounced to her feet. "Sir Job, I would love to go. I am 18 years old, and I am ready for a change. Please include me."

"What do your parents say?" Job asked.

"I think they will permit it. After all, I am 18 and not married."

A lady in the back stood. "As her mother, I give my permission for her to go. Her father is working and is not here, but he will not object."

"Is there perhaps another lady that would like to go?" Job asked.

"I would like to go." A tall buxom woman that appeared middle-aged stood. "My husband died last year, and I have no one to be obligated to."

"All right, we will take you. I think that makes enough for this trip. Jamie, the two ladies are Irene and Josephine. You met Jacob and Joseph before. How soon do you want to leave?"

"As soon as possible. We would like to get home early. Pack only some extra clothing for a week and what personal things you want. If you forget something, we can find it for you there."

"Would some of the ladies pack individual lunches for seven people?" Job requested. "We might want something to eat on the way."

Jamie and Brian made their way back to the planes, discussing the flight as they went.

"I believe that I have plenty of fuel to go nonstop home," Brian said. "It can't be more than four hours from Calgary."

"Sounds good to me. I'll stay with you. We can divert to Vancouver if it looks like you might run low. How about taking the young lady with you?"

"Sure, that's OK by me," Brian agreed.

The planes were inspected and ready to go by the time their passengers arrived. They were all in typical Mennonite dress, the women in plain mid-calf dresses with scarves over their heads and the men in black hats, trousers and jackets. Each carried a bag of some sort and well-used paper bags with lunches for all.

Jamie did not ask who would like to ride where. He assigned Irene to ride with Brian. He helped her board the passenger seat of the 206 and get her safety harness hooked up properly, then told Brian to be on his way. He placed Job in the copilot's seat of the Caravan, got the other passengers installed in their seats and strapped in. The caravan had eight passenger seats, four on each side of a center aisle.

* * *

Brian looked at the girl beside him as he swung the plane into position and prepared for takeoff. Her teeth were clenched, and her hands gripped the seat belt so hard that the knuckles shown white. She's scared to death, he told himself.

"Relax," Brian said. "Everything is going to be OK. We will bounce around some on this rough road, as we must get to 60 miles an hour to take off. Don't worry, just relax."

Irene's eyes were squinted shut. Cautiously, she opened them, then hastily shut them again as she saw the ground receding below her. She felt the engine slow as Brian retarded power to climb setting. Again, she opened her eyes and peeked out the side window. They were unbelievably high in the air.

"How high up are we going to go?" Irene asked.

"Much higher," Brian responded. "The higher we are the safer we are. Just relax and enjoy the view. It keeps getting better the farther west we go. This airplane is safe, and I've been well trained in operating it. Please relax."

Brian didn't tell her that she was the first passenger he had ever taken up. He glanced across at his passenger and saw Jamie pull alongside and slow to keep pace. Josephine was waving from one of the windows.

"Look out to the right," Brian requested. "Josephine is waving at you."

Irene turned her head, and cautiously raised her hand to wave back. Visibly, she began to relax.

Brian busied himself with the radio, contacting Stan with an estimated time of arrival. He set his ETA at 2:10 PM; pretending to be busy with his charts and flying the airplane, he stole covert glances at his passenger. She was small, possibly five feet two inches and maybe 110 pounds. It was hard to tell what was under the plain shapeless dress of heavy, coarse material that she wore. He wondered if it was homespun from wool raised on the ranch. The only part of her that was visible was her face and hands. Her face showed possibilities of beauty. A short, slightly upturned nose and a broad mouth highlighted her features. Her skin was clear and unblemished, and her large brown eyes had an interesting sparkle. The single lock of hair that had escaped from under the scarf that covered her head was a brown to match her eyes. Her hands were long and slender but showed signs of abuse. The nails were short and broken, and there appeared to be calluses on her fingers. He wondered what he could talk to her about.

"You said in the meeting that you were 18 years old," Brian said. "I sort of gathered that you would like to get away from the colony. Is that true?"

"Yes," she answered hesitantly. "My dad was trying to arrange a marriage for me with the people back east. I did not want to marry some man I had never seen before, but he said I had to. Then we could not contact them anymore, and he and Job tried to figure out whom I could marry within the colony. There was no one except for an older man that had lost his wife. I did not like him. He was old and rough and not very clean."

"Would your dad force you to marry a man like that when you didn't want to?"

"My dad said that it was my duty to do as he told me. I must follow his orders, or the orders of Job."

"I think you should stay in New Island," Brian said. "There are a number of young men there that don't have wives."

Irene's face reddened in a blush, and she looked down to hide her eyes. "I do not think that Job would let me stay. He does not like to have people leave his colony unless they go to another Mennonite group."

"Well, maybe we could change his mind. I think you would be a good addition to our country, and I'll bet that you can attract a lot of attention from the young men, if you could get into some better looking clothes. I think you might be beautiful if you had the chance. I'll bet Mary Jorgenson would help you with some fixing up, and Jamie's daughter, Kelly, would like to help. She's only ten years old, but you can't believe how smart she is."

My God, Brian thought, I'm prattling along here like some teenage Romeo.

Irene looked closely at the face beside her. His face was nice, she reflected, even though it was black. His features were uniform, the nose a little broad and the lips full. He was pleasant and obviously extremely capable. She decided that she would like to know him better.

"You are being nice to me," she said. "I am a complete stranger from a different culture than you are accustomed to. There is no reason for you to be so nice."

"That's reason enough," Brian replied. "We all have to live together in this world, and if we meet people that are different, it is important to be nice to them and make them feel a part of our world. Look below, we are crossing over the Rocky Mountains;

they are the Continental Divide. From here on, all the rivers we will see flow into the Pacific. Some of them take a long ways around to get there, but they eventually become a part of the western ocean."

Brian took time out to report to Stan and checked with Jamie. Jamie requested him to contact Stan again and have him call Mary to make arrangements for housing their guests. Jamie had a spare room with twin beds; he would keep the two women. Stan called back in a short time. Mary would take the two young men, and Joe Gardner would host Job. They would be at the airport to meet them.

Irene was beginning to relax and enjoy the panorama of mountains and valleys that they were flying over. The air was crystal clear, a real plus for a first flight, with only an occasional bump as they passed over the high mountains. Their conversation became more relaxed as they got used to each other. Irene's formal English, so precise with none of the contractions that he was accustomed to using, fascinated Brian. The time went by rapidly, and they had their first glimpse of salt water.

"Brian, how is your fuel supply?" Jamie was on the radio.

"We are in good shape," Brian replied.

"OK," Jamie replied. "I'm going on ahead. I'll see you on the ground."

"Roger," Brian replied. "I won't be too far behind you."

He watched as Jamie went to full cruise power and started his letdown. Brian trimmed his own plane for power descent and watched as the bigger plane pulled ahead.

"What is happening?" Irene asked.

"Jamie's plane is faster," Brian explained, "and we are letting down for home base. He has been flying his bird slower to keep us company, but now he can get on the ground and out of the way in time for us to land. We can gain some speed by starting our descent a long way back."

Brian made a long straight-in approach and a faultless landing. He taxied up to the hangar to find a crowd around the Caravan, admiring the new plane. Introductions were over, and Mary was getting Jacob and Joseph herded to her car. Bob Elder was talking to Job and getting ready to go.

Jamie spoke to Irene. "You and Josephine are going to stay with me. I have a spare room with twin beds. I hope you do not mind sharing."

"Not at all," Josephine said. "At home, single women have to share a dormitory with several others."

Brian walked with them to the car. "Irene, I will be seeing you soon, I hope."

"I hope so too," Irene said, a blush coloring her face.

Chapter 35

Jamie pulled the car into the parking place alongside the house to be greeted exuberantly by Dawg, who came bounding off the front porch. Jamie opened the door, and Dawg waited for the pat on the head and the ear scratch that he knew were coming. He accompanied Jamie around the car, where Jamie opened the door for Josephine. Irene, in the back seat, opened her own door and got out. Dawg was obviously surprised by the strangers and backed up to look the situation over, then approached Irene with his tail wagging.

"Oh, what a beautiful dog," Irene exclaimed as she patted Dawg on the head. Dawg rubbed his head against her thigh in approval.

It's amazing, Jamie thought, how Dawg immediately recognized and responded instantly to someone who liked dogs.

"Come along inside," Jamie said, retrieving their bags from the trunk and leading the way through the kitchen door, "and I'll show you to your quarters. My daughter, Kelly, will be home from school shortly."

The two women stared in wonder at the luxury of the home, unconsciously comparing it with their own austere quarters.

"This is your bedroom," Jamie said. "And your bathroom is here. You will have to share it with Kelly. She has a tendency to spend a lot of time in the bathroom, so stand up for your rights. Please make yourselves at home. My house is your house while you are here. If you would like to have a shower and freshen up a bit, please go ahead. There is plenty of hot water, so you don't have to conserve. There are towels in that cabinet. Please help yourselves." Jamie turned and left the room.

The two women stood looking at each other in consternation.

"I did not know that people actually lived in houses like this," Irene exclaimed. "I have seen pictures of such places in magazines, but I did not know that ordinary people lived in them. I thought that it was only very rich people."

"Maybe he is very rich," Josephine said. "But I doubt it. I think that this is the way most people live here."

"I cannot believe it," Irene replied, "but it must be true. And the people are so friendly and nice. They do not seem to consider us different or strange. The young man that flew the plane was unbelievably nice. I sure would like to try out that shower. Do you think we should?"

"Mr. Jamie said to. Let us do it. You can go first, if you want to."

"Help me figure out how to make it work," Irene requested.

"I think I can figure it out. Let us see."

Josephine worked with the shower controls until she understood them. "This knob turns on the hot water and this one the cold. You have to adjust it where you want it, then get in, slide the door closed, then pull up on that button to start the water through the shower. And I have seen toilets like this. You just turn that knob after you use it."

"Yes, we had toilets like that in the school, but I never knew that people had them in their homes."

"I think that we both have a lot to learn," Josephine said. "Now go ahead and take your shower. That bottle has shampoo for your hair. Go ahead and get your hair really clean. I will go out, sit on that wonderful front porch, and look at the valley."

Josephine went to the big living room and continued out the open front door to the porch. Jamie was sitting there, with a cold beer on a table at his elbow.

Turning, as he heard Josephine approach, Jamie indicated the chair on the other side of the table. "Please join me," he requested. "Could I get you something to drink? I presume that you don't use alcoholic beverages, but we have soft drinks."

"Just water would be very good," Josephine replied.

Jamie came back in a minute and set a tall glass of water on the table beside her. The water had ice cubes floating in it.

"Thank you, Sir Jamie," Josephine said. "I am not used to having ice water served to me. And to be served by a man is different than I am accustomed to."

"You are my guest," Jamie replied. "And I would like you to drop the 'Sir' business. I am just plain Jamie."

"But as leader of your country, are you not entitled to the title of Sir? We always address our leader as Sir."

"I don't think leadership should be provided any special treatment. I just happen to have some capabilities in that respect, but that shouldn't grant me any special privileges. We have many people who have special abilities, and they are treated equally. We all try to look after each other the best we can, and use any special capabilities of any person for the good of all. That person putting forth his special capabilities should earn respect from the rest of us, but no special consideration. Everyone contributes what he or she can in his or her own way."

Josephine sat for several minutes, reviewing in her mind what Jamie had just told her.

"It is almost beyond my comprehension. I have been taught that we must call our leader Sir, and obey his every wish. No one ever disobeys him. He is like a king, except that he does not take more than his share of the goods we produce. At least, I do not believe he does. Perhaps. I am not very sure. We do not have much personal life. He has to approve a marriage, and in most cases, he arranges marriages without much consultation with the ones getting married. He tells us whether or not we can have babies and where we will work. He is completely in charge of our lives. He says that that is God's will."

"I don't think that the people here would put up with a God that exercised that kind of control. I know that I wouldn't."

"You said when you talked to us this morning that women are treated with full equality. Is that really true?"

"Yes, it is," Jamie told her. "My vice president and secretary to the council is a woman. She lost her husband to cancer a year before disaster struck us. When we were forming our new leadership group, I asked her to serve as secretary. As such, she is a member of the council and has the same vote as other members. Then recognizing her capabilities and realizing that there should be some one to take my place if I were unavailable for any reason, I proposed to the council that she be elected as vice president. She was approved by the council and then by the entire population. Since then, she has proven her worth. There are many other women here who are very capable, including my daughter, Kelly. She is only ten, but has all of the capabilities of a woman of 15. You will meet her soon."

"All of this is very hard for me to assimilate. Arrangements were made for me to marry my husband when I was 13. He was 40 years old, more than three times my age. We had little in common besides belonging to the Mennonite community. I had the equivalent of an eighth-grade education, taught to me by my mother. I was never able to go to high school; however, my mother taught me as much as she could when we could find time to be together. I was never able to become pregnant, and my husband put all of the blame on me. That was an excuse to make me work harder at the many jobs necessary to keep the colony going. He died a year ago, and I was unable to grieve very much. There was no other man there suitable to be my husband. Since then, I have been trying to find a way to leave the colony. Do you think it is possible for me to stay here?"

"I am sure the New Island people would welcome you to our community. I would like to have you stay, but it would be up to the council to decide. There may be a problem if Job objects strongly. I hope he doesn't. But here comes Irene. We will talk more later."

Irene came running through the door, her waist length brown hair flying behind her. "Oh, Sir Jamie, it was wond..."

Josephine was staring at her aghast. "Your hair! You have not covered your head."

"My hair is still wet, and I thought it would dry faster if..."

Jamie interrupted. "Josephine, you are in New Island now. Irene, you do not have to cover your hair here. Besides, it is much too beautiful to cover up. Please be comfortable the way you are."

"Josephine," Irene said, "I knew it was much different here than at home. Brian told me much about life here while we were flying over. You better go and take a shower now. It is wonderful. I feel so clean. I want to stay here and always be able to feel this way."

"All right, child," Josephine replied. "I guess we have a lot to learn in this wonderful new country. I have told Jamie that I would like to stay, also. I hope that we both can. Now I will go and try that shower."

* * *

Irene was enthralled with the view. Jamie explained as much as he could about the small farms that crowded the valley. It was green everywhere, with patches of woodlands mixed in with farms. There were trees and shrubbery around every farmstead and flowers were visible. "I have never seen a place so beautiful. But then I have never seen any place other than Little River Valley, where we live. Does it get cold with lots of snow in the wintertime?"

"Not very cold," Jamie explained. "Sometimes it snows, and it freezes a little, but nothing like the country you are from. We have a very mild climate here."

A car stopped at the entrance to the property, and Kelly piled out, a bundle in her arms, and come running up the driveway. She abandoned her package on the steps and threw herself at Jamie.

"Jamie, I'm so glad to see you home. I don't like it when you are gone for so long."

"Hey, I was only gone two nights."

"Well, it seemed a lot longer."

Suddenly, Kelly became aware of the girl seated across the table from Jamie.

"Kelly, this is our guest. Please meet Irene. She will be with us for a few days or a week."

Kelly stared at the girl for a minute. "Oh, what beautiful hair," she exclaimed. "I am glad to meet you. I hope you enjoy your stay with us. Where did you get those clothes? They look like they came from a long time ago."

"Kelly!" Jamie stated. "It is not courteous to criticize people's clothes. That is all that was available where she came from."

"I'm sorry, Irene," Kelly was contrite. "But they don't look very good. We will have to get you some decent clothes as soon as possible. Jamie, would you take us to the Zeller's store?"

"I can understand your disapproval, Kelly," Irene interjected. "But all women wear these kinds of dresses all the time at home. We wear cloths over our heads and tied under our chins. I would never be allowed to come outside with my head uncovered."

"How horrible," Kelly exclaimed. "I'm glad I don't live there. Jamie, what are we going to have for dinner? I brought some fresh bread home from Pat's."

"I put a roast in the oven." Jamie told her. "And there are fresh carrots and lettuce in the garden. I think we'll be OK."

"All right," Kelly replied. "It's early yet. Let's go get Irene some clothes. Give me a minute to freshen up." Kelly started for the door.

"Hold on," Jaime demanded. "Your bathroom is in use. Josephine, our other guest, is taking a shower. You can use my bathroom. By the time you are ready, she will probably be ready too and then both women can go."

Josephine returned to the porch, her damp hair uncovered and hanging to her waist. It was a darker brown than Irene's and shaded with gray. She is an attractive woman, Jamie thought, and certainly looks much better without that drab head covering. Her face showed the ravages of extensive exposure to the weather, but her features were regular with high cheekbones and a wide mouth.

Kelly reappeared, and Jamie introduced her to Josephine. "We're going to get some new clothes for you two," Kelly told her. "We're going right now, if you are ready."

"But I have to get my hair dried and my head covered before I can go out."

"Go like you are," Kelly ordered. "You look wonderful with your hair down. Besides, there is no one in the store to see you. Let's go, Jamie. I'll get the lantern."

Jamie explained to the two women that the store was abandoned and unlighted. The two younger women got in the back seat with Dawg between them, and Josephine rode in front. Jamie parked the car in front of the huge empty store, explained that people could shop at the store without paying, as long as merchandise lasted.

"Dawg and I will stay here while you ladies do your shopping," Jamie told them. "Have fun."

Kelly led the women into the store, switching on the battery-powered fluorescent lantern. She knew her way to the women's clothing department. "What do you want?" she asked. "Pants or dresses or skirts and blouses?"

"Do grown women wear pants?" Josephine asked. "I saw a lady at the airport that was wearing pants, and I could not believe it."

"Yes, we all do." Kelly explained. "It's much more comfortable if you are active and outdoors a lot."

"I think we should stay with skirts," Josephine said.

"I guess we should," Irene agreed, starting to sort through a rack of skirts. "How do we know what size?"

"Take off that thing you are wearing," Kelly instructed, "and we'll figure out your size and you can try them on."

"Take it off right here?" Irene asked. "Right here in public?"

"Sure," Kelly told her. "There's no one here but us."

Reluctantly, Irene pulled the shapeless dress over her head and dropped it on the floor.

Kelly moved the light to see. "My God!" she exclaimed. "Is that what you wear for underclothes?"

"Yes," Irene responded. "This is all we ever have."

The girl was dressed in a tight fitting knit undergarment that went to mid-thigh, buttoned up the front and had a buttoned flap on the back for toilet convenience. It extended to the base of the neck and was sleeved to the upper mid-arm.

"Get that thing off," Kelly commanded.

"But, but…"

"No buts about it. Take it off." Kelly was emphatic.

Reluctantly, Irene unbuttoned the garment and slid it to the floor.

"That's better," Kelly exclaimed. "You are beautiful. Get those shoes and socks off. Here are the panties, over here. You're not much bigger than I am. This size should fit. Here, try it on."

Irene stepped into the garment and pulled it in place.

"Perfect," Kelly approved. "Here are six pair, three pink and three white. Now let's see about brassieres." Sorting through the rack, she selected one for trial. "Nope, it's too small, here try this one." She helped Irene get the garment on, hooking the fasteners in the back. "How does that feel? Is it comfortable?"

"It feels wonderful," Irene exclaimed. "But it makes my breasts stand out."

"That's what it's supposed to do," Kelly told her.

"But we were always told to keep our breasts flattened out as much as possible. It was immoral to let them be seen."

"How do you expect to get a man that way? Men like to see them. Show them off, if you have something to show, and you have." She selected more brassieres and led the way back to the skirts.

Josephine stared at Irene in amazement, but held her tongue.

A light blue skirt just hitting the knees and a matching knit top that fit loosely and did not emphasize her breasts, but still let it be known that they existed, was the first selection. Two other outfits followed, then shoes. Kelly picked out a pair of open-toed sandals, then a pair of oxfords and several pairs of short socks.

Then Kelly went through the same routine with Josephine. She had to talk a bit to get Josephine to accept the underwear, but finally succeeded. Josephine's first pick for outerwear was a mid-calf denim skirt with a matching tuck-in shirt. Josephine knew what pantyhose were and took several pair. She refused the open-toed sandals but selected two pair of oxfords.

With the selections, plus old clothes and footwear bagged up, Kelly led the way back to the car to display the transformation of the two women. Jamie was amazed at the difference proper clothes could make and lavished his praise on Kelly and her protégés.

* * *

Joseph and Jacob were astounded at the female that was shepherding them to a car. They had never seen anything to compare. Taller than either man, she was very slender with long jean-clad legs, a covering of very short blond hair on her head and an angular face that was on the verge of being beautiful. They were not accustomed to seeing women in pants and without scarves over their heads.

In turn, Mary had reservations about the two bearded men with black broad brimmed hats and coarse clothing. They were obviously young. They had been introduced by their first names only. She wondered what nationality they were and assumed that they were of some kind of religious sect that mandated their manner of dress. She had noted that the women wore head coverings and long dresses.

There was complete silence in the car as Mary drove the few miles home. On arrival, she was delighted to see that Dave was home. She would leave Dave to cope with the strangers. She had called him on the cell phone to tell him that they were coming to stay for a few days. Dave met them on the front porch, and she introduced him to the two men. She didn't know which one was which, so she just said Joseph and Jacob and decided to let Dave sort it out.

Dave escorted the two into the house and figured out which one was which, although he had a hard time keeping track. They were very similar in appearance, and he learned that they were first cousins. He asked if they would like a drink, and they accepted water. He brought each of them a glass of ice water.

"Water with ice," Joseph said. "We never have that at home. We do not have any ice."

Jacob put in, "If we had ice, we would not be allowed to use it in water. That would be unnatural. The only ice we see is in the winter, and then there is too much of it."

"I've been places," Dave said, "where they didn't have refrigeration, so they put up ice in the winter in special buildings, insulated with sawdust. It would last all summer."

"No, we would not do that. It would be against the scripture that says we may not go against nature."

"What do you do about keeping food for winter?" Dave asked. "You must have some way of preserving food."

"Yes, that is different," Jacob said. "We are allowed to put food in jars and cook it, or dry food. In the wintertime, we freeze meat outdoors. That is permitted."

"Does the Bible tell you all of these things?" Dave asked.

"According to Sir Job, it does. He keeps the good book and reads sections of it to us every Sunday, then tells us what it means. He does not allow us to read it ourselves."

"Sir Job. Is that the older stern looking man that came with you?"

"Yes Sir," Joseph said. "Sir Job is our leader, and we must do what he says. We were very surprised that he let us come. I think he expected that we might find wives here. You see, there are no women in our colony that are not related to us. Before the world came to an end, he would have arranged marriages for us with our kind in Pennsylvania."

"I don't think he will have much luck here. We do not arrange marriages. If you want wives here, you will have to ask them for yourselves. I doubt that any woman here would leave our freedom to live in a religious cult of some kind. We have too many comforts here and, besides, there is a shortage of women. The only way you could find a wife here is to stay here, adapt to our ways, and court the girl of your choice."

"But we do not know the ways here," Jacob said. "And Sir Job promised that we would be back within one week."

The conversation went on for an hour, as Dave probed for answers about the Mennonite colony at Little River. He was astounded at what he learned. It seemed impossible that in modern times, there could be a group of people so far behind the times. Mary occasionally stood in the door for a while, listening to the conversation and then went about her household chores. Dave finally took the two men out to show them the farm, and an hour later came back to the house.

"Dave," Mary greeted him, "I have not had time to gather the eggs. And I think that you should milk the cows before dinner. I'll have dinner ready soon."

"Do you mean that men gather eggs and milk cows?" Joseph asked. "That is always women's work at Little River."

"I think you people are at least a hundred years behind the times," Dave told them. "In the modern world, at least in New Island, there is no distinction between women's work and men's work. There are some physical differences, but that is all. We

241

share in everything, and if you want to be a part of this country, it would be worthwhile for you to change your thinking as fast as possible."

With the eggs gathered and the two cows milked, it was time for dinner. Dave showed the men to the bedroom they would share, and the adjoining bath where they could wash up before dinner.

* * *

Joe Gardner looked at the bearded man seated beside him in the pickup. That beard must be very uncomfortable, he thought. It would be a job just washing it every day. I wonder if he does wash it every day. Probably when he takes a shower. Does he take a shower every day? I think that I smell evidence to indicate he may not bathe regularly.

"Tell me, Sir," Dave requested, "what kind of community do you have in Alberta?"

"There are 48 of us in the valley," Job replied. "We all live in one compound and share in the work and the proceeds of the work. We all worship God, and we have prayer meetings almost every evening. We are almost fully self-sustaining. We are able to sell enough grain and other farm products to get the things that we cannot produce from our land. Most of these things we order from our brethren Mennonites in Pennsylvania. That is the way it was until the world came to an end. Since then, we have had no contact with them. Now, we will have to learn to do without the things we bought from outside."

"I understand that you are the leader of your group?"

"Yes, God selected me to be the leader and to give directions to the others who are not as strong, so that we can live up to the expectations of God."

"So what made you decide to come here with Jamie for a visit?"

"He offered the opportunity, and after a long meeting with my followers and much prayer, God suggested that I come here with Jamie and see what it was like. Perhaps we can establish trade relations to benefit all of us. And all of our people are so closely related that we cannot find mates for our young people. We used to arrange marriages with our eastern brethren, but now that seems impossible."

Bob pulled the pickup to a stop in front of his house. Ten-year-old Susie come bouncing out of the house to greet him, but was somewhat taken aback at seeing the bearded stranger getting out of the car. Bob introduced his daughter to Job, and the youngster curtsied politely.

"Where did you come from?" Susie asked. "I have never seen a man with a beard as big as you have."

"All of the men where I came from wear beards. I am from a small place in Alberta, and Sir Jamie brought me here in his airplane."

"Why do you call him Sir Jamie? Nobody here calls him that. We just call him Jamie, or maybe Mr. Jamie."

"Sir is a mater of respect when one is the leader of their country. Everyone calls me Sir because I am their leader. That is required."

"That is a funny requirement," Susie said. "Are you the king of your country?"

"Some people call me that, but my real title is Sir Job."

"Sir Job. Job. That sounds like a name out of the Bible."

"Yes. Job is a biblical name. Many of our people have names that originated in the good book."

"OK, young lady," Bob interceded. "You have asked enough questions. It is not very courteous to ask questions that way. I'm sure Sir Job will tell us all about his country in good time. Let's go in the house and introduce your mother to our guest."

Susie skipped up the path ahead of them and held the door open for them. "Mom, come and meet Sir Job. He is a stranger that Jamie brought from far away, and he is king of his country."

Ronda came into the room, looking a little astonished at the visitor. She recovered her poise quickly and advanced to shake hands. "Welcome to our land. I hope you enjoy our little country. We don't have a king here, just an elected president."

"Thank you for your welcome," Job said. "I am not really a king, but sometimes my followers call me king. But they are only required to call me Sir, which is the title required by God for the leader of a group such as ours."

Ronda was a little taken aback by Job's response. "How large a country are you king of?" she asked.

"There are 48 of us now, but a few years ago there were 75. We hope to build the population back to its original size, or larger."

"Please forgive me," Ronda said. "I am not being very courteous. Please be seated. Would you like a cold drink? We have cold beer in the refrigerator."

"No, lady," Job responded. "Our people are not allowed to use alcoholic beverages. A glass of water would be appreciated, though."

"We have cold lemonade," Susie interjected. "It is non-alcoholic. Even us kids are allowed to drink lemonade."

Job hesitated, started to speak, and then appeared to change his mind. "No, the water will be just fine," he insisted.

Susie handed him the tall glass of ice water. Job accepted it, hesitating a minute before taking a sip of it.

"We do not enjoy ice water in our country. We do not have ice available, and God would frown on it. It is not natural to have ice in the summertime. But I am sure God will understand if I drink it under these circumstances."

Bob and Susie both looked at him in surprise. They both started to speak and then held it back for fear of saying the wrong thing.

Chapter 36

Jamie did not know what to do with his guests while Kelly was in school Friday. Discussing it with Kelly, the girl provided the perfect suggestion. Why not take the two women to the school for a day? It would give them a chance to see something of New Island's education system and get a better understanding of New Island culture. Jamie called a couple of the teachers, and they thought it was a good idea. Kelly's teacher insisted that the younger girl attend her class, and the other teacher agreed to have Josephine visit for the day. She would try to specialize for the day on different cultures and get Josephine to talk to the students about her life in Little River. The two women were at first reluctant, but finally agreed that it would be a good way for them to get a better view of the people of New Island. However, they both insisted that they be permitted to wear the dowdy clothes that they arrived in.

"If we are going to talk about the culture of the place we came from," Josephine insisted, "we must portray ourselves as we are in our home land; we must wear the clothes that we would be wearing there."

Jamie had to agree with her logic and overrule Kelly in her desire to make the women more presentable. She did get her way, though, in Irene's hairstyle. She braided the long locks into two braids, which she coiled around Irene's head and pinned in place, instead of the bun on the back of the head that she ordinarily wore. She would still wear the scarf over her head.

Kelly led the way into the school and to her room well before the nine o'clock starting time. Jamie introduced the two to Mrs. Darwood, an ebullient plumpish woman with short gray hair, dressed in a simple sheath that reached her knees. Mrs. Darwood hugged Irene, much to her embarrassment, and welcomed her as a guest of the class for the day.

Mrs. Darwood had placed extra chairs at her desk. "Kelly, I am going to ask you to sit in the chair to my left, and Irene will take the chair on my right. I am going to have you two share in teaching for the day."

In the next classroom, Jamie introduced Josephine to Mrs. Hogan, a tall dour looking woman that was much less forbidding than she appeared. Mrs. Hogan asked Josephine to share her desk for the day. The two teachers had obviously agreed on the method of handling their guests.

* * *

The bell rang, signaling time for nine o'clock classes to begin, with Mrs. Darwood behind her desk. The children quieted down immediately, recognizing that something out of the usual was in store for them, with Kelly on one side of their teacher and a strange looking woman on the other side.

"Children," Mrs. Darwood started, "I am not going to call role today. I can see that there are no empty seats, so everyone is here. We have a special treat for you today. You remember that last week we were discussing ethnic groups, minorities and various religions and how necessary it is in our community to in no way discriminate against any of them. Our President Jamie emphasizes in almost every public meeting how important it is that we consider everyone equal, regardless of skin color, ethnic background or religious beliefs.

"Today, we have a special guest. Jamie and Brian brought her, along with some others, from a group of people that live in an isolated spot in Alberta. This is a religious minority group that to us may seem to have some strange religious beliefs and customs. Regardless of how different they may seem, they are entitled to be treated with the same courtesy and respect that we would extend to any other guest. Kelly, would you please introduce our guest?"

Kelly stood. She was accustomed to speaking before the class, was at ease and spoke like an adult. "We really have a very special guest. Jamie has been flying all over looking for people that are still alive after the world disaster. He found a remote religious settlement in Alberta and brought five of the people back here for a visit. I would like to introduce one of them. Please welcome Irene from Little River Valley."

Irene stood to a round of applause and whistles. "I do not know what to say," she stammered. "I have never appeared before a group of people so large, especially when they are strangers. I am very scared."

"Don't be," shouted a boy from the back of the room. "We won't eat you."

"I am sure you will not eat me. I would not be very good eating. But, if you would like me to, I will tell you what I can about Little River Valley and the community that I am from.

246

However, I do not know how to start, so I will answer questions if I am able."

"Miss Irene," a girl from the front row asked, "how come you wear funny looking clothes and have a scarf over your head?"

"I somehow knew that that would be one of the first questions. According to Sir Job, our leader, this has been the accepted dress for all women for hundreds of years. God says that women must dress modestly, and show as little as possible of their skin. At one time, we were required to wear veils to cover our faces, but that custom was relaxed a long time ago. The clothes we wear are the ones ordained by God. They are required to be simple, with no fancy materials or decorations."

"What church do you belong to, Miss Irene?" another girl asked.

"We belong to the Mennonite religion, which is much like the Amish, or the Huterite religions. In our community, we do not have a church but worship in our community dining hall."

"Do you have a preacher?"

"No. Sir Job, our leader, acts as a preacher and reads scriptures to us regularly."

"Do men wear funny clothes, too?" a boy asked from the rear.

"I suppose you would call them funny clothes. The men wear mostly black pants and jackets and broad-brimmed black hats. They never cut their hair but wear it in braids down their backs. They all have full beards. They do shave off their mustaches. Our religion says that we should never cut our hair."

"What is Little River Valley like and where is it?" a boy asked.

"Little River Valley is about two miles wide and ten miles long. It is in the foothills of the Rocky Mountains and is about 80 miles west of Lethbridge and 35 miles south west of Claresholm. Because we have no cars or trucks, it takes a long day with a team and wagon to get to Claresholm."

"How come you don't have cars or trucks?"

"Our leader says that it is against the will of God to have any mechanical things, other than wagons or buggies. We do not have electricity, but use candles and coal oil lamps for light."

"Do you have schools?"

"We have a one-room school in our community which goes to the eighth grade. Most children finish schooling at that time. Some of us were able to go to high school in Claresholm. We had

247

to ride a bus for more than an hour to get there. In the wintertime, the roads were snowed in, and the bus could not get to our community, so we did not get much high school. Sir Job said it was a waste of time, anyway, because we did not need more education for our way of life."

"You talk kind of funny," a boy piped out. "You never say *don't* and *it's* and other words like that."

Mrs. Darwood interrupted. "This young lady speaks the most perfect English I have ever heard. Don't and it's are contractions, combining two words into one. She has been taught to use the formal form of English rather than the informal form that we have grown accustomed to. I will bet that she has never said 'I don't got' or 'I've got.' I would love it if all of you would speak as she does. I have been lax about the way I speak, but I am resolved, as of this minute, to emulate Irene and speak the English language as it should be spoken. Maybe some of it will wear off on you people."

Recess time arrived, and the class was dismissed for a 15-minute break. Kelly escorted Irene to the rest rooms, where she discovered the privacy afforded by the toilet stalls. She reveled in the comfort of and convenience of the soft panties that she wore instead of the crude underwear that she was accustomed to wear. When the two women decided to wear their conventional clothing for the day, Irene was unable to convince herself to give up her new underthings. No one will know the difference unless I show them, she reasoned.

The rest of the morning went the same way, with the students seeming to have an inexhaustible reserve of questions, indicating their extreme interest in this strange girl from over the mountains and the conditions under which she lived. Irene entranced the students, and their liking for her increased by the minute.

As noon approached, Mrs. Darwood announced that they would return to their regular studies for the rest of the day, and thanked Irene for her patience in answering questions for the entire morning.

* * *

Dave went out to milk the cows while Mary prepared breakfast. He was frustrated with his visitors. The evening had not gone as well as he would have liked. The two men were so far removed from the realities of life, as he and Mary knew it, that it was difficult to carry on a conversation and get on any kind of common ground. He decided that he would take them with him on an inspection trip to Elk Falls. Back in the kitchen with a full bucket of fresh milk to take care of, he talked it over with Mary. Mary agreed that taking their guests with him for the day was the best thing. "I don't know what I could possibly do with them," she told him. "They would not be interested in the work I do in the office. It would all be far out of range of their knowledge and capabilities."

Mary called them to breakfast. The men looked more presentable than they had the evening before. Their clothes appeared fresh, and they had obviously taken a shower. Their beards were still damp; their upper lips freshly shaved, devoid of the dark stubble that had been obvious the evening before. When told of the plans for the day, both men were enthusiastic about seeing more of the country.

Midway through breakfast, Dave's cell phone rang. Jacob and Joseph watched in amazement as Dave removed the phone from the case on his belt and answered. It was Joe Gardner, who was planning a barbecue for their guests and host families at his place in the evening. Dave agreed to be there and asked what he could bring. Joe was getting a supply of fresh ground beef from Ted Parks, along with the fresh baked buns. He would furnish the salad. They would have cold drinks and beer on hand—plus ice water for the visitors. Brian had been invited because of his involvement in bringing the visitors to New Island.

With the three men squeezed into the front seat of Dave's pickup truck, they headed up the Old Island Highway. Jacob and Joseph were astounded at the number of good-looking unoccupied small farms along the way.

"Is there no one to take care of all of these places?" Jacob asked.

"We do not have enough people to occupy all of them," Dave explained. "If you decided to come here to live, each of you would have the privilege of taking your choice of the vacant places. You would be registered as a citizen of New Island, which would endow you with that right. Plus you would be given a car or truck plus $100 of New Island money to get started."

"You mean that we would own the farm as our own and not have to share it with anyone else?"

"That is right," Dave assured them. "It would be registered in your name. You would be expected to share it with a wife and family, if you had any. You would also own the farm equipment and household furnishings left on the place. It would all be yours. Your only obligation would be to eventually pay taxes on the property to help support the government and the public services we have established."

"Who runs the government?" Joseph asked.

"The New Island council runs the government, under mandate from the people. President of the council is Jamie Morgan, and my wife Mary is the Vice President and secretary. The council is elected by a vote of the people, and that council in turn elects one of their members to be President and another to be Vice President. This is about as true a democracy, as it is possible to have. We all have a say in what happens to our country."

"If we decided to stay here, could we find a woman and get married?" Jacob asked.

"That would be up to you," Dave said. "It might not happen for a while, because there is a shortage of women in our community. But if you found one that was willing, that would be your privilege. You would have to convince the woman of your choice that you would be the best husband for her."

"You mean no one arranges marriages? You arrange your own?"

"That is correct," Dave assured them. "Mary and I fell in love and got married less than a month ago. We are very happy. Meg and Ted Parks were the first couple to get married. They are real young people. I know of at least two more marriages that will take place soon. There are probably others."

"If we had a farm here, could we sell things off of it to get money to buy other things we needed?"

"Yes, if you could find someone to buy it. You could also work for other people who need help and get paid for it."

Jacob turned to his companion. "You know, Joseph, if there is a heaven, this place sounds about as close to it as you could ever get. I wonder if we could convince Sir Job to let us stay here. I would love to have a farm of my own to manage my way. I would work hard to make it prosper, and in time, I would be able to find a woman to share it with and raise a family. Even if it took many years, I would be willing to wait for the opportunity of selecting a woman who wanted me, not one that our leader selected for me. I think that would lead to real happiness."

Dave completed his inspection at Elk Falls Power Plant and made notes to talk over with Andy the problems that Andy thought might exist, showing the two boys what he was doing as he went. He then drove back to Campbell River and stopped in the plaza in front of an outdoors-clothing supply store.

"You fellows' boots don't look in very good condition. Is this the best you have?"

"They are all we have," Jacob answered.

"Let's see what we can find here," Dave told them, leading the way through the unlocked door and on to the shoe department. "What size do you wear?"

Neither man could answer.

"Looks to me that about eight would suit you both. Get those old shoes off, so you can try on new ones."

"You mean that we can take new shoes? How do we pay for them?"

"This store has been abandoned. We can take what we want if we need it as long as the supply lasts. Now get those old boots off."

The boots came off, and Dave was astounded at the socks that they had covered up. They were hand knitted, patched and darned on top of patches and darns.

"Get the socks off, too," Dave demanded.

The men shed the socks, and Dave picked one up to inspect it, wrinkling his nose. "Whew!" he said. "They are not only worn out, but they smell like they haven't been washed for a while."

"We don't have enough socks to wash them often," Jacob explained.

Dave reached to a display of work socks and tossed a pair to each man. "Get these on, and we will try on boots."

Selecting a box numbered size eight of a medium-weight work boot, Dave handed the box to Jacob. Another box of a similar style he passed to Joseph. "Try these on," he commanded.

"I believe these are just right," Jacob said.

"Lace 'em up and walk around. Be sure they are comfortable," Dave told him.

"I think mine are a little tight," Joseph said.

"OK, here is eight and a half. Try these."

With the boots fitted, Dave handed the extra pair of size eight to Jacob and found an additional pair to fit Joseph. "These will keep you going for a while. Now, take 'em off, and we will find pants for you. Both of you look about 32 waist and 30 long. Get your pants and shirts off."

Dave went to a display of jeans, found the required sizes, and returned. The two men were standing in their underwear.

"Jesus Christ!" Dave exploded. "Is that what you wear in the summertime? How do you stand it?" Both men had old-fashioned long johns on with the buttoned drop seat.

"This is all we ever wear, summer or winter," Joseph told him.

"Get those off, and we will find something more suitable for you." Dave returned with Jockey-style shorts to find the men standing self-consciously in their birthday clothes. "Here, try these on. They are mediums and should fit."

"Is this what men wear here?" Jacob asked.

Dave unbuttoned his pants and let them drop. "It's what I wear," he said, pulling his pants back in place. "I don't wear undershirts in the summer, but you can if you want to. Here are medium work shirts. Try them on. I think they will fit. And here are jeans."

The sizes were okay, and the men dressed and pulled their new boots on and laced them up.

Dave found a luggage display and returned with a pair of zippered tote bags. "Here, put your old stuff in these. You should have about eight pair of socks each and eight shorts. Here are two more shirts each and two extra jeans. Pack 'em all up, and we will be on our way."

"I do not know what Sir Job will say," Jacob worried. "He might not let us keep all of these things. He will probably say we do not need so much."

"I think it is about time you men started thinking for yourselves," Dave exploded. "Your Sir Job doesn't own you, I hope. Let's go home. We have a party to go to tonight."

* * *

Joe and Ronda did not have an easy time of it that evening. They found that they had little common ground with Sir Job on which to establish a conversation. It seemed that every item that came up led back to religion and what God's commands were. They showed Job to his room and went to bed early.

In the privacy of their bedroom, they discussed their frustration with their visitor.

"Damn!" Joe exclaimed. "I'd hate to live in that guy's community. If I tried to live up to all of his requirements, I would soon be as nuts as he is. He acts like a religious dictator."

"I think," Ronda replied, "that he is even worse than the Puritans were in the early days of North America. I cannot believe that there are people still living in the modern world under those conditions."

"Those two women seemed nice enough, from the little I saw of them at the airport. They might actually be attractive if they got out of those horrible clothes and got into some decent togs. Maybe you should try to get some new things for them."

"They are staying with Jamie and Kelly," Ronda responded. "Knowing Kelly, I'll bet there is no time lost in getting them into something more appropriate. She won't be happy until she gets them made over."

"If she changes them too much," Joe said, "our Sir Job is apt to have a fit. Let's say we get them all here, with their host families, for an outdoor barbecue tomorrow evening? If there have been any makeovers, we might see some sparks fly. I'd like an excuse to take that opinionated bastard down a notch or two."

"I think that's a good idea, but be careful what you do or say. After all, these people are guests in our community and we have to treat them as such."

"You have to admit that I behaved well this evening," Joe said.

"Yes," his wife replied, "you were marvelous. But I could see the frustration boiling very close to the surface. What are you going to do with him tomorrow?"

"I think I will take him on a tour of the valley and show him some of the farms, perhaps introduce him to some of the farmers. I would like to see what kind of response he gets from Teresa Blunt. Then I'll take him out to the docks to meet our Indian friends and introduce him to Little Bird."

"If you get through all of that without an explosion, you'll have had a very full and successful day. I wish I had time to go along and watch the fireworks. Let's get to bed. You'll need a good night's rest to get you ready for tomorrow."

Joe started his tour with a circuitous route around the valley, visiting several farms where he introduced Job and let him see the people at work. They spent some time at Chuck Marshal's dairy where Chuck took them on a tour of his operation.

Their next stop was at Teresa Blunt's farm. They found Teresa shoveling manure in the cow barn. Teresa was wearing a tattered straw hat, well-worn jeans and a shirt that barely buttoned over her ample bosom. Natalie Jim sat on a stool, nursing her baby. Job's face reflected shock as he took in the scene.

Joe introduced Job to the two women, and Teresa responded in her normal ebullient way.

"So, you are the preacher that Jamie brought home with him from his last trip?"

"No ma'am," Job replied. "I am not really a preacher, but I have been directed by God to lead the people of our community and see to it that they live by the teaching of our ultimate leader, God Almighty."

"How did you get the message from God to be boss of your people?" Teresa asked bluntly.

"It came to me in the middle of the night when my father was dying. I was very young, but I felt that I had to accept the responsibility of directing our people in the way that God ordained."

Teresa regarded the man for a minute, then, with an exaggerated shrug of her shoulders, turned to Joe, and spoke loud enough to be sure Job could hear. "Lars is off in the north pasture fixing some fence. He has become so attached to that baby that he insists that Louise stay here, so he can see the baby as much as possible. You'd think the kid was his instead of a woods colt. Louise doesn't like to be alone, so she follows me around and helps wherever she can. She has to stop now and then to feed the kid. We have all decided that the wedding shall be next week if Jamie is available. Just as well make it legal for the girl to be living here."

Job was aghast. "You mean that the child was born out of wedlock?"

"She sure was, and a better piece of humanity you will never find, regardless of her parentage."

"In our community, a thing like that would never happen."

"I take it," Teresa said, "that the people in your community are not human. These things happen everywhere, regardless. It's human nature."

"It does not happen where people are governed by the God that created them. If it did, those people responsible would be excommunicated and forced to leave our community. Our people must maintain the purity that God demands."

"I'll be damned!" Teresa exclaimed. "I had heard that there were people like you in the world, but I never expected to meet one."

Joe interjected. "Teresa, this gentleman is a guest in our community, and we should treat him as such. I know that his beliefs are different from yours or mine, but we must be tolerant. Everyone is entitled to believe the way he wants, and the rest of us must honor those beliefs."

"I'm sorry," Teresa said. "I shouldn't have blown my stack that way. But when he says that the baby I love and her mother should be kicked out because a couple of young people made a mistake, I don't like it. He can believe as he wants, just so he keeps those beliefs to himself. I am entitled to believe as I want, too, and won't inflict those beliefs on anyone else, but I sure as hell will not listen to a guy like this when he spouts off. OK, I'm sorry. I guess we better drop it."

Job had heard enough and stalked off towards the car.

Teresa watched him for a minute, and then broke into loud laughter. "Whew, I guess I better learn to curb my temper better. But I have a hard time tolerating a sanctimonious ass—like that guy. I hope Jamie doesn't bring him here to live."

Joe joined in her laughter. "If he did, you would soon trim him down to size. That's the reason I brought him by. I hoped you'd lay into him."

"You laid out the bait," Teresa chuckled, "and I grabbed it like a hungry coyote. You better get out of here before I take you to the cleaners."

"I'm on my way," Joe exclaimed, heading for the car.

"Be careful of that guy, Joe," Teresa called after him. "I'd hate to see you converted to his way of thinking."

Joe got in the car and started the engine. "I don't think you made a very good impression on Mrs. Blunt."

"If that woman lived in my community, she would have to change her ways and learn who is in charge. I would not put up with a woman who did not recognize her place. She is obviously immoral and unfit to live among God-fearing people."

"I guess we are not God-fearing people in New Island." Joe was gritting his teeth, trying to hold his temper. "We consider Mrs. Blunt an outstanding citizen. She is a little outspoken, but she has a very big heart, and I consider it a privilege to be her friend. That girl made a mistake, and if there is a God giving directions, that God arranged for Teresa's son to fall in love with that girl and her baby. He will make a home for her, and her baby will grow up without any stigma attached to her because she was illegitimate. Now, we better forget all of this and go and meet some more people."

Joe drove to the docks where he led Job to the seafood market that had been set up by the Indian families. The market was small, but clean and neat. Live crabs and live prawns occupied circulating tanks of salt water, and fresh oysters and clams were on display in a refrigerated showcase. Job was totally unfamiliar with any of the products. The only fish he had ever eaten was pike and catfish from the local waters where he lived. Johnie Jacob came in, and Joe introduced him to Job.

The two men looked at each other for several minutes before either decided to speak. Then Johnie broke the ice. "You are the Chief that Mr. Jamie brought home with him the other day?"

"I am the leader, of our people. Four of them came with me to visit your country."

"Leader? That means Chief to our people. So you are the Chief of your tribe like Mr. Jamie is Chief of our tribes that have banded together here to form a new and more powerful tribe. I was Chief of my tribe until there became too few of us to survive and we had to join other tribes. Our last move was to join Chief Jamie's tribe, and he is the greatest of all chiefs."

Job continued to study the old Indian. He did not know what to make of the shrunken figure before him. His copper-colored face was shriveled and worn by many decades of Pacific Coast weather and straggly gray hair hung to his shoulders. In spite of his apparent age, his flinty black eyes were sharp and penetrating. He seemed unusually healthy and spry.

"I presume you are Indian?" Joe detected a slight edge of disdain in Job's voice and decided to not let things get out of hand.

"Johnie, is Little Bird available? I would like our guest to meet her."

256

"I'll get her," Johnie said brusquely as he stomped out of the store.

A few minutes latter, the tap of a cane on the deck planks announced the arrival of Little Bird. Johnie followed her with a folding chair, which he placed on the deck for her. Little Bird disdained the chair until she had thoroughly appraised the stranger and acknowledged his introduction, and then folded herself cautiously into its seat.

"This old woman does not get around too well anymore. I am sure that I will not be here to greet many more of the strangers that the great Chief Jamie rescues from around the world. Tell me Sir, where did Chief Jamie find you?"

Job was nonplused by the old woman. She seemed disdainful and showed none of the respect that he was accustomed to from women.

"Sir Jamie landed his airplane in the road that runs along the north boundary of our property. A black man accompanied him. He convinced us that he meant no harm, and we invited him to stay overnight. He talked to our people about your country of New Island and offered to take in any of us that cared to move here. I decided to come here for a visit, with the agreement that he would take us back within a week. I brought four of my people along. I find this community quite uncivilized. I have been treated without the respect I deserve as the leader of our people and a member of a great religion. I shall request that we be taken home as soon as possible."

Little Bird was quiet for minutes before she replied. "I do not know if you are a great leader or not. I have the feeling that, unlike our Chief Jamie, you are a despotic ruler that depends on religion to enforce total subjugation of your people. I think I will be happy to have Jamie return you to the place you came from as soon as possible. I do not think you belong among the freedom-loving people of New Island. Good day, Sir."

The medicine woman struggled from her chair and, with her cane tapping as an accompaniment, hobbled down the dock.

Job's face was scarlet with rage as her turned to Joe. "Please take me back to my room. I will spend the rest of the day in prayer for the non-believers that live in this colony, and I shall leave it as soon as possible."

"I am sorry that you feel that way, Sir, but perhaps that is best. I doubt that you have the understanding to interact with people who do not subscribe to your beliefs. Let's go."

Back at his farm, Joe shut off the engine of his car and turned to Job. "Sir, we are going to have a barbecue here for all of your people and their host families this evening. It will be a further opportunity for all to get to know each other better. I think it would be very advisable for you to spend the next hours in meditation and try to come to terms with yourself. Our culture is obviously much different from yours, and you should make an effort to understand and accept, as Jamie did when he was in your community. People here are not used to having an all-powerful ruler trying to inflict his ideas on them. This is a democracy, people are free to act and think as they wish, as long as it does not conflict with the public's good. Please think about it."

Job got out of the car and stalked into the house without answering.

* * *

It was well past five o'clock, and Joe was in the kitchen helping Ronda to prepare for the evening festivities when Sir Job emerged from his room and approached Joe.

"Mr. Gardner, I guess I should apologize for my unseemly brusque treatment of some of your people today. I am accustomed to not having people recognize me as the bearer of directions from the Almighty God. I will try to be more receptive to your hospitality and ignore the ignorance of some of your people."

Ronda glanced at Joe and saw the fire building in his eyes, and the muscles of his jaw tense. Stepping forward, she gripped Joe by the arm, squeezing hard. "It is nice of you to apologize, Sir Job. I can understand your frustration at being with people who do not understand your greatly different culture. But you must understand, also, that our people are not ignorant, as you imply, but certainly not educated in your way of thinking. I accept your apology for Joe and myself. I would request that you be very prudent in the way you respond to things this evening. I would like for all of us to finish the evening as good and understanding friends. You are now in my home, and I have a right to have a peaceful and pleasant evening."

"I am sorry, Miss Ronda," Job replied. "I will try my best to control myself while I am in your home."

"Here come our guests," Joe exclaimed. "Let's get out and greet them."

Meg and Ted Parks were the first to arrive. Ted had insisted that he would prepare the meat and man the barbecues to be sure it was cooked just right. Ted went to inspect the two barbecues that had been set up for him. The charcoal was already starting to form gray ash around the sides and would soon be ready. He had already formed the ground meat into patties and was ready to start as soon as everyone was available.

Mary and Dave Jorgenson were the next to arrive, with their guests, Jacob and Joseph. Job turned from watching the preparations for the meal to see his two young men dressed in their new blue jeans and checkered shirts. He appeared to grow two inches in stature, and his eyes were on fire. Ronda, watching him, held her breath. He opened his mouth to speak, seemed to reconsider, and shrunk back to his normal size.

Wow! Ronda thought, that was a close one. I hope we don't get any other surprises like this. She had to admit that the two young men looked a lot more presentable in their new clothes.

Jamie's Lincoln pulled up at the front gate and Jamie got out, starting around the car to open the passenger door. Josephine opened the door before he got there and stepped out. Irene and Kelly emerged from the back of the car, and the group came through the gate and proceeded towards the people gathered around the porch.

Kelly, her blond hair cascading around her shoulders, was wearing a figured summer dress. Irene's deep brown hair, glimmering in the sun, flowed almost to her waist. She wore a snug blue skirt that ended above her knees and a pale blue blouse that left no doubt about her gender. Josephine, her long gray streaked hair flowing almost to her hips, but bundled at the nape of her neck with a light blue ribbon, was wearing a soft gray skirt that barely covered her knees. Her blue blouse stretched snugly across her ample bosom.

Job stared aghast at the women. Josephine led the way towards him, and Irene, obviously frightened, followed closely behind. Kelly stayed at Irene's side.

In a harsh, belligerent voice, Job spoke out. "I do not believe what I am seeing. You women look like a group of streetwalkers. You have violated all of the precepts of our God. You are subject to excommunication from our church and exclusion from our community."

"Sir Job," Jamie's voice was unusually brusque, "you have just compared my 10-year-old daughter and these other women to prostitutes, and you are completely out of line. I ask that you apologize at once."

"But their mode of dress is completely wrong, as mandated by our God. It is not allowed for women to expose themselves so blatantly. They should go home immediately and get themselves properly garbed."

"If there is a God, he is completely different from the God of New Island. I am waiting for your apology."

"Mr. Jamie, I am sorry if I have offended you. But this display of ..."

"Leave the buts out, Sir. I asked for an apology to these young women and myself for the remark you made comparing them to prostitutes. No excuses are acceptable."

"But, Sir Jamie," Job blustered. "You do not understand..."

"I understand only one thing, Mr., and that is that you made an extremely derogatory remark about these ladies. Now, there will be no more excuses. Your apology, please."

"All right," Job conceded. "I used the wrong words and apologize to you and your daughter. But these young women cannot be accepted back into our society until they have returned to a proper mode of dress."

"Sir Job!" Josephine spoke emphatically. "I am not going back to Little River. I have had a taste of freedom and do not choose to return to the domination I have experienced for the 38 years of my life. I have asked for the privilege of staying in New Island."

"I have also asked to stay in New Island," Irene declared.

"The only way you could stay here is if you were married to a man from this community. No one has come to me with such a request."

Brian Veary stepped to the front. He had come around the house in time to hear the entire altercation. "I wish to marry Irene and will do so immediately if she will accept me, and Jamie will perform the ceremony."

Irene was instantaneous in her response. She ran to Brian and threw her arms around his neck. "Of course, I will marry you. I fell in love with you during the flight over here. Nothing would suit me better."

"Then he will have to request that privilege from me or your mother and go through the proper procedures."

Jamie interceded. "He does not have to get permission from you or anyone else. This is a free country. The young lady is 18 years old and a free agent. I will be happy to marry them at any time they desire. I would only suggest that they wait to be sure that they are not entering into marriage under duress in order for Irene to escape from Little River. I am asking our council to grant citizenship in New Island to both of these ladies, and I am sure that the council will concur. There will be no more discussion on this subject. We are here to have some fun and relaxation, so let's proceed."

The tension evaporated from the crowd as they gathered around Jamie and the girls, chattering enthusiastically. Josephine grabbed Jamie's hand. "Thank you so much, Jamie. I may not have a husband, but I will be a good citizen of New Island. I promise."

Chapter 37

On Saturday morning following the barbecue at Joe Gardner's, Mary called Jamie on his cell phone. The two young men who were staying with her wanted to meet with Jamie as soon as possible. Could she bring them over?

"Right away," Jamie told her.

A few minutes later, Mary and Dave pulled into the driveway with Jacob and Joseph, and they congregated on the porch.

"What can I do for you gentlemen this morning?" Jamie asked.

"Jacob and I stayed awake half the night talking about what happened at the party last night," Joseph led off. "We were embarrassed very much by the actions of Sir Job. We felt that he was entirely wrong in his condemnation of Irene and Josephine. As I said, Jacob and I spent half the night making our decision, but we have decided that we would like to remain here. Miss Mary said that your council meets tomorrow afternoon, and we wanted to be considered at the same time as Irene and Josephine."

"Jacob, do you agree with Joseph?" Jamie asked.

"Yes, Sir Jamie, I agree fully. In fact, we decided if we are forced to go back, we will leave and try to find another place to live. We have not been allowed to live lives of our own under the dictatorship of Sir Job. If we have to set up our own place in the wilderness somewhere, it would be better than the life we are now living. We might starve to death, but we will chance it."

"Are you both willing to keep your religious orientation to yourselves and not try to inflict it on the people of New Island?"

"Yes, Sir," Joseph said. "We would even renounce our religion if it was necessary to be approved for admission."

"That isn't necessary," Jamie told them. "Just keep it to yourselves. Don't go preaching it to others. I don't think there will be a problem with accepting you into our community after you have been presented to the council. I hate to interfere with the affairs of Little River, but it looks as if there is no choice. Mary, would you try to contact all council members and ask them to meet at two o'clock rather than three to give us more time to deal with these requests? Also, we would like both of you fellows to be there so that the council can see whom we are talking about and hear your reasons for wanting to join us."

"Would it help if we cut our beards and hair?" Jacob asked. "We do not believe that it is necessary to continue wearing them this way."

"That is up to you," Jamie replied. "You are certainly free to do as you wish. But you might look a bit more presentable if your hair and beard were at least trimmed a little."

Mary spoke up. "I have had some training and experience with hair management. I think I can take care of it—if they wish."

"If Miss Mary can get rid of this bush for me, I will be eternally grateful," Jacob said.

"I will join in that," Joseph agreed.

"Sir Jamie," Jacob said. "I understand that, if we are allowed to stay here, each of us will be given the opportunity to have one of the vacant farms."

"That is true," Jamie replied. "You will each be allowed to select a vacant property. You will be able to keep any livestock and equipment that may be on the property, along with household furnishings."

"That is wonderful," Jacob enthused. "If hard work will make it possible, we will succeed."

Dave spoke up. "I know of a couple of properties that I think would be just right for them. I'll take them out and show them this afternoon, and if they like them, I'll get the descriptions for Mary and she can record them if they are accepted as citizens."

"Good deal," Jamie concurred. "I'll see you at the council meeting tomorrow afternoon."

* * *

Mary could not wait to get at the surplus hair on the two men. As soon as they arrived home, she set a chair in the backyard and brought her barber tools.

"Who wants to be first?" she asked.

"I will be first," Jacob said, his voice a little tremulous.

"Do you have any idea of what you want?" Mary asked.

"I just want it off," Jacob told her.

Mary had some trepidation as she picked up the scissors. What if the hair had not been washed for months? Could she stand working with it? Dave had told her about the socks. She lifted one of the long braids. It seemed clean, and there was no odor. He must have washed it when he took a shower yesterday. She grasped the scissors, and with a few snips she had the braid off. The other one followed and was tossed on the ground with its mate. She ran a comb through the hair and found it relatively free of mats. Thirty minutes later, the hair was neatly trimmed, full on the sides and tapering to the base of the head in back. It was a little long, but neat, and, in Mary's opinion, looked good. Then she started on the beard. She left it less than an inch long, neatly trimmed.

Going in the house, Mary returned with a hand mirror. "How does it look?" she asked.

"My God! Is that me? I think it is great. Joseph, how do I look?"

"Sir Job will be greatly shocked, but I think you look like a human being instead of a wild animal of some kind. Can you do the same for me, Miss Mary?"

"Come on, we'll try." Mary had the feel now, and she soon had Joseph looking like a brother to Jacob.

Dave returned from an errand and was astounded at the change in the two men. "Wow," he exclaimed. "It looks like a bear tangled with a cyclone from the amount of hair scattered around here. You guys look great. Hold on here a minute." Going in the house, he returned with a pair of baseball caps. "Here, try these on. They'll be a lot more comfortable than those hats. Let's go and look at farms."

The two farms were north of the properties occupied so far and walking distance from the Merville store. The farms were 80 acres each and well developed. The small houses and outbuildings were in the corners of the plots, adjacent to each other. Stopping at the first of the two places, they went to investigate. Several chickens were scratching in the yard around the barn. A milk cow in a pasture behind the barn had a new calf, possibly four days old. Her udder was swollen with milk, the calf unable to handle it all.

"Looks like you have a milk supply," Dave commented. "Seems like one of you said milking cows was women's work. Do either of you know how?"

"Sure," Jacob said. "We both do. Boys do a lot of women's work until they get grown up. That cow sure needs milking." Crawling through the bars of the gate, he approached the cow. She stood still as he patted her on the back, ran his hand down her thigh and squatted beside her. Grasping a tit in each hand, he squirted milk on the ground. Returning to the others, Jacob told them, "We should find a bucket. That cow needs milking very badly. She might get milk fever if she is let go."

On the back porch of the house they found an outdoor sink and several buckets nested underneath. Dave pulled a bucket out and turned on the tap. Water flowed. The electricity was still on, and the pressure pump hooked on the well was working. Dave handed the bucket to Jacob, and the man went back to the pasture and spent ten minutes milking the cow, returning with the bucket half full of milk.

"What are we going to do with the milk?" Jacob asked. "I hate to waste it."

Dave tried the kitchen door. It was unlocked. Inside the kitchen, it looked as if it had just been vacated. The refrigerator was working, and spoiled food was evident when they opened the door.

"You have to clean this thing out before you use it. Maybe you could give the milk to the chickens." Back outside, they went to the hen house beside the barn. "Chick, chick, chick," Dave called. A number of chickens came on the run, and Jacob poured the milk into a feed trough.

"You mean we can really have this place with everything on it?" Joseph asked.

"Yes," Dave said. "It can belong to one of you if you want it. Let's go see what the other place is like."

At the neighboring farm they found several horses in the pasture that came trotting up to them when they approached the gate. They were in good condition. A water trough with a float control had kept them supplied with water for the several weeks that they had been abandoned, and the grass was lush in the pasture. There was a pond off the garden patch and a mother duck had a clutch of ducklings. In a shed alongside the barn, they found an old-fashioned buggy. Harness hung on the wall. Further back in the shed was a mower and a hay rake. The house was similar to the one they had just left.

"What do you think fellows?" Dave asked. "You could live together in either of these houses and work both farms."

"No," Joseph retorted. "We are first cousins and good friends and get along well. But I think that we want to live individually. We can work together and maybe eat together and share equipment, but I think that at the end of the day we would prefer to go to our own place and be alone."

"We have had enough of living together with a lot of other people," Jacob agreed. "Now, with a taste of freedom, we want to be individuals. I would like to have a place to call my own."

"How are we going to decide which place each of you gets?" Dave asked.

Jacob picked a stick up from the ground. One end had a short fork on of it. "We will throw this stick in the air. When it comes down, I will take the place that the forked end points to and Joseph will take the other. Agreed, cousin?"

"Agreed," Joseph said.

"Will you throw the stick, Mr. Dave?"

Dave tossed the stick high in the air. It came down with the forked end pointing to the first farm that they had visited.

"All right," Jacob said. "That is my place, and this is yours. Are you happy?"

"Absolutely," Jacob agreed. "That was a fair way to make the decision."

* * *

Job made his appearance at breakfast and silently ate the eggs and toast offered to him. With hardly a word, he retired to his room and stayed there all morning. When lunch was ready, Ronda knocked on Job's bedroom door and called him for the midday meal. Job emerged and joined the family, eating in almost total silence. As they finished lunch, Job seemed to make a decision and spoke.

"Mr. Joe, I believe that we should have a conference. I would like to talk to you for a few minutes, if you can spare the time."

"Come on out on the porch, and we can take as much time as you want," Joe told him.

Seated in chairs on the front porch, the two men were silent for several minutes. Finally, Job spoke.

"I have been reviewing in my mind the things that are happening here, and I am deeply distressed. I am fearful that the four people that I brought along to visit your country are going to request permission to stay here. I am fearful that if I refuse that permission, which I am bound by God to do, the results will be serious conflict."

"Sir Job," Joe replied, "I am gong to be frank with you. I don't believe that it will do any good to refuse permission for them to stay. I've been informed that they are all going before the council tomorrow afternoon to request permission to be admitted to citizenship in New Island. I'm certain that the council will look on their requests with favor. Once they become citizens of New Island, you no longer have any control over them."

"But Jamie did not tell me that he was going to recruit my people to abandon their home and come here to live."

"Jamie has had nothing to do with it. He told you while he was in Little River that anyone from your valley would be welcome in our country. You didn't realize what a taste of freedom could do to your people. I don't believe that there is any way you can reverse the course of events at this time. You had just as well accept it. If you persevere in your efforts, you will cause enmity that will alienate your people irreversibly. If you accept things as they are, you may be able to retain their friendship for the future. It would be much better to have friendly relations between our people than to have them enemies. I urge you to think it over carefully. Next week, Jamie will take you home. It would be nice if you could part friends. There are too few of us in the world now to allow for hard feelings among us. Accept the inevitable, and we will all be better off. Tomorrow afternoon, Jamie has asked me to have you appear before the council at three o'clock. The rest of your people are appearing at two o'clock. Now I have had my say. It is now up to you. Please think it over before you make any rash decisions."

* * *

After lunch, Jamie took Kelly and her charges to the Zeller's store and waited outside with Dawg. It was almost two hours before the three reappeared, burdened with bags and boxes. At home, they disappeared into the house and a half-hour later, they started parading their acquisitions for him. They modeled jeans and shoes for farm work and hiking, with jackets and caps. Skirts and dresses were conservative and reflected Kelly's good taste and what she felt would be approved by Jamie. The women were both very attractive, Jamie decided, and would certainly be a desirable catch for any single man.

Jamie had settled down on the porch when his cell phone buzzed. It was Brian. "Jamie," he requested, "could I come by for a few minutes? I would like to talk to you about the radio for Little River, among other things."

"Sure, come on over and stay for dinner. I think my harem is getting ready to start preparing it."

"That's wonderful," Brian replied. "I'll be right there."

A few minutes later, Brain joined Jamie on the porch, and Kelly brought cold beers for them. After a few minutes of casual conversation, Brian told Jamie that Stan had rigged up a radio that he thought would work well for communications with Little River. He had an aerial and the connecting cables necessary for its installation and had found a small generator to power it.

"That all sounds great," Jamie said, "but you had something else on your mind?"

"Yes I did," Brian admitted. "First, I wanted to apologize for butting into the altercation that was going on with Sir Job last evening."

"There is nothing to apologize for," Jamie said. "I was about in a position where I needed some interference. That sanctimonious ass was just about to make me lose control of my temper."

"You had every reason to be upset with him. I think if I had been in your position, I might have thrown a punch at him."

"I was tempted, but that is not the answer to a problem. Punching someone out should only come as a last resort, when all else fails."

"Most importantly," Brian said, "I wanted to tell you that I meant what I said about wanting to marry Irene. I had been wondering how to go about proposing to her ever since we got home. I didn't dream of doing it in such an unorthodox way in front of a crowd of people. I'm sort of bashful when it comes to girls and wondered if it was proper for a black man to propose to a white girl. But I forgot all of that when His Honor Sir Job started spouting off. I threw caution and propriety to the wind and jumped in with both feet and tried to see how big a splash I could make."

"You made a big splash all right. At least you gained everyone's attention, including Job's. I think it is wonderful if you two get married; I have no concern about you being black. I still think you should wait a while until you are sure you really want to."

"I'm as sure now as I'll ever be," Brian told him. "Nevertheless, I agree that we should wait awhile to be sure Irene wasn't carried off her feet by her desire to get away from Little River. I would hate to have us get married, only to find out that she couldn't tolerate a black man."

Kelly came out to tell them that dinner was ready. She directed Irene and Brian to seats on one side of the table, with Josephine and herself across, and Jamie at the head. Brian was obviously enthralled with Irene in her new clothes. He could not keep his eyes off of her during dinner, and he was oblivious of the conversation of the others. Immediately after dinner, Brian asked Irene if she would like to go for a walk. Irene agreed, and the two disappeared down the driveway, not to reappear for almost two hours.

* * *

The earthquake hit at five in the morning. It was already daylight. The screeching and squalling of the tortured building brought Jamie out of a sound sleep. It sounded like every nail was being pulled from the wood. Crashes sounded from somewhere, like dishes dumped in a garbage can. There was a rolling motion, interrupted by jarring jolts that felt like the building was being lifted up and dropped from several feet. Jamie staggered from his bed and wrapped himself in a robe, concerned for the safety of Kelly and his guests.

His bedroom door was jammed shut, and he had to use all of his strength to open it. Charging into the living room, he met Kelly coming from her end of the house, Dawg close at her heels.

"Hey Jamie," she stammered, "that one scared me a little bit. That was the worst one we've had yet. Are you OK?"

"I'm fine," Jamie told her. "But we had better see about our guests."

Jamie tried the door to their room, but like his own bedroom door, it seemed frozen in place.

"You girls OK?" Jamie shouted through the door.

"We are all right," a frightened sounding voice replied, "but we cannot get the door open."

"Stand back," Jamie shouted. "I'm going to kick it open." Twisting the knob to be sure it was unlatched, he threw his weight against the door. It crashed open, slamming violently against the wall. The two women, in their nightgowns, were huddled together a few feet from the door.

"Are you two all right?" Jamie asked.

269

"We are fine," Josephine answered in a tremulous voice. "But we are surely scared."

"Was that an earthquake?" demanded Irene.

"That was an earthquake," Jamie told them. "And it was a good one, too. Let's take a look and see what damage has been done."

"Is it safe to stay in the house?" Josephine asked. "It sounded like it was being torn apart."

"Yes, it is safe," Jamie told her. "A wood frame house is almost impossible to tear apart, unlike houses made of bricks or blocks. The sounds you heard were joints moving and nails pulling a bit."

Jamie hit a light switch. The lights came on, and Jamie was surprised that the power was not interrupted. In the living room, a bookcase had turned over, spilling books across the room. A large potted plant had upset, the pot breaking, its soil spilled on the carpet. In the kitchen, food from the refrigerator was spilled on the floor, but the refrigerator door was closed. It was the same with dishes. Dinnerware dumped on the floor, but the cupboard doors were closed.

"How did that happen?" Kelly demanded. "Everything spilled, but the doors are all closed."

"I guess that the doors flew open," Jamie said, "and stuff fell out and the doors swung shut again. Either that or some little men were here and shut the doors. Let's get dressed and clean this place up."

* * *

Dave Jorgenson awoke to feel Mary grasping frantically at him as the building swayed and rattled. He grasped Mary in his arms to reassure her, wondering how the house could make so much noise without coming apart. "It's OK, Mary," he said, trying to calm her as he pulled her tighter against him. "It's only another earthquake."

"It was only another earthquake that almost killed me." Mary reminded him.

"It wasn't the earthquake that hurt you," Dave said. "It was the tree falling on you."

"But the earthquake caused the tree to fall."

"We better check on our guests," Dave said.

Mary sprang from the bed and started for the door.

"Hold on there," Dave said. "Hadn't you better get something on before you charge out there?"

Mary paused, running her hands up and down her sides. "Yeah, I guess it would be a good idea."

Dressed, they made another start. Mary couldn't open the door, and Dave gave a pull on it. The door opened reluctantly. "I guess the house settled and distorted the door frame," he explained.

Entering the living room, they found their guests emerging from their bedroom fully dressed and showing little excitement.

"I guess we had an earthquake?" Joseph asked.

"We sure did, and it was a strong one," Dave told them.

"Well, there is no end to the new experiences we are getting in this new land," Jacob said. "Do you suppose it did much damage or hurt anyone?"

"I doubt it," Dave replied. "I think everyone in the valley lives in wood houses. They are flexible and can stand a lot of stress. Mary got hurt in an earlier quake, but it was because a tree fell on her. She just happened to be in the wrong place at the wrong time."

* * *

Dogs barking woke Joe Gardner from a deep sleep. I wonder what they are excited about, he thought. Then the house started to roll like a ship on the ocean.

"What's happening?" Ronda asked.

"Another earthquake."

They lay quietly, listening to the house groan and squeal as the ground went through a myriad of contortions under it. The shaking stopped, and a loud yell emanated from the living room. Ronda and Joe sprang out of bed, grabbing for robes and headed towards the source of the sound. They found Job frantically trying to open the front door, jumping up and down in his efforts. He was dressed only in his long johns, the rear flap unbuttoned and flapping at his thighs.

"What a sight," Ronda giggled.

"Hey, Job," Joe called out, "settle down. You can't open that door unless you unlock it. And there is no purpose getting outside anyway. It's all over now. Settle down."

"But we better got out of here." Job's voice came out a high falsetto. "We may all be killed."

"Too late for that now." Joe reassured him. "The excitement is all over. You had just as well go back to bed. At least cover up your ass."

Job suddenly realized his position, grabbed the flap, and holding it up with his hands, raced back to his bedroom. Joe and Ronda collapsed on the couch, laughing hysterically. Twelve-year old Bruce came running down the stairs, demanding, "What's going on down here? What's so funny about an earthquake?"

"You just missed the show of a lifetime," Joe told him. "I'll tell you about it another time. Better get back to bed and get some more sleep. Is Susie OK?"

"Yeah, I looked in her room. Nothing wakes her up."

* * *

There was a full crowd in the hall when Jamie called the general meeting to order.

"I know there is not much news that I can bring to a meeting. The grapevine in New Island is the most effective news distribution network that I have ever experienced." Jamie paused and an appreciative chuckle flowed over the room.

"Most of you know that I brought five people back from our last trip, the trip to Alberta. What you do not know is that four of those people applied for asylum in New Island. They didn't use those words, but that is what it amounted to. They asked to be allowed to stay in New Island. They made their requests to the council at a special meeting held for that purpose this afternoon. They are two women: one a 38-year-old widow and the other an 18-year-old girl. The two men are cousins, both 22 years old. After interviewing the applicants and listening to their stories of why they wanted to stay in New Island, the council was unanimous in granting their requests. Now, I would like you to meet your new neighbors. Would the four of you please come forward?"

Starting with Irene, Jamie introduced the four newcomers and told something about each of them. When he was through, the crowd gave the foursome a rousing welcome.

"One further introduction that I would like to make. The leader of the religious group from which these people came is also with us. We have agreed that we need to establish friendly relations between our two groups and help each other out when there is a need. There is a definite need of some medical services in their community, and Sir Job, their leader, has requested aid of a doctor. Our Dr. Ron has agreed to go with us on Tuesday, when we return Sir Job to his flock. Ron will conduct a one- or two-day clinic, and we will return later in the week. Now, I would like you to meet Sir Job Navolsky, the spiritual and de facto leader of the Little River Valley community. Sir Job."

Sir Job stepped forward and raised his hands to stop the applause. "In our community, we do not applaud. We are not demonstrative. We prefer quiet, which is the will of God. God governs our community with a firm hand. He governs through his devoted servant, myself. He makes known to me what his will is, and I relay it to our people, who are obligated to obey his every command.

"Unfortunately, the four people who accompanied me over to your country saw fit to completely disobey the will of our God Almighty. They applied to stay in this Godless country, which I am sure is the reason for the terrible convulsions of the earth early this morning. While I have agreed with Sir Jamie to maintain friendly terms with our two countries, I will be glad to get back home where God gets the respect He deserves. I find this community that shows no respect for the messenger of God impossible to tolerate. I especially find it hard to understand the disrespect shown by some of the women for their betters. They will roast in hell if they do not change their ways."

There was a shout from the back of the room, and Teresa Blunt was on her feet.

"You sanctimonious asshole," she shouted at the top of her strident voice. "It's a good thing you are going back home. If you stayed here, the women of this valley would probably string you up to a tree and cut off your manhood, if you have any."

The crowd went wild, whistling and shouting for several minutes. Job stood uncertainly until Jamie led him away.

"What did I do wrong?" he muttered. "I was only trying to impress on them the necessity of obeying the will of God. I am used to having my word accepted."

"You are in the wrong place to preach your doctrine," Jamie told him. "I warned you about trying to tell these people how to act. It is obvious that you know nothing about democracy. Now, I would suggest that you lay low until we are able to get you out of here. Teresa Blunt might just get angry enough to follow through with her threat, if you continue to preach around here. Here's Joe.

Joe, take Sir Job home, keep him under wraps until Tuesday morning, and bring him to the airport. He doesn't seem to know how to keep his mouth shut."

Chapter 38

Brian and Stan were doing a final check on the Cessna Caravan when Jamie arrived at the airport Monday morning. The two new pilots were watching and taking notes on the inspection procedures. The cowling was off, exposing the PT6A turbo power plant, and inspection plates were off on wings and fuselage.

"We didn't get to give this bird a full inspection when we picked it up," Brian said. "We thought we should go over it real carefully before we fly it anymore. So far, everything is good. Another hour and we can button it up, and you can take it for a test flight."

"Now, as for tomorrow," Jamie said. "Besides you and me, we will have Stan, Dr. Ron and his wife and our precious Sir Job. Dr. Ron will have some medical supplies, but weight shouldn't be a problem. I would suggest that you throw in sleeping bags for all of us, in case there're not enough accommodations there. Also our regular quota of food and water in case we get stranded somewhere."

"Will do," Brian said. "I wonder if those people have any dental problems. Maybe we should take our dentist along, too."

"Good idea. Dr. Lang has been busy setting up an office at the hospital. He's had no customers yet, and he has plenty of time. I'll ask him."

"Fine," Brian said, "I'll have everything ready to go in the morning. Maybe I should rig an escape hatch, and we could eject Sir Job somewhere over the mountains. His God should let him float to an easy landing, and he would be out of those poor people's hair. Maybe if we could find a parachute for him, he'll jump on his own, if you bounce the airplane around enough. We'll be sure to warn him to have his underwear flap buttoned."

"OK," Jamie said, "let's plan on takeoff about nine. I'll come out this afternoon, and we'll flight test the bird."

* * *

Jamie was back at the airport at three o'clock and found the Caravan sitting on the ramp, ready to go. Brian and Stan as well as the two junior pilots were sitting in the shade of the wing, waiting for him.

275

"Does anyone know if there is an instrument flight hood kicking around here anywhere?" Jamie asked.

"Yeah," Stan said, "there are a couple of them hanging in the back of the office. I'll get one for you." He was back in a minute. "If you are going to do some instrument practice, let's check out the instrument landing system. I think it is working OK, but I'd like you to air check it, so we know for sure."

"Kevin and Randy want to go with us," Brian said. "Is it OK?"

"Sure, come along. You might get a rough ride with me on the gauges. It has been a long time since I did it, and never with a plane this big. Stan, I am going to climb over the airport to 5000 feet and practice some steep turns and full stalls. Then we'll go off to the southeast and see if we can pick up the Instrument Landing System and make a straight-in instrument approach."

"OK," Stan said, "I'll get everything turned on."

Jamie went carefully through the checklists. The engine fired readily, and a few minutes later they were climbing in a long spiral over the airport. Leveling off at 5000 feet, Jamie flew a series of gentle turns to get more feel of the plane, and then went into a maximum bank 720-degree turn, adding power to compensate for the loss of wing lift. Watching his altitude carefully, with the plane on the edge of a stall, he made the first turn and got a substantial bump as the plane hit its own prop wash. "Good job," Brian praised. "Right on the button. And you lost less than a hundred feet when you hit the prop wash and you recovered that quickly. You are doing OK flying a strange plane."

"Let's go for a full stall," Jamie said. Throttling back to minimum power, he held the plane level, pulling back harder and harder on the yoke. The plane shuddered as it warned of an impending stall. Then, violently, the nose dropped. Jamie released the backpressure on the yoke and held his heading with the rudders. The plane recovered quickly. Jamie advanced the throttle and started to climb again. They had lost less than 500 feet.

"That was all OK," Brian said. "The plane does what it's supposed to do, and you do the same. I think it is a good combination. Congratulations."

"Thanks," Jamie replied. "This is a mighty fine bird. I think we will get a lot of use out of it. Give me that hood." He fitted the hood on his head so that he could see nothing but the instrument panel. "OK Brian, you are the radar operator. Give me directions to intercept the ILS."

"Roger, Sir. Turn right to 135 degrees. Descend to and maintain 4000 feet."

"Turning to 135 degrees, descending to maintain 4000. Level at 4000."

"Turn left to 315 degrees," Brian directed. "Descend to and maintain 3000."

"Turning left to 315 degrees and descending to maintain 3000. Level at 3000."

"Maintain 315 degrees to intercept the ILS, descend to 2000."

Suddenly the ILS needle started to swing from its position at the left of the dial. Jamie was slow on starting his turn to the right, and the needle moved to the right of center. Jamie corrected to the right and cautiously brought the needle to center.

"You are now established on the ILS." Brian instructed, "Slow to 100 knots and descend at 500 feet per minute. You should break out at 500 feet."

Jamie watched the altimeter unwind. Eight hundred feet— 700—600—500. He flipped the hood up and spotted the runway directly in front. Slowing to 90 knots, he brought the plane to a smooth landing.

"Bravo," shouted one of the guys in a seat behind him.

"I'll fly an instrument flight with you anytime," Brian said. "It may have been a long time, but you have lost none of your skills."

* * *

His crew and passengers were already gathered when Jamie arrived at the airport at 8:45 Tuesday morning. "Fuel is topped up, and she is ready to fly as soon as I load the luggage," Brian told him.

Dr. Ron had four large boxes, and Dr. Marvin Lang, the dentist, had one. All of the passengers had one bag each. With everyone in place, five passenger seats were occupied.

"We're in good shape," Brian said. "We could probably fill all the seats and with full fuel, still be OK. This bird carries a lot of weight."

* * *

"We are about 40 miles out," Brian told Jamie. "We are past all of the high country. If you want a high speed letdown, we can start now."

"Here we go," Jamie replied, trimming the nose down. A few minutes later they crossed the last range of hills, and the valley loomed before them. Jamie was feeling exuberant as he pushed the nose down more and watched the airspeed indicator pass the 210-knot line. He crossed over the buildings at about a hundred feet, the jet engine screaming as he pulled up in speed killing climb.

"Hey, I bet you woke them up down there," Brian said. "That was great."

Jamie retarded the power and held the nose up until they were approaching a stall and kicked left rudder. With the stall horn screaming, the nose came down rapidly, leaving everyone hanging in their seat belts. A wild scream came from the back seat where Sir Job had secluded himself during the flight. Jamie neutralized the controls, and the plane was in a glide lined up with the road, about a thousand feet from the touchdown point. The landing was as smooth as could be expected on the crude surface, and Jamie brought the plane to a stop opposite the main gate.

As the passengers disembarked, Marguerite McIvor stepped close to Jamie and whispered in his ear. "Jamie, you should be ashamed of yourself. I think you almost scared Sir Job to death. He might even have messed his long johns, if odor is any indication." She stepped back, laughing lightly to herself.

"Is that your standard approach to an airport?" Marvin Lang asked, his eyes twinkling. "That should jar a few teeth loose, so I don't have to pull them."

Sir Job was out of the plane and, without a word to anyone, headed through the gates toward the buildings. His followers, coming toward the plane, stared after him questioningly.

An older man approached Jamie and held out his hand. "My name is William Broder. I have been in charge since Sir Job left. He seems greatly disturbed about something. You have brought us more visitors, but what of the four people who departed with you?"

"All four of them have chosen to remain permanently in New Island. They have been accepted as citizens of our country."

"That does not surprise me much. They all had become restless, and I could sense their dissatisfaction with our lot here. I cannot say that I blame them, although I am sure that Sir Job was not happy about it."

"No, he wasn't happy. He threatened them with excommunication and all sorts of dire things. But nothing would change their minds. And Job was not happy with some of our people because they refused to treat him as a superior being. Our people are independent, and they do not respond well to anyone that starts preaching to them."

"I understand," William said. "Job is set in his ways, and he is not accustomed to having anyone cross him. It is too bad that he failed to make friends with your country."

"We agreed to continue our friendship," Jamie reassured him. "In spite of the disruptions that he caused, I've brought a doctor and a dentist, and they'll conduct a clinic to see if they can be of help to anyone in your community who is ill."

"That is great. There are several people who need attention, and we have one man who I fear is seriously ill. He has been experiencing severe stomach pains off and on for weeks."

"Be sure that he sees our Doctor Ron while he is here," Jamie told him. "Let me introduce you."

Jamie made introductions all around, and then William called on a couple of men to help unload the equipment. Dr. Ron explained to William that he needed a room to set up his clinic, and that Dr. Marvin should have a room for his dental examinations.

"About the only place we have is in the dining room. We can move the tables over some and hang curtains to make small spaces along the side of the room."

"God," Ron erupted, as he entered the dining room, "this is the best you have? No electricity—no running water—no sanitary facilities. You people are living a hundred years behind the times."

"Yes, Dr. Ron, you are right. Our people have followed the dictates of Sir Job. He refuses to let us modernize in any way. He swears that God has told him to follow this path. I must admit that there are some doubters beginning to make themselves heard."

"Now what am I going to do for hot water?" Ron asked. "I need to sterilize equipment after use. I should have a place to boil water."

"There are stoves in the adjoining kitchen. You could have hot water there and boil your instruments."

"I guess that'll have to do," conceded Dr. Ron. "We'll need two examination rooms, one for me and one for Dr. Marvin. I should have a cot of some kind, a small table and a couple of chairs. Dr. Marvin will need a couple of chairs and a small table."

"I think we can arrange all of that. We will have it ready for you to start right after breakfast in the morning. We will announce tonight that you are here and get the names of the people that want to see you. Also, if any of you would like to sleep in here, it would be all right. There is an outhouse a short way from the kitchen door."

"No," Ron replied, "I think we will sleep out by the plane. If we could have that little room you use for guests, we could use it for our personal needs. We can pack hot water from the kitchen for shaving and washing."

"I am sorry that we are so lacking in facilities. I will do the best I can to accommodate your needs. Now, I should get on with getting things ready for you. We will have dinner in this room at seven this evening. I will see you all at that time."

"William," Jamie said, "we have a radio to install so that we can maintain communications with our home base. I brought along an expert to set it up for you and teach someone to use it. Do you have a place for it?"

After a minute's thought, William replied, "How about the guest room where you slept before? That is about the best spot that I know of, and it is not needed for guests anymore."

"Do you suppose Job will approve of all of these arrangements?" Jamie asked.

"Job put me in charge of the colony when he left, and he has not rescinded those instructions yet. Until he does, I will carry on using my own judgment. If he objects, we will worry about that when the time comes. Let us get on with what we are trying to do. I appreciate your efforts, especially under such trying conditions. I will see you at dinner this evening."

* * *

William was waiting for Jamie and his group when they entered the dining room. "I have had the men's table extended to accommodate all of you. Lady McIvor, I know it is your custom to eat at the same table as you husband, so I have provided room for you."

"No, William," Marguerite said, "I'll eat with the ladies. I would prefer to adapt to your customs when I am your guest."

"Thank you," William replied. "I will make the arrangements; come along." He escorted Marguerite to the women's table and introduced her to his wife, Mary Broder. Mary immediately made a place for her beside her own place at the head of the table.

Jamie wondered about the absence of Job, but kept still, waiting for events to evolve.

The meal was finished, the dishes picked up, the children dismissed, and the women returned to their places when the front door opened and Job entered the room. There was complete silence as he made his way to the head of the men's table. William slid his chair aside to make room for him.

"My friends." Job's voice seemed a little tremulous. "We have come to a great divide in our history. I have returned from a trip to the beautiful New Island country with their leader, Jamie, who you have met before. I failed you miserably on that trip. In spite of my exhortations, I lost four of our people to the appeals of that Godless country. I also failed miserably in my public relations efforts with the Godless citizens of that country. In spite of my failures, New Island's President Jamie treated me as a gentleman, even though he was in extreme disagreement with my actions, and has offered his friendship and help to our people. In view of the failures that I have experienced in the past few days, I find it necessary to withdraw as your leader, hoping that God will forgive me. I will spend the rest of my days in seclusion, praying to the one and only God for the souls of our people. After tonight, you will not see me again. I am asking Sir William to assume my post as your leader. I hope that you will all obey his dictates as prescribed by our God Almighty. I exhort you to obey his commands as you have obeyed mine. Farewell and God bless you all." Turning, Job hurried from the room.

The dead silence in the room had stretched into minutes when William rose to his feet. "Although I knew that something was afoot, and had a faint idea how things were headed, I had no inkling that we had reached this crisis. I am not sure that Job has the right to appoint his successor without at least some consultation with his subjects. We have with us tonight the leader of the New Island country that Sir Job alluded to as beautiful but Godless. I question that the people of that country are Godless. At least the ones that I have met demonstrate that they are considerate and caring people. I wonder if it is not time to change our thoughts and perhaps emulate to some extent the people that Sir Job has criticized so harshly. With that in mind, I would like to have Sir Jamie tell you something of his government and the customs of his people. Sir Jamie."

Jamie rose to his feet and surveyed the crowd. "The first thing that I would like to make clear to all of you is that I don't care to be called Sir Jamie. That seems to designate one as some superior being, entitled to special treatment. I am plain Jaime, and that is what I wish to be called. My official title is President. The term president denotes, to me, an ordinary man who is elected by his peers as the temporary leader of a country, or organization. By temporary, I mean that he can be voted out of office by the people if another person can offer the people better leadership.

"Another thing. In New Island, women have equality with men. Women vote the same as men. Anyone over the age of 16 is entitled to vote. Women are not segregated as they are here. In our country, women, and in most cases the children, would join the men at the dinner table. We take every opportunity to enjoy each other's company. We also prefer to have our meals in a leisurely manner. We eat, laugh, tell stories and otherwise enjoy our meals. So much for some of our basic customs. Now, on to government.

"New Island is governed by a council of seven. The council is elected by the vote of registered citizens. The council, once elected, elects one of their members to serve as president. Another member is designated vice president and secretary-treasurer. This council has the power to conduct routine business of the country, but must go to the people for approval of anything out of the ordinary. In our case, we have regular general meetings in which I, as president, report to the people. This works well for us. This is radically different from your own conditions, and I don't know if it would work here or not. Are there any questions?"

A woman from the middle of the table held her hand up. "Am I permitted to ask a question?"

"While I have the floor, I will conduct this meeting as if it were in my own country. Yes, you may ask a question."

"In your country, if I thought you were doing something wrong, could I say so?"

"Yes, you would have that right. And if you were supported by the majority of the people, I would have to change to suite the majority, or get out of office."

"I can hardly believe that such a country exists."

A hand was raised at the men's table, and Jamie nodded acknowledgment.

"Do you really believe that women have the same capabilities as men to make decisions on major issues?"

"Sir, if you asked that question in a general meeting at home, you would probably be booed out of the room."

"Can you tell us about the four people who went over with you last week and decided to stay?"

"Yes. I don't think there is any secret about it. One reason is that all of them are unmarried people and have no chance of finding mates in this community because everyone is related to them. One of the ladies already has a proposal. The main reason is that they got a taste of freedom, which they have never had before. The council approved their applications, and that was the end of it."

William stepped up. "What would all of you think of establishing a government here similar to that of New Island?"

After a long silence, someone spoke up. "Do you mean that such a thing is possible?"

"Yes, it is possible if you people want it and think you can cope with it. It may be a challenge because none of us have any experience with self-government. I do not wish to continue the dictatorial regime that we have had. I believe in a God, but He certainly has not given me any instructions as to how to govern, and I do not think that He will in the future. How many of you here would be in favor of us setting up a government similar to that of New Island?"

Every hand went up at the men's table. The women did not move.

"The men all appear to be in favor. But what about the ladies?"

"You mean we get to vote too?" a voice called out.

"Yes, you have a vote."

Every hand went up at the women's table.

"What I would like to do, if Jamie will consent, is to have him direct us and serve as an advisor for an election. Will you do that, Jamie?"

"Yes, I will," Jamie consented. "I would like all of you to think about it and discuss it. We'll have another meeting here tomorrow evening to see where we are going."

* * *

As the group dispersed from dinner, William followed Jamie from the room. "We have other problems here besides health," William said. "There are some supplies, that in spite of our self-sufficiency, we have to buy from outside sources. Heavy merchandise, such as sugar, we must go to Claresholm for. That is about 35 miles away. To go there and back with a team and buggy takes about three days. Sir Job would not consider letting us get a truck of some sort, saying that was against the will of God. Have you any suggestions?"

"Can anyone here drive a motor vehicle?" Jamie asked.

"I can," William replied. "And there are one or two others here that say they can drive."

"Then we should get you a truck and a smaller car of some kind."

"How would we possibly do that?" William asked. "We have very little money."

"No problem. We have to fly the plane to Lethbridge to get fuel. You come with us, and we will find a vehicle and you can drive it home. All the people are dead, so we can take anything we want."

"Is that ethical?" William asked.

"I don't know, but I can see no reason not to take advantage of it."

* * *

Nick Shushkoff was Dr. Ron's first patient. His wife practically dragged him into the examination room. "He not want be examined," she explained. "He say he all right, we just leave alone. He hurt all time and not eat many days. He not able work. Something bad wrong with him."

"Let's take a look," Dr. Ron said. "Let's get that shirt off."

Nick unbuttoned his shirt and removed it, revealing the long underwear.

"Where does it hurt?" Ron asked.

"Down here." Nick indicated the right side of his lower abdomen.

"Lay down on that bed," Ron ordered.

Reluctantly, the man stretched out on the cot. Dr. Ron unfastened his belt and undid his pants, opening them wide. Unbuttoning the underwear, he felt of the man's lower abdomen, pressing lightly. Nick winced in pain and gritted his teeth. A large lump was evident to Ron's exploring fingers.

"OK, you can get up and fasten your clothes, then sit in this chair." Sticking his head out a gap in the curtains, Ron asked Marguerite for a thermometer. She fished one out of a jar of sterile solution and handed it to him. "Have you ever had your temperature taken?" he asked.

"No," Nick replied.

"Open your mouth," Ron commanded. "This goes under your tongue. Close your mouth, but don't bite down on it. Just hold it there for a bit." Pulling the thermometer from Nick's mouth, Ron held it up to get better light and made a note on a pad. "You have a temperature of 103," he reported.

"Is bad?" Nick asked.

"Yes, it's bad. You have an infected appendix."

"You have medicine make well?"

"No," Ron told him. "I'll have to operate. There is no other way. It is not a serious operation, but I can't do it here. I'll have to take you back to my hospital in New Island."

"You mean you cut me. No, I not be cut."

"Then you will die. Sooner or later, you will die."

Nick's wife intervened. "How soon he die?"

"I don't know how soon. The appendix is badly swollen, and it is likely to rupture anytime. If that happens, the poison goes through your body and you will die within a few days. If we take it out, we get rid of the inflammation and you will be well soon."

"But I no want you cut. I never been cut. I afraid."

"You big baby," declared Mrs. Shushkoff. "You take him on airplane your house do cutting?"

"That is right. I will have to make arrangements with Jamie, but I am sure he will agree. I need to get him there as soon as possible. It's risky to wait."

"All right. You take him. I go, too, make him behave. OK?"

"All right. I will ask Jamie if you can go along. I am sure that he will agree. Now, he should go home and rest. Give him one of these pills now and another before bed, then another in the morning. We will go either tomorrow or the next day. So long."

Marguerite brought in the next patient. The man pulled off his shirt and unbuttoned his underwear to pull it from his shoulders.

He had a huge boil under his arm. Dr. Ron lanced the boil; drained out the pus that it contained and placed a sterile dressing over it.

His next patient was a woman who had had her regular period, then continued to bleed for three weeks. Reluctantly, she disrobed and allowed Ron to examine her. He found a uterine cyst and decided to remove it. He didn't like the conditions, but decided the operation should be done as soon as possible and didn't justify taking her to New Island. Marguerite agreed. They used a local anesthetic, and an hour later the woman walked out with instructions to rest for at least three days. By then, the morning had disappeared.

Dr. Lang spent the morning pulling teeth. Several patients had come in with broken, rotten teeth for which the only remedy was extraction. One woman had an abscessed tooth, and her jaw was badly swollen. She reported that it had been that way for a month, and Dr. Lang marveled that the infection had not spread to other parts of her body. The two men took their used instruments to the kitchen where they put them in a pot of water to boil, making them ready for the afternoon.

* * *

Jamie and Brian were at the plane immediately after breakfast. William was waiting for him, along with another man who he introduced as Thomas Skrylak. "Could I bring Thomas along?" he asked. "He is also able to drive a car."

"Sure, bring him along," Jamie consented. "There's plenty of room."

The two men looked apprehensive as Jamie showed them how to buckle their seat harness. Neither had ever been in an airplane before. Jamie let Brian take the left-hand seat, and a few minutes later they were airborne and headed east for the 25-minute flight to Lethbridge. Brian made a couple of low altitude circles over the area before landing, to give them an idea of the layout of the city. They found the fuel station, and Brian disconnected the regional power and hooked up the generator in order to activate the fuel pumps.

With the airplane serviced, and Brian carrying his tool kit, they started out to find a vehicle for Little River. They decided to try the parking lot where they found a late model Chevrolet Suburban.

"Let's look at that one," Jamie said. "That could be the perfect vehicle for these fellows."

The driver's door was open, and a badly decomposed body, swarming with maggots, was on the tarmac at its side. A key ring was on the pavement a few inches from the body. Gingerly, holding a handkerchief over his lower face, Brian approached the gruesome corpse, snatched up the keys and retreated. Going to the other side of the car, he opened the passenger door, got in and slid across the seat to reach the driver's door and pull it shut. Inserting the ignition key, he tried the starter. The motor came to life, and Brian backed the vehicle out of the parking stall and moved a short distance away. The others came forward to examine it. The unit was four-wheel drive, with a winch mounted on the front. Only 20,000 kilometers showed on the odometer.

"This should be an ideal rig for you fellows," Jamie said. "I don't think we are going to do any better. At least, this is a good start. Let's gas it up, and you guys can take it home."

"Let's go see if we can find a grocery store first," William said. "We are almost completely out of sugar. I think there is a big wholesale kind of place not far from here."

"OK, William. It's your car. Brian and I will ride in the back seat."

William was a little awkward with the vehicle, but with no traffic to contend with, he managed well enough. A couple of miles toward town, they found a big box grocery outlet, and William parked close to the front door. The parking lot was empty, indicating that no one was around when the poison gas struck. Brian had a little trouble with the door, but managed to get it open. With shopping completed, they headed back to the airport, where they dropped Jamie and Brian and started the hour and a half drive home. They were all home for lunch.

* * *

Over lunch, Dr. Ron told Jamie of the bad condition that Nick Shushkoff was in. "I'm really worried about him. If that appendix ruptures, it is going to be very bad. If I get to him fast enough, I can probably save him, but it is hazardous. If I can get in there before it breaks, there is nothing to it."

"Maybe we should load him up and get him to the hospital today," Jamie said. "We can do it if you think it is advisable."

"It is very advisable, but I hate to push your schedule."

"To hell with the schedule. Let's go see your man."

William directed them to the Shushkoff living quarters. They found Nick on the bed, wreathing in pain, sweat running down his brow. His wife was frantic. "I can no do nothing help," she sputtered. "He hurt worse all time."

Jamie took one look and made up his mind. "Let's get him out of here. The plane is ready to fly. We have to round up our people. Leave all your stuff here, and we will be back next week or sometime and you can finish your clinic."

"That's the best thing we can do," Ron said. "Let's hurry!"

Jamie found Brian and William and explained the situation. "We need to lie him down, if we can."

"I can pull two seats out of the plane and leave them here. That way, we can lay him flat on the floor and strap him down with the safety belts. It will only take a few minutes. I'll be ready before you can get him out."

"I will get help to move him to the plane. I know where there is a cot that we can use as a stretcher." William was off at a run.

By the time Jamie had rounded up the rest of the crew and explained the situation, William had the cot with three men to help at the Shushkoff quarters. Ron gave the patient a shot, hoping to ease the pain, and supervised moving him onto the cot. With a man on each corner of the makeshift stretcher, they headed for the plane. Marguerite came running with Ron's medical kit, and Marvin Lang was right behind her. They maneuvered the cot through the wide door of the cabin and strapped it in place. Ten minutes later they were climbing towards the mountains.

Brian got busy on the satellite phone. Randy answered. "How's the weather there?" Brian asked.

"We have a heavy overcast, about a 1000 foot ceiling and good visibility."

"Any wind?" Brian asked.

"Not a bit," Jacob told him. "Dead calm."

"We'll be there about three o'clock. Have Dr. Bill there with an ambulance. We have a very sick man onboard." Brian turned to Jamie. "We will have to make an instrument approach. I'll set up a GPS marker about 20 miles southeast of the field in line with the runway, and you can make a straight-in from there. Should be a cakewalk."

"Thank God I made that practice run," Jamie said. "I'd feel pretty nervous if I hadn't had that opportunity to try it out. I'm a little nervous, even so, but there is no alternative."

"It's no problem," Brian assured him. "I have every confidence in you being able to do it."

"I hope these other people feel the same way," Jamie said.

"We won't tell them till we get in the soup; they will think you have been doing it every day."

* * *

In the back of the plane, Marguerite was having trouble with Mrs. Shushkoff. The woman was frantic, both with fear for her husband and fear of the airplane. Marguerite was trying to reassure her. "We will only be about three hours, and then your husband will be on the ground and in the hospital. After that, it won't take long for Dr. Ron to fix him up."

"But maybe all die before get there," Mrs. Shushkoff exclaimed.

"We are perfectly safe," Marguerite explained. "This is a very good airplane with a fine pilot. I will ride anywhere in the world with Jamie flying the airplane."

"But maybe engine stop. We fall."

"No," Marguerite tried to reassure her. "If the engine did quit, we would not fall. Jamie would fly the plane like a big glider and find a spot to land it. We would be safe." Then in an effort to change the subject. "Were you born in Little River?"

"No. I born Rooshia. Nick born Rooshia. That why we not talk good. We learn many words, not all words. We talk Rooshia good, but no one here talk Rooshia. English hard."

"Do you read and write English?' Marguerite asked.

"No. Nick—me no read Rooshia—English. We no write."

"How long have you lived in Little Valley?"

"We live camp Poland many years. Then government send us Canada. Then we come here. Very good. Camp no good."

Marguerite decided that Mrs. Shushkoff was settled down and went to check on Nick. He seemed to be sleeping, but was groaning and sweating. He was obviously in bad shape. She hoped that they would get him to the hospital in time.

* * *

Brian was busy with a pad and pencil. "We'll be coming up on the marker any minute now. At the marker, turn to 320 degrees. At 120 knots, you should make the field in 10 minutes. That means that you can let down at 1000 feet per minute. Here's the marker now."

Jamie swung the plane to the new heading, slowing and trimming to the required speed and letdown. The ILS needle was showing on the right side of the dial, and Jamie edged right a little, watching as the needle slowly moved to the left. As it neared the center, he turned back to the left to stop the needle. The glide slope needle made its appearance at the top of the dial. He was high, so he pulled in 10 degrees of flaps and throttled back to increase his rate of descent. Suddenly, he was in clear air, and the runway was in front of him. With a thrill of accomplishment, he completed the landing and taxied rapidly to the ramp where the ambulance was waiting. In minutes, the patient was transferred to the ambulance and, along with the patient's wife, Dr. Ron and Marguerite, was on its way to the hospital.

Chapter 39

At the hospital, they wheeled Nick to the operating room. "Get his clothes off and prepare him for surgery," directed Dr. Ron. "Dr. Weaver will handle anesthesia. Marguerite will be surgical nurse." The patient was already in a semi-comatose state from the shot Dr. Ron had administered before landing. Rapidly, they stripped his clothes.

As they slid the long johns off his body, Marguerite exclaimed with disgust. "Christ! I wonder how long since he's had a bath. This underwear stinks worse than a pigpen. Look at the brown stain in the seat. They must not have any toilet paper there. We better give him an antiseptic sponge bath. His whole body must be crawling with bugs."

In spite of her objections, Nurse Dianne had parked Mrs. Shushkoff in the waiting room, commanded her to stay there and went to help with cleanup of the patient.

Dr. Bill rigged up an intravenous drip and was ready to put the patient under. Dr. Ron returned from scrub up and slid into a surgical gown and rubber gloves. "Are you ready?" he asked.

"We're ready," replied Dr. Bill.

Ron held his hand out, and Marguerite slapped a scalpel in it. Sliding his finger along the course he wanted to cut, Dr. Ron followed it with the scalpel, making a five-inch incision through the skin and muscle of the abdominal wall. Nurse Dianne at his elbow sponged blood as Ron cut through the peritoneum. The appendix was readily visible, swollen many times its normal size and colored a nasty dark-blue black. "God, we're lucky. It hasn't broken yet. But it sure couldn't go much longer. Now to get it out without breaking it and spilling that mess. Sponges, please." He inserted the sponges under and around the swollen pouch, and with a pair of tweezers, grasped the neck of the pouch close to the bowel and snipped it loose with scissors. Holding up the swollen gland for all to see, he exclaimed, "We got it, and it didn't break."

Twenty minutes later, the incision closed and a dressing over it, the patient was ready to go to his room.

"We better get his wife cleaned up before we let her see him," Marguerite said. "If she is half as dirty as he was, she'll contaminate everything she gets close to."

"She's about my size," Dianne said. "I'll go round up an outfit and see if I can get her in a shower and some clean clothes on her."

Returning to the waiting room, she explained to Mrs. Shushkoff, "Your husband is fine. The operation was successful, and he will be regaining consciousness in a short time. But before you go in the recovery room, you will have to take a shower and change clothes."

"I no have other clothes," Mrs. Shushkoff objected. "This all."

"You are about the same size as me," Dianne explained. "I brought you an outfit of mine. It will do until we can get some clothes for you." Leading her into the bathroom and showing her the shower, she asked, "Have you ever used a shower?"

"No. We bath tin tub."

"All right," the nurse told her. "Get those clothes off and I will help you."

"I take all off?" The woman was reluctant.

"Yes, everything off," Dianne said emphatically. "If you want to see your husband, you have to get cleaned up."

Slowly, Mrs. Shushkoff began removing her clothes. The nurse turned on the shower and adjusted the temperature. Turning to the woman, she pushed her into the shower. "Here is shampoo. You use it on your hair. Scrub it good with the shampoo, rinse it out and use the shampoo again. Use this soap on your body. Use it all over, everywhere, and rinse. Here are towels to dry yourself. Now, get at it."

Out of the shower, Mrs. Shushkoff toweled furiously, obviously enjoying the sensation of being clean. She had gotten over her reluctance at being nude. Dianne noted that, in spite of her age, which she judged to be around 60, Mrs. Shushkoff appeared to be in remarkable physical condition. Her face showed the ravages of weather, but her body was well muscled and firm, even her breasts showing little sag. Her waist length hair was a dark brown with only touches of gray. Dry, she turned to reach for the clothes the nurse was holding out for her. She recoiled in horror at the scanty underpants and the brassiere. "You want me wear that?"

"Sure," the nurse told her. "It's what I and other women wear. Look," she lifted her knit top over her head. "All women wear this kind of underthings. Go ahead. Try them on."

Reluctantly, Mrs. Shushkoff pulled the panties on, and the nurse helped with the brassiere. The panties were loose, but the bra fit fine. The sturdy knee-length skirt had an elastic waistband that was self-adjusting, and the knit top fit nicely. A pair of flip-flop sandals completed the outfit.

Mrs. Shushkoff looked at herself in the mirror. "Feel naked," she exclaimed. "Not proper."

"It is proper in New Island. It's all I have for you now. To-morrow, we will take you to get more clothing. You look very good. Come on, I will take you to your husband."

Entering the room, they found Nick already coming out of the anesthesia. Groggily, he stared at his wife. "I have dream." He said, "You may be my wife."

"No dream," his wife replied. "It me. I just have bath, new clothes. I same woman."

"You beautiful," he murmured and drifted into sleep.

* * *

The next morning Jamie went to see Nick Shushkoff. He found him sitting up in a chair, the remains of a breakfast on the table beside him. He was still hooked to an intravenous drip, but he appeared much better than he had the day before. Dr. Ron had just finished taking his temperature. "Everything looks good," Ron reported. "His temperature is almost down to normal. He is going to be fine in a short time. He was dehydrated and undernourished, so I have him on an intravenous hydration and feeding program, along with antibiotics. He should be able to continue on his own within a day or two."

"He good doctor," Nick spoke up. "He cut me, I not know. I much better now. I feel good."

"He is a very lucky man," Dr. Ron said. "His appendix was swollen to many times normal size and was full of infection. Another day or two, it would have ruptured for sure, and he would have been a dead man. Thanks for getting us back here so fast."

"No problem," Jamie said. "Thank that beautiful Cessna Caravan for performing so well. That is one fantastic airplane."

"Of course one fantastic pilot had nothing to do with it. Where did you learn to fly instruments?"

"Oh, I picked it up when I was flying up and down the coast for many years. I knew what happened to pilots that blundered into clouds when they were not prepared for it, so I figured I better learn how to do it. It came in handy yesterday."

"You did a fine job yesterday," Ron said. "I was nervous when you dropped into those clouds, but happy when the runway showed up in front of us. That was well done."

Mrs. Shushkoff came into the room, and Jamie was amazed at the difference in her looks. Her hair was shiny and clean looking, and hung in a braid down her back. With her borrowed outfit, she looked as if she could fit into any New Island gathering.

"You look very good, Mrs. Shushkoff," Jamie said approvingly. "How does it feel to join the modern world?"

"Me feel much good. Husband like."

Nick spoke up. "I not know I have much beautiful wife. She not look much so good before."

"You folks don't speak like the rest of the people at Little River," Jamie commented.

"No," Nick explained. "We Rooshian Doukhobor. We kicked out. We not burn schools and go naked to town. Sir Job take us in. He say we must obey him. Sometimes much hard. We talk Rooshian good. Not English. We learn much English words. Much English words we not learn. It hard."

"You speak enough English to be understood," Jamie told him. "Where was the Doukhobor colony you were kicked out of?"

"Over mountain west. Bountiful."

"Yes, I have read in the newspapers about Bountiful. They are more law abiding there now, I think. Or were before everyone died."

* * *

With little else to do, Dianne took it upon herself the transformation of Flora Shushkoff. She took her to the Wal-Mart Store and outfitted her with a good supply of outdoor work clothes, boots and rain gear, plus an assortment of better clothing for indoors and special occasions. With no winter underwear available, Dianne convinced Flora that if she was going to wear what she had been wearing, it should be in cold weather only, and the underwear should be washed at least once a week.

"But take much water," Flora objected.

"But your husband likes the new you and says you are beautiful," Dianne observed. "If you want him to keep on liking you, you must be beautiful all the time. To be beautiful all the time you must be clean and smell good. You can't wear underwear for weeks and not take baths and smell good. You smell like a cow, only worse."

Dianne introduced her to toilet paper and body powder, to toilet soaps and hand creams, and a limited amount of cosmetics and how to use them judicially. By the end of the week, Flora was a new woman and the pride of Dianne as she showed her off every chance she got.

Dave brought Joseph and Jacob to visit Nick on Friday. Nick was up and walking the halls and getting restless. After talking to Nick awhile, the two convinced Dave that he should help Nick get clothes like they were wearing.

"What people say I go home?" Nick objected.

"They will probably envy you and want the same things." Dave told him, "I understand that Sir Job is no longer in charge and that you are considering setting up a government like we have here. You will be able to show them how we dress here."

"Maybe Jacob or I should go along for a visit, so they know how happy we are to be free."

"Sounds like a good idea," Dave said. "I'll talk to Jamie about it. Maybe you should both go."

"No, one of us has to stay here to look after the farms," Jacob said. "We could draw straws to see who stays. We just want to be sure that whoever goes is able to come back."

* * *

They were ready to make the return trip to Little River Monday morning. Jamie had had to refuse passage to Jacob because the six seats that remained in the Caravan were taken. The two doctors, with Marguerite and Stan, plus Nick and Flora Shushkoff filled all of the seats. The rest of the space was crammed with cargo, including two cases of toilet paper that Marguerite had insisted on. "We'll get toilet paper over there," Jamie told her, but Marguerite reasoned, "Now that I have two of them converted to the proper way of cleaning their butts, I'm going to be sure they have the means to continue and can pass it on to others."

"How's our load?" Jamie asked Brian.

"We are under allowable gross by close to a hundred pounds," Brian replied. "I weighed everything. You may be just a little tail heavy, but not enough to bother."

At 11 AM, Mountain Time, they touched down on the road at Little River.

"That landing was a little more civilized than the last one we made here," Marguerite kidded as she disembarked. "How come?"

"I didn't have anyone onboard that I really needed to impress," Jamie replied.

William was running from the gate to greet them. He seemed surprised to see Nick Shushkoff climbing from the plane in apparently good health. "You get healed without the operation?" he questioned.

"Dr. Ron cut belly open, fix, sew me up good. He good doctor. I feel good. He say one week, I work like always."

With the plane unloaded, it was time for lunch. William led the way to the dining room and stood back to see Jamie's reaction, which was one of complete amazement. The tables had been rearranged to form a U, with places reserved at the base of the U for the guests and William and his wife. Kids were placed at the ends of the tables and men and women were intermixed at the remaining spaces.

"Hey, this looks great. How do people like it?"

"They are having the time of their lives. Everyone is happy. They adapted to it almost instantly. I think it is one of the best things we could do to revive friendships and the spirit of cooperation. People are working harder and enjoying it. You cannot believe the difference it has made in only a few days. Now, they are waiting for you to tell us how to go on with self-government and how to make this place a better place to live."

They settled into their places, and there was a sudden quiet as the group realized that their company was back. William stood to speak. "You are aware that Jamie and his crew and the good doctors are back with us. Also, Nick and Flora are back. Nick and Flora, please stand up." There was a gasp as people saw the change in the two. "The good doctor Ron saved Nick's life by operating on him to remove his appendix. Nick is almost fully recovered and can resume his regular duties within the week. But also look at the new clothes they wear. And Nick has had his hair cut and his beard trimmed. Do they not look mighty fine?"

An enthusiastic round of applause indicated the people's approval.

Jamie stood to another round of applause. "I cannot believe the difference in this group since we left a week ago. You look

296

like a bunch of happy, well-adjusted people rather than the bunch of grouches that you appeared to be last week. What has made the great difference?"

A man stood near the middle of one of the tables. Jamie recognized him as Thomas Skrylak, the man who had gone to Lethbridge with them last week.

"It's good to see you again, Thomas. You have the floor."

"You are the reason, Jamie. You talked to us, and we realized that we had not been living a good life. With Sir Job gone, and you to tell us how to get organized, I think we are going to be a new people."

"I am glad for you all," Jamie said. "Perhaps you will join William and Brian and me this afternoon to go over some ideas, then I will present my ideas to you all at dinner this evening. Let us now enjoy our lunch."

Again, there was applause as several women got up and went to the kitchen to serve the meal.

* * *

Jamie, Brian and Stan met with William Broder and Thomas Skrylak outside the dining hall.

"What can we show you and what do you want to know?" asked William.

"First off," Jamie said, "we would like to know about your water supply."

"Our domestic water comes from a well. Come, I'll show you." William led the way to a small fenced enclosure behind the buildings. "This well is 60 feet deep, hand dug. The water comes up about 30 feet in it. We have the pump set at 50 feet, so we have never been able to pump it down."

The pump, setting on a platform a couple of feet above ground level, was an ancient hand pump with a handle about three feet long that actuated the pump rod that connected to the pump cylinder deep in the well. Two boys, one on each side of the handle, were using most of their strength to pull the handle down, and then up. Each downstroke produced a gush of water from the pump outlet to rush down a wooden trough, through the fence to empty into a water tank for livestock. Inside the fence, several large tubs could be filled for domestic use.

"How about irrigation water?"

"The water rights on the river are held by farmers about 20 miles downstream, so we have not used much irrigation. We have garden plots and orchards along the river, which seem to be adequately subirrigated for most things. The higher ground is all dry land. We get good crops of wheat, oats and barley most years. We always carry enough over to see us through lean years. Other land along the riverbank grows hay."

"Do any of you know what an old-fashioned pump jack looks like?" Jamie asked.

"Yeah, I have seen them," William said, "pumping water with a gas engine."

"I wonder if we could find one," Jamie said.

"There might be one in Claresholm at the farm supply store. They carry a lot of things."

"It would be worth looking into," Jamie commented. "If we could find one, plus a gas engine to operate it, it would save a lot of hard work."

"Where does the river come from?" Stan asked.

"There is a small lake in the foothills about six miles west." William told them, "It comes out of the lake over a waterfall and down the valley."

"A waterfall!" exclaimed Brian. "How high is it?"

"Probably 30 or 40 feet."

"We should bring Andy and Dave over here. They might be able to put a power plant on it and provide electricity for the whole place."

"Worth looking into," Jamie said. "But let's follow up on a pump for this well first. I think we can make life a little better for people here by installing new conveniences a step at a time. Let's say we take your van and drive into Claresholm and look around?"

"All right, let us go," William said.

"Tell the folks that we will be back in time for dinner," William told the boys who had quit pumping to listen to the conversation, and then led them towards the barn where the car was parked.

"Let Thomas drive," Jamie suggested. "I want to visit with William about some more ideas. Stop by the plane, so Brian can get his tool kit and the generator."

They were back at Little River in time for dinner, bringing with them not only the pump jack and engine but also a new two-ton flatbed truck.

Chapter 40

Jamie had barely arrived home from his last trip to Little River when his cell phone jangled. It was Teresa Blunt.

"We have made the decision. The whole damn family is going to get married at one time. Well, not quite the whole family, but half of it at least. That's Lars and Louise and Pat and me. We'd like to do the deed on Saturday, if you are available. What about it?"

"OK by me," Jamie consented. "Just tell me where and when."

"The where might be the problem. You know that Pat is a man of the sea. He mentioned one day that he would like to be married on a nice sandy beach looking out over the Pacific. Georgia Strait isn't big enough. He wants the open ocean. You know; he's sort of a sentimental old reprobate. Anyway, I thought that was a good idea. There is an airport at Tofino and a beautiful beach."

"Yes, there is an airport at Tofino, so that is no problem," Jamie told her. "But the weather could well be a problem. Also, the airport is about six kilometers from town. I think, if you have your hearts set on this, I better take Pat and fly over there tomorrow, see what weather conditions are and try to find some transportation from the airport. We still couldn't be sure of the weather a day ahead, but we would have a better chance. What do you think?"

"Sounds good to this old woman," Teresa replied. "I'll talk to Pat about it and call you back as soon as I can. I don't know when he'll be home, for sure, but sometime this evening."

"OK. I'll be waiting for your call."

Dinner was over when Teresa called back. "We have had a big family conference, and everyone is gung-ho on the project. Pat will meet you at the airport in the morning at whatever time you set. We won't formalize any plans until you get back and we know what the conditions are."

"Tell him to be there at about 9 o'clock," Jamie told her.

* * *

Jamie found Pat waiting for him at the airport when he arrived. Brian had the 206 out and ready to go. In a few minutes the plane was in the air. Jamie headed southwest over Comox Lake, then swung directly south through the gap between the Beaufort Range and Strathcona Park. With Pat marveling at the beauty of the rugged country, they crossed over the middle of Great Central Lake. The long narrow lake stretched for miles in either direction in its confining valley. They picked up Highway Four as it crossed the divide and twisted down the Kennedy River. Thirty minutes after takeoff, they had crossed over the Tofino Airport and were circling the village of Tofino. There appeared to be no activity anywhere, so, after another circle, Jamie headed back south towards the airport, flying at 500 feet above the terrain.

Pat came suddenly to life. "Jamie, look, there's a car down there."

The car was moving down the highway. Jamie made a circle to come over the car again. The passenger was hanging out the window and waving frantically. Jamie waggled the wings to acknowledge that he had seen her and continued on to the airport. By the time they got on the ground, the car, a late model SUV, was at the ramp to meet them.

As Jamie shut the engine down, a man and a woman were running to greet them. "Damn," the man exclaimed breathlessly, "there is someone else in the world besides us."

"My God," the woman gasped, "it's good to see you. Where are you from? Who are you?"

"I'm Jamie Morgan, and this is Patrick Holden. We are from the Comox Valley, just across the island from here."

The man stuck out his hand with a forceful grip. "I'm Harry Haynes, and this is my wife Janice. We were here when everyone started getting scared and leaving because some nitwit said the island was about to sink or something. We thought everyone was nuts, so we left on a fishing trip. We were out on the ocean for a week and came back to find everyone gone, with no radio, TV or telephone."

Jamie outlined for them the story up to date of the New Island settlement and what they had accomplished, with the supposition of the gas that had killed off everyone, except a few scattered pockets. Apparently Tofino was included in the north island area that had been spared.

"It sounds like we were just on the south border of the clear area," Harry reasoned. "We were going to drive to Port Alberni, but up Kennedy Canyon a little way we found a big semi jack-knifed, completely blocking the road. The driver was dead. We took the boat to Bamfield and found a number of dead people there. It looked like they had gone to sleep wherever they happened to be. There is no one, as far as we know, in Ucluelet or in any of the camps or Indian villages in the area. We are all alone."

"Well," Jamie told them, "you are no longer alone in the world. We would like you to join us in New Island. We will provide a farm for you, or if you don't want to farm, we'll find another place for you to live. We have room for lots of people in our community."

"I'm not much of a farmer," Harry said. "I've spent my life on the water. I was 20 years on a deep-sea tug, and then quit that to become a commercial fisherman. Do you have room for a fisherman in your community?"

"We have some Indian families living on our dock that are fishing people. We don't want to displace them. They have been providing all of the sea food the community can use."

Pat interrupted. "You say you are a tugboat operator. We don't have anyone that is competent with a tugboat and that might be a valuable skill in the future, in that we are living on an island."

"I was captain of a tugboat for ten years," Harry said. "I hauled as far as Hawaii and the Aleutian Islands. I've been up and down the Inland Passage hundreds of times, and in and out of the Frazer River."

"We'll find some place for you in our country for sure," Jamie told him. "At the present, we don't seem to need a tugboat operator, but we might well need you in the future."

"There might well be a job for you right soon," Pat said. "I was going to bring it up at the council meeting Sunday. This possibly solves some problems I was worrying about."

"Anyway, let's get on with our present project," Jamie said, and went on to explain their purpose in coming to Tofino.

"No problems there," Harry reported. "It's only a short way to the beach, and we have the transportation. Come, and we'll show you."

After a short ride down the highway, Harry turned onto a side road that led to the beach. There, spread out before them were miles of white sand, with the big Pacific waves rolling halfway up the beach.

"Perfect," Pat exclaimed.

Back at the airport, Harry and Janice decided that they would like to keep their 50-foot fishing troller, which they had spent years of rehabilitation work on, and would sail it around the island to Comox. They could live on the boat at Comox until it was decided what they would do. Nevertheless, they would wait until after the wedding to start out, and would be there with the car to provide taxi service.

* * *

The wedding party filled the Caravan to capacity. The two couples to be married, plus Mary and Kelly to act as bridesmaids, and Dave and Nils Blunt as best men filled the available seats. A couple of large coolers and several baskets were stuffed into the baggage compartments. A flight over the village alerted Harry and Janice, who were soon at the airport to meet them. It took two trips to ferry the party to the beach, where they found picnic tables above the high tide line.

Jamie made quick work of the ceremony, using the same basic lines that he had improvised for the marriage of Ted and Meg just after opening the settlement at New Island. With congratulations, handshakes and hugs over with, the coolers were opened. One contained several bottles of champagne and the other stocked with beer. Glasses were produced from one of the baskets and a round of toasts proposed and executed. Jamie and Brian refused the next round. "We don't drink and fly," Jamie explained.

The other baskets contained food. Cold meat and fresh sliced homemade bread with creamy butter, and an array of pickles and relishes, followed by an assortment of cakes and cookies provided the wedding feast. With wine and beer flowing freely, the party was soon feeling little pain. After a couple of hours of fellowship and drinking, Jamie decided he had better get them home.

* * *

All members of the council were present when Jamie called the meeting to order on Sunday afternoon. In addition, Pat Holden and the now Teresa Holden were at the table.

Jamie started the meeting. "Pat, from a comment you made Friday, I assume that you have something you want to put before the council."

"Yes, I do have something we need to discuss. Lately, I have had a number of people ask me what is to become of the submarine Denver. We should have brought this up before, but there has been so much going on in the development of this new country that I was reluctant to add to the burdens that you people are carrying. To make the story short, the Denver is not in a proper place for permanent storage, plus there is always the remote chance of radiation danger from her nuclear reactor."

"I thought," Jamie interrupted, "that the Denver was due for refueling very soon."

"That is true. We would take her into the base, and the depleted fuel rods would be removed and new rods installed. Nevertheless, those depleted rods are still radioactive, and will be for generations. Therefore, we can't take any chances with them. They must be put in a safe place. That doesn't mean that we can go down there and remove them. We wouldn't live long to tell about it. In order to dispose of the used fuel rods, the only answer is to dispose of the Denver. The safest thing we can do is tow her into the Pacific and scuttle her in the deepest water we can find. Then, even if the fuel rods were released, they could do no damage to human life. My proposal is to tow her out beyond Cape Flattery and open her seacocks over one of the deep canyons out there."

"Do the little tugs we have around here have the capacity to do the job, and do we have anyone that could operate them safely?" Charlie Johnson asked.

"No, it takes a seagoing tug to venture out in that water with a tow as big as the Denver. But the man that we met over at Tofino says he has had 20 years in big tugs on the ocean. We just have to find a tug big enough to do the job. I'm sure that if we went over to Vancouver we could find something."

"I haven't had a chance to tell you about Harry and Joyce Haynes," Jamie intervened. "We found them over at Tofino when Pat and I flew over there Friday. They were out fishing northwest of Tofino when the big disaster hit, and somehow, they were missed. They are on the way here now with their deepwater troller and should be arriving at Comox dock tomorrow. I think he could do the job if we can find a boat for him. I have been out and talked to the people on the dock, and they will be watching for them and make them welcome. They will live on their boat until they decide what they want to do."

"Well, that's the story that I wanted to talk to you about," Pat said. "What is the opinion of the council?"

"I move that we turn the whole problem over to Pat and make him responsible for solving it," Charlie Johnson said.

"I'll second that motion," Pat Draper said.

"That's how we get things done around here," Jamie said. "Delegate the responsibility to someone best qualified and forget it. The process works. Now the monkey is on your back, Pat. Talk to Harry as soon as you can and report back to us next Sunday, if possible. Now, something else. The people at Little River are gung-ho to modernize, but they have little mechanical knowledge of how to go about it. They have elected a council kind of government like we use, under my directions. We got them a gas-powered pump for their well, and that is the first step towards modernization. They asked if there was anyone here that would go over there to live for a period of time to help them get out of their primitive age and get up to date. I'll announce it at the meeting later this evening, but if any of you have any ideas, I would sure like to hear them."

Teresa spoke up. "I might have a solution for that, Jamie. My oldest boy, Nils, is getting restless. There just isn't enough work to keep him busy on our place, and with the additions to the family, we are running out of room. He might jump at the chance to do it."

"He is awfully young," Jamie said. "Do you think that he could handle a job like that?"

"He's not quite 23 years old, but he has more capabilities than a lot of men twice that age. He worked with his father on the tree farm starting at about 10 years. He finished grade eight but refused to go to high school. He just wanted to work with his dad. We had no help whatsoever on the farm. If something broke, his dad fixed it, showing Nils how to do it at the same time. They built and operated a sawmill. We all lived in a two-room shack, so they cut lumber and built on to it. They tapped a spring up the mountain, and we had running water. When power became available, Nils bought a book on wiring and did all the wiring himself. When his younger brother started high school, Nils studied with him. He learned algebra and trigonometry. He finds something he can't do; he gets a book and learns how. I think he'd jump at the chance to go over there and help those people, just so he doesn't have to join their religion. He'd kick up his heels at that."

"Okay, Teresa," Jamie said. "If he's interested, I'll talk to him about it. There is one more thing to look at over there. There is a waterfall a few miles from the compound at Little River. I would like to take Andy or Dave, or both of them, over there to see it and see if it has any possibilities for a hydro project. About the only other possibility for electricity would be a steam-powered plant fired with coal. They have a coal mine a few miles from the ranch."

"When do you want to go over again?" Bob Elder asked.

"I'd like to go this week, probably Tuesday. I would suggest that we take both of them over there at once, if they are willing. Anyone disagree?"

There was assent from all.

"OK," Jamie said. "It's potluck time. Let's close this meeting till next week."

Chapter 41

Jamie took the copilot's seat and let Brian fly the plane. There were cloud buildups over the mountains and thunderstorms to circumnavigate, resulting in some extreme turbulence. Brian handled it well, demonstrating improved proficiency with the plane. Some of the passengers were uneasy, but Nils, sitting behind the pilot, seemed to enjoy every bump. I believe that guy could become a good pilot, Jamie thought to himself. Maybe I should give him some instruction.

They landed promptly at noon (one o'clock Mountain Time) and found most of the population of Little River out to meet them. After introductions, William informed them that sandwiches were waiting for them in the dining room. William and Thomas sat with them while they ate, and they started plans for the afternoon.

Andy and Dave wanted to make a preliminary visit to the falls that afternoon and asked Thomas to guide them. Nils expressed a desire to see around the complex in order to get an idea of what was needed. William agreed to show him and Jamie everything that he could. Brian asked if he could follow, and permission was granted.

William asked Nils what he would like to see first.

"I want to see the houses first, inside and out. I want to know what your living conditions are."

William led the way. There were four houses, spaced in a row, close together. The grass and weeds around them were dry and brittle. No effort had been made to garden in any way. The houses were old wooden two-story structures, the paint peeling from the clapboard siding, the cedar shingles on the roofs curling and splitting.

Nils stopped and studied the houses appraisingly. "Have you ever had a fire here?" he asked.

"We lost a barn a few years ago when a lantern was dropped," William said. "We managed to get all the stock out, but it was nip and tuck. It had been raining, so the fire didn't spread."

"If the kitchen, or one of these houses caught fire the whole shootin' works would go up in an instant. You'd be lucky if people got out alive. Those buildings would burn like kindling

306

wood." The young man was obviously concerned with what he saw.

"I suppose you are right. I guess we have just never given it any thought."

"What do you heat with?" Nils asked.

"Mostly coal. We have our own coalmine a few miles away. The men work in the mine during the winter when there is less other work to do and get enough out to last for the summer. We use some wood in the summer because it burns out faster and does not heat the kitchen up so much. In the winter we use wood to start the coal burning. It is easier to get coal than it is wood."

"Let's see inside," Nils requested.

William led the way. Most of the first floor was taken up by a large common room, furnished with a skimpy amount of old-fashioned and well-worn furniture. A double set of bunk beds sat along one end, with drapes strung in front of them. At the other end was a room that William said had been designed as a kitchen, but since the communal kitchen had been started, it was used only for bathing and laundry. A large wood range provided the source of hot water to fill the round tub sitting in one corner. A trapdoor in the middle of the floor with an iron ring handle was obvious.

"What's under here?" Nils asked.

"That is a cellar for storing our winter food where it will not freeze." William grasped the ring and lifted. The door came up and swung back against a leather strap that kept it from folding down to the floor. A musty odor came up from the darkness of the cellar.

"I'll have to get a lantern if you want to go down there now."

"Never mind," Nils said. "I'll see it later."

Nils looked out the back door. Obviously, wastewater was disposed of off the step just outside. There was a space where the vegetation had been killed by the soap in the water.

A large drum stove in the middle of the room heated the main room. A metal chimney went through the ceiling above the stove. An open stairway led them to the second floor. A hallway went down the middle, with the iron stovepipe going through the center. Three bedrooms opened off each side of the hall. The bedrooms all contained old-fashioned iron bedsteads with sagging springs.

"I've seen enough," Nils said. "Are the other houses all the same?"

"They are all about the same," William said. "You appear distressed."

"I am distressed. These places are a disaster waiting to happen. I expected a big challenge in getting this place modernized, but this is far worse than I expected."

"This place was built just after World War I, and nothing much in the way of maintenance has been done since. What do you suggest we do about it?"

"I have to do a lot of thinking and have some advice from others to come up with a solution," Nils said. "My first thought would be to get all the people safe and touch a match to it, and then start over from scratch. I know we can't do that, so we have to give it a lot of thought."

Nils led the way downstairs and out the back door. A few paces from each back door was a scroungy privy. Nils opened the door to one and was assailed by a powerful stench and a swarm of flies.

"Where is your water supply?" Nils asked.

William pointed to the well about a hundred feet up a slight rise and led the way to it. "We got a gasoline pump on it last week, courtesy of Jamie and Brian. It has been great to have all the water we can use without hours of labor pumping it." A half dozen round washtubs were lined up, all full of water waiting to be packed away in buckets. "We are planning on building a wooden flume to carry the water to near the houses, but we have no lumber that is proper for it, and there hasn't been time to go get any. Besides, I am having a hard time driving the big truck. I keep killing the engine or getting it in the wrong gear. I need someone to teach Thomas and me to drive it."

"That's no problem," Nils told him. "I can teach you to drive it. But why build a wooden flume rather than pipe?"

"We could build a wooden flume, but we do not know how to build one of pipe."

"That's what I'm here for," Nils said. "Let's see the rest of the buildings."

William led the way through a gate in the fence that divided the living quarters from the barnyard. A long shed outside the fence covered an assortment of machinery, all designed for farming with horses, and all showing the wrath of ages. Two large barns appeared to be in reasonable condition. One barn was for cows and the other for horses. They were clean inside, the manure obviously shoveled out on a daily basis. Large lofts were filled with hay. Behind the barns was a granary, better built than the other buildings. It contained a number of bins for storage of wheat, barley, oats and rye. A chicken house was to one side of the granary, and chickens were scattered around the yard foraging for what food they could find. Farther along was a pigsty capable of housing a couple of dozen pigs.

"Where does the stock water?" Nils asked.

"The stock that is kept up water at a trough up by the well. The other stock goes to the river for water."

"What about the pigs and chickens?"

"We carry water for them from the well."

Nils shook his head, a look of disbelief on his face. Jamie, who had not spoken a word during the entire tour, looked with approval on the young man. He had displayed an extraordinary ability to absorb the deficiencies of the place, and Jamie felt that there was no doubt about his ability to do the job assigned to him. It would take a good deal of time, however.

"Let's see the rest of the land," Nils requested.

"Let us take the truck," William said. "You can show me how to drive it." He led the way back to the machine shed where the truck was parked under one end.

"I'd like to see the rest of the place, too," Jamie said. "Brian and I will ride in the back." He clambered over the side of the rack and stood behind the cab. Brian joined him.

Nils got in the driver's seat, and William climbed in beside him.

Nils studied the truck for a minute, then explained the shift pattern to William, and showed him how to maneuver the stick to engage the different gears. Starting the engine, he demonstrated as he slipped the shift into reverse. "Hold the clutch down," he explained. "Add throttle slowly. You will feel it start to take hold. Add more power as you remove your foot." The truck backed smoothly out of the shed.

"It looks easy," William said.

"It is easy. You just have to practice until you get the feel. This truck is real nice. Where do we go?"

William conducted a tour of the two sections of land, and they parked the truck back in its stall in the shed. "What do you think, Nils?"

"The land looks good. We can arrange for pumps to irrigate the bottomland during dry years. You should have no problem with raising enough food. The things we need to look at are your living conditions and safety. No one should have to live in the conditions you have here."

"I guess we never realized that we were bad off. We did not know any differently and were not allowed to find out. Now that a few of our people have been exposed to the outside, we are beginning to realize what we are lacking. What do you suggest?"

"Modernization and rebuilding. We need to get electricity in here somehow, that is the most important. We need to replace your living quarters. They are terrible firetraps, as well as presenting serious health problems. What do you think, Jamie?"

"You have summarized the situation very well," Jamie replied. "I think there are two alternatives. You follow through on Nils' suggestions, or you can abandon the whole place and move over to our valley. We would be happy to have you do that, but if you decide to stay here, we will help you in every way we can to fix things up here."

"We will have to put it to the people," William said. "I have an idea that they will opt to stay here. I think they would be very reluctant to move to a strange land. They are going to have enough challenges to cope with modernization here."

"That's probably the best," Jamie said. "It might be good for us to have two widely separated communities for security sake. We need a lot more thinking and conferences with your people. Here come our electrical engineers. Let's hear what they have to say. What did you find?"

"We found a beautiful waterfall," Dave reported. "A beautiful little lake and probably the most perfect spot for a small hydro project you could ever find. We'll go back tomorrow with our instruments and make a rough survey. Then we can come up with a preliminary draft of what you can expect. It should be a relatively simple project to build. We would have to build about six miles of power line to service the community here. Finding the generating equipment will be the big job, but I'm sure it can be found."

* * *

Dinner over, William stood and spoke to the assemblage. "I would like all of you to meet our new technical adviser, Nils

Blunt. I have spent the afternoon showing Nils our property here, and he is preparing to make recommendations on what we can do to improve our lives here. Would you like to give us a bit of advance information on what you think and what we can do to improve things?"

Nils got reluctantly to his feet. "I am not used to talking to a large group like this, so you will have to excuse me if I stutter a little, or have a hard time otherwise. I may be a little harsh in my statements. I don't know how to be a diplomat. Or a politician. I will probably say it like it is and hope you will not be offended.

"I am not prepared to make any recommendations yet. I have to think about it, study it some and talk to Jamie and the others. But I can say this. You have a beautiful piece of land here, and with very little help it will return you a good living. With the placing of some irrigation pumps to insure good crops of potatoes and other produce, even in the driest years, you have security of your food supply. I will have no problem with helping you with that.

"However, I am appalled at the condition of your living quarters and the sanitation. If a fire was to start in the kitchen or one of the houses, there is no way you could possibly stop it. They are too close together, and the dry grass around them adds to the danger. Fire in one and they will all be gone. Until that can be remedied, you must be very careful of fire. I am surprised that you have gone all of these years without a major disaster.

"Tomorrow, Jamie is going to fly us to Lethbridge. I want to see what is readily available there and in Claresholm to start modernizing. Also, tomorrow, Andy and Dave are going to survey the falls up the river and see if they can come up with a plan for a hydro plant to furnish electricity to the compound. That would be the biggest possible advance and make many other improvements easy. That's about all I can tell you tonight. Thank you for listening. Are there any questions?"

A man held up his hand and Nils nodded. "You seem to be very concerned about fire. I guess we have never thought about it much. Could we form some kind of a fire brigade to fight a fire if it should happen?"

"It wouldn't do much good. Even with the new pump on the well, you couldn't get enough water with a bucket brigade to accomplish much. As close together as these buildings are, one catches on fire and the fire will be so hot that the others are bound to burn. They catch fire, the best thing to do is grab your pants and run like hell. Don't stop to put 'em on, just run."

"Do you think it is possible to do anything to remedy these conditions?" another man asked.

"Of course it is possible. That is the reason we are over here, and I am going to stay for a while. We will do everything we can to make things better here. But we have to decide the best way to go about it—before we start making recommendations. I'll talk to you again tomorrow night."

* * *

They were down to 1000 feet above the ground, flying along the highway approaching Lethbridge when Nils yelled from his seat behind the pilot. "Hey, Brian, there's a big mobile home factory down there. Can you circle back so that I can see it better?"

Brian nodded his head and started the circle.

"Drop us down to 500 feet," Jamie said.

Brian slowed the plane and established the new altitude, flying a left-hand pattern around the factory.

"Jamie, can we come back and look at that place?" Nils said. "That may solve our housing problem. I've seen enough for now. I need to see it on the ground."

"Let's get to the airport and see if we can find a car."

A few minutes later Brian parked the plane at the fuel station. While Brian tended to the fuel, Jamie went for a walk along a row of hangars. A couple of cars were beside one of the hangars. One of them was an older model Buick sedan and had the keys in it. A few minutes later, he had it back at the fuel station. The gas tank was low, so they filled it with 100 octane. "That ought to make the old critter run like a new," Jamie said. "All aboard. Where do we go first?"

"I'm sure anxious to see those mobile homes," Nils said.

It took half an hour for Jamie to find his way through the city and out onto the freeway to the northwest. They found the factory on an access road, and Jamie drove onto the large display lot. Several models were on display, set up as model homes. Parked at the back of the lot were eight singlewide units, all identical models except for a variety of exterior paint schemes. There were numbers on the front of each unit, one to eight. Number one had a tow truck attached.

"Looks like a special order getting ready for delivery," Jamie remarked. "Let's go to the office and see what we can find out."

Brian made short work of the locks on the office. After some rummaging around, Jamie came up with a folder. The units were on order, all completely furnished, for a mining company in the northern part of the province. All the keys and the paper work were in the folder. Taking the folder along, they walked out to the units. Number eight had a set of access steps by one of the doors. Brian found the proper keys and they went in. The unit was fourteen feet wide and seventy feet long, with two bedrooms and a bath with a shower over it, plus a washer and dryer. A coal or wood stove was in the living room, as well as electric heat, with electric appliances in the kitchen.

"Hey," Brian enthused, "these could go a long way towards solving the housing situation out there. It would be no problem to move them all out there. Then if the guys get electricity in, these would house quite a few in modern comfort."

"But if we don't get the electricity, they are not of much use," Jamie cautioned. "But it is sure something to think about."

"Why don't we take that unit that's hooked up to the truck and set it out where we park the airplane?" Nils asked. "Then we can use it for sleeping quarters. It would beat sleeping on the ground, especially if the weather got bad."

"Can either of you guys drive that rig?" Jamie asked.

"Let's go look at it," Nils said. "I think I can handle it. I helped a guy move one about that size and set it up onetime. He borrowed a truck something like that to move it with."

They went to look at the truck. Nils climbed into the cab. The keys were in the ignition. He started the truck, waited for air pressure to build up in the brake system, and then moved it forward a few feet. Shutting off the engine and getting out, he stated, "Yep, I can handle it OK. There is no traffic, so I can use the entire road. Do you want me to take it? I think it's a good idea."

"Do you want to go with him, Brian?" Jamie asked. "I'll fly low and see how far you've got when I start home. If you get in trouble, we will come and get you with the van."

"Sure," Brian consented, "between the two of us, we will get it there. How is the fuel in the truck?"

"The gauge says full," Nils reported. "Let's go."

Jamie stood back and watched as the big rig left the lot. Nils made the proper wide turn to get it onto the access road, and a moment later he saw it headed up the freeway.

Jamie kept the plane at a low altitude as he followed the road that Nils and Brian would be taking on their way to Little River. Near a place on the map marked as Fort McLeod, he spotted the big trailer moving up the deserted highway astraddle of the centerline. Jamie passed over them at a hundred feet, waggling his wings as he pulled up to a more comfortable altitude and took up a heading direct to Little River.

* * *

Brian and Nils pulled the mobile home onto the lot near where the airplane was parked and by dinnertime had it on temporary blocks, with steps up to the door and the truck unhooked from it. It created a sensation as the inhabitants of Little River trooped through on tours of inspection. The house provided luxury beyond conception to the people of Little River who had never experienced even the rudiments of modern living.

Everyone was waiting expectantly when William called the evening meeting to order. He lost no time in turning the meeting over to Jamie. "I have talked to all of the people involved and will relay their thoughts to you as best I can. First, the power plant. Andy and Dave have made a preliminary survey and assure me that there is no problem in building a power plant that will provide all of the power needed in a community of your size. We only have to locate a generator that can handle the load. They think they can do that, but it may take awhile. There is no use in starting construction until we are sure that the generator is available. They will go ahead with drawing up plans while we search for the generator. The rest of the material should be readily available from Lethbridge or Calgary. The wire for the transmission lines can be salvaged from existing lines if we can't find new material. I don't know how many men you can dedicate to construction. I believe that I can find several in New Island. It would take a couple of months to build it.

"Now, the other thing that we found today. You have all seen the portable home parked over beyond the airplane. We found eight like that that were ordered for a mine up north. It is easy to move them up here. The thing is, would you people be interested in going back to family-style living rather than the communal setup that you have now? Those houses would not be of any use if you want to continue the commune. If you do, we will have to come up with another alternative. The living conditions you have now are not satisfactory. The decision is one that we cannot make for you. You must make it for yourselves."

Ann Broder held up her hand. "Do you mean that you could get enough houses for all of us to have our families separate?"

"That is correct. The eight we have now are probably not enough, but I know we can find enough to do the job."

Another woman spoke up. "It would sure be nice to have my own house. I would very much enjoy keeping house for just my own family. We have two boys."

"Jamie," William asked, "what is the time frame for getting a project like this done?"

"I cannot make a definite commitment, but I think we could finish before severe winter weather sets in."

"What is the feeling about such a project with you people?" William asked.

"What would be expected of us in return?" a man asked.

"Nothing at all," Jamie assured him. "We want to develop a New World of free people. In the future we might need your help as much as you need ours now. You have a beautiful and productive little valley here, and I would like to see it preserved. The only alternative to what we are proposing is to move to our valley. While we would welcome that, it may not be the best for you."

"This seems too good to be true," Anne Broder interjected.

"The thing is, do you people want to do it?" William said. "And do you want to go back to family-style living? These are decisions that you must make. Do you want to think about it for a week or two, talk it over among yourselves? This is a drastic decision, and you must not make a mistake."

A man stood in the back of the room. "May I speak, William?"

"Yes Armond," William told him. "It is your privilege."

"These people are offering us a great opportunity to put things right in Little River. It is going to be difficult to get the work done before snow comes, and then we would suffer through another winter of blizzards blowing through the shacks we are living in. Also, I can feel the anticipation that my wife has for a home of her own. If I understand the rules, I may make a motion. Is that right?"

"That is right," William assented.

"I move that we accept Mr. Jamie's offer to build the power plant and to bring in individual houses for the people of Little River to live in. That means that I move we get away from communal living and only operate the land on a communal basis. Thank you."

"Is there a second to that motion?" William asked.

Several hands went up, and William selected one.

"I second the motion," the man said.

"All in favor hold up your hands."

Hands were up all over the room.

"Opposed?"

One man raised his hand. "May I speak against the proposal?"

"The proposal has been approved, but I will allow you to have your say."

"This goes totally against the teachings of Sir Job. We have followed those teachings for more than eighty years. Do we want to throw that all away for the sake of a little luxury that we may not be deserving of?"

"I think that we have found the teachings of Sir Job to not be in the best interests of the people of Little River. We note your objections, but the decision has been made. Jamie, do you want to say anything?"

Jamie stood to a round of applause. "I am going to take charge of the project, so I will be here off and on for the rest of the summer. I am going to designate the mobile house parked out by the airplane as a headquarters and place to sleep for my people until the project is finished. I hope none of you objects to that arrangement. We will move the new homes in as fast as possible, but no one may move into them until water, sewer and electricity are hooked up to them. We will eat with you here. We are going home tomorrow, but we will be back and forth all summer. Nils is going to stay here indefinitely. I hope that you will give him and the rest of us the fullest cooperation possible." Jamie sat to a round of applause.

Chapter 42

Jamie picked Kelly up at school and found Pat Holden waiting on the front porch when he arrived home. Kelly ran to see if Irene and Josephine had anything planned for dinner, and the two men relaxed in the deck chairs.

"How was your trip to Little River?" Pat asked.

"It was a good trip, and we made some progress. Andy and Dave think they can put in a hydro plant if they can find equipment for it. That's going to be a problem, I'm afraid. They surveyed the falls, and there is enough water and enough head to run a turbine that will produce enough power. Finding the turbine is the problem. Turbines don't sit on shelves at Wal-Mart. But how is your project coming?"

"Harry Haynes and his wife arrived Tuesday afternoon and tied their fishing boat up at the dock. I went to see him yesterday morning and explained our problem. He says he can handle the tow and even knows about a tug that could do the job. It's tied up at the docks at Ucluelet. It's an old boat and should have an engineer and a deck hand to help him operate it. I think that Brian could handle the engine room, and Robert Dick says he will be a deck hand."

"Could we get everyone together this evening?" Jamie asked. "Let's try to meet in the boardroom at about seven o'clock. Maybe we should have some of the other council people there, too."

"All right," Pat agreed. "I'll get on the phone and round them up."

* * *

The group was there when Jamie entered the boardroom. Harry Haynes stood and shook hands with Jamie. "It's good to see you again, Jamie. Did you have a good trip?"

"Yes, mine was fine. How about yours?"

"We had a little rough weather getting into Juan de Fuca, but it wasn't too bad. That area can get very rough at times. Anyway, we are glad to be here. Your valley is beautiful."

"Let's sit down and get to work," Jamie said. "Harry, tell us about the tug you have in mind."

"It has been working out of Ucluelet for the past year. There wasn't much work for it, but the guy who owned it only wanted enough to pay for moorage and upkeep. The boat is very old, but seems to be in good condition. I have been on it several times. The engine is a big six-cylinder job and only turns about 300 revolutions at cruise speed, and makes about six knots regardless of the load it is pulling. To start it, you have to start a smaller diesel engine that runs an air compressor. When the air pressure is built up, you turn a valve that sends it through the big engine and turns it over. The engine usually starts almost immediately. Once started, it will run forever. There has to be a man in the engine room to put it in forward or reverse and handle the throttle. There are no remote controls on it."

"It sure sounds primitive," Bob Elder remarked. "Don't you think it would be better to go over to Vancouver and try to get something more modern?"

"It is primitive," Harry admitted. "But we know it is in good working condition, and I believe that I can operate it without too much trouble. We just have to find someone to handle the engine room."

"I think I can do that," Brian Veary spoke up. "I have been around diesels a bit, and they are all fundamentally the same. A diesel is a diesel, regardless of how old it is. A lot of the old-timers had to use auxiliary power to start them. I am willing to try, if you want me to."

"I can be a deck hand," Robert Dick spoke up. "I have crewed on tugs a bit. I could probably handle the engine room, too. I have been around some diesel engines."

"Can you operate with that small a crew?" Jamie asked.

"Three is absolute minimum," Harry said. "That leaves no relief for anyone. It will take about 24 hours to bring it around the island, so we should have some relief."

"I know a couple of fellows from the submarine that would be able and probably delighted to go," Brian reported.

"I'll go," Pat Holden said, "and I'll ask Bill Portman. He is a mechanical engineer and should be capable."

"When do you want to try this venture?" Jamie asked.

"'I would like to go as soon as possible," Harry told them. "Tomorrow would suit me fine."

"What about transportation from the airport to the harbor?"

"I had a hunch something might come up," Harry replied. "Our neighbor had an old car sitting in the driveway, and he left the keys in it. Janice and I took it out to the airport and left it there for future use—should we need it."

"All right," Jamie said. "If you want to go tomorrow, I'll be at the airport ready to go at nine AM. Is that OK, Brian?"

"I'll have the bird ready. Looks like we'll have about a full load."

"Maybe I'll take Kevin or Randy along to ride back with me and start getting used to the Caravan," Jamie said.

* * *

Jamie was amazed at the size of the ancient diesel engine that powered the North Star. The crankcase appeared to be eight feet long. Six huge cylinders were bolted to the crankcase, and an overhead camshaft was set to open and close the valves. A small diesel engine was running, and pressure was building up in an air tank. Brian picked up a speaking tube and held it to his mouth. "This is the engine room, ready to start engine."

"OK to start engine," came the voice from the bridge. Brian turned a valve. There was a rush of air, and the big engine started to rotate. One cylinder fired, then another. Then all cylinders were firing and a gauge indicated 30 revolutions per minute. Harry's voice came from the speaker tube. "All ashore that's going ashore. Prepare to cast off bowlines."

Jamie hurried up the steel ladder to the low deck and sprang to the dock. Glancing up at the stack, he could see perfect donuts of gray smoke erupting with each explosion in the cylinders below. "Cast off bowline." The order came from the bridge. Randy Earheart lifted the loop of the bowline from the bollard and tossed it to the deck where Robert Dick started coiling it in place. In the wheelhouse, Harry swung the wheel to the left. "Ahead slow," came the order to the engine room where Brian pushed a big lever forward. Water stirred under the stern as the big wheel started to turn, pushing the water against the rudder that was deflected full left. Slowly, the bow edged away from the dock. "Cast off stern line," Harry ordered. Jamie tossed the stern line to Pat Holden on the deck, and the big boat moved slowly away from the dock. "Quarter speed." The exhaust donuts blended together as the engine turned faster.

"Well," Jamie spoke to Randy, "they're away at twelve o'clock. I guess we had as well head for home." A half-hour later they were in the air. Jamie swung south, and they spotted the tug well out into Barkley Sound, churning a big wake in the blue ocean water.

* * *

Patrick Holden was on hand when the council convened on Sunday afternoon, and Jamie called on him immediately for a report.

"The North Star is older than I am, but it is in surprisingly good condition. That old engine never missed a beat. It's dirty and messy, with oil leaking everywhere, but it just keeps plugging along. It's a dependable old critter, and I think it will get the job done fine. Brian and Stan are busy installing a satellite radio. They said they could probably have it done today, so we could leave as early as tomorrow morning. With decent weather and good luck, we should make the run out and back in three days or less. Janice Haynes will take their fishing boat along for a standby. Johnie Dick will be deck hand for Janice. I think we will take her inside Denman Island, then right out around Saturna Island, through Boundary Pass and Haro Strait. I don't want to cross the Comox Bar. That way we keep out of the narrow passages and their currents and away from shallow reefs. Harry agrees with me on that."

"Sounds like you're getting organized okay," Jamie said. "It's up to you and Harry. Go when you are ready."

* * *

The North Star was ready to go at noon on Tuesday, and a large contingent of New Islanders was on the Comox docks to see her off. Johnie Dick was at the controls of the big cable reel on the stern. A bridle had been secured to the bow of the Denver, and the steel towrope was shackled to the bridle. Lines were cast off both boats, and the tug edged ahead cautiously, swinging her bow away from the dock. The line tightened gently, and the submarine began to move. A cheer went up from the audience on the dock. The North Star headed south down Baynes Sound. Johnie gradually eased out more line until several hundred feet of cable separated the North Star from the Denver. The heavy cable would drag deep in the water, providing elasticity to compensate for the shock of waves or currents.

Stan kept someone on the radio constantly to monitor progress of the North Star. At ten PM, the ship reported abreast of Parksville and at three AM Wednesday abeam Gabriola Island. At five AM, they reported rounding Saturna Island. At ten AM, they were off of Victoria and picking up a brisk head wind in Juan de Fuca Strait.

At noon, Jamie talked to Pat Holden. "Everything is going fine," Pat reported. "The water here in the strait is getting rough but is giving us no trouble so far. The Denver is following along like a well halter broken mustang. I don't think she knows where she is going. We should clear Duntze Rock off Cape Flattery by nine tonight and then about six hours southwest should put us in about a thousand feet of water. That's where we will say good-bye to Denver."

Pat's report turned out to be optimistic.

* * *

There was little to do onboard the North Star, so boredom was starting to have its effects. A traffic lookout was unnecessary. Joyce Haynes in the fishing craft Halibut King took turns at the helm with Robert Dick, who felt right at home on the vessel. They maintained a position about a hundred yards off the starboard side of the North Star. Boredom soon disappeared as they neared the open Pacific. They made their estimated time at Duntze Rock, but as they rounded the rock and established their new heading to the southwest, the wind increased. They were headed directly into the wind, and giant waves lifted the tug high in the air and let her down with a thud as they rolled under the hull. Every third or fourth wave seemed higher and broke over the bow, sweeping the deck from bow to stern.

"We better get some more line out on that tug," Harry told Johnie. "But be careful out there. Get a safety line hooked up."

"I'll let out another 500 feet," Johnie agreed. "That should ease her off and put about a ton of cable between us to absorb the shock."

Johnie, dripping water, reported to the bridge 20 minutes later. "It's getting really wild out there. Those waves are something else. How are Janice and Robert doing?"

"I just talked to them," Harry replied. "They are OK. The King has seen some mighty rough weather and did OK. I suggested they stay farther away. We don't want them drifting in between the Denver and us. Janice has set up her GPS to put her about a mile away at our destination. We can close up then. I just get an occasional glimpse of her mast light. Christ! There's a big one."

The North Star slowed as she climbed the face of the monster wave, teetered over the top and plunged forward, stern in the air. The boat raced down the backside of the wave, pulling slack out of the tow cable, to slow suddenly as she hit the trough and raised her bow to the next wave.

"I guess we better slow up," Harry said. "We don't want to break that cable. We'd never get hooked up again in this stuff."

"There's no hurry," Pat replied. "There is no way we could get aboard the Denver to open the seacocks in this kind of water. We had as well go slow as possible, just try to keep control, until this storm dies down."

"Agreed," Harry said, picking up the speaking tube. "Engine room. Are you OK down there?"

"OK so far," Brian replied. "What are you trying to do with this thing? Aerobatics?"

"Yeah, but I'm not going to try a loop. Reduce speed to half."

"Half speed it is," Brian agreed.

The boat slowed perceptibly.

"King, do you read?" Harry spoke into the radio mike.

"King here," Janice replied.

"Did that big one hit you?" Harry asked.

"Sure did. Thought we were never going to stop going up. When we hit the next one, I thought King had turned into a submarine. Water came clear over the wheelhouse. Are you OK over there?"

"Yeah, we're OK. But we've slowed to half speed, only showing between two and three miles per hour. Maybe not making that much over the bottom. We gave a hell-of-a-jerk on the cable on that big one. Don't want to take a chance on breaking it if we can help."

"I don't think I can slow up that much, but I'll keep in contact."

"That gal is one big time skipper," Harry said to Pat. "She can handle a boat better than any man I know. She'll be OK."

At three o'clock, when they had expected to be on their position for release, they were halfway from Duntze Rock. At six o'clock, in a misty daylight, Janice came within sight on their starboard about 300 yards away. The King was visible on top of the waves, but disappeared as she plunged into the trough. Janice reported that she could see the tug, but only an occasional burst of spray marked the location of Denver. The seas were subsiding by nine o'clock as they finally reached their destination.

The North Star suddenly surged ahead and picked up revolutions.

"Christ!' Harry gasped. "We've broken loose. Johnie, get back there and reel in the cable." Grabbing the microphone, he called King. "King, do you read. We have lost the tow. We are reeling in the cable and can't do anything until it's in. Will you get back there and keep the sub in sight until we can join you?"

"We're on our way," Janice replied. "Meet you there."

It took several minutes to reel in the cable. Johnie secured it and came to the bridge to report. "The shackle that hooked us to the bridle wore right through. It was old and rusty. Lucky that it lasted as long as it did."

As Harry got the tug turned around and headed back, Janice called, "I have the sub. I'm about a hundred feet to the starboard. Almost every wave sweeps over it. The deck is only clear between waves."

"OK, we have you in sight," Harry told her. "We'll go back by you and turn to come up on your starboard. Keep the sub in sight."

"No problem," Janice reported.

It took half an hour for Harry to bring the North Star abeam the Halibut King headed into the seas. "This critter doesn't maneuver well at all in tight places." He told the others. "It's too slow to get from forward to reverse, and it doesn't respond fast at all. I'm used to a much more agile boat like the King. How many men do you have to put on the sub to get the seacocks open?"

"I can do it myself," Pat said. "If you can put me on the boat."

"King," Harry spoke into the mike, "could you put a man on that sub?"

"I could put him in position to get on, but I don't know if he could stay on. Almost every wave sweeps the full length of it. He'd have to be agile and fast."

"Let me have the mike?" Pat requested. "Janice, if I come on the King, could you put me in position to board the Denver?"

"Can do," Janice replied. "I'll come alongside the Star. You will have to jump fast when the time is right."

"OK, I'll be ready." Turning to Harry, he said, "I'll need a good length of light line, and I better have the Zodiac. We'll toss it aboard the King before I go over."

"Get into a survival suit. You're trying a mighty dangerous job, and you could well get dunked in the ocean."

A few minutes later, Janice eased the King up to within a few feet of the Star. Pat and Johnie had a line attached to the Zodiac. They tossed the line to Robert on the King. As the two boats seemed synchronized for a few seconds, they heaved the boat forward and Robert pulled in the line. The rubber boat slid over the rail, and Robert secured the line to a cleat.

"I'm next," Pat called.

Janice again maneuvered her boat to within feet of the Star and Pat jumped, sprawling on his face on the deck. Picking himself up, he staggered to the wheelhouse to talk to Janice.

"Because the deck of the sub is round without much to hang on to, I can't jump like I did to get here. I have a lightweight nylon rope. I'll have one end tied to the Zodiac. The other end I'll use as a lasso and try to snag the periscope on top of the conning tower. If I can, I'll make the jump and have the rope to hang on to. I'll put a short loop of rope around my waist and tied loose to the main rope. If I fall, I can't lose the main line, and the dinghy will be on the end of it for safety. Get as close as you can, but try not to smash me if I fall."

"I have both bow and stern thrusters," Janice said. "The second you jump, I'll use both to push me away."

Janice again eased the King close to the sub. When the boats were both in the trough between the waves, the periscope was much too high to enable the lasso trick. The Star rode the waves much higher and put the periscope within range as she topped the wave crest. It took three tries to get the looped rope over the periscope. Pat took in as much slack as he could. Janice eased the King to within a few feet of the sub. As the King went up on a wave and the sub, because of its much greater tonnage, stayed stationary, Pat leaped. His right hand gripped a bar on the side of the conning tower, but a rush of water dislodged him, and he fell between the boats as the King's side thrusters pushed violently to shove the boats apart. Pat held onto the line grimly and fought his way up the rounded side of the sub. Janice watched as he climbed the conning tower, opened a hatch on top and disappeared inside the boat.

In the sub, Pat made his way to a stern compartment where he opened two seacocks. Water started gushing into the boat. Quickly, he went forward and opened two more, then un-dogged a hatch and flung it open. A deluge of seawater greeted him. Fighting his way back through compartments, leaving doors blocked open, he climbed back out the conning tower where he lifted the line off the periscope and secured it around his waist. The Zodiac was tugging strongly on the rope a hundred feet away. Pulling the rubber boat up to the side of the submarine, he jumped. He hit the boat, but it flipped from under him, dumping him in the sea again, but he held on to one of the safety lines that were secured along the gunnels. Rapidly, they floated to the rear of the submarine. Pat rolled himself into the Zodiac, sat up and waved to the King.

Janice brought the King around and approached him upwind. As the big boat came alongside, he tossed the line to Robert. Robert secured the line, pulled the dingy closer, and Pat climbed aboard. "Damn," he groused. "I think this suit is plumb full of seawater and it's cold. Help me get it off."

"He's back onboard," Janice reported to Harry. "That guy has more balls than a dozen ordinary men. On top of that, he has brains enough to figure out how to get away with the impossible. He's all man."

Robert found dry clothes for him, and he changed. His side was bruised from falling against the side of the submarine, and he wondered if maybe he had cracked a rib. It hurt when he breathed. Otherwise, he had suffered no ill effects.

Back in the wheelhouse, he found that Janice was holding a position about a hundred feet from the submarine. The North Star was a few hundred feet away.

"How long will it take for her to go down?" Janice asked.

"I don't really know," Pat told her. "I opened four large valves, and the hatch on the forward deck is open. Every time a wave goes over, water spills in there. It might take several hours. There's a lot of space in there to fill up. I'd like to stay here and see her go down. I hope we don't drift too far before she sinks."

"We are close to the location you wanted," Janice said. "We are not drifting very fast. The wind is dying down some, and the seas are subsiding a little. I don't think it is going to get much better, though, so it's good that you got her on her way."

"What's the story?" Harry asked over the open radio. "Is the mission accomplished?"

Pat picked up the mike. "Mission accomplished. But I would like to stand by to see the end. It might take awhile."

Janice took the mike. "Why don't you head for home, Harry? We can catch up to you pretty fast. I think we have about twice the speed you have."

"Hey," Harry answered, "I hate to leave you out here all alone in this weather."

"The weather is getting better, and you know me—I can get us home fine and dandy. I'll catch up in a few hours."

"OK," Harry replied. "I know you are capable of getting home. We'll be on our way. Maintain radio contact."

They watched as the North Star got underway and set a course to the northeast. Two hours later, they watched as the Denver settled lower and lower in the water. The waves were washing constantly over the deck. Then the bow sank lower and they could see a whirlpool form as the sea rushed through the open hatch. The end came soon, and there was nothing but bubbles boiling up as water displaced the air in the sub.

"Goodbye to a valiant ship," Pat said. He blinked his eyes, trying to keep the tears back.

Janice looked at her depth gauge. "She's resting in 978 feet of water," she reported. "That should be a comfortable place for her. Let's go home."

Chapter 43

Nils and William were torn from their conversation inside the door of the workshop by a horrific scream of agony. They burst through the door into the barnyard to see a man, totally enveloped in fire staggering away from a ball of flame that was erupting from the end of the machine shed where the trucks were parked. Nils, followed closely by William, covered the 100 or more feet in seconds. Nils knocked the burning man to the ground and started rolling him over and over with no effect. Tearing his shirt off, he attempted to smother the flames. William joined him with his shirt, but their efforts were fruitless. The man's clothing appeared to be soaked with gasoline, and the fire was determined to burn itself out.

"My God, it is Job," William yelled.

Nils felt the heat intensifying on his bare back and looked over his shoulder to see flames soaring high into the air. "Christ Almighty," he shouted. "We have to get people out of the houses. It's all going."

"Job is gone," William said. "Nothing we can do for him. Let's go."

* * *

Nils was a little nervous as he watched the plane climb out to the west and disappear. He was on his own in a strange environment for the first time in his life. He had committed himself to a project that was far beyond anything he had ever tried in his 23 years. Was he capable of it? He had begged Jamie for a chance to prove that he could handle it, and now he was in the hot seat. He had to go ahead and prove that he could accomplish what he had promised. Bringing Little River into the modern century would be an awesome challenge.

Turning to William and Thomas, who had been with him to see the plane depart, he spoke quietly. "Do you gentlemen have any ideas on how we should get this project underway?"

William lost no time in answering. "I think that that is going to be up to you. We are placing ourselves completely in your hands."

"That's an awesome responsibility that I've agreed to take on, but I'll do the best I can. I hope that I'll be able to justify your trust in me. The first thing I'd like to see is what you have in the way of tools to work with."

"Come with me, and I will show you what we have in shop and tools." William led the way back across the road and to the far end of the machine shed, where a space was closed in. Opening half of a set of double doors, he motioned Nils in. An old-fashioned coal-burning forge occupied the center of the room, and a heavy anvil was attached to a block of wood nearby. Tongs and hammers hung on the side of the block. A water bucket for tempering iron was beside the anvil. A workbench along the rear wall had a heavy-duty vice attached. Punches and chisels were in racks over the bench, and other tools hung along the sidewall. There were few carpenter tools. A couple of handsaws and a carpenter's square, a spirit level and a few hammers and chisels were about the extent of wood working tools. A heavy six-foot crosscut saw suitable for cutting large logs and a splitting maul hung in a corner. Nils noted that both the handsaws and the big crosscut were sharp and well set.

"Nick Shushkoff is our best blacksmith and tool man." William told him, "He can fit and place horseshoes and sharpen saws and do a lot of other blacksmithing chores. He is a handy man with tools and does a fair job of carpentry. He is also a good leather man and has a bench in the horse barn where he repairs harness."

"Sounds as if he is a good man to have around," Nils commented. "I'd sort of like to have him as my number one helper."

"He's the best we have, and I will assign him to help you whenever you need him," William agreed. "Otherwise, his main job is looking after the horses. He really has a way with horses. However, other people can look after the horses if Nick is too busy, just so he has time to supervise the horse care."

"I'd like to get a privy built out behind the mobile home. It's a far piece away to the nearest one; I found that out in the middle of last night. I think I would like to take the truck to town this afternoon and get a load of lumber to get started with. We'll need lumber for a lot of things as we get going here. If you would like to go with me, I'll teach you more about driving the truck as we go."

"Sounds good to me," William agreed. "I'll go let others know that we are going. If you would like to locate a spot for the privy, we can have someone start digging the hole. Nick can look after that."

* * *

The days went fast as Nils struggled hard to make improvements to living conditions in the complex, both for the residents and for New Island people that would be assisting. The new privy was built a short way behind the mobile home. The radio was moved to the mobile home and installed in the front of the living room, the antenna attached to a long piece of timber secured to the side of the house. Water pipe had been installed to bring water from the well to the kitchen door, an unbelievable luxury to the women who were responsible for water. Nils and William were discussing how to pipe water to the barnyard to serve the chickens and pigs when disaster struck.

* * *

The pine boards of the machine shed, loaded with pitch, burned with the ferocity of gunpowder. Half of the building was already fully involved in fire when Nils got around the end to where he could see the dining building. Super-heated air from the fire was carrying shards of burning wood to drop on the roofs of other buildings and the surrounding area.

The roof of the dining hall was already burning furiously when Nils plunged through the door shouting, "Fire." There was no one in the dining room, but several women working in the kitchen looked up in amazement as Nils dashed through the door.

"Get out! Fire! Get out now," Nils shouted. "Move it. Get going."

As Nils pushed the women out the door, William dashed past and entered the first house, which was already heavily involved.

"Run to the barnyard to get away from this grass," Nils yelled at the women. Patches of grass were burning furiously. The women lost no time in dashing for the barnyard.

Nils was at the door of the second house in seconds. He ran through it shouting loudly, but there appeared to be no one in it. William was into the third house, and Nils continued to the last house, which already had most of its roof in flames. Bursting into the kitchen, he found two women, completely nude. One was standing in a tub of water, and the other was scrubbing her back.

The women screamed in dismay as the frenzied man interrupted their bath.

"The house is on fire," Nils shouted. "Get your shoes on. We have to get out." Snatching the women's dresses from a chair he dunked them in the tub and shoved the garments at them. "No time to lace your shoes. Get these on. We got to get out of here."

The two women pulled their dresses over their heads, and Nils had them out the door before they could get them down over their hips. Grass was burning all around them.

"Go this way and run," Nils instructed, leading them through the burning grass. "Be careful. Don't lose your shoes. We'll try for the road."

In seconds, they were clambering through the fence and were out on the road and clear of the fire. Both women's skirts were smoldering, and Nils pushed them to the ground, so he could beat the embers from the cloth. With the badly frightened women back on their feet, they turned to survey the fire. The first house was almost completely consumed. The upper story of the second was completely involved in flames when a scream issued from the building. The scream was cut off when the entire upper story crashed through the lower story, and a huge ball of fire erupted into the air.

"My God," Nils exclaimed. "There was someone in that house."

"It must have been John and Jenny," one of the women gasped. "They were sick. They had bad diarrhea all night and were throwing up all of the time. They decided to stay in bed and sleep today. They must be dead now."

"Come on," Nils suggested. "There is nothing we can do now. Let's get down next to the mobile home. We need to watch that it doesn't catch fire. The ground is bare there and we should be safe."

People were gathering on the bare ground, coming in from the fields where they had been working, dumbfounded at the extent of the fire. The barns and outbuilding were now all ablaze. Squeals of terror and pain emanated from the pigsty, which was totally aflame. Everything was burning.

William hurried up to the group gathering in front of the mobile. "Nils, are you all right? Your hands and arms look burned, and your shoulders are awfully red."

"I'm OK," Nils replied. "I have some minor burns, but they will be all right. How are you?"

"About the same," William said. "I think we lost at least one person. An old lady who was an invalid was upstairs in the first house. I tried to get up there, but it was totally engulfed in fire. There was no way I could get there. I was lucky to get out before it caved in."

"I think that we lost two more. I heard a scream from the second house. These ladies tell me that a couple of people were sick and stayed in bed. I was in and yelled as loud as I could, but I didn't go upstairs. They must not have heard me. If I had gone up, I might have been able to get them out."

"But then you would not have gotten us out. I am Gladys, and this is my mother, Gwen. We had no time to spare and could not have possibly gotten out if you hadn't arrived when you did. You saved our lives."

"You saved a lot of lives." Ann Broder had just approached. "If you had not arrived when you did, it is doubtful that any of us in the kitchen would have gotten out. Thank you. You are a real hero."

"But God," Nils mumbled, "how I feel to have lost those others. That scream will be with me for the rest of my life. Now I better see if I can call New Island. It is sure lucky that I moved the radio over to the mobile."

Chapter 44

Andy Blankenship and Dave Jorgenson were at the council meeting to report on their efforts to find a hydro plant for Little River.

"Small hydro electric plants are mostly bought on an order basis," Andy told them. "With the unit designed for the place, it will be used. We located one that was built for a mining camp up on the West Coast. I found a record of it in files at the BC Hydro office. The company that was going to put it in proposed that they sell any excess power to BC Hydro. However, the location was too remote, and the plant not nearly large enough to be of any value to the company. An outfit from California was going to develop a gold prospect there and had this plant lifted in by helicopter to provide power for their camp. The company went broke and never got the camp going. The hydro plant, as far as I can ascertain, is still in there. I don't know what kind of problem it would be to get it out."

"How about a gas or diesel generating plant?" Bob Elder asked. "I believe that there are lots of them around."

"Going for diesel is shortsighted," Jamie said. "We don't know how long useable fuel will be available. Waterpower is permanent. Did this outfit have any kind of camp established up there, Andy?"

"I think they had a temporary camp at the mouth of the creek that they were going to use for power. The mine site was higher on the mountain. I don't know how much development work they had done."

"Do you have an exact map location for the place?" Jamie asked.

"Yes," Andy replied. "I even have the GPS location for where the helicopter set the plant down. It's about as remote as you can get, in Malksope Sound. That's just south of the Brooks Peninsula."

"Let's fly over there tomorrow and take a look," Jamie said. "Both you and Dave should go along. Make it Tuesday. I'll go up to the Campbell River Spit and see if I can find a floatplane. There's no place to land on wheels there. I'll have the plane at the dock here, if I can find one."

"OK," Andy replied. "We'll be at the dock at nine on Tuesday."

* * *

Two floatplanes were tied to the dock on the inside of the Spit at the mouth of the Campbell River.

"There's a Beaver and a Cessna 185," Jamie reported. They had loaded a battery charger, generator and Brian's tool kit into the trunk of Jamie's car and driven to the Campbell Spit. Stan came along to return the car. "I would like to take the Beaver. I have several hundred hours in a plane identical to this one. That's what I flew up and down the coast for years."

"OK," Brian replied. "The gas tanks are full. Let's see if we can get it started. Get onboard and give it some prime, and I'll pull the prop through a few times to get some fuel in the cylinders."

Jamie felt right at home as he entered the cabin and settled into the pilot's seat. Brian balanced on a float and pulled the prop over, then stepped back to the dock. Jamie hit the starter, and the big radial engine started with a cloud of blue smoke exiting the exhaust stacks. Letting the engine run for a few minutes to settle down, he motioned a thumbs-up to Brian. Brian released the dock tethers and climbed aboard, giving a push away from the dock on his way. Jamie taxied the plane out of the river mouth and added throttle. The takeoff was smooth, and Jamie felt comfortable, as though it was last week rather than 30 years since he had flown a Beaver. Twenty minutes later, he touched down in the Comox harbor and tied up at the floatplane dock.

* * *

Jamie found Brian tinkering on the Beaver when he walked out on the dock the next morning. "Is everything ready to go?" he asked.

"Yeah, I guess so. I have the emergency gear all onboard, and there is plenty of fuel. But I haven't had time to give it a real inspection. I think it's using oil quite badly. I put two quarts in. I really need about a week to go over this bird before I will be confident in its operation."

"Well, we'll only put a couple of hours on it today, and then you can have all the time you need to tinker on it. Here come the other guys; let's go and get back here."

The flight to Malksope Sound was uneventful. The GPS led them to the location where the machine had been dropped. A big square wooden crate in the middle of a clearing seemed to be what they were looking for. A hand-cut trail led to the beach where a bulldozer sat in the middle of another clearing. The water was calm in Malksope, and Jamie set the plane down smoothly. Approaching the sandy beach, he shut the engine off, and the plane coasted to a gentle landing. Andy and Dave looked the box and its labels over carefully, as well as boxes of other equipment nearby.

"It looks like a good deal. The plant is labeled for 60 kilowatts, which is adequate for the Little River job. The creek here doesn't seem as large as the creek at Little River, so I am sure that it would operate all right over there. We just have to figure out how to get it out of here."

"That is not too much of a problem," Jamie told them. "Especially if we can get that bulldozer to work. It would only take a couple of hours to doze out the trail to the beach. We can build a stone boat to drag the equipment out to the beach. We have to find a tugboat and a barge with a loading ramp, and then the cat can drag the load right onto the barge."

"The label says that one crate weighs more than 1000 pounds," Andy said. "That's not something to be tossing around with impunity."

"We can figure that out OK," Jamie told them. "We just have to bring adequate tackle along to rig a hoist. I've figured out much more complex problems than that. Let's see if the cat will start."

Back in the beach clearing, Brian looked the bulldozer over. "It has a small auxiliary engine to start the big engine," he reported. "If I can get the auxiliary to go, I think the big engine will start OK."

The keys were missing for the small engine. Brian spent a few minutes looking it over, then went to the plane and brought his toolbox. Disconnecting a wire, he held it to the positive terminal of the battery. The engine turned over rapidly and started. After a time for warming up, he engaged the clutch that connected to the big diesel. The diesel started with a positive sequence of explosions that soon settled down to a steady rumble. "She's all OK," he reported, hitting the kill switch.

"Let's head for home," Jamie said.

They were over Gold River and entering the pass through Strathcona Park when Brian spoke up. "I think we are losing oil. There's a streak of oil along the side of my window. I don't know where it's coming from."

"Oil pressure is still OK," Jamie said. "We should be home in 20 minutes. There's Upper Quinsam Lake. It won't be long now. Keep a close watch. I'm going to start letting down. See if Stan is on the radio."

Brian keyed the Mike. "Stan, are you there?"

"Big as life," Stan replied.

"Stand by. We are losing oil. We are just past Upper Quinsam lake and are letting down for Comox."

"Damn," Jamie exclaimed. "Oil pressure is going down."

"There's smoke coming out of the engine," Brian reported.

"Shutting her down," Jamie reported calmly. "It's dead stick from here in. I think we can make the harbor."

"Stan," Brian reported, "engine is down and we are losing altitude rapidly. We are trying for the bay, coming in down the river. Jamie says he will land in the river just below the bridge at the lumber mill. It looks close. If we can't make the river itself, we'll try for the big field in the river bottom."

"Hang on," Jamie cautioned. "We're going to make it." They skimmed over the bridge with feet to spare. The tide was out and the channel narrow with mud flats showing to the left. Pilings marked the channel.

"We are OK, Stan," Brian reported. "Oh hell! There's a log and we are going to hit it."

The left pontoon caught on the log, and the plane was jerked to the left and into the mud bank. For seconds, it seemed that they were going to slide over the mud without a problem, but the float had been damaged by the log and dug into the mud. The plane went up on its nose and gently toppled over to come to rest on its back, leaving its occupants hanging upside down in their safety harness.

"Damn, I goofed on that one," Jamie said angrily. "It's going to be tough walking in that mud."

"Better the mud than the bush," Brian replied calmly. "Try to hang on to something when you release your seat belts. Otherwise you'll fall on your heads and it could hurt."

Jamie got loose first, scrambled to get right side up and pushed the door open. Brian got his belt loose and helped the two in the back to get free. They climbed out onto the bottom side of the inverted wing.

"Get that rope out of there. We might need it in case we hit a soft spot in this muck."

Brian retrieved the rope, and his toolbox. "There are some of my favorite tools in here," he said. "And I don't want to lose them. Let's start walking. I'll lead the way. The rest of you space yourselves out along the line and don't walk in each other's footsteps. Each step in this gook softens it up for the next."

Brian stepped off the wing, sinking above his ankles in the muck. The others followed, their feet making sucking sounds as they pulled them laboriously from the ooze. It wasn't far too solid ground, but it seemed like a long way to the struggling men. They were halfway to shore when a car came speeding down the road that paralleled the channel. The car slid to a stop, and Stan, Kevin and Randy piled out to stand on the bank watching them. A pickup with Charlie Johnson in it followed. Brian reached the bank and handed his toolbox up, then clambered up himself to turn and help the others up.

"What happened?" Charlie asked.

"We developed an oil leak," Jamie told him. "Those engines don't run worth a damn without oil. Then I hit a log just after landing, and it threw us into the mud. Let's go someplace and wash this mud off."

"You better ride in the back of my pickup," Charlie said. "It will be easier to wash the mud out of the pickup bed."

"Listen," Stan said, "I have important news for you. Just before Brian called in, I had a radio conversation with Nils. They have had a terrible disaster over at Little River. They are completely burned out, including their cars. They need help badly."

"I guess that means we go to Little River this afternoon. Was anyone killed in the fire?"

"Nils wasn't sure, but he thinks three people died."

"Did everything burn?" Jamie asked.

"Yes, everything is gone, except the mobile home. Nils had moved the radio and generator to the mobile home and jury-rigged an aerial, so it wasn't lost. The fire started in a truck in the machine storage shed. It spread rapidly to the cookhouse and the rest of the houses. Then the gas tank blew up on the truck and sent embers over the barns. They lost all of their food, and both vehicles burned, so they have no way to go after more food. Nils said it is 35 miles to the nearest town and will take more than three days to get there and back with horses."

"OK, we better get cleaned up, have some lunch and be on our way," Jamie declared. "Charlie, will you get some help and round up a batch of food? We can carry close to a ton. Get a bunch of beans and rice and a lot of canned foods. Stan, call them back and tell them to sit tight. We are on our way with relief supplies. Brian, you fly the 206 and take Kevin with you. I'll fly the Caravan and take Randy."

"What about that airplane?" Charlie demanded. "The tide is coming in, and it will be swamped in a few hours."

"Let it be," Jamie said. "We have more important things to worry about. We need to get over to Little River. Charlie, we better get a bunch of sleeping bags and blankets, too, whatever you can find."

"OK," Charlie agreed. "I'll take you all back to the airport and then start rounding up supplies. I'll get Bob Elder to help. And Mary will want to be in on it. We should have a load for you as soon as you are ready to go."

The four men piled into the back of Charlie's pickup, and Charlie headed for the airport, his cell phone at his ear as he called for help in rounding up supplies. At the base they headed off to the officers' quarters to shower while Kevin and Randy rounded up clean clothes for them. Stan went to his radio room to contact Little River and tell them that aid was on the way.

By the time they were cleaned up and had lunch, trucks and vans were pulling in with supplies. Mary was with them, supervising the supplies they selected. "She even insisted that we include a case of toilet paper and a case of paper towels," Charlie told them. By two o'clock, the planes were loaded and ready to go.

"Don't wait for me," Brian said. "You can get there a good half-hour ahead of me. Go ahead. I'll keep in contact by radio."

"Go ahead and get going," Jamie told him. "I'll be off close behind you and go on ahead. See you in Little River."

* * *

Jamie touched down at Little River just after six o'clock Mountain Time. Nils, with William and Thomas, were in the forefront of the group that was gathered to meet them. Jamie was astounded at the total destruction of the complex. Only smoldering ruins remained.

"How did the fire start?" was the first question Jamie asked.

William answered, "Sir Job sneaked in and set the truck afire. Apparently, he opened a five-gallon can of gas that was stored in front of the trucks and splashed it over everything. When he touched it off, he made a human torch of himself. Nils and I heard him scream and ran to try to put the fire out. We were too late, and he died almost immediately. Nils burned his hands badly, and I did some, trying to put the fire out. I think that Job wanted to destroy anything modern that we had. The fire in the truck was so intense that we had no chance of stopping it, and it spread in all directions. It was like Nils said, if ever a fire started, it would get everything. Even though the barns and other outbuildings were farther apart, they caught and burned like they had been doused with gasoline."

Jamie noted that the mobile home that Nils had moved from Lethbridge was still in place beside the plane parking area, and there was a new privy behind it and a pile of fresh lumber nearby. Nils had been busy.

"Did you lose any lives?" Jamie asked.

"Yes," William replied. "Three people are missing. An older couple and a lady who was sick in bed are unaccounted for. We have not yet been able to search the buildings for any remains. We are sure that they perished. We buried Job this afternoon, and said a prayer over him."

"All right," Jamie said. "It is too bad to lose lives, but we must get on with living. Let's get busy. Get us some help to unload the plane. We'll spread everything out here so we can see what we have. Brian will be here right away with the other plane and it is loaded too."

Mary had done a good job selecting supplies. The first things out of the plane were boxes with large cooking pots and frying pans and boxes of paper plates and plastic tableware. Then out came boxes of canned food and bags of beans, rice and flour. Brian arrived and started unloading. Stacks of blankets and more food came out of the 206, with a couple of large dishpans and bottles of dish detergent and kitchen towels and washcloths.

"Did anyone here have lunch?" Jamie asked.

"No," William answered. "The fire started before noon."

"Where is the best place to set up camp?" Jamie asked. "We need to round up firewood and build cook fires, so we can fix some supper."

"Maybe best right here," William suggested. "This bare ground is safe to build a fire on."

"Sounds good. Where can we store all of this stuff? A storm could do a lot of damage."

"There is no building left standing except the trailer, and we have no tarps."

"We will put what we can in the trailer and stack more under it. Who is your best organizer for the kitchen?"

"Probably my wife, Ann," William said. "Here she is right now."

"Hello Ann," Jamie said. "Would you go through this stuff and get out food for dinner and utensils to cook it? We're going to set up camp right here and move everything else into the trailer for protection in case we have a storm."

"I'll get some people to help," Ann said. "On short notice, let us just use canned goods tonight. We will heat up enough to feed everyone. Then we can get better organized tomorrow."

Ann proved her leadership ability as she organized several women to help with preparations for the evening meal. She soon had what she needed sorted out, and the men began packing the balance to the trailer, where other women organized its storage. A couple of sawhorses appeared, and planks from the new lumber pile created a worktable. An hour later, dinner was ready. A big container of pork and beans, another of canned corn and plates of fried bread were on the table. Stacks of paper plates and piles of plastic tableware were handy. A bucket of fresh well water and a stack of Styrofoam cups completed the dinner setup.

Dinner over, William called the people together. "We must give thanks to the people of New Island who rushed to our aid on such short notice. It is hard to accept that we have lost everything we have—our homes and barns and even three of our people. We have lost our reserve supply of grains, our chickens and pigs. There is nothing left except the horses and cattle and the un-harvested crops. We have lost the winter fodder stored in the barns to support our livestock. It is doubtful, at this date, that we can harvest enough to feed the stock through the winter, especially if we have a hard one. I think we are going to have to depend on

President Jamie to suggest what we should do and lead us towards getting it done. Jamie, would you take over?"

"Let me express my sorrow for the three people that you have lost, and my dismay at the total loss of your facilities here. When I got word of the disaster here, Brian, Andy, Dave, and I had just returned from a trip to the west coast via floatplane to look at an electric plant. I called people to help in getting organized to fly supplies over here immediately. With the super organizational abilities of my vice president, Mary, and Charlie Johnson, we had the supplies gathered up and ready for takeoff by two PM. It's three hours over here, so we arrived at six PM your time. That was only made possible by a lot of highly organized help.

"I don't know what we should do now. We had planned on having a power plant in before winter and a better housing setup, but the situation is different now. You folks have to give a lot of thought about what to do. It will be very difficult to get this place ready to live in before winter, but if that is what you want, we will do our best. I cannot suggest that you try to relocate anywhere in this area because of the danger of disease created by the dead bodies everywhere, both human and animal. The only safe place is our own country, which you may relocate to—if you choose."

Nick Shushkoff stood. "I not talk much good, you know that. Joseph, Jacob, have farms their own. Could we all have farms too?"

Thomas Skrylak was next to speak. "I think quite a few people here would like to have their own farms. If we choose to move to your country, is it possible for all of us to move there? How would we get there?"

"Five trips in my airplane would move all of you over there. I can make two trips per day."

"Could we get horses for our farms over there?" Thomas asked.

"No," Jamie answered. "We are short of horses."

"Is there any way we could move our horses?" William asked. "You cannot take them in your airplane."

"That is a difficult question to answer. It would be hard, but we are prepared to not only do the difficult, but we also will try the impossible. We would have to find some big stock trucks and plan out a route to travel. I know that some roads have been made impassable by volcanic action. We would have to fly over routes to see what roads are open. Then we will have to find a tugboat and barge to move them to the island. That scenario is probably much easier for us than rebuilding your facilities here. You people should talk it over and make up your minds as soon as possible."

"I think we must consider it very seriously," Thomas said. "Could I ask that you and the other fellows from New Island go for a walk while we have a discussion among ourselves without your influence?"

"Come on," Jamie said, "let's walk down to the lower pasture and have a look at the horses."

The five New Islanders left the meeting and made their way past the smoldering ruins of the barns and down a quarter mile to the horse pasture. Brian let them through the gate, and they walked on towards where the horses were feeding. The horses became aware of them, and several came to meet the men. A big Clydesdale mare with a colt tagging along came up to Jamie and nuzzled his pockets, obviously looking for treats. Jamie scratched her ears and talked to her while Brian petted the colt.

"These are beautiful horses," Nils told them. "I haven't seen anything finer, and they are perfectly broke to any job you put them to."

"What a fine bunch of horseflesh," Jamie agreed. "There's no way we can leave these horses here. We need them desperately in New Island."

"You wouldn't leave them here," Brian said, "even if we didn't need them. You'd bust a gut to keep them from being abandoned. You're as softhearted about animals as you are people. We'll figure out a way to get them home, along with all the people. Let's get back to the meeting."

They found the people sitting on the ground in small groups, talking among themselves.

William greeted them. "The decision has been made. There are 40 people here, and 38 voted to accept your hospitality and relocate in Little River. The two that voted against it will go along with the majority. Now, it is up to you, Jamie, to organize the move."

"Thank you, William, for your trust in me. I can succeed only with the help of many trusted companions. We have decided that we must move the horses. They are vital to your and our survival at New Island. We will have to find trucks and survey a route to move them by. We will take most of you over in the airplanes, but some will be required to help with handling the horses en route, which could take several days.

"Tomorrow, we will fly to Lethbridge and find a vehicle for use here until we make the move. We will also start the search for trucks. I think we will need at least two. How many horses do you have, William?"

"Of the workhorses, there are eight matched teams, plus the stud that we work only as needed. Two of the mares have foals. That makes 19 work stock. Then we have six other horses for use as buggy horses and for riding. That adds up to 25 head. I do not know how many will fit in the big trucks. We lost all our harness, so we need to try to replace that. There is a demonstration farm outside Calgary that I have heard of. We may be able to get harness there. We have people that can make harness, if we can find leather. Or we can make our own leather, if we can find hides."

"All right, we will start working on that tomorrow. With sundown, there is a chill setting in. Let's get the blankets distributed. We are all going to have to sleep on the ground tonight, out here in the open. We will try to find some tents tomorrow for temporary shelter. This one outhouse is going to have to serve all of us, so there may be a lineup."

"The ladies left the beds available in the trailer," Nils reported. "There is space for all five of us in there. Two will have to share the big bed. There are bunk beds in the small bedroom and room for one on the couch."

"Maybe we should make them available for some of the women," Jamie said. "We can sleep on the ground."

"No," William objected, "we will all sleep out. We are just thankful to have blankets to keep us warm."

* * *

The air was chilly as the sun came peeking over the distant horizon. Ann and her crew were preparing breakfast. Stacks of pancakes were coming out of the pans, and syrup and margarine were on the table. Jamie realized that Mary had done an outstanding job getting supplies ready in such a short time.

William approached. "What are the plans for today, Jamie?"

"We'll fly over to Lethbridge and start our search there for a truck. We also need to bring back some transportation for here. And we need some tents for temporary shelter, here. You people may have to live in the open here for a few days until we get things organized."

A few minutes later, they were in the air with Brian flying the Caravan. Jamie was attempting to get as much experience as possible for the junior pilot. Kevin, Randy, William and Thomas were along. At the Lethbridge airport, they found the old Buick they had used before and drove it to a car dealership they had spotted on the road into town. There, Jamie found a late model Chevrolet extended cab pickup with a winch on the front and four-wheel drive. In the truck yard, they found a delivery van with a 20-foot box on it. Jamie decided these two vehicles would fulfill their transportation needs for the present. In the office, a telephone directory revealed the address of an outfitting company that advertised tents and other camping supplies.

At the outfitting store, they found four 12-foot by 16-foot tents, which they loaded into the truck, along with two wood burning camp stoves, several large plastic tarps and a supply of rope. Again, referring to the yellow pages, they located a farm supply store. After fueling the larger truck, they sent Kevin and Thomas on their way to Little River. With the smaller truck, they searched out the farm supply store. They found two sets of new heavy draft horse harness and two sets of lightweight harness in the used department, along with an assortment of used horse collars, a variety of hardware and tools for harness repair and two whole cowhides that had been made into leather. They gathered up bridles and bits, two saddles, a number of feedbags and other odds and ends related to horse handling and maintenance. Piled in the pickup, the load was so high that it needed securing. A couple of saddle blankets and a length of rope solved the problem.

Randy and William dropped Jamie and Brian at the airport and headed for Little River with the pickup load of supplies. While Brian refueled the plane, Jamie searched the yellow pages some more. Under livestock trucking, he found the address of a company that claimed they could move cattle anywhere at any time. They listed an address on Highway 3, east of the city.

Jamie took the plane when they left. He picked up the highway east of the city and flew at 500 feet. A short distance out, Brian spotted stockyards and a pair of big trucks near a nearby building. Jamie circled and dropped to two hundred feet for another look. Carcasses of cattle littered the yards. The trucks, large semis, were equipped with stock racks. Jamie guessed them as about 40 feet long, and it appeared that either of them would handle the entire horse herd.

"I think that we have solved the transportation problem," Jamie told Brian. "I believe we can land the 206 on the highway without any problem." Back at Little River, they found a crew already at work erecting the tents. The two camp stoves were in place with smoke flowing from short stacks and women preparing lunch. A crew under the direction of Nils was putting the finishing touches on some rough tables and benches to make eating more pleasant.

William met Jamie as he left the plane. "People have searched the ruins most of the morning and have found no sign of bodies. The fire was so hot that everything was consumed. Even the metal bedsteads were melted into globs of iron. We are going to hold a religious service for those who were lost, probably tomorrow. What are your plans, now?"

"I think we should go to Calgary this afternoon to look at that demonstration farm. We are going to need a lot more harness and equipment for the horses. Then I think I will send Brian and Kevin home with the Caravan tomorrow. If you want to send some people ahead, they can take eight passengers. I want to take the 206 and survey the roads to the coast. I may take a couple of days to get home.

"In the meantime, you can start getting your people ready to go. I'll fly you and Nils to Lethbridge in the morning, and we will look at the stock trucks we located there. If one is satisfactory, I think Nils can drive it, you can bring it home, and Randy and I can continue on our road inspection trip. Here's Nils now. Nils, can you drive a big semi stock truck? It looks like about a 40-foot diesel rig."

"If it has wheels on it, I can drive it," Nils affirmed.

"I think we can find eight people to go ahead," William said. "We should send the older people. Some of them are not doing too well sleeping on the ground."

"How many farms are we going to need to accommodate all of your people, William?" Jamie asked.

"I've been thinking about that. We have ten families here. That includes children and some older parents. The biggest group is six and the smallest two. People here keep their parents with them."

"OK," Jamie said. "I am going to arrange to talk to my vice president tonight to start making arrangements over there."

Going to the airplane, Jamie contacted Stan on the radio. "I would like you to get hold of Mary and have her at your radio room about eight this evening. I would like to talk to her so that she can start making arrangements to receive people there."

"Hold on," Stan replied, "she and Dave are out front now. I was just talking to them, and they wanted to know what I had heard from you. Stay put, and I'll see if I can catch them." It was only a minute when Stan came back on the radio. "Here she comes, hold on."

"Hi, Jamie, this is Mary."

"You are our problem solver," Jamie replied. "Brian and Kevin are bringing the Caravan home tomorrow, and they will have eight passengers. We need a place to house them until we can get the rest there and get them located. There will be 32 more coming later. In total, there are ten families, and we will need to find ten farms for them, preferably closely grouped, so they can work together. They are horse farmers, so we are going to truck their horses over for them. We have found a truck, or two, if we need them. Randy and I are going to use the 206 to survey a route for the trucks to follow. That might take two or three days, or even longer. When we get a route surveyed, we'll go over and move the rest of them to New Island. I'll leave it to you to take care of that end."

"Sounds like a big project," Mary replied. "Have you given up on rebuilding their place over there? You just found a power plant for them."

"They lost absolutely everything—all of their buildings, chickens, pigs—even three people. It's not worthwhile trying to rebuild here for their diminishing population. It's better for all concerned to integrate them into our society. They are intelligent people. They will adjust."

"Can Brian handle the Caravan on his own, with a load of passengers?"

"He has been flying it a lot with me in the right-hand seat. He will do fine."

"All right," Mary agreed. "I will start organizing things on this end. Dave will help me. I'll get some of the others involved, too. Be careful doing your road survey. I assume that means flying close to the ground. You have already wrecked two airplanes. That is enough."

Back with the others, Jamie spoke to Brian. "Are you comfortable with flying the Caravan home with Kevin as your copilot?"

"Sure," Brian replied. "You have been letting me fly it a lot. No problem."

"Let's find William. We are going to Calgary."

"Here he comes now. William, Jamie says we are going to Calgary."

"Do you have any idea where that demonstration farm is?" Jamie asked.

"It's on the highway a few miles east of the city. They say it is marked with a big statue of a Hereford bull about 20 feet high. Should be easy to find. Why don't you take Thomas instead of me? I would like to stay here and figure out who is going out tomorrow on the plane. He knows as much as I do about harness."

"That's OK," Jamie agreed. "Get him so we can be on our way. It's only about an hour up there, so we should be back early."

A few minutes later, with Brian flying, they were on their way. They found the main highway east out of Calgary, and Brian dropped to 300 feet to the left of the highway to give Jamie the best chance to find the Hereford bull.

"There it is," Jamie exclaimed. "That is one lot of bull. The highway looks clean here, turn back and drop to about a hundred feet, and we'll check for wires."

Brian followed instructions.

"There is a power line across the road up ahead. Turn back and we will see how far it is clear the other way. Turn back and set her down on the eastbound lanes."

"You want me to land it?" Brian asked. "I've never landed on a highway before."

"Just like landing on an airport," Jamie said.

A few minutes later, Brian parked the plane at the entrance to the driveway marked by the big bull. The smell of death greeted them as they left the plane and made their way towards the big barns. Its source became evident as they approached the barns and their adjoining fields. A number of horse corpses were decaying in the field. When they opened the door of the first barn, the stench was overpowering. Several dead horses were in the stalls. Backing away, they went to the other barns, opening doors. The third one was set up as a mini showroom, with banks of seats on each side. The odor was less prevalent here, but there was little of interest.

"If there is any harness here," Jamie commented, "it must be in the other barns. Hold your breath and we'll take a look."

A large tack room was in each barn with a plentiful supply of harness hanging from wall pegs. One room held a workbench where harness-making tools, including a power sewing machine and numerous hand tools were evident. Back outside, breathing was easier.

"That is rough in there," Thomas growled. "I could not stand much of that. But there is surely a lot of good harness and tools. I think we need to recover it all if possible."

"It will take a good-sized truck to haul it all," Jamie said. "Let's open up more doors on the barns, so they can air out some and come back for the harness another day. We don't have time to find a truck today, load it up and get back in reasonable time tonight. Also, we have to fuel the airplane on our way back."

"We know it is here," agreed Thomas. "We can unload the truck the other harness is in and drive it up here to get this lot. We will probably have to have another truck, or else get a bigger one, to haul all of the stuff from both lots. We can decide that later."

"Has Brian shown any of you how to get gasoline at service stations?" Jamie asked.

"Nils knows, and I think William does," Thomas told them.

* * *

Jamie and his crew were back for the evening meal. They were able to sit on benches at the crude tables that had been constructed during the day. Bowls of rice and a savory stew made from canned beef and an assortment of canned vegetables and fresh pan bread provided an adequate meal. Four tents had been set up, and everyone would be able to sleep undercover tonight.

Jamie told William of the harness they found at the demonstration farm, and it was agreed that they would go after it with the big van as soon as possible. Jamie was going to drop Nils off on his way out in the morning, so he could drive one of the stock trucks back to Little River. They talked about the cattle. Only two cows were milking, and their calves could be turned back to them. The cattle were not worth transporting, considering that there were plenty of cattle in New Island. They would cut the fences and leave them to their own devices.

"Maybe they will be a start for a herd of wild cattle to populate the plains like the buffalo once did," Jamie suggested. "Be sure and cut fences in all directions, so they can go where they want. Maybe you should go down country a ways and cut the fences that lead into some of those big meadows. There are probably no more predators alive, so they would have the country to themselves."

Jamie called home and found Mary waiting at the radio room. There was plenty of room to house the new people in the officers' quarters at the base, and the Navy cook would feed them until they got located. They had been looking at farms north of the present settlement, and there were plenty of good locations for the newcomers. Everything was taken care of.

* * *

The next morning, Brian had the Caravan ready to load as soon as breakfast was over. Jamie helped strap the frightened passengers in their seats, and Brian and Kevin were on their way. A few minutes later, Jamie and Randy, with Nils and Nick Shushkoff as passengers, followed. Jamie landed the 206 on the highway in front of the livestock transport place, and they got out to examine the trucks.

Nils walked around the outside of the two trucks. They appeared to be in good condition. He climbed the ladder at the rear of one and undid the ramp that let down for loading. It let down with a rope on a winch device that made it easy to handle. Sides erected on each side kept stock under control.

Climbing to the cab of the first truck, Nils studied the controls for a few minutes. The keys were in the truck. He turned the key, waited for the glow lights to come on, and activated the starter. The big diesel engine came to life and sounded good. He climbed down and tried the other truck. It was equal to the first. He shut it down, checked oil and fuel in both trucks, and pronounced them both acceptable.

"It looks good," Jamie said. "You better get on your way. Keep things under control at Little River. I'll be back in a few days."

The two men shook hands, and Nils climbed into the first truck and started the motor. Nick took the passenger seat. It took a minute for the air pressure to build up for the brakes. Nils then shoved in first gear and eased out the clutch to get underway. He went slowly out the driveway and turned into the highway. Jamie saw a puff of smoke from the upright exhaust pipe as he shifted up a gear, then another as the big rig gained speed. Another puff of smoke and Jamie turned away. He had no doubt that Nils could handle the truck.

Jamie sat in the plane and showed Randy the route they would take on highway maps. "We will go southwest on route 5 to Cardston, then south on number 2 to the Montana border, flying low enough to see that the highway is clear. In Montana it becomes Interstate 89. We follow that to Kiowa and pick up a shortcut to East Glacier Park where we pick up Route 2. We stay on two all the way to Spokane, where we switch to Interstate 90. That takes us to Seattle—if we are lucky."

The weather was good, and they penetrated the pass over the Rocky Mountains with no problem. At Columbia Falls they turned south, and the highway became four lanes. Jamie had just made the turn to the south when he spotted a small corral complex in the corner of a pasture and what looked like a loading chute. He turned back and dropped to a hundred feet to get a better look. The corrals appeared sound and the loading chute in good condition. A pasture of about 40 acres was lush with grass and had a good-sized pond near the center of it.

"Looks like a perfect spot for our first night's camp. We can unload the horses and let them graze on green grass. No feed or water problem."

They landed at Spokane to refuel and continued on. The four-lane highway all the way to Ellensburg was wide open. They landed at the Ellensburg airport for fuel, where Jamie had to rewire the fuel pumps in order to hook up their generator. While Kevin filled the gas tanks and checked the oil, Jamie stood gazing at the airport. Grass grew knee-high between the runways.

"This might be a good place for our second night's stop," Jamie told Randy. "There is lots of grass. Let's go see if we can find water close. I think I saw a creek just outside the entrance."

They walked out the main entrance of the airport and down the road towards town. A hundred yards from the airport entrance, a bridge crossed a small stream. Beyond the bridge was an entrance to a farm with access to the creek from the farmyard. The farm appeared not to have been active. No dead stock was in evidence, and they didn't notice any odor.

The next day, they went over Snoqualmie Pass and well into the metropolitan area of Seattle before they ran into trouble. The dead traffic had got steadily more congested after North Bend, until by the time they were over the intersection of Interstate 5 with State 405, the roads had become impassable. All four lanes were blocked by eastbound traffic that was in total disarray. There was no way that they could get through this area on the ground. Going back to North Bend, they headed north on rural routes and, with some difficulty, charted a route to intersect I-5 and on to Bellingham.

The extensive low altitude flying and backtracking looking for suitable routes had used a lot of fuel, so they landed at Bellingham to refuel. Jamie turned the fueling over to Randy and went for a walk along the row of hangars. He stopped in front of an open hangar and was surprised to see a Cessna Caravan parked inside. Looking closer, he found the logo of the U.S. Border Patrol; apparently, it had been used for border surveillance work. The plane was unlocked with the keys in the ignition. He turned the key to start, but the battery was low. Back at the plane, Kevin had finished fueling.

"Take us home," Jamie told Randy.

Chapter 45

"Golly, I thought you were never coming home." Kelly was almost crying as she flung her arms around Jamie. "You've been gone so long. I worried about you all the time."

"Hey, I'm glad to see you too, sweetheart," Jamie exclaimed. "But you shouldn't worry about me. I take care of myself pretty good."

"Yeah!" Kelly groused. "You take care of yourself by wrecking airplanes. This is the second time you've scared us by wrecking an airplane. No wonder we worry about you."

"I have an inclination to agree with her," Mary, standing behind her, agreed. "None of us are excited about you going around piling up airplanes."

"All right," Jamie told them, "I've been properly lectured. I promise to have Brian inspect any airplane I fly in the future. Airplanes are safe, when properly inspected, like this one. It has done a good job the last two days. Now, let's get out of the way, so Brian can get it serviced and ready for some more safe flying. I'm tired and hungry. We have had a hard two days."

"All right," Kelly agreed. "Let's go home. Brian said you probably wouldn't eat very well. Irene will have some lunch for you as soon as you get home, and we are going to have a big dinner tonight with Mary and Dave and Brian and Irene and Josephine all there, and then you can tell us all about your flight to find a road for the horses to come home on." Kelly stopped, gasping for breath.

"You better learn to talk a little slower, youngster," Jamie said, "or you'll run out of breath and not be able to talk at all."

"Well, I've got so much to say..."

"Hold on," Jamie interrupted her. "Remember what we said about that 'got' word? Have you forgotten about 'have'?"

"Well, no, not really. I just forget sometimes when I'm excited. I just have so much to say that I run out of breath trying to say it all."

"Umm, that sounds better." Putting his arm around her shoulders, he started for the car. "We have to keep harping on those things till they come naturally. Let's go home and get that lunch you promised Irene would have ready."

"I'll see you tonight," Mary called after them.

* * *

They were all there ready for dinner when Jamie emerged, greatly refreshed from a good nap, a hot shower and a fresh shave.

"It's great what some sleep and a bath can do to rejuvenate your outlook on life," Jamie commented, as he took his place at the table. "It's great to see you all here."

Josephine set bowls of food on the table, and they started the rounds. Everybody was busy for a few minutes, loading their plates according to their individual appetites. Jamie's was loaded substantially. This was not like the food he had been getting for the past week, especially the two days on the road during their return trip.

"Tell us about your trip home," Mary requested. "Brian brought us up to date on what happened at Little River, but we don't know anything about whether or not you found a route that we can get the horses over okay."

"And what is so important about getting those horses over here?" Dave wanted to know. "I understand the necessity of getting the people here, but why the horses?"

"You probably never had a chance to really see the horses while you were there. They are some of the finest workhorses I have ever seen—far superior to anything we have here in the valley. We are likely to be dependent on live horsepower for our farming and transportation in the future, and this stock is suburb. There is a stallion that is a beautiful piece of horseflesh, probably weighing better than 2000 pounds, and gentle as a kitten. There are eight teams, mixed mares and geldings. Four of the mares are carrying, and two have colts at their side, one a beautiful stallion that was conceived at another farm, so is a breeding stud for the future without inbreeding. All of the horses are well trained and will work at any kind of a job. Then there are six head of light stock for riding and buggy transport. They are fine-looking stock too. The people were eager to accept our offer to emigrate here, but they were reluctant to leave their horses."

"What about the cattle?" Mary asked. "Didn't they want to bring the cattle too?"

"There are plenty of cattle here of better quality than the ones over there. Their cattle are mixed breed, not anything to get

352

excited about. They will cut the fences and let them go on the open range. There is a good chance that they will survive and be the foundation for a strain of wild cattle that could conceivably populate the plains like the buffalo once did."

"You have to face it," Brian said, "Jamie fell in love with those horses. I think he would walk them over here by backcountry trails if he couldn't have found a road to bring them over. He is the world's champion softy when it comes to people—or horses—that are in trouble."

"That's the reason we all love him," Mary interjected.

"We found a big stock truck near Lethbridge, and Nils took it to Little River. He drove it out of the stockyard, like he had been driving it for years. There are 25 horses, and I think they will all fit in one truck. We have found a lot of harness and supplies to replace what was lost in the fire. We will load that on another truck. I will lead the caravan with a four-wheel drive pickup that has a winch on the front. I think I will draft Brian to help me, because of his special expertise in anything that comes up. With a couple of more people that can help us handle the horses on overnight stops, we should be OK.

"The roads are clear by way of highways number 2 and number 90 through the states. We have located good overnight stops in Kalispell, Montana and Ellensburg, Washington. It gets a little sticky around Seattle, but we found back roads that are not too badly blocked. We might have to shove or tow a few cars off the road, but we can get through to Blaine, just south of the border. There is a barge ramp there where we can load. We have to find the barge and tug. We'll leave that to Harry Haynes and the Dick men and Pat.

"We will go back to Little River and start moving people over by air. Brian can take care of that; he brought the initial load over with the Caravan and is qualified to haul passengers now. Incidentally, Brian, there is another Caravan down at Blaine that the Border Patrol was using. I think we should go down, have a look at it, and bring it home—if it's a good one. It has a dead battery."

"If the Border Patrol was flying it," Brian said, "it is probably in good condition, well maintained. It would be nice to have a spare."

"When are you going back to Little River?" Mary asked.

"Probably Monday or Tuesday, if we can get things lined out here OK. Let's go down to Blaine in the morning and see about that Caravan. If it is OK, we will bring it home."

"Can I go along, Jamie?" Kelly asked. "I haven't had a chance to fly for a while, and I would like to ride in the Caravan."

"I don't see why not," Jamie responded. "We might need you to fly the other plane home."

"Oh, Jamie, don't make fun of me. I just want to ride along. But I want to learn to fly as soon as I'm big enough."

"OK," Brian said, "if we are through telling lies here, Irene and I would like to go for a walk."

"All right," Jamie agreed. "Just be sure you don't get lost. We want to leave for Blaine about nine in the morning."

"I'll be there," Brian agreed. "And if Kelly is going along, how about Irene too? Then I wouldn't have to fly home alone."

* * *

The flight to Blaine was uneventful, and the two girls enjoyed the comfort of the Caravan's seats. Jamie stopped by the hangar where the Border Patrol plane was parked. Brian walked around the plane, inspecting it carefully.

"It's a nice-looking bird, Jamie. Let's get a fresh battery in it and see what happens. I don't see any sign of a booster around here, so the battery has to do the job."

Twenty minutes later, Brian had the new battery in place and climbed in the pilot's seat.

"Clear," he shouted. The engine wound up and fired. "I'm going to take it for a test flight." He shouted out the open window. Without waiting for an answer, he taxied towards the runway. A few minutes later, he was in the air, climbing in a tight spiral over the airport.

"Was that in the plans?" Irene asked. "I think he took that plane up without permission from you."

"Well…It needed to be tested before we started home with it. I was going to test-fly it, but he beat me to it."

Ten minutes later, Brian was on the ground and parked at the fuel pumps. "It's a nice bird," he reported. "Let's bring the other plane over here, and we will fuel both of them up."

"We need to take a look around here and see if we can locate a place to feed and water the horses before we load them on the barge. They'll need an overnight rest here. There's a Border Patrol vehicle in the hangar with the keys in it. Let's go patrol some border."

In a short time they had located a pasture north of the airport. It had good grass and a lake and would be a good place to overnight. Back at the airport, they refueled the planes, parked the SUV in the hangar and got ready to go.

"Brian," Jamie said, "you and Irene go ahead, and Kelly and I will follow. Give me a radio check when you're ready."

Brian taxied to the runway and did his preflight check. Jamie was close behind him.

"Jamie," Brian's voice came over the radio. "Border Patrol ready for takeoff."

"Let her rip," Jamie responded, "I'll be right behind you."

With Brian only a hundred feet down the runway, Jamie followed. With Brian established in a steady climb, Jamie spoke on the radio. "Brian, let's practice a little formation flying. I'm coming up on your port side. Just hold everything steady and I'll follow your moves."

Jamie added a little power and eased up on the other plane until he was established with his wing tip about six feet from the wing of the other plane.

"Gee, this is fun," exclaimed Kelly. "I didn't know planes could fly so close together."

"Sure," Jamie told her, "planes are like cars. You steer them the same way. We can get closer if we wanted to. I just like to be far enough away to be comfortable." Keying the radio, he spoke to Brian. "Let's level off at 8000. Start your letdown when ready. I'll stay with you."

"Roger," Brian acknowledged. "Level at eight and I'll start the letdown."

The air was smooth and time went fast. Brian tipped the nose down and, without reducing power, started the letdown. Jamie followed so faultlessly that it appeared one pilot controlled both planes.

"Brian, call Stan and tell him we're coming. Let's give them a high-speed flyby down the runway. I'll break first after the pull up and come around to land. You follow close as you feel comfortable."

Air speed increased to 200 miles per hour as the planes descended. Brian had his letdown gauged perfectly and flared out over the end of the runway. The two planes screamed the length of the runway as though attached to each other. Brian pulled up into a steep climb with Jamie in close synchronization. Without reducing power, Jamie turned steeply to the left and came back past the airport at cruise speed. Reducing power, he flew a short pattern and was on the runway and slowed enough for the turn to the hangar. Brian was close behind him.

Mary and Dave were there to meet them, as well as Stan, Kevin and Randy.

"Hey, you guys put on quite a show," Stan exclaimed. "You can start putting on air shows anytime you want to."

"It looked dangerous to me," Mary complained.

"No," Kelly objected, "it was lots of fun, and when Jamie is flying, it isn't dangerous. He's the best pilot in the world, even if he does wreck a plane now and then."

"No, it wasn't dangerous," Brian reported. "All I did was fly normally. Jamie was the one that demonstrated skill. His plane seemed to know what mine was going to do and followed perfectly. We have to have some fun now and then."

"Yes, we need to relax now and then." Jamie agreed. "All work and no play make Jack a dull boy. But we have a council meeting soon and we had better be there."

* * *

The council convened at the regular three PM Sunday afternoon time, with a full contingent of members, plus Harry Haynes and Brian.

Jamie brought the group to order promptly. "I suppose what you would like first is a full report from me. I have had an eventful week. You know part of it, but I will review everything in detail so you can understand what's going on."

The next thirty minutes was spent on that report. Jamie told them of conditions at Little River and the total loss that the people had suffered there. He continued with a detailed breakdown of his trip home and the route he had mapped out for bringing the horses home.

"In conclusion," he reported, "I think that Bellingham is the best spot to put the horses on a barge. There is a good place to load there. The area is not too congested with dead cars and people or animals. There is a good place to overnight the horses, and it will only add an hour or two to the barge time. So, have you folks found a barge and tug suitable for the job?"

"Yeah," Harry Haynes reported. "Richard Dick has one all lined up. It's an 80-foot barge with a lift ramp on the stern. The tug is plenty big enough to handle the load; it has been towing log booms from the north island area to the mill here and to Crofton. I think we should build a corral for the horses on the barge. We can do it in a day or so, and the horses will be a lot more comfortable. They will have enough room to move around a little and lay down if they wish. It can take up to 14 hours for the trip."

"There's no danger in them getting thrown against the side or otherwise hurt?" Jamie asked.

"No. Horses adapt to sea movement readily. That's the way they transport them on ships where they are out for days or weeks at a time. We throw a good lot of straw on the deck to make them more comfortable. We can use less than half the deck space for the pen, and there is still room for several vehicles. I don't think there is any reason to bring the big stock truck across."

"Sounds like you have everything worked out," Jamie admitted. "If everyone agrees, go ahead and build the corral and get everything ready. I'll go back to Little River with Brian Monday or Tuesday, and we can start moving people. With another bigger plane, we can move people faster. Are you ready for the people here?"

"That's my department," Mary said. "We have ten farms marked out for them all close together at the north end of the occupied places. They are all about the same size, and all of them have good two- or three-bedroom houses on them. Two of them have additional small cabins that might be good for in-law suites. I think we should employ a lottery like we did before except that we should give preference to extended families for the places with extra space. We will house all of them in the officers' quarters at the base until we get things organized. Right now, we have the four kids and the two older couples that Brian brought over located with families. We had people that wanted to take them, and they will keep them until everyone is moved in. I need to get them over here and register all of them in order to get organized properly."

Chapter 46

Brian had both airplanes on the ramp ready to go when Jamie arrived at the airport. Stan was there with a box of equipment and tools. He was going along to install a satellite radio in the truck that Jamie was going to drive back.

"Did you feel the earthquakes last night?" Brian asked.

"Yeah," Jamie responded, "they were strong enough to wake me up and make a few things rattle. I didn't keep track of how many there were. Kelly said she counted six."

"That's about right," Stan reported. "I felt at least six. There may have been seven. They were spread over about a two-hour period."

"Well," Jamie said, "let's start fires in these birds and be on our way. We are coming back with a load of people this afternoon, if the weather doesn't clobber up on us. This southeast breeze could stir something up. Go ahead and take off, Brian, and I'll be right behind you. Stan, you can go with Brian, if you like."

Brian leveled off at 10,000 feet and Jamie established himself about a hundred yards off his port side. They had barely established their cruise altitude when Brian came on the radio.

"Jamie, look at those volcanoes. It looks like both Garibaldi and Baker are set on some activity."

"Looks that way," Jamie agreed. "Maybe they were the cause of the earthquakes last night. There appears to be plenty of space to fly between them. We just need to be sure we don't fly through any ash clouds. That volcanic ash can raise hell with these jet engines. Brian, do you want to call the boys at home and alert them to keep an eye out and let us know if the wind comes up more and starts moving the ash clouds towards home?"

"Will do," Stan replied.

At just after 11 AM, Brian set his plane on the dirt road at Little River, followed by Jamie. Nils and William were out to meet them.

"We have 18 people lined up for you to take back to New Island," William told them. "We will have some lunch and then they will be ready to go."

"Sounds good," Jamie replied. "Nils, how's it been going here?"

"Just fine," Nils told him. "We found another van, so we can divide up the load of harness and stuff we have gathered up. William has been learning to drive it. We tried loading the horses in the truck. Nick put a halter on the stallion and led him up the ramp. The others followed just fine. I took them for a short ride to get them used to the idea. When we came back, Nick called to the stallion, he marched out calm as could be, and the others all followed him. We won't have any problems handling the horses. Nick is a master horseman and knows how to handle them."

"Good," Jamie said. "It looks like you are ready anytime we are. We'll get this load home tonight and come back with one plane tomorrow. That will account for 27 people, leaving six to go with the trucks, including you. Brian can take the load home tomorrow and bring back the 206 with the other two pilots. They're ready to go it alone on the 206, so Brian can stay with us. You can drive the big truck. I'll take the pickup. Brian can drive one of the vans and William the other. We should have Nick along to handle the horses. There will still be three people to come with us on the trucks."

"Nick's wife insists on going with Nick," William said. "I think that is a good idea. My wife wants to come too. Thomas will fill out the crew."

"Sounds like you fellows have it all organized OK. Let's get lunch over with and load up. We have to go by way of Lethbridge to fuel up."

By noon, the two planes, fully loaded, were ready to go. By the time they got to Lethbridge and refueled both planes, it was after one o'clock when they got away. They leveled off at 10,000 feet, and Jamie called New Island on the satellite phone. Kevin answered.

"What's going on there?" Jamie asked.

"The wind is coming up pretty strong, but it has switched around and is coming directly from the south. We think we can see smoke on the horizon to the west."

"That means that we better head south of Mount Baker to keep out of the smoke. That will add about thirty minutes to our flying time. We should arrive about 4:45 PM. We will keep you informed. Let us know if there is any drastic change in conditions."

Changing to the aircraft radio, Jamie called Brian, "Did you hear my conversation with Kevin?"

"Roger, I got it OK. I have some scared passengers here that I've been trying to settle down. I had the speaker on, and they heard it too, so that didn't help any. What's our new course?"

"Set your GPS for the Mount Vernon area. That will keep us well south of Mount Baker. We'll keep our eyes open and be prepared to go further south if we need to. We'll go to Mount Vernon and then fly up the coast. I gave an ETA of 4:45."

"That sounds about right to me," Brian agreed.

Jamie dropped back and let Brian lead. Over Mt. Vernon Brian changed course to the north and Jamie followed.

"Jamie, are you there?"

"I'm here, Brian. We seem to be doing OK."

"I figure we will be about 45 minutes from here. Your estimate sounds good. I'll call base and let them know."

"This is Comox base. We hear you on 121.1. We will be expecting you at 4:45. Everything is ready for your passengers."

"Good," Jamie replied. "They'll be ready to get on the ground. None of them have been in an airplane before, and they are a bit uneasy."

Mary had brought Kelly to the airport to meet them, and as usual, Kelly welcomed Jamie as though he had been away for an extended time. Kelly was full of news to relay to Jamie. "We had another earthquake today, and it was stronger than the ones we had last night. It shook a pot of stew off of the stove and made a terrible mess, but Dawg helped clean it up. He gulped down most of the stew as though he hadn't had anything to eat for a week. I think it burned his tongue a little bit because he was anxious to get water afterwards. But he only ate the meat out of it, and Irene and I had to clean up the rest of the mess. Josephine was out working in the garden, and she was scared; she said it shook hard enough that she had a hard time standing up. There, I told you the news without running out of breath."

"So you did, Kiddo. You are learning. I've flown almost seven hours today, and I'm tired. Let's get home and get some dinner. Did you make another pot of stew?"

"Yeah, but we had to put canned meat in it, and it isn't as good. But it is pretty good anyway. I put lots of onion and some fresh garlic in it out of the garden. Irene said Brian should come to dinner, too."

"OK, you go tell him and then we'll go home. I'd like to shower before dinner."

Jamie had finished his shower and changed into clean clothes. Josephine and Kelly were busy getting dinner ready. He wondered where Irene was, but decided not to ask. Someone would tell him, sooner or later. He picked up a book that he had been reading and settled into an easy chair, but, somehow, it was hard to pick up where he left off in the book. Dropping the book, he went to the entertainment center, popped a disk into the player, and went back to his chair. As he settled back to enjoy the classical music, the front door opened and Irene and Brian came in.

Brian seemed nervous. "Jamie, we would like to talk to you a minute. Do you have time?"

"Of course, I have time."

"Irene and I want to get married."

"So what about it?" Jamie asked. "There's nothing new about that, is there?"

"No, but we have been putting it off too long. I've been so busy that it just seemed like there wasn't time, but we have decided we don't want to wait any longer. We want to get married tonight. Will you do it?"

"Of course, but if you would wait until we get this project over with, you could have a few days off."

"I don't really want a few days off. We have too much to do, and I want to do my share. But we decided we would like to squeeze the wedding in between times. We have a house up at the base, and it is all ready for us to move into. We have been getting it ready for some time. We will be gone for several days, and we don't want to wait till we come back."

"You agree with all of this, Irene?" Jamie asked.

"Yes Jamie. I have been insisting that we do it soon. I do not want to wait any longer, either."

"You know that we are committed to flying tomorrow. There is no way we can change it. We have to get the rest of those people over here."

"Yes, I know. I'll be ready to go as early as you want to."

"All right. We better get the others in here and tell them and get this ceremony over with."

"They already know," Irene said. "We talked it over while you were in the shower, and then went for a walk to get nerve enough to ask you."

"I didn't want you to think I was trying to get out of doing my job," Brian explained.

"Gee, I never thought I was that much of a nasty old man. I didn't think anyone was scared of me."

"That's not it," Brian said. "You have a tremendous job to do, and it is my duty to help you in every way that I can. I want to do my job better than anyone else would do it. I have to live up to your expectations."

"Kelly! Josephine!" Jamie called out. "Get yourselves in here. You knew all about this and didn't tell me. Call Mary and tell her and Dave to get over here. Is there enough food to have them for dinner, too? We need Mary to record this ceremony, and Dave can be best man. Kelly, you can be bridesmaid."

"I've already called them," Kelly admitted. "They'll be here any minute, and they are bringing the wine."

"Looks like I'm tail-end Charlie in this operation. Are we going to have the ceremony before dinner or after?"

"Before," Kelly replied. "Dinner won't be ready for close to an hour. We had to change everything when we found out it was going to be a wedding feast."

"You didn't have any doubts, did you? What if I had said no?"

"Brian was a little worried about it," Kelly admitted, "but I knew you would agree."

"You know me pretty well, don't you? Or at least you think you do. Someday, I'll surprise you."

"No, you won't," Kelly said. "I really do know you. Here come Mary and Dave."

Mary appeared even more radiant than usual as she came through the door. Her blond hair was an inch or more long and looked like static electricity had set it all on end. The scars no longer showed on her scalp. She wore a light blue sheath dress that ended above the knees and emphasized her thinness, and the slight bulge that was beginning to show in her stomach, but somehow added a touch of beauty to her gangly form. "Hey," she said, "we have to get this gal dressed properly for a wedding. Dave, would you bring in the bag I left in the car? How much time do we have, Kelly?"

"'Bout half an hour. Dinner will be ready in an hour."

Dave returned with an overnight bag, and Mary and Irene disappeared into the bedroom.

"I have some other clothes in the car," Brian said. "I suppose I better change, too."

"Damn," Jamie grumbled. "That means I have to get dressed up too."

"Well," Dave told them. "I had to. Mary made me put on a suit and tie. You guys are no better than I am. When you have a bossy female in charge, you go along and do as she says."

"Gosh," Jamie muttered. "I sure do feel sorry for you. But you brought it on yourself, so don't tell me your troubles."

Thirty minutes later, Mary led Irene into the room.

"My God," Brian exclaimed. "She is even more beautiful than I thought. Look at her."

"Wow...ee!" Kelly exclaimed. "You really are beautiful, Irene."

Color flared up in Irene's face as she ducked her head in embarrassment.

"Don't let these oafs upset you, girl," Jamie told her. "Of course, you are beautiful. I knew that all the time. It's too bad you have to get gussied up for the rest of these nitwits to understand it. Mary, you did a good job."

Irene's deep brown hair shone brightly, coiled in a mass on top of her head, emphasizing her clear, olive-tinged complexion and her slender neck. The form-fitting white dress, ending mid-thigh, showed her generous curves and the slim legs to perfection.

Jamie took the lead. "Now that we have this beauty queen in the notion, let's get this critter that she has agreed to marry up here and get them hitched. Enjoyable as it is, we can't stand here all night gawking at the best looking girl in New Island. Brian, get up here. Irene, stand here beside him. Kelly, take note how this is done; you'll be doing the same thing someday, and you will be just as beautiful. Your place is beside Irene. Dave, you are best man. Get up here beside Brian. You can commiserate with him after we have the job done."

With the ceremony completed, toasts drank, congratulations, handshakes, hugs and kisses over with, they sat to a dinner that was remarkable for having been prepared on short notice; they all returned to the living room for a final after-dinner drink.

"I hate to break up a fine party," Jamie proclaimed, "but we better decide what we are going to do tomorrow. We are committed to going to Little River, so we better get organized. Brian, I had planned on leaving at six in the morning, but let's put

363

it off until nine. Then you can bring back the last load of cargo and be home tomorrow night and come back to Little River with the boys in the 206 the next day. That will give you two nights of honeymoon. We will be several days getting back, so Irene had better come back here to stay, so she doesn't have to be alone. Does that sound OK to you?"

"That's wonderful, Jamie." Brian was enthusiastic. "But you didn't need to change your plans on account of us."

"I know," Jamie assured him, "but I wanted another day to get ready to start the trip home with the horses. This will give us more time to get things ready. Now it's time to take this gal to her new home. Good night—see you at nine in the morning."

* * *

Jamie was finishing breakfast at eight o'clock when Stan called on his cell phone. "I just had a satellite call from Nils. It's cold over there; froze hard last night. You better take a warm coat and some winter clothes, also some gloves. Nils said it looked like it would stay cold for a while."

"Thanks Stan. Will do. Better warn Brian, too."

"Already done," Stan replied.

"I just thought of something else, Stan. You don't by any chance have some CB radios available?"

"Yeah," Stan replied. "I have four or five in the storeroom."

"Any chance you could come with us today and install them in the vehicles? You could come back with the boys when they return tomorrow."

"Yeah, I can gather them up and be ready to leave when you are. I have another fellow who will monitor the radio here while I am gone."

Jamie went back to his room and added some warm clothing to the bag he had packed. As an afterthought, he picked a small thermometer from his bedside table and tucked it into a side pocket on his bag.

The airplane was out and ready to go when Jamie arrived at the airport. Kevin and Randy were there, helping wherever they could.

Jamie called them together. "Brian will come back this afternoon with nine more passengers. I'll be staying in Little River.. Randy and Kevin, both of you will come back to Little River tomorrow with Brian in the 206. You two will have to bring the 206 home alone. Do you feel ready for it?"

"Sure do," Kevin replied. "If we are not ready now, we better quit flying. You've trained us well."

"OK, Brian, let's saddle up and head east. We will probably have to go south around the volcanoes, but we can take a peek before we decide. We'll keep home base informed. See you fellows tomorrow."

* * *

They immediately noticed the cold when they opened the plane doors at Little River. Even with a hazy sun shining, a light breeze sent the cold penetrating their clothing. Jamie pulled his heavy coat from the plane and shrugged into it, then fished the thermometer from his bag and held it exposed to the air. It only took a minute for the thermometer to establish itself in the new environment; it registered 25 degrees Fahrenheit.

"Wow!" Jamie told the others. "It's seven degrees below freezing, with the sun shining in the middle of the day."

"Yes," William said, "it is very cold. It was much colder during the night. I think everything is frozen. The garden is all turning black. If it gets colder tonight, all crops that are left will be ruined. It is one disaster on top of another."

"Well, there's no need to let this one worry you. You are all getting out of here fast. Let's get this airplane loaded and on its way. The other boys will bring Brian back tomorrow, and we will get ourselves on the move the next day."

"Here come the rest of the people that are going out," William reported. "They are reluctant to get in that machine. None of them have ever been in an airplane before. We have tried to reassure them, but they do not listen very well."

"OK folks," Jamie announced. "We are ready to load this airplane up. Meet your pilot, Brian. He looks young, but he knows how to operate this machine. Who wants to sit in the front seat with him and help him out? What, no one wants to volunteer?" He took a youngish looking rather plump woman by the arm, ushered her to the right side of the plane, helped her in, and fastened her seat harness. "When Brian needs help," he told her, "he will tell you what to do."

Finally realizing that she was being kidded, she gave a nervous laugh. "You can depend on me. I will be sure to panic before anyone else does."

"That's the spirit," Jamie told her. "All right folks, all aboard. You now have a capable copilot that will get you home if your regular pilot can't. There is absolutely nothing to be afraid of. I'll see all of you next week in New Island."

A few minutes later, the Caravan was airborne, on its way to Lethbridge for fuel before starting the trip to New Island.

"Thanks for the bit of humor, Jamie," William said. "I think you lightened their fear a little. That, and the fact that everyone else has gotten to their destination safely, makes things a little easier."

Chapter 47

Shivering from the cold, Jamie watched the airplane disappear in the haze. "How are we fixed here?" he asked. "Are we pretty well set to go? Stan is going to install CB radios in all the rigs, so we can talk to each other when we are on the road."

"Yes," William assured him, "we are just about all ready. The radios sound like a good idea. This cold does not help any. Luckily, we went up to the mountain and brought down a load of wood yesterday afternoon. Some of the people huddled around the fire most of the night. Even though we have lots of blankets, they were having trouble keeping warm. This is like midwinter, almost, except that there is no snow."

"Let's go over things," Jamie requested. "Where's Nils? Ah, here he is. Are we well equipped for everything we may need on our way?"

"I think so," Nils replied. "Let's check, though. What do we need?"

"Shovels, pick, ax, heavy hammer, saws, log chains."

"I missed the heavy hammer. We should have one, as well as carpenters' hammers. We have only one. We have two log chains, about twenty feet each, with a grab hook on one end and a round hook on the other and a snatch block."

"OK," Jamie said, "let's make a list. One big hammer, maybe two, a couple more chains and some repair shackles for them. We should throw in a few pieces of timber from the pile there, some two-by-fours and two-by-sixes. Better have some spikes and some smaller nails."

"I think we're ready otherwise," Nils said, going over his list. "I didn't make any arrangements for spare fuel. I assumed we could get that along the way."

"Sounds like you are well prepared," Jamie said. "I believe we will get out of this cold once we cross the Continental Divide. Let's keep our minds open to anything else we might need. Although I have flown over the route that we will take, we never know how conditions might change before we get there. This volcanic action that is going on is very unpredictable. It could affect the weather, too. We need to be prepared for anything. Let's get inside. It's getting cold out here, and I'm beginning to feel it."

The others were all huddled in the comfortable warmth of the wood stove. Stan followed them in, rubbing his hands to bring the feeling back into them. "I have radios in the pickup and one van. There is already a good one in the big truck. I'll get the other van ready as soon as I warm up a little."

"Good deal," Jamie reported. "It's getting colder out there; it's down to 24 degrees, and the sun is still shining."

"I have never seen anything like this," William reported. "I have been living here for 30 years. I've seen frost at this time of the year, but never killing cold like this."

"How about the livestock?" Jamie asked.

"The horses are in the small pasture at this end," William told him. "There is a clump of trees down by the creek that offers some protection. They will be OK. We turned the cattle loose yesterday morning and started them down the valley. We have opened gates and cut fences into the meadows in the lower valley. We also took down the fences around some haystacks. That is about all we can do for them. We just have to hope for the best."

"I go fix supper," Flora told them. "I cook outside, but we all eat here. It more comfortable."

"Can I help you?" Jamie asked. "I'm not much of a camp cook, but I can follow instructions."

"No," Flora replied. "My old man follow instructions too. He do it. You stay here keep warm."

"I'll go get the other radio in while dinner is cooking," Stan said. "I'd like to finish tonight; it's likely to be colder in the morning."

* * *

Jamie awoke stiff from his night on the living room floor. Someone had stoked the wood stove, and the room was reasonably warm. But when he stuck his head outside, he received a shock. The little thermometer he had left on the table registered 12 degrees Fahrenheit, or about minus eleven Celsius.

Flora was preparing breakfast on the camp stove, bundled up with all the clothing she could get on. "It much cold," she said. "Much more cold. I never seen summertime."

Nick came from the pasture. "I use ax, cut hole in ice so horses drink."

"Are they all right?" Jamie asked.

"Yes, they all good. But everything ruined. Even potatoes in ground froze solid. It good you taking us away from here. We would starve this winter. There nothing left us here."

They were ready to go. Brian had arrived in the 206, and Stan had gone home with the two young pilots.

Nils started the diesel truck and warmed it up. Nick led the big stallion up from the grove where they had spent the night. The stallion walked calmly up the ramp into the truck, and the other horses followed without question.

"I'll lead with the pickup," Jamie told them. "Nils will follow in the big truck, and the two vans will come behind. You all have radios. Keep them on and call me if there is any problem, regardless of how small." Nick was in the big truck with Nils, and Flora rode with Jamie. Brian drove one of the vans, and William drove the other, with Ann beside him. Things went well, and by noon they were transiting the Rocky Mountain divide. Jamie stopped, and they all got out to stretch. The cold didn't seem as bad here as it did at Little River, in spite of the altitude.

The weather warmed up steadily as they moved off the mountain and westward. It was fairly early when Jamie led the way off the highway to the corral beside the road near Kalispell. Nils backed the truck up to the loading ramp and let the gate down. The horses moved gratefully down the ramp and into the corral. Nick opened the gate, and the stallion ventured cautiously out, and then broke into a wild gallop across the pasture, the other horses galloping exuberantly after him. They made a great turn around the pasture, then stopped by the lake, waded in and drank their fill. Coming back from the water, they started to graze on the lush grass.

"They much happy," Nick said. "You pick good spot for horses."

"Thanks Nick." Jamie retrieved his thermometer. It was 63 degrees. They had definitely departed the cold country.

They were on the road early the next morning and arrived at the Ellensburg Airport without further trouble. Nick led the stallion down the road to the farm where they could reach the creek. With their thirst quenched, the horses followed Nick back to the airport, where he put the stallion on a picket line. The horses started grazing contentedly.

"Any danger of them wandering off during the night?" Jamie asked.

"Not as long as the stallion is here. They won't leave him unless they were panicked or something."

The women set the camp stove up on the tarmac and cooked supper. They took their beds inside the terminal building and slept on the carpeted floor of the waiting area. The next day, they were on their way early under a leaden sky that obscured the mountains to the west. An hour later, they stopped in dense fog at the top of Snoqualmie Pass. They all gathered around the front of the horse truck while Nick climbed up and talked to the horses. They seemed restless and nervous, more so than they had at any other time on the trip.

"Wonder what's eating on the horses?" Jamie questioned. "They haven't been this way before. I wonder if they know something that we don't know."

Suddenly, there was a rustling in the dead still air as a slight breeze stirred the fog. The breeze strengthened, and the fog began to swirl and dissipate and was gone in minutes. Jamie looked up to see broken clouds racing overhead, swirling around the mile high mountain to the south of them. In the truck, the big stallion snorted and stamped his feet.

"What the hell is going on?" Nils ask.

Then they heard it—a low rumble, like distant thunder and the ground beneath their feet began to tremble. It didn't shake, like an earthquake. It was more of a vibration that they could feel through the soles of their shoes. The horses seemed even more upset, and Flora climbed up beside Nick and began to sing, her voice soft and melodious in her Russian language. Her voice had a soothing effect on the horses. The vibration grew worse, and the rumble was increasing to a roar, like a freight train coming down the tracks at high speed. Then the rotten egg odor intruded on their senses.

"What is happening?" William asked.

"I think it is a volcano erupting," Jamie told them. "The odor is sulfur gas which is common in volcanoes. I think Mount Rainier is blowing up. It's only 30 or 40 miles south of us here."

"Don't you think we better get out of here?" Ann Skrylak demanded. "I am scared."

"I am too," Jamie told her. "But panic is the worst thing we can do. Panic always leads to catastrophe. We just have to wait a few minutes and be sure of what we are doing."

Brian was on the satellite radio to New Island. "There doesn't seem to be anything unusual going on there," he reported.

"Let's get the rigs turned around and headed the other way. If we have to run for it, that is likely to be the best way."

Nils jumped in the big truck, swung it in a circle on the parking lot, and headed it east. The others fell in behind him, got out, and gathered around Jamie again. The wind was increasing from south-southwest, and ash was fouling the air.

"I believe it is time to go," Jamie told them. "Nils, you go ahead with the horses as fast as it is safe. Don't take any chances with too much speed. The rest of us will follow. I'll bring up the rear. I may wait here a few minutes to see what's going on if possible."

The big truck roared off down the slope to the west, the others following. The ash was getting thicker in the air, and visibility was deteriorating rapidly. "Guess we better get going too, while we can still see," Jamie said to Ann, who was riding with him.

"I'm with you," Ann replied. Jamie drove as fast as visibility would permit. Ten miles down the road, the ash began to lessen, and another ten and the air was clearing. Jamie picked up the CB mike. "Nils, do you have your ears on?"

"Yep," Nils replied. "I hear you."

"Where are you?" Jamie asked.

"Just past intersection 78," Nils reported.

"OK, I think you can slow down now. We are in the clear. Let's go on to our last camp at Ellensburg and settle down till we can find out what's going on."

"Sounds good to me," Nils replied. "I'll see you there. Should we unload the horses?"

"Yes, we might be there for sometime."

When Jamie pulled into the airport, Nils already had the ramp down. The horses seemed to have settled down and followed the stallion out of the truck. Nick put the stallion on a picket line nearby where the grass was good, and the others gathered around him and started grazing. The women set up the camp stove and got ready to prepare a hot lunch. The sun came out, and the day warmed up to a comfortable level.

To the west, some sixty miles away, a huge gray cloud swelled into the air and spread northward. There was no question as to the source. Mount Rainier was in full eruption.

"Get your toolbox, Brian," Jamie said, "and let's go and look in those hangars and see if there's an airplane that's usable."

A number of small hangars were spaced along the far side of the field. Jamie took the pickup and drove over to them. The first three were unlocked and empty. The fourth had a padlock on the small door at the side, and the main doors were obviously locked on the inside. Brian made short work of the padlock, and they entered to unfasten the main doors and slide them open. An older model V-Tail Beech Bonanza, looking shiny and well cared for, glistened in the sun that came through the doors. The plane was locked, as was a sturdy locker to one side. Brian popped the padlock on the locker and swung it open to reveal a cabinet with supplies for maintenance of the plane. The keys hung on a nail. A maintenance manual and an operations manual were on a shelf.

Brian unlocked the plane and slid inside. He found a logbook in the glove compartment. It showed that the plane had had a hundred-hour check in February and had only flown five hours since then.

"Have you ever flown one of these?" Brian asked.

"No, I haven't, but it has wings. It must fly like most other planes. I can't see any problem."

"I've heard they have some special characteristics," Brian said. "I think you should read the flight manual before you try it."

"I agree. Let's see if it will start. If so, we will take it over by the terminal, and I'll start studying it."

Brian pulled the prop through a few times. Jamie turned the switch on. He looked to see that Brian was clear, eased in a bit of throttle and activated the starter. The engine turned over a few times and started. Brian pulled the chocks from in front of the wheels, and Jamie eased the throttle in and taxied out of the hangar and along the perimeter taxiway to the terminal, where he shut down and started in on the manual. At two o'clock, he crawled out of the plane and declared himself ready to fly it.

"OK," Brian said. "Let's go."

"All right. Tell the others we are going. Ask Nick to be sure and keep the horses away from the main runway. We'll fly locally; shoot some landings and things like that."

Twenty minutes later, they were at the end of the runway. Jamie spent some time running the engine up, testing everything and explaining to Brian what he was doing. "Here we go," he said. The plane gathered speed readily. At 70 miles indicated, he started easing back on the yoke, and at 90, the wheels came free of the runway. With the plane flying solidly, he hit the gear switch, and the growl of the motor retracting the gear was evident. The gear snapped into place in the belly of the plane, the doors closed over them and the plane accelerated as it freed itself of the drag of the landing gear. Jamie throttled back a little and trimmed to climb at 120 miles per hour. He put the plane through its paces: slow flight, steep turns and stalls. After a series of landings, he taxied to the fuel pumps. "Let's top that right tank off. We will want full tanks to go exploring tomorrow."

Brian spent the rest of the afternoon checking everything he could on the plane.

Chapter 48

Jamie and Brian had the Bonanza in the air early the next morning, getting a closer look at the volcano. Great clouds of gray smoke were belching from the top of the mountain and streaming off to the north as far as they could see. Torrents of water and mud from the melting snow were rushing down every channel leading from the summit. The entire west side of the original crater had been blown away and rock and debris scattered for many miles to the west. The forest was gone, only occasional fire marking where the land had not been completely covered with debris. The Puyallup River was a raging mud-laden torrent that was spreading over the lowland. The flood had completely inundated the city of Puyallup and was spreading on downstream and pouring into the bay at Tacoma. The Nisqualli River was also flooding, and a huge wall of water was sweeping across the lands of Fort Lewis and spreading into Olympia. Further north, the Carbon River and the White River were in full flood, overflowing their banks and spreading mud and debris everywhere. As they went further north, it began to rain and the rain soon became so heavy that they had to turn back. Continuing to the south, they found that Mount St. Helens was also erupting, and the Toutle River was in full flood, laden with mud and debris. The crater was spewing a steady column of smoke.

"Let's go on up the Columbia River," Jamie suggested, "and see if there is a chance we can get down one of the roads. There's a two-lane road on the north side of the river and a four-lane along the south side."

"Sounds good," Brian agreed. "How's our fuel?"

"Should be OK. There's an airport at Hood River. We'll fuel there."

At the Hood River Airport, they found the fuel station with no trouble. The flight to Ellensburg was uneventful, and they were back in camp early afternoon.

Jamie went on the satellite phone to call Stan. He reported the results of the day's flying. "I think we are completely blocked from any route by way of the Seattle area. It appears we may be able to make it down the Columbia River. If so, we should be able to get through on Highway One, up the coast, which would put us in Port Angeles. The only problem is the Portland area. Brian and I will survey that route tomorrow and let you know tomorrow night."

* * *

The whole group was participating in a round-robin discussion about the project.

"One difficulty is moving dead cars out of the way," Brian commented. "Too bad we don't have a dozer blade on the front of that big truck."

"Hey," Nils said, "that pickup Jamie is driving has a pretty good push."

"Only trouble is," Jamie told them, "it would be easy to damage the radiator if something came loose on the car we were pushing."

"How about putting a big, extra strong brush guard on it?" Brian asked. "It has a big heavy steel bumper that the winch is mounted on."

"Who's going to make an installation like that?" Jamie asked.

"I saw a machine shop over near the access road," Brian said. "Let's take the pickup over there and see what we can find."

At the machine shop, Brian pried the lock off the double doors at the front and swung them open.

"Pretty junk place, but there is an acetylene welding outfit. If it works and we can find some iron, we'll be home free. Here are all kinds of scrap. If Nils will help, we can make a guard in no time. Let me see if that torch will work?" A minute later, the torch flared alive. "We are in business."

The next morning, Jamie and Brian were off early. The freeway south to Yakima was open. They found a traffic snarl on the freeway going through Yakima but managed to chart a way around it on secondary streets and get onto Route 97. From there, it was clear all of the way to the Columbia River where they were able to pick up the freeway routes 30 and 94. There was heavy congestion on the eastbound lanes, but the westbound appeared passable.

They landed at Hood River and topped the tanks, then continued flying along the freeway. Everything went fine until they hit the Portland area where they found total blockage of the last mile of the freeway before its junction with Interstate 5, which was jammed for miles both north and south. The bypass Route 405 was equally impassable. They spent an hour flying back and forth until they finally charted out a torturous route that swung far south of Portland. By turning off of the freeway at Troutdale, they could follow country roads south and then west and finally intersect Route 47 that would take them north to Route 30. Jamie estimated that it would take them an extra 75 miles to make the detour.

Route 47 proved to be open, and they turned down the Columbia River over Route 30 to Astoria where they found some congestion in the area entering the approaches to the bridge across the Columbia. They circled several times and decided that they could probably get through all right. They found gas at the Astoria Airport, and after eating sandwiches that Ann had prepared for them, they continued up the coast over Highway 101. Although a tortuous route, they found no serious blockages that they were able to see. At Port Angeles, they flew the waterfront, and it appeared that there was a spot in the Coast Guard complex on the spit that enclosed the harbor where they could load a barge.

Over Nanaimo, Jamie tried a call on 121.5. Stan answered immediately. "We are over Nanaimo," Jamie reported, "and will be landing in a few minutes. What is your wind?"

"Wind is southeast at 15," Stan reported.

"OK, we'll land from the northwest," Jamie told him.

As they were pulling onto the ramp, they saw a car rush through the gate to park by the hangar. Kelly, Irene and Mary piled out of the car and came running towards them. Jamie wondered how they got to the airport so fast. Kelly ran to the pilot's side of the plane as Brian opened the passenger door and stepped out onto the wing.

"There's no door on that side," Brian called to Kelly. "He'll be getting out this side."

Kelly raced around the tail as Jamie stepped down from the wing. "Jamie! Jamie, you've been gone forever. What took you so long? I thought you were never coming back."

Jamie picked her up and swung her around as he gave her a terrific hug.

"I left Monday, this is Sunday," Jamie told her. "That's only a short week. I admit that I have missed you too."

"Please don't be gone so long again. I really miss you ever so much. And with school not going, it's even worse."

"Come on, let's go home. Brian and I have had a long hard flight. Brian, let the other fellows service the plane and take your lady home."

"No," Brian replied, "they are not familiar with this bird. I'll stay long enough to be sure they know what to do. It will only take a few minutes."

They were in the car on the way home when Jamie asked Kelly, "How did you get here so fast? You had no way of knowing when we were coming in."

"Mary was at our house. We suspected that you would be in most anytime because Stan said you had left early this morning. Then when you called on the radio, he called us and we rushed out in time to meet you."

"So what's been going on while I was gone?"

"Not much. One day the wind blew from the southeast, and we had a lot of that nasty smell and some ash from the volcanoes. Another day, Jacob rode over with two extra horses and took Irene and me for a ride. I like riding horses. I'd like to have one someday."

Mary had followed them home in her car and pulled in the driveway behind them.

Getting out of the car, she asked, "Are you coming to the council meeting, or do you want me to handle it and take a rest? I know you must be tired."

"I'll come to the council meeting, but I'd like you to handle it. I'll make a report on the week."

"Can I come too?" Kelly asked. "If Mary is going to be chairman, she'll need a secretary, and I can do that. I've done it before."

"Of course," Mary told her. "I'll need someone to take notes and you always do a good job. I better get on home now. I'll see you both at three. It's well past two now, so you don't have much time to rest."

"We'll be there," Jamie said.

* * *

The full council was present when Jamie and Kelly walked in. Jamie was greeted with enthusiasm.

"We didn't expect you to be here today," Charlie Johnson said. "From what I heard from Stan, you were exploring the Portland area looking for a route through."

"That's right, but we told him that if we wound up closer to here, we would come on in for the night and go back tomorrow. I have a newly married young man flying with me, and I have to give some consideration to his wife."

"Let's call the meeting to order," Mary requested. "Then Jamie can make a complete report to all of you. You're on, Jamie."

Jamie spent 20 minutes on an outline of his activities for the week.

"So the country is really frozen up over there?" Bob Elder asked.

"Yes, it was really cold when we left, down around minus 12 Celsius. It had been getting steadily colder every day. Absolutely everything in the way of crops was totally destroyed. I don't know how far it extended, but I have a feeling it is all of Alberta, and possibly all of the plains and far south into the States. It is all held, however, east of the Continental Divide. As soon as we got over the mountains, we ran into normal temperatures."

"The volcanoes have really raised hob, you say?" Bob Elder asked.

"Yes, I wouldn't have wanted to be living anywhere near the west side of Rainier. The whole west side blew out of the crater and scattered rock and debris for 30 miles or so. It is really scorched earth. Then beyond that, the runoff from the melting glaciers and snowcap has flooded everything towards Tacoma and Olympia. The floodwaters are loaded with silt and trash of all kinds. Farmlands are ruined, and many towns have been totally destroyed. Mount St. Helens has erupted also, but not so violently as the last time, but flooding is extensive. If there had been people living in the area, casualties would have been extensive. Now, I think Mary would like to get on with routine business. I will make a further report to the general meeting tonight."

"Thanks Jamie, for your report. Now let's hear from council members. Bob, I'll call on you first."

* * *

Jamie and Brian had the Bonanza in the air early Monday morning, heading south for the Seattle area. The Rainier eruption seemed to have subsided; only a lazy spiral of smoke drifted upwards in the still air. They decided to look at Snoqualmie Pass in case it was open. Not far down the western slope, a giant mudslide had cascaded across the highway, blocking all lanes. They flew on through the pass and were on the Ellensburg Airport before eight o'clock where they found the crew preparing for the road. Stan had forewarned them over the satellite phone that they would probably be early and eager to go.

"You must have been up before breakfast, this morning," Nils greeted them.

"Yeah," Jamie agreed, "and this little bird is fast. Less than ninety minutes getting over here. Let's put it in the hangar. Who knows, we might want it again someday."

The convoy was on the road before nine and across the Columbia River before noon. They pulled off the highway at The Dalles where they found a truck stop and refueled all of the vehicles. The day was still young when they hit the Troutdale turnoff and started south on country roads. The pace was slower here, however. Sometimes Jamie had a hard time determining which road to follow, especially as they went through small towns where the route changed directions in the middle of the town. It was near five o'clock when Jamie hit a stop sign to a major road.

"Hold here for a bit," Jamie instructed by radio. "There's a park that shows on the map a short distance down this road. I'll check it out and give you a call if it is OK for overnight."

Jamie found the day use park, along the shores of a creek, only a short distance off of their route. Grass had grown tall, and there was adequate feed for the horses. Jamie called instructions on the radio and was in position to flag the big truck to a spot where they could unload the horses that were eager to get on solid ground. They drank their fill of water and started grazing on the tall grass. Ann and Flora set up their kitchen at a group camping facility shelter for cooking, and they had the luxury of sitting at a picnic table to eat their meals.

They spent most of Tuesday working their way through the rural areas south of Portland, going through villages, such as Logan, Fishers Mill and Four Corners, then west on rural roads to Canby, on 99 East. Once, they found a truck and trailer loaded with baled hay overturned in the ditch. They loaded as many bales as they could on Jamie's truck. When they stopped for the night, they would muck out the stock truck and spread fresh hay on the floor.

From Canby, they had four miles to go southwest on 99E. Twice in the four-mile stretch, Jamie pushed cars off the road, tumbling them into the ditch, ignoring the badly deteriorated corpses inside. The guard that the fellows had built on the front proved effective in protecting the front end of the truck. At the intersection of State 282, they went north, then under Interstate 5 to follow along the Willamette River. Through the village of Champoeg, Jamie spotted another picnic ground. Although it was early, they decided to stay for the night because they were assured of feed and water for the horses.

The next day, in a drizzly rain, they made good time to Newberg, on to Yamhill where they intersected Route 47 north. They had some trouble getting through Forest Grove, but made good progress the rest of the day, winding up at Svensen, a small village about 15 miles east to Astoria. There was a freshwater creek where the horses could drink and plenty of forage along the shoulders of the road.

Jamie and Brian decided to go ahead to Astoria to try to clear a way through the traffic jam that they had seen from the air, leaving the others to unload the horses and set up camp. The blockage was not extensive, but it took them an hour to push their way through it. Jamie used the truck like a bulldozer and got the job done. They returned to find camp set up in the middle of the highway.

"We were going to camp in a schoolyard just down the road," Nils told them, "but there were several dead animals in the field next to it, which still had a bit of odor, and the horses didn't like it. They seem happy here munching away along the side of the road."

The next morning, they were on the road again at eight o'clock. Nils had some trouble navigating the big truck through the path they had cleared through the jam in Astoria, but he managed with only a few more scratches on the truck. The rest of the day went easy, and they made fair time up the coast route. About 20 miles west of Port Angeles, they found a good spot to camp near a ranger station in the Clallam National Forest. Jamie raised Stan on the radiophone and reported their location and requested that Harry Haynes call back. Jamie sat in the tuck and relaxed. Thirty minutes later, the call came from Harry. Jamie told him where they were and that they could be in Port Angeles any time that was agreeable to Harry.

"How about eight tomorrow?" Harry asked.

"That's fine," Jamie replied. "But you're going to have to run all night to get here and then run all day to get home. When are you going to rest?"

"That's no problem," Harry replied. "I'll have Johnie Dick along. We can take turns on the wheel. Both of us have gone days at a time on a two-man boat. We'll be fine. Johnie is getting the boat ready now, and we can be on our way in less than an hour. Unless we get bad weather, we'll be there. If we can't make it for some reason, we'll call Stan and he can let you know."

Jamie led the way into the Coast Guard Station before eight o'clock the next morning. The tugboat was in the harbor, snubbed up to the side of the barge and pushing it towards the sea wall. The tide was high, and Johnie Dick was on the barge lowering the ramp to the edge of the sea wall. In a short time, the horses were in the corral; the two vans and Jamie's truck were in place on the stern of the barge. Johnie had the ramp up, and Harry was maneuvering away from the shore. As Johnie placed blocks to prevent movement of the trucks, he called to them to get aboard the tug while it was still tied alongside.

"I stay here with horses," Nick said. "I want be here if they scared. I talk to them."

"I stay too," Flora declared.

"We will be several hundred feet in front of you, and we can't talk to you." Jamie explained. "We will be underway all day."

"That OK," Nick said. "I be with horses."

"I fix lunch from truck," Flora said. "We be OK. I wave flag we need help."

The rest of them jumped from the barge to the tug. Johnnie stayed on the barge, cast off the lines that secured the tug to the barge and went to the bow. Harry maneuvered the tug into position to back up to the bow of the barge; Johnnie secured the towline and jumped on the tug as Harry started moving it away. Johnnie manned the big reel of cable, gradually allowing more of it to pay out until the barge was a satisfactory distance behind them. They were out in the Strait of Juan de Fuca and on their way home.

* * *

It was getting dark when Harry pushed the barge against the bank in Comox to unload. The three trucks were backed off. Nick opened the gate to the horses, put a halter on Commander and led him off the barge. The rest of the herd followed quietly. Bob Elder was there to lead the way to a paddock about a half-mile away that had been prepared for the horses. Thirty minutes later, the horses were in the paddock, drinking from a large trough of fresh water. Nick gave the big stallion a pat on the neck, uttered some words in Russian, removed the halter, and stepped outside the gate. The stallion whinnied and went to the trough to drink.

"He OK now," Nick said. "They little nervous first, then settle down. I glad be here."

"I'm glad to have you here," Jamie told him. "We'll go to the base where you all can stay for a short time until we get you settled on your farms. Perhaps tomorrow, we can decide where to move the horses to."

Several cars picked them up, and a few minutes later they were at the base. Kelly was there to greet Jamie with her usual enthusiasm, and Irene was waiting for Brian. Bob Elder got the newcomers installed in the officers' quarters with the rest of the Little River people. It was agreed that they would have a meeting in the morning to start the process of sorting out the farms and getting the newcomers settled.

Chapter 49

They were all in the officer's clubroom at nine AM, along with the entire New Island Council. Jamie stood and looked with satisfaction at the group he had rescued from probable death in Little River Valley.

"I am delighted to see all of you here," Jamie told them. "It has been a bit of a hassle, but with lots of cooperation, we succeeded. We have found about ten farms that we think will be satisfactory, but we have done nothing about allocating them. That is going to be up to you. I think that your own leadership should continue, at least for the present. If, later, you wish to place yourselves under the leadership of the New Island Council, we will welcome you. I might suggest that we use the same kind of lottery that we used in locating people here in the valley. If you wish, our vice president, Mary, will tell you how it worked and will help you with it. Now, I would like to turn this meeting over to William, your own Council President. William, please take over."

William stood. "Thank you, Jamie. You and your people continue to amaze me. You have rescued us from serious trouble and brought us, at great effort, to your country. After all of that, you offer us self-government. Well, I don't think it would work very well, and after we get ourselves sorted out, I am sure that we will place ourselves under your leadership. Miss Mary, will you take over and help us get started on allocation of the farms?"

By noon, the farms had all been assigned to their new owners.

* * *

They were back in the hall after lunch, and Mary went to the front of the room. "Will the family who has farm number one please stand?" A family of four stood. "Bob Elder, will you please escort these people to their new home?" Bob led the family out of the room to a van in the parking lot.

"Dave Jorgenson, will you please take number-two family?"

Mary continued until all of the families were assigned escorts. The last one, she reserved for herself, an extended family of a couple with two boys and the wife's parents. Loading them into the van that she had borrowed for the occasion, she headed off to the valley. Fifteen minutes later, she pulled into the driveway of an attractive house surrounded by trees. A barn and several outbuildings were evident in the rear. They got out of the van, the entire family gawking in disbelief.

"You mean that this house and land is ours?" the woman demanded.

"Yes, it is all yours," Mary told her. "Come on inside."

They trooped through the front door into a well-furnished living room. The furniture was old but in reasonable condition. Area rugs were spread over a hardwood floor; a dining area was to one side and an up-to-date kitchen beyond. Teresa Holden came in from the back porch and introduced herself.

"My name is Teresa. I am here to show you some of the things in this house that you might not understand." She turned and yelled out the back door, "Hey Pat, get in here. Take the men out and show them around the outside, while I spend some time with the gals in here." She gave a boy of about twelve a push. "Go with the men and learn about this farm. You have a lot of work to do here."

The boy, awed by the newfound wealth of the family, stumbled after his father and grandfather.

The same experience was involving the other nine families. All of them had been provided with mentors to teach them something of their new environment. And all of them were equally astounded at their good fortune. Jamie made the rounds of the new residents to see if they were taken care of properly and was swamped with messages of gratitude wherever he went. At the farm allotted to William Broder, he spent a little more time.

"I would like you to attend our weekly council meeting on Sunday afternoon at three o'clock," Jamie told William. "I am going to ask the council to appoint you to a seat on the council. I am sure they will agree. That will enable you to represent your people here and act as sort of liaison man between our people. Will you accept if the council agrees?"

"I would be highly honored to serve on your council, and I am sure that our people will be happy that I have been appointed to such a post. Ann and I are delighted with the farm you have given us. It is far beyond our expectations. We will be able to live well here."

"It will take awhile to get organized," Jamie told him. "It is late in the year, and that will make it hard to get any crops. There may be some planted that can be harvested. It looks like a good crop of hay out there if you get at it right away. Joe and Jacob have been putting up hay on their places, and they have a horse-drawn mower and rake. I am sure they will help the rest of you. I'd go talk to them if I were you."

"I will," William said. "Ann says there are some winter vegetables that we can still plant if we can find seed. All our seeds were lost in the fire."

"I'll come by tomorrow and take you to where you can find some seeds. Bring Ann along. You can probably pick up seeds for the other people too. I'll be here about ten in the morning. Now, I'll be on my way and let you get settled. See you in the morning."

* * *

Jamie had picked up William Sunday afternoon to bring him to the council meeting. He was surprised when he entered the room to see Chuck Marshal there, sitting alongside of Bob Elder. Mary came in and took her place at the table.

"Let's call the meeting to order," Jamie requested. "The first thing I want to do today is introduce William Broder, Chairman of the Little River Council." He went around the table, naming the rest of the council. They all greeted William with messages of welcome.

"Now," Jamie said, "I would like to tell you a little about William. William was the first person the Little River People picked for their council. When the rest of the council was elected, they insisted that William sit as chairman. He is highly respected by all of his people and is a natural leader of exceptional capabilities. For this reason, I would like to appoint him to serve on this council. We need someone to represent the new people that we have brought in. They are of a different culture than ours, and we need someone that understands them and also is open to change. William can serve that purpose admirably. What are your thoughts?"

"You have been working with him," Bob Elder said, "and your recommendation is good enough for me. I move that we appoint Mr. Broder to serve on this council until such time that an election is called."

"I'll second that motion," Pat Draper said.

"Question?" Jamie asked.

There was no response. "All in favor of the motion so indicate." All hands went up.

"Carried unanimously," Jamie said. "Welcome as a member of the New Island Council."

"Thank you, Gentlemen, and thank you, Jamie. You honor me greatly. I will try to justify your confidence in me. I would like to express my great appreciation for all that Jamie and you people have done for us. Without your help, it is doubtful that we would have survived the disasters that hit our little community. We will try hard to earn a place here and, someday, be able to repay you for your help. I have never experienced such widespread goodwill and helpfulness."

"What's next on the agenda?" Jamie asked.

Bob Elder spoke up. "I have brought Chuck Marshal today. He has something that he wants to talk about."

"You have the floor, Chuck," Jamie told him.

"As you know, I am a dairyman. When things broke last spring, I took over the big dairy farm I am now operating, but at the same time I seriously considered the University Farm up at Oyster River. I, at one time, worked on that farm. Not wanting to see it go to waste, I have been doing what I could to preserve the livestock. I put calves with the milking cows and turned them all into pastures with adequate grass and water. I have checked on them regularly, and they are in good condition. This is my idea. There are at least ten cows up there that have calves sucking. The calves could be weaned, and the cows brought back to producing milk. There are another ten cows that are dry but are carrying calves that are due during the next few months. To end it, there is a prize bull. All of this stock is gentle and most are halter broken. I propose that we turn this herd over to the new people here and let them divide it up to suit themselves. The bull should be available to all. That chore would be up to you to handle, Mr. Broder. Does it sound reasonable to you, Sir?"

"First, would all of you please call me William? Yes, I think it is a marvelous idea. It would be a great aid in bringing our people to self-sufficiency. I would certainly welcome the opportunity to handle the project. I just need to know where the cattle are. My people will take care of the rest."

"Does any of the council have any objections to this project?" Jamie asked. "If not, it is all up to you, Chuck. Can you find time to take William up to Oyster River and get him started?"

386

"Can do," Chuck assented. "We will start on it tomorrow."

"Good," Jamie said. "Another thing, William, what about the horses? They are still in the paddock over by the dock. They are OK there for a while, but they will have to be moved soon."

"I was not sure, Jamie, what your intentions were. Whom do the horses belong to, now that they have been rescued?"

"They belong to Little River people, of course," Jamie said. "Are you going to keep them as a community herd, or are you going to divide them up among the farms?"

"Commander, the stallion, should be given to Nick. He really loves that horse. However, his services as a stud should be community property, yours included. This is my idea, but I will have to take it to my people. I am sure they will agree. The rest of the horses should be spread out over our farms, but subject to helping each other, and you folks, as needed. I will handle all of this and bring it to this council for final approval. It is not too far, so we will walk the horses up to our places. The same with the cattle, if it is not too far. We will walk them down the road to our farms."

"Sounds like you have a capable leader here," Chuck Marshal commented. "There is another thing I will show you at the farm tomorrow, William. There are a couple of rubber-tired wagons up there that you could probably find useful. Also, there is a bunch of old farm machinery stored in a warehouse that was being saved for a museum. A lot of it looks good. There are mowers, hay rakes and plows, even a thrashing machine. It might be that your people could use a lot of it. I'll show it to you when we go up to look at the cows."

"Wonderful," William said. "I cannot believe how lucky we are to be here and find such wonderful people. We are very good at making old machinery work. We never had any money to buy new. We will make it work."

Chapter 50

Suddenly Jamie was wide-awake and sitting up in bed. He glanced at the bedside clock: it said 5:10 AM. Then Dawg was bounding into the room, barking furiously. The big dog jumped on the bed, turned and jumped down, leaving the room, still barking. Jamie swung his feet to the floor, grabbed a robe and ran after Dawg.

Something must have happened to Kelly!

Dawg was in Kelly's room, still barking, when Jamie plowed through the door. The girl was sitting up in bed, rubbing sleep from her eyes. "Dawg! What's wrong?"

"Are you all right?" demanded Jamie.

"Yes, what's happening?"

"I have no idea. Something has Dawg shook up. Come on Dawg, settle down!"

As Jamie turned and left the room, Dawg following him, he became aware of a roaring noise. It sounded like a freight train coming. He was in the middle of the living room when the quake hit. It was sudden and violent. Jamie's feet were whipped from beneath him, and he found himself sitting on the floor, Dawg at his side. The big picture window shattered and crashed to the floor as the house heaved and shook.

Jamie, on the floor, could see out over the valley. What looked like lightning flashing was the arching of electrical wires as they swung together. The flashing was up and down the valley, everywhere, and then they were all out at once. There were more crashing sounds and a scream from Kelly. It felt to Jamie like the house was on a turbulent ocean, with waves coming under one end of the house, lifting it high, the house bending and twisting as the wave progressed, only to be followed by another wave.

It seemed like many minutes before Jamie was able to regain his feet and get back to Kelly, who held onto him sobbing her fear. Jamie sat on the bed with his arms around her, and Dawg huddled close to her on the other side. Finally, it was over.

"It's OK, Kelly. We are OK. It's over with now." Kelly straightened up and wiped the tears away with her knuckles, as Dawg massaged her cheek with a rough tongue.

"Gee, Jamie," she whimpered, "I'm sorry for acting like a baby. But I have never been so scared in my life. That must have been the big one we've been talking about."

"I agree," Jamie admitted. "If that wasn't the big one, I sure don't want to be around when the real 'big one' hits. Come on, get some clothes on and let's see how we stand."

A few minutes later, Jamie was dressed, back in the living room. Kelly joined him, and in the early dawn light, they surveyed the damage. The picture window, its glass in huge shards, was scattered over the living room floor. Pictures were off the wall; frames and glass smashed on the floor. In the kitchen, the refrigerator lay on its face, blocking the aisle. Overhead cabinets were ripped from the wall, their contents in a jumble of broken glass and spilled condiments on the floor. Tremors continued almost constantly.

Kelly held tightly to Jamie's hand and ogled the damage. "Golly, what a mess. But you were right. The house didn't collapse, but it sure did get shook up. Do you suppose it is safe to keep living in it?"

"It has to be," Jamie said. "We have no place else to live. Let's take a look outside."

Jamie wrenched the front door open and cautiously peered out. The front porch had been torn loose from the house, and a gap of about a foot showed between the porch floor and the house. Two of the uprights that supported the roof had broken loose, and the roof sagged at an angle on one end. The other supports were angled away from the house. The roof of the porch was still secured to the house.

Kelly peered around Jamie. "Gosh!" she exclaimed. "I never did see such a mess. What are we going to do?"

"We are going to take our time and figure things out. We are still alive and unhurt. That is the important thing. We have to get out of here and go see how other people are doing. There may be many people that need help. Let's try the back door."

With a great deal of difficulty, Jamie got the back door open only to be confronted with a wall of debris. The roof of the back porch had pulled loose from the house and collapsed, totally blocking the egress.

"Guess we have to go back to the front," Jamie said. "Let's see if we can get across that porch without the roof falling on us." Jamie held on to the doorframe and pushed his foot against the edge of the porch floor. It felt solid. "Stay here," he told Kelly, as he cautiously stepped over the gap and moved to the front edge of the porch. The several wooden steps leading to the ground had been broken loose and were flat on the ground, with a three-foot drop to the top step. Jamie sat on the edge of the porch and got his feet solidly on the collapsed steps, then moved to the ground alongside.

"Come on, Kelly, step easy."

Kelly made an exaggerated step across the gap and came forward. Jamie reached up and swung her to the ground. Dawg was close behind and jumped down to stand beside her. They walked around the house, and it all appeared to be intact, except for the porches. The car and the truck that Jamie had brought from Alberta were parked at the side of the house. Both were undamaged. The power lines were still attached to the house.

"I had better go back in and shut off the power," Jamie said. "If it comes on and there is a short somewhere, it could cause a fire. I don't think, though, that we will have power for a while." He was back in a minute; the master breaker shut off.

"With no power, what's going to happen to all the food we have in the freezer?" Kelly asked.

"If it's off for more than three or four days, we will lose it all," Jamie replied. "Let's go see about other people. We better take the truck. It is better if we find damage on the road."

There was damage. About halfway to the schoolhouse, a section of road had subsided, leaving a bank about a foot high. Cracks ran away from the road in each direction, and the foot high bank was readily visible, even through the brush on each side of the road. Jamie got out and looked carefully. The road seemed solid beyond the drop, so he eased the truck forward and let the front wheels drop off the bank. The back wheels dropped off with a thunk, and they went on.

"Good thing we took the truck," Jamie said. "The car wouldn't have handled that very well."

"What caused that?"

"Probably a fault line deep under the ground. That's a line where the earth crust is cracked, and one side settles or the other side raises up."

"Is that what caused the earthquake?" Kelly asked.

"Possibly, but I think there were other causes. I don't think that one would have caused as severe a quake as this was. I think that a greater quake triggered this one, and it let loose at the same time, or maybe a few seconds after."

They arrived at the school and found the building intact except for a number of broken windows. Two vehicles were already in the lot, and they found Andy Blankenship and Dave and Mary in the office.

"We must have had the 'big one,'" Andy commented, as Jamie walked through the door. "Do you think it was?"

"I'm afraid everyone is going to ask me that," Jamie replied. "And there is no way I can answer, except guess. I sure hope it was. It was bigger than I ever imagined an earthquake could be."

"Did you have much damage?" Mary asked.

"Quite a bit," Jamie replied. "But the house is still intact. We have a hell of a cleanup job inside, and both front and back porches are torn loose. How about you?"

"Same thing. I don't see how the house possibly held together. But I believe it is fundamentally solid."

"How about you, Andy?" Jamie asked.

"About the same situation. Everything out of the cupboards, pictures smashed on the floor, a couple of windows out. The power is out all over the valley, I believe. We may have a major job in getting it back on. I guess we best start at the Puntledge dam and trace things out from there. Do you want to fly the lines again, Jamie?"

Bob Elder burst into the room. "Hey, I'm glad to see you guys. Anyone hurt?"

"Not among us, but we haven't checked much, yet. We better fan out and start checking for casualties. Our cell phones are not working, so we are back to having to run personal contact."

"The Super Store collapsed," Bob reported. "It looks like the roof fell in, and it is burning. There go the tons of frozen foods we stored in the big freezers."

"There's nothing we can do about that, but let it burn. Have you been in contact with anyone else?"

"No. I saw the smoke and drove over there to look, then came directly here. What's next?"

"Guess we better fan out and visit as many places as we can," Jamie said. "Bob, do you want to take charge of that? Mary can stay here and help. Assign routes to all of us, and we will check and report back here. Here's Charlie Johnson and Gary. How are things on your side of the river, Charlie?"

"Pretty bad, but no serious casualties. Young Jim has some glass cuts, but Anne is patching him up. If there are not too many others worse hurt, we'll take him to Dr. Ron later. The bridge across the river is in bad shape. It settled partway into the river, and it is hard to get across. It takes a four-wheel drive rig to make it. There are some trees down along the road, but we managed to get around them."

"Let's start with Charlie and Gary," Bob said. "Is the bridge dangerous?"

"I'm not sure," Charlie responded. "We didn't take time to look it over good, but it could be, especially for a car."

"Why don't you and Gary take responsibility for the west side? Check out all the people that live on the west side, and then check the bridges in town and the one up the river. If they are OK, barricade the main bridge until we can look it over good and make it passable. Check back here as soon as possible."

"Jamie, how about you checking the airport and the dock? Stop by the hospital on your way."

"Dave, will you take the upper end of the valley? Check on the new people from Alberta and work your way down to here, and Andy, how about you starting here and work towards Courtenay? Let's try to all be back here as soon as possible. Let's get going."

"Kelly, you stay here and help Mary and Bob. I'll let Dawg go with me. See you soon." Jamie was out the door before Kelly had a chance to protest.

Jamie found the hospital staff sorting out the chaotic start of the day. Their standby generator was furnishing power. The building itself had suffered little damage, but the contents were well shaken up. Dr. Ron met them and said he had everything under control and had already admitted two patients. One was an elderly woman who had fallen and broken her hip. They had her stabilized and would make repairs to the hip later. The other was a little girl who had received a bad glass cut. Dr. Weaver was stitching her up. "We are trying hard to get everything organized," Ron said. "We are very likely to get a substantial number of casualties out of this. I think this must have been the 'big one.' "

"We have people fanned out over the valley to look for anyone that may be injured," Jamie told him. "I'm on my way to the airport and the docks. See you later."

At the airport, Jamie found Brian, Randy and Kevin working on the hangar door. The big door had jumped the track, was sitting solidly on the concrete, and could not be moved. They were rigging big hydraulic jacks to lift it to where the carriage wheels could by shifted over the track. Timbers had to be bolted to each side of the door to provide a lifting spot for the jacks. None of the airplanes had been damaged, although they had shifted around some. "Good thing we had wheel chocks under most of the wheels," Brian said. "We have to get this door open before we can use any of them, though. But we will have it on the rails in jig time."

Jamie headed on to the docks where he found everything in reasonable order. There had been a series of rough choppy waves that shook things up a little. Jamie was on the deck of one of the houses, talking to Little Bird and Johnie Dick when Sweet Grass came bursting out the door. At the same time, Dawg started barking, ran up the dock, turned around and came back, still barking.

"Something's happening," she exclaimed. "The water is coming up fast. I could see a big wave from the upstairs window."

"Jesus Christ," Jamie yelled. "Tsunami. Get everyone off the docks and up the hill. Hurry!!!" He grabbed Little Bird from her chair and flung her over his shoulder as he leaped to the dock and began to run. He was amazed at how light she was. He doubted if she weighed more than 80 pounds, still a load for a man in his seventies. The dock seemed to go on forever, then the long blacktopped ramp that led to it. His truck was on the lot at the side of the ramp, and Jamie headed for it, and then changed his mind, deciding that he could reach high ground faster if he kept running. Dawg was barking frantically somewhere behind him, but he couldn't look back to see. The Dick girls, fleet-footed as deer, fled past him, followed by Sweet Grass.

Fighting for breath, he came to the up slope of the road that led to the dock and charged up it. Partway up the hill, he caught up with the girls, who had stopped and were looking back. Gasping, he slowed and turned. Johnie Dick and Robert Dick had Julia Jacob by the arms and were practically dragging her along while Angela Dick had her father, Johnie Jacob, by the arm urging him to move faster.

The tide had been low when Jamie had arrived on the dock. Now it was at the high tide level, and he could see a huge wave rolling up the bay. "We better get higher," he yelled as he started another push up the hill.

"I think we're OK now," Johnie Dick gasped. Jamie stopped and turned again. The big wave was at the end of the dock, lifting the dock and boats high as it surged under them. A 14-foot aluminum skiff broke from its moorings and tumbled wildly along the docks. The water surged over the decks of the houses before their floatation could lift them, knocking out windows and filling rooms with water. The wave progressed up the ramp, across the parking lot, completely submerging Jamie's truck and several other vehicles on the lot at the foot of the hill. It surged up the road like high surf up a beach, finally expending itself only yards from where the group of people had stopped, and started its rush back to the sea. The aluminum skiff was left upside down just yards from their feet.

"You can put me down now, Big Chief." Little Bird's voice was not as strong as usual. "I've had all my innards displaced with the jolting you gave me."

Jamie eased the old woman to the ground and straightened up, still gasping for breath. Little Bird grasped Sweet Grass's hand to steady herself. She didn't have her cane. "You are a rough riding critter," she continued, "but I thank you for taking care of this old woman and saving a life that was not much worth saving."

The water was flowing back down the hill. A couple of cars on the parking lot were overturned and rolled in a pile against Jamie's truck, water gurgling out of them as the wave receded. The houses were still in place, except for one that had broken partly loose and was trying to follow the outward rushing water. One line still held the house to the dock. Several sections of finger docks for small vessels had broken loose and were headed down the harbor, but for the most part, the docks were still intact as were the fishing boats and the barge and tug that had been tied to it. The wave had rolled over them, but had not completely swamped them.

"Our lovely houses are all ruined," moaned Julia. "What are we going to do?"

Grandson Johnie Dick answered her. "We are going to go back, dry them out and go on living. Think how lucky we are to be alive. If Sweet Grass hadn't warned us, we'd all probably have drowned."

"Don't go back for a while," Jamie commanded. "There could be more waves following for several hours. I have read quite a bit about tsunamis. They are very unpredictable."

A pickup came roaring down the road and skidded to a stop. Brian got out and surveyed the scene in amazement. "You are all OK?" he asked. "That was some wave. It came right up on the airport and plowed all the way to the hangar."

"We better go see how far it went up the river and if anyone got flooded out. Can we take your truck, Brian?"

"Sure, come ahead. Let's go." Brian jumped back in the truck and started the engine.

"Should I come along?" asked Johnie.

"No," Jamie replied. "You stay here and take care of your people. Find a place for Little Bird to rest until it is safe to go back on the dock. I'll come back later and bring some food."

Getting in the truck, Jamie didn't have time to get the door closed before Brian had spun the truck around and smoked rubber starting up the road. In only minutes, they were on the hill leading down to where the road paralleled the river. The big expanse of wetland field at the foot of the hill was covered with water that was draining through the culverts back into the river.

The Super Store at Ryan Road was still burning, throwing up a lot of smoke, in spite of the fact that water had covered the parking lot. Nevertheless, that seemed to be as far as the wave had penetrated. "Let's see if the Fifth Street Bridge is OK," Jamie requested.

The bridge was undamaged, but water had covered the park that extended on both sides of the bridge along the river bottom.

"It doesn't look like the flood went far enough up the river to do any harm to any of the farms," Jamie commented. "Let's go on up to the schoolhouse and see if there are any problems reported."

Back at the school, reports were coming in. A tree had fallen on one house, crashing through the roof and trapping the occupants in the bedroom. They were unhurt, but it took several men an hour to get them out. Another house had burned to the ground when the wood stove in the kitchen had been upset and embers spilled out onto the floor. One man had a broken arm. There were several casualties from glass cuts, and all had been transported to the hospital for care.

By noon, most members of the council had arrived, and they held an impromptu council meeting. Jamie listened to reports from everyone and then summed up the situation. "It seems to me that we have been very fortunate. We have survived what I believe was 'the great one.' We have had no fatalities and only a few injuries, none of them extremely serious. We have all suffered a fair amount of damage that will take us awhile to clean up. We have lost two homes, and we should make every effort to get them replaced, or the occupants settled in other housing as soon as possible."

"Jamie," Bob Elder interrupted, "both families have been taken in by nearby neighbors and I'm assured that they will be welcome until their situation is resolved."

"Thanks Bob. We really have great people here willing to help out wherever it is necessary. I think the troubles we have gone through have brought people much closer together. Now to go on from here. A priority is to see if we can get power back as soon as possible. Andy, that is up to you and Dave. It's too bad that we have lost our cell phones, but we will have to make do. I'll take Brian and go out to fly the lines this afternoon, if the boys have gotten the hangar door open. We can keep in touch with base by our aircraft radios, so they will know where we are and what we are doing at all times..."

Kelly came bursting through the door, carrying a large platter of steaming ground beef sandwiches, followed by Meg with a big coffeepot. Ted followed with a stack of paper plates and coffee cups.

"God, that looks good," Bob Elder exploded. "How in the hell did you manage this?"

"Well," Ted explained, "we knew that none of you had had time for breakfast, and it is lunchtime, so you had to be hungry. I have an outdoor wood-burning grill rigged up and lots of ground meat in the freezer, so here we are. If we don't get power back, we'll lose the meat, so we had just as well use it up before it spoils."

"See what I say about wonderful people helping out?" Jamie said. "Thanks a million, Ted. We sure appreciate it. Let's chow down and get back to work."

Conversation died for the next twenty minutes as each of them devoured at least two tasty hamburgers.

"Brian, how long would it take to install VHF radios in vehicles for Andy and Dave?" Jamie asked.

"Not long," Brian replied. "I can jury-rig a system pretty quickly, just set the radio on the seat and hook up some wires. I can rig an antenna somehow. Stan will know more about that than I do. Let's get the vehicles to the base, and I'll see what we can do."

"Will someone take me home? I need to pick up my car. Also, we need a shovel and pick to repair a break in the road, so I can get the car over it. If we had a four-wheel drive truck, maybe we could drag the back porch out of the way so I can get in."

"I'll come with mine," Dave volunteered. "I have tools in it. If Andy would go along to the base, the boys could get started on the radio for Andy's truck."

"Bob," Jamie said, "will you coordinate efforts to get people settled? Get plywood or tarps to cover windows until we can get glass replaced; do whatever you can to move things forward."

"Will do," Bob agreed.

* * *

At the road break, Dave pulled a shovel from the truck and handed it to Jamie. Equipped with a pick, he started breaking the blacktop while Jamie shoveled it down to form a ramp that a vehicle could get over. At the house, Dave looked critically at the back porch. "I don't know what kind of damage we'll do if I pull that mess loose."

"To hell with the damage," Jamie said. "Let's just get it moved, so I can get in the door."

Dave had a winch on the front of his truck. Pulling out the cable, he carried it to the opposite end of the porch and flipped the cable over the top of the debris. With a short chain, he found an anchor spot and hooked the chain to the cable. Back in the truck, he started the motor and engaged the winch. With a splintering of broken wood and the squeal of pulling nails, the porch roof tore loose from the house, and the entire mass moved toward the truck. Jamie waved for him to stop. The porch floor was still in place and access to the door was established. Jamie unhooked the chain and guided the cable back into the winch. The two men went inside and heaved the refrigerator back to an upright position.

"OK," Jamie said. "We'll take it from here. Let's get on to the airport."

At the base, Jamie found the 206 on the ramp ready to go. Stan had just finished a temporary installation of the radio in

Andy's truck and had one ready for Dave's. "I found out why we lost the cell phones," Stan reported. "The tower toppled over and smashed the equipment to smithereens. I am not sure if we can recover it or not."

"Thanks Stan, we will worry about that later. Keep your radios on, fellows," Jamie told Andy and Dave. "I think I'll go take a look at Elk Falls first. We'll fly the main line on the way. We will report anything we see that you should know about."

A few minutes later, they were in the air and following the main power line north. A short distance north of Oyster River, they spotted two of the big steel towers that had gone down. They were a twisted mess of steel. At the Elk Falls power plant, major problems had developed. One of the huge pipes that fed water to the powerhouse had ruptured, and a torrent of water was cascading down the mountainside.

Jamie climbed away from the area and circled over Campbell River. The Discovery Mall Shopping Center built on fill land only a few years ago had suffered extensive damage. The entire back wall of the huge Zeller's store had caved outward and let the roof collapse. Other buildings were distorted or leaning crazily like disoriented drunks. The fill material had partially liquefied from the shaking and left the buildings unstabilized. The Tyee Plaza, also built on fill, showed extensive damage. The tidal wave had apparently petered out before reaching this far north. There was little evidence of flooding. Calling Andy on the radio, he reported what he had observed.

"It doesn't look like we'll be getting much power from there for a while," Andy said. "However, the Puntledge plant is OK. We will try to trace the main line down to the valley from here. Then we will just have to follow every line out until we find the problem."

Jamie spent another hour flying the lines in the valley. They found two trees down across lines, and a power pole had broken off and was lying across the adjacent road. They made notes of the locations and reported the results to Andy.

"I think we have done enough for today," Jamie told Brian. "Let's go home. I have an awful mess to clean up at home."

"Do we have plans for tomorrow?" Brian asked.

"Yeah, I would like to fly down and take a look at Victoria, and maybe over to Vancouver. We might get an idea if this was really the so-called 'big one' by seeing what damage has been done to the cities."

"Let's take one of the Caravans," Brian said.

"OK by me," Jamie responded. "See you about nine in the morning."

Jamie stopped by the school to pick up Kelly. Charlie Johnson was there and informed him that they were going to try to get school operating in the morning. Plywood had been nailed over the broken windows and the glass shards cleaned up. "I think it's important to get the kids in school," Charlie told him. "It offers more continuity for them, and they are less likely to be affected by the quakes. There have been seven strong aftershocks today, and I suppose we'll keep getting them for sometime."

"Have you had a chance to check on the people at the dock?" Jamie asked.

"Yeah," Charlie responded. "We took some food out to them and offered to move them somewhere else until they could get things straightened out, but they refused. They were busy mucking out the houses and had tarps nailed over the broken windows. They are very self-sufficient people."

Jamie found Kelly in the office. Mary was getting ready to go home. "I was going to take Kelly with me if you didn't show up, but now she can go with you. She says you have a real mess."

"Yes," Jamie agreed, "but we will manage. We got the roof of the back porch pulled away, so we can get in the house. Our beds are fine, so we have a place to sleep. We have an outdoor barbecue that we can cook on, or we can build a fire in the fireplace. How about you?"

"We have a wood stove in the kitchen beside the electric one. We didn't get too much damage. I'll be able to sort it out all right. I think Dave will be home soon to help."

* * *

At the house, Jamie and Kelly stood for minutes surveying the damage in the kitchen. "Golly damn," Kelly exclaimed. "Where do we start?"

"We start by trying to clear out the kitchen. I'll bring in the big garbage can." With the trash can in place, they started. "Anything that is broken or badly damaged goes in the can," Jamie instructed. "Anything we can use, stack up on the back of the counters. I'll get these broken cupboards out first."

Jamie tugged a cupboard loose from the debris and carried it out to the backyard where he sat it against the wall of the garage. The rest followed as fast as he could get them out. Most of the Dura-Wear dinner dishes were undamaged, and Kelly was stacking them along the back of the cabinet. The glassware was smashed to fragments, and Jamie got a shovel and began dumping it into the trash can. Baking powder and soda were spilled and mixed with vinegar and oil. Kelly sorted out dishes that were unbroken but soiled and stacked them in the sink. Finally everything of value was off the floor, leaving a sticky mess. Jamie went to the backyard and came back with a bucket full of sand, which he spread over the floor, then worked it back and forth with a broom. Pushing it into a pile, he shoveled it into the trash can, which he dragged out the back door.

"There, we can at least get in the kitchen," Jamie said.

"Shall I start washing those dishes?" Kelly asked.

"No, we don't have any water, so they will have to stay dirty. You can load the dishwasher full, but we can't run it. At least that will get some of them out of the way."

"What are we going to do for water?" Kelly asked.

"I have two five-gallon cans full in the garage, and there is a case of bottled water in the utility room. That has to last us for a while. There will be no showers. We can't use the toilet, so we have to use the outhouse. Except for beds, we are going to be rough camping for a few days. Think you can manage that?"

"I can manage anything if you are here to help me," Kelly declared.

Jamie brought in another garbage can, and they swept up glass from the rest of the house, along with broken picture frames and a few ornaments that had been displayed around the house. Books that had been tipped from the shelves were put back in place.

They were finishing up when a pickup stopped in the driveway. Bob Elder got out and pulled a sheet of plywood from the truck and shoved it onto the front porch, then clambered up after it. "I think this will cover that picture window," he told Jamie. Five minutes later, the window was secure, and Bob was on his way.

"Well, at last, it looks like we have the place livable." Jamie told Kelly, "It should be a first-class camping spot, now that we have the trash moved out."

"But now I'm hungry," Kelly complained. "What are we going to do 'bout that?"

"Could you do with a steak?" Jamie asked.

"I think I could eat two big steaks," Kelly replied.

"I'll go get a fire started in the barbecue. Could you stand a cold drink?"

"I sure could. Is the refrigerator working?"

"No, but it should still be at least partly cold."

After a dinner of steak and canned beans and dried apricots for dessert, they called it a day.

* * *

Jamie dropped Kelly off at school. Teachers were in place, and kids were dribbling in. Things were getting back in order. At the airport, Jamie found a Caravan on the ramp ready to go, and Brian fussing with a few last-minute inspections.

"If you are ready, let's get underway," Jamie requested.

"I'm ready," Brian replied. "I have charts onboard, the fuel tanks are full and everything looks good."

A few minutes later, the wheels left the runway. Jamie held the plane low and swung over Courtenay. He was amazed to see most of the older buildings centered on Fifth Street totally demolished with bricks and debris toppled into the streets. "That was not a gentle earthquake that we had," Jamie commented.

"It sure wasn't," Brian agreed. "In fact, it was anything but gentle. Golly, look at that." The almost new big-box Wal-Mart Store had collapsed. It looked like some giant had stepped on it and squashed it flat.

"Wow! I thought they built stuff to be earthquake-proof these days," Brian exclaimed.

"Earthquake resistant, I believe is the terminology," Jamie replied. "That doesn't cover monster earthquakes. I'm becoming more convinced that this was really the 'big one.' "

Jamie lifted the plane higher in the air and continued south. In Nanaimo, the big hotel in the center of town was toppled to the ground, and the entire old business district seemed to be totally demolished. "The farther south we go, the worse it looks," Jamie said. "We might have sort of been on the edge of it, or farther from the epicenter. Let's go on to Victoria."

Victoria was worse yet. The area around the harbor, including the Empress Hotel, looked like a war zone. Many high-rise buildings had been toppled over, as though they had been constructed of a child's building blocks. The waterfront everywhere had been scrubbed clean by the tsunami, with buildings, docks and boats flung high ashore or sucked out to sea by the backflow. The two men were speechless as they looked down on the metropolitan area.

"Let's go look at Vancouver," Jamie finally broke the silence. Brian didn't answer.

They dropped low to come in over the Vancouver Airport. The runways were littered with debris of every description. A battered 747 was sitting astride the freeway east of the airport. The tsunami had rolled on over the lowland that comprise the delta of the mighty Frazer River, sweeping everything before it and dropping much of it haphazardly as the water returned to the ocean. Flying over the city, all they could see was destruction. What the earthquake had not destroyed, the tsunami had finished off.

"Let's fly over Port Alberni on the way home," Jamie said, "and around the coast to Gold River."

Chapter 51

It looked like everyone was there for the general meeting on Sunday evening. Jamie waited till all were seated and settled down, then stood and waved for attention. The room immediately became silent.

"I do not know if there is a God, but if there is, I am genuinely puzzled about his actions. It would be easy to say that we are here alive and well today because we are his chosen people. But to say that would be the height of egotism. Yes, I think we are special people, but no more so than millions of others that used to inhabit this world. I cannot imagine why he destroyed so much and left so little. I am not saying that you should not believe in God, but if there is a God, he is making it very difficult for me to believe in him. Understand, I am not saying there isn't a God, but the events over the past few months sure make it difficult for me to accept him, or her, unquestionably.

"There are about 500 of us here, and if we are the chosen few, we certainly were properly chosen, for I think it would be impossible to find a better group of people—people that are caring, kind, compassionate and just plain good. But I believe that if we had randomly picked 500 people most anyplace else in the world and subjected them to the same conditions, you would find that they were much the same as the people here. It takes conditions like we have here to bring them together and make them realize that they must depend on each other or perish. So, regardless of their background, with a few exceptions, they would respond in much the same way as we have.

"Maybe, if there is a God, he lives in the minds of people—of human beings. Humans are animals, physically much like all the other animals of the world. But there is one big difference. All animals have brains, that glob of soft tissue surrounded and protected by bony skulls. But only humans have minds, developed within the confines of the brain to provide us with the ability to think, to reason, to plan. So if there is a God, that is possibly where he resides.

"Now, I think that is enough of philosophy. I will try to get down to facts. I am not sure that I can give you genuine facts, but they are as true as it is possible for me to make them. I will have to

403

admit that the good Dr. Wolfgang was not as far off the beam as I first thought. He predicted much of what has happened. He just was not very well informed and got some of his predictions mixed up with a desire to gain attention, to shock, to scare people into panic. And panic is disaster in the making.

"My own predictions have been much more accurate. He predicted the great earthquake was eminent. I said all along that it was sure to come, but there was no way of knowing when. That was the consensus of all of the scientific people that were engaged in the study of plate tectonics and earthquakes. I also said that I doubted that the severity of the quakes would be anywhere near as great as he would have had you believe.

"Well, 'the great quake' arrived. I have no question about that. And we were fortunate to be in a place that was affected very little in comparison to effects in other areas. I have experienced a number of quakes, some as strong as 7.4 on the Richter scale. But this one, at this point, was far stronger, probably about 9, or maybe 10, on the scale. But this wasn't the epicenter of the quake. I think that the quake originated along the overlapping plates about 60 or 70 miles off the Pacific Coast, and its strength there must have been fantastic. But the west coastline of Vancouver Island failed to be raised the 30 feet or more that Wolfgang predicted. It might have risen a few inches; we have no way of knowing. And the east coast of the island certainly didn't sink 30 feet. That just didn't happen, or you would not be here listening to me hypothesize about what did happen. I do know that we had a local quake that was quite strong that was probably keyed by the big one. That resulted in a fault line about a foot high that runs along the valley between here and my house. The ground either raised a foot on the east side of the fault or dropped a foot on the west side. We do not have instrumentation to determine which. I saw a fault line in California that was three feet high and 50 miles long. A whole mountain range was raised three feet.

"Now, to really let you know how severe this quake was, I will try to tell you about what Brian and I saw when we flew over Victoria and Vancouver. There are high-rise buildings that look like they had been made by a youngster stacking up his building blocks until he got them out of balance, and they toppled over. They didn't crumble to the ground in a heap. They were upset and dumped full length on the ground, like a fallen tree. Most of these buildings were constructed under the latest earthquake codes to withstand the strongest of quakes. The area around the inner harbor in Victoria looked as if some giant had set his thousand-ton foot on it, and it went squish. Then the tsunami came and washed all the debris up in piles hundreds of feet from the shore. Along with the giant wave went docks, boats and buildings of every description. The Vancouver area was worse. The water rushed over the airport with such force that we saw a battered 747 sitting across the remains of the highway east of the airport. Downtown Vancouver is a total disaster. If there had been people living there, few could possibly have survived.

"Then we decided to take a look at the west coast. We went to Port Alberni, which has ceased to exist. The tsunami had destroyed all but the highest parts of the town. Huge piles of debris were pushed far up the valley. The wave or tidal bore had striped the shoreline of the Muchalat Inlet for probably a hundred feet above high-tide line. Huge piles of trees and other debris were deposited in every cove or sheltered spot. Out in Barkley sound, we found numbers of islands that had supported substantial forests swept clean. All vegetation was gone, and they were polished like gemstones.

"Up the outer coast the destruction was unbelievable. Waves had washed hundreds of feet up steep slopes, dislodging trees and rocks, and then sucking loose materials back into the ocean. We came back over Gold River and found the same thing. The docks and the old Uchuck freight and passenger boat was swept several hundred yards up the river and dumped in a pile, the Uchuck upside down.

"So that is the story of the 'great earthquake' and the tsunami that followed it. Why we were not affected more here, I don't know. I think that we were saved from the major effects of the tsunami because of the islands in the Strait of Georgia that acted as buffers. Also, we had a very low tide. That gave us an extra 15 feet of space to be filled before the water came ashore. We have survived in surprisingly good shape. We have had no fatalities, and the damage has not been nearly as great as I would have expected.

"I think the tsunami originated at the source of the quake out in the Pacific Ocean, probably 60 or 70 miles from shore. That is probably the main reason we were spared here from its maximum power. We are a hundred miles up the Georgia Strait from where the wave rolled out of the Strait of Juan de Fuca and continued on to the Vancouver area.

"Now, let us get to our own situation and what is going on here. Our electrical supervisor and his chief aid, Andy and Dave, restored our electrical service in an amazingly short time. A number of repairs were temporary, but we have the juice. They can finish up at their leisure. Andy tells me that the Puntledge power plant was not hurt. All the damage was along the lines, caused by trees falling or poles breaking off. The Elk Falls Plant suffered more and has been shut down. Andy thinks they can get it in service again eventually.

"All but two of the broken windows have been replaced, and those two will go in tomorrow. We lost two homes: one burned and the other was crushed by a falling tree. New mobile homes from a sales lot in Courtenay have been moved in to replace those houses, and the owners are already getting settled.

"Our reserve food supplies took a serious hit. We had several tons of frozen foods stored in the freezers at the Great Canadian Store. That building collapsed and burned. Several other grocery stores were severely damaged, and salvage of food from them may be questionable. But our crops have been good, and most people have plenty of food stored up for the winter. Our dairy plant and our meat processing plant are doing well. I see little danger in anyone suffering from hunger. By next year our farming knowledge will have improved, so I think our living is insured for the future.

"Our gasoline-powered equipment is still operating, but I must warn that there is no insurance of it continuing. Gasoline is known to deteriorate in storage. Old gas forms a gum that fouls up filters, and carburetors and engines refuse to run. However, there are quite a number of you already farming with horses, and those people have agreed to help the non-horse farmers until horses can be obtained for every farm.

"We are in better condition with our airplanes. Brian discovered a supply of fuel additives for jet fuel that prevents the growth of bacteria in the fuel and formation of sludge. There is not a great amount of it, but it will enable us to keep flying for a while at least. I am eager to conduct more exploration and see if there are other people alive in the world.

"So, all in all, everything looks good for us. We have before us an opportunity to develop a new society in the world, starting fresh with the knowledge of all the mistakes made by the old one. If we are strong enough, and I believe that we are, we have an opportunity to avoid many of those mistakes and build and repopulate the world with a society that we can be proud of. I am projecting far into the future, now, about our children, our grandchildren and our great-grandchildren. It is up to all of us to steer them properly. I know that we can do it."